"Sarah Schulman's *The Cosmopolitans* is richly imagined, observantly written, and stunningly researched. It's a cascade of such insights rendered vividly and movingly—so much so that it may be as popular with people who weren't there as with folks like myself who were. Novels about the past that can celebrate it with intelligence rather than nostalgia are rare and are themselves to be celebrated."

—**SAMUEL R. DELANY**, author of
Through the Valley of the Nest of Spiders

"A deep, smart, and satisfying novel."

—**RABIH ALAMEDDINE**, author of *An Unnecessary Woman*

"*The Cosmopolitans* is Schulman's best—the heartbreaking, beautiful, exquisitely researched evocation of a lost time. She has saved what history has forgotten, and miraculously presents the voices and stories of the unheard. A sensational work of fiction."

—**ANDREW SEAN GREER**, author of
The Impossible Lives of Greta Wells

"Balzac and Baldwin are the named influences here, but as I read Sarah Schulman's remarkable new novel, I couldn't stop thinking of Douglas Sirk and John Dos Passos. *The Cosmopolitans* is a beguiling balancing act, a melodrama with a wide-eyed social analysis, and a polemic with a heart as generous as its politics."

—**DALE PECK**, author of *Visions and Revisions*

"This novel is book club gold. *The Cosmopolitans* is a great group read—weighty dilemmas, unforgettable characters, and a roller-coaster plot!"

—**TAYARI JONES**, author of *Silver Sparrow*

"What a vision—Sarah Schulman sees everything, from cultural details that create the immersive world of this novel to the intensely personal. The psychological insights she shares with artful simplicity will shatter your heart. A masterpiece."

—**MICHELLE TEA**, author of *How to Grow Up*

Also by Sarah Schulman

NOVELS

The Mere Future

The Child

Shimmer

Rat Bohemia

Empathy

People in Trouble

After Delores

Girls, Visions and Everything

The Sophie Horowitz Story

NONFICTION

Israel/Palestine and the Queer International

The Gentrification of the Mind:
Witness to a Lost Imagination

Ties that Bind: Familial Homophobia
and Its Consequences

Stagestruck: Theater, AIDS, and the
Marketing of Gay America

My American History: Lesbian and Gay Life
During the Reagan/Bush Years

PLAYS

Enemies, A Love Story *(adapted from IB Singer)*

Carson McCullers

Manic Flight Reaction

Mercy

The Cosmopolitans
Sarah Schulman

THE FEMINIST PRESS
AT THE CITY UNIVERSITY OF NEW YORK
FEMINISTPRESS.ORG

Published in 2016 by the Feminist Press
at the City University of New York
The Graduate Center
365 Fifth Avenue, Suite 5406
New York, NY 10016

feministpress.org

First Feminist Press edition 2016

 This book is supported in part by an award from the National
Endowment for the Arts.

 This book was made possible thanks to a grant from New
York State Council on the Arts with the support of Governor
Andrew Cuomo and the New York State Legislature.

First printing March 2016

Cover and text design by Drew Stevens
Cover and interior photos by Robert Otter © 2005 Ned Otter

The Feminist Press gratefully acknowledges Ned Otter for sharing his
father's photography. RobertOtter.com

Library of Congress Cataloging-in-Publication Data

Schulman, Sarah, 1958–
  The cosmopolitans / by Sarah Schulman.
    pages ; cm
  ISBN 978-1-55861-904-3 (pbk.)–ISBN 978-1-55861-910-4 (hardback)–
  ISBN 978-1-55861-905-0 (ebook)
  I. Title.
  PS3569.C5393C67 2016
  813'.54–dc23
                    2015017798

For Claudia Rankine

"The past is never dead. It is not even past."

—WILLIAM FAULKNER

New York City, 1958

Chapter 1

Bette's windows framed a movie of the world in lacerating color, solitary black and white. All was below, and yet knowable, from the second floor. Real theaters charged fifty cents for matinees and were easy to attend. But, sunken in the seats of Loews or the Eighth Street Cinema or the film house on Bleecker, looking up instead of down, she was diminished and felt controlled. Bette could never ignore the simple fact that what passed on the screen had already been seen by multitudes before her. Each time the projector clanged its reels, the characters reached an identical conclusion.

How can one story unfold the same way under so many different circumstances?

It could not. She didn't care for it.

She preferred the art cinema near Sixth Avenue, down the block from Nedick's hot dogs and orange drink. The films there were in French and Italian, with inadequate explanations in small print below the action or slapped across the actors' faces. It was more like

1

life, where she could come to her own understanding of events by assessing gesture, facial expression, and body language. Her apartment's windows offered this gift as well, but in panoramic variation so that the simultaneity of our lives became irrefutable. That we're all in this together. Musical, drama, romantic comedy, cartoon, suspense, cops and robbers, animal tale, even stag. Silent and talkie. Who needs Hollywood when there's Tenth Street? The show is always playing and it's always up for free.

As a girl in Ohio, it had to come from within. The dirt was so clean, it shouldn't be called dirt. It was empty, she could wash in it. No sign of man and his use of life. No passersby. There was a magic lantern show and then a nickelodeon. The newsreels rolled in with the war and she attended regularly, searching systematically for signs of her brother in France until he came home unscathed, with no stories, having only learned to smoke. The banality of it all turned her away from movies and made her a fan of the stage. Real life in real time, whether a carnival sideshow at the Ashtabula County Fair or Carousel on Broadway. Act One. Intermission. Act Two. Change is inevitable. What looks like nothing can become cataclysm. And then, of course, resolve. In Ohio, transformation was an elusive desire, but in the city, the theater of change constantly displayed itself before her. She'd have her coffee by that window, following the high jinks of those beloved weedy city trees, survivors who grow, sway, shade, bend, lose and build their leaves like matinee idols. The stars of the street were the streets. Surrounded by architectural forests. The trunks of buildings turned dark with rain, burned dry, skidded with ice, and then preened in calm camaraderie. There were canyons for folks below who navigate natural ravines that float, freeze over, and sizzle the path to each person's dream. Set, costumes, soundtrack, and special effects all by chance. No dirt. It was all constructed with something in mind. An idea.

Almost time for the 6:00 p.m. show, so Bette sat up in her chair by the window. First on was Mrs. O'Reilly, sending seven-year-old Margaret to Joe's Fish Market across University Place. Bette saw Mrs. O'Reilly slap wet arms out on her windowsill, propelling her neck and then head, hovering over the street. Their building was a ship and Mrs. O'Reilly's profile their masthead, as the whole structure sailed forth behind her. Downstairs, on the corner, Margaret stood, pigtails tight, fist clenched around two dollars and a list of what to buy. Bette could see Joe through the plate glass windows of his shop, big belly, black mustache, thick glasses, shoveling fishy ice aside to haul up a slab of cod, expertly wrapping it in an old page of the Daily Sun. All the actors were in place, waiting for the streetlight to let them go.

And then it began. Mrs. O'Reilly seized the green moment, stretched even farther into the air over Romanoff's Pharmacy; the light flashed and she yelled out, "Cross!"

Margaret obeyed, knowing she was safe this way. Margaret liked to do as she was ordered and always would because she had her own concerns, and obeying made it easier to engage them secretly with passion. Outside responsibilities were assigned and she followed, ever imagining that she'd be a nurse and someday ride a horse. That her father would come back to them and that school would magically and mercifully end. That her mother would get a radio and then a telephone, and that her green jumper would be miraculously clean by the next morning and more instructions would await on her breakfast plate. She did not understand the trance in which she lived as a warm hearth protecting her from her mother's sadness. But it was.

Joe saw her coming and waved up to Mrs. O'Reilly with his favorite hand signal, a-okay, as he opened the front door in welcome. A shopkeeper should treat his customers with love. They needed that and so did he. His son was in Korea, and Joe hoped someone was being kind to him. That's how it worked—*I see you and then you see him.* Recognition, that's the key. Joe gave fishtails away to the poor and special ordered a whole striped bass when someone had a wedding or anniversary or graduated first in their class. When his son came home, his wife would make the boy a whitefish stew with peppers and onions and a baked potato with butter. Bluefish was the local crop, right off the coast of Long Island, as plentiful as stray cats. Thank God for Catholics, they have to have their fish. And the Jews chop theirs up once a year with some blistering horseradish.

Joe wasn't religious himself, but he knew that faith created order, and order was necessary to avoid the kinds of confusing wars that had sent his son away. He loved his Joe Jr. He didn't know how a person could live hating their own children, but there was plenty of evidence of that everywhere he looked. He loved Margaret O'Reilly and he loved his fish. Margaret's mother had a hard time of it and had buckled down to her task. He wished she could show her child more love, less duty. Joe enjoyed it all, and he wanted Mrs. O'Reilly to feel the same way. He loved his apron and his cleavers and his old fedora and the keys that locked and unlocked the front door of his shop. This was the life.

Bette watched these relationships, filled with promise and threat. They all lived in front of each other, together. There was no pretending one was better than the other. Too late for that. "Everything has two faces," Balzac wrote. "Even virtue." That was one good thing about Ohio, it had made her a reader. *Wuthering Heights* and *Jane Eyre* and little David Copperfield all grown up. There would never be a paucity of good books. It was something always to look forward to. As dependable as the coming of evening's shadow.

Bette leaned a bit farther out the window to scan down the avenue, past Rubin's Deli, toward the singing, swinging, loafing branches of Washington Square Park. She checked to see if Earl had chosen that route home.

Rubin had lox for sale, bagels, bialys, pletzel. He had fresh wet farmer cheese in wax paper to cradle herring, smoked whitefish, smoked carp. Global purple onions exploded with demands next to the complimentary red tomatoes and hanging, greasy smoked kippers that the old men loved to eat. Next door to him sat the watchmaker, wild white hair, a single eyepiece, and devotion to minutiae. On the diagonal was Barney Josephson's new hamburger place, the Cookery. He used to run Café Society and his wife Gloria worked for the poor Rosenbergs. Everyone in the neighborhood knew her, and everyone in the world knew them. Bette and Earl had discussed their fate, followed it closely in the newspapers. There was so much to understand. What is a spy? Can *any* person be one? Treachery is wrong, but which loyalty is more important, to the present or to the future? How could a secretary, like Ethel Rosenberg, outwit the United States? Bette was herself a secretary and it didn't seem possible. That's a small life. She knew it for a fact. If she wanted to betray her country, she wouldn't imagine where to begin. That's top information, not bottom.

Earl thought they were innocent, but Bette thought it was more complicated than that. They could have done "it" and still be innocent. She and Earl had listened to the radio together the night the Americans incinerated Hiroshima, and they both knew immediately that this was wrong. Now that the Soviet Union had the atom bomb, *we* Americans could never do that again. *We* could not take that much life at one time because then it would happen back to us. Tit for tat. It was a balance of power that keeps everyone civil. That's why Joe is nice to Margaret and Mrs. O'Reilly can buy on credit from time to time. Because we all have the ability to hurt each other equally, and as long as that's so, neighbors have incentives to stay on their best possible behavior. To be friends. Or at least friendly. At least to try. The Rosenbergs, dead for five years now, had been incinerated like Japan. But the Josephsons have a new baby boy, named Eddie. Life apparently goes on.

One of the most significantly positive occurrences in Bette's life was getting a corner apartment on the second floor. She could move to the bedroom and hear the children playing, the neighbors gossiping, and the birds hovering window height in the trees. The Italians liked to sit outside on folding chairs, even in the winter. They loved seeing who was coming home from work and hear everyone's grocery report. One boy, eight-year-old Salvatore, had a lemonade stand, two cents a glass. He also tried his hand at fortune telling, staring into an overturned cereal bowl, rubbing its contours. He had a future, this Salvatore, there were no limits to his entrepreneurial desires. Bette put down her penny, gave him a shot.

Sal furrowed and stretched in imitation of concentration. He caressed the bowl and closed his eyes. He took no chances, this Salvatore. Even he knew that Bette was a woman of a certain age, and so her life was in place and somewhat prescribed. Yet, there was still room for one last big adventure. One last enjoyable transformation before all the losing began. She wondered if this change would actually take place or just loom and then one day be surpassed.

"What do you see?" Bette asked the boy.

"I see . . . that you . . . will . . . go for a walk," he said.

"I think you're right," Bette nodded, reassured. "What else?"

Sal closed his eyes. First tight, but then a vision appeared internally, and he seemed to read its prophecy on the insides of his own lids. "Wait!" His tiny pink lips pursed and then relaxed. "I see a . . . big change."

"You do?"

7

"I see a stranger, a mysterious stranger."

"Is she bearing gifts?" Bette chuckled to herself.

"No." Sal opened his eyes. "Her pockets are empty. She only brings herself."

"And that will change *everything*? Her . . . *self*?"

"Yes," Sal said. And smiled, once again turning into a little boy with a delicate future.

"Okay," Bette said. "I'll keep a lookout."

It was dinnertime now all over the Village. Not too many takers for Salvatore's fresh squeezed. But always working until the last moment, the boy waited for his mother to come home before finally closing up shop. There she was! Back from the slaughterhouse on Sullivan Street with her fresh killed rabbit, soon to be dinner. She paused on the corner of Ninth, at Readers Stationery Store to pick up a copy of the *Mirror*, then smiled at her son, the cue for him to swallow the last rewarding drop.

On Tenth between University and Broadway, an art gallery had a wealthy visitor. A beige Bentley pulled up, then stood idling as the Negro chauffeur stepped out. He looked left and right at the folks on the street and then entered, hat in hand, through the gallery's front door. He had grace and training, this chauffeur. Clearly, he had prepared for some other profession. The Italians stared at the car, staying fixed in their folding chairs, postponing dinner preparations to enjoy the special event. Chauffeur was a good-looking man, his uniform matched the car.

The bells at Grace Episcopal Church finally tolled six. On cue, the poor and rich artists, the middle-class and destitute painters and floating sculptors climbed out of their studios, scruffily distracted and ready for cocktails. Beer beckoned for now, followed later by whiskey, and right before dawn, a handful would have a great idea and stumble back to easel, floor, and wall. Willem de Kooning and an unknown would come to fisticuffs in about six hours, somewhere in the back of the Cedar Tavern. It could be over a girl they were both lying to or about, or a painting that really mattered.

The lady gallery owner and the chauffeur emerged from her store. They had obviously conferred. He opened the car's back door, and she climbed in to discuss with the sedan's mysterious owner. It was a mobile office for someone too grand to roam the streets. Too special to be seen. The car's windows were tinted black, so the neighbors could not peek inside. Children started to gather, and Salvatore daringly tried to press his nose against the glass. He decided right then and there that he, too, wanted a Bentley, and that when he had one, he would never come out, never satisfy the desires of others. Chauffeur did his duty and kept the bewitched children at bay. Finally, the gallery owner, a prim, muscular lady with a seductive smile, flowing hair, and a special suit, hurried out of the car so fast that Chauffeur didn't have a chance to hold open the door. She turned out the gallery's lights, locked up, and glided right back to the sedan with her purse and hat. This time he was ready and secured the sanctuary with an assured and assuring move. The car whisked away on its own cloud and this allowed everyone else to get back to their tasks of cooking, drinking, and loving. As they cried and celebrated together and alone.

The Italians and the artists? They meet over commerce. The artists rent from the Italians or live next door. They buy their vegetables and both overhear each other's travails. Every now and then, an artist speaks some Italian because he studied there, or romanced a girl, or his mother back home in Philadelphia was from Calabria. Once one sculptor and his neighbor enjoyed a recording of Maria Callas singing *Norma* together and shared a pack of cigarettes, but that was more out of a novel than for real. It was a *LIFE* magazine moment, and yet it happened. Mostly the two worlds rarely met, just passed each other by on the same quiet street, coming and going to opposing destinations. More likely, Salvatore and a painter's daughter would both go to Washington Square Park, tear off their clothes, and run into the same water fountain to dance around topless in their underpants when it got too hot for decorum. Would they recognize each other and wave? Yes. Maybe later Sal will grow to love paintings and cross the line. Maybe the girl will despise the men who lied to her mother in the back of Cedar Tavern and find a nice reliable Italian boy to marry and feed.

There is the tailor in his shop window. Bette could see him pull on the sewing machine cover, fasten its snaps. He cares for that machine, oils it and dusts it. All his dreams are there, his children's futures, God willing. Every night he rolls his shirtsleeves back over his concentration camp number, locks up for the night, and goes home to Washington Heights. As he pulls the front door shut and puts on his outside hat, the guests at the Albert Hotel next door are just beginning to roll out of their cages. Last night's mascara still running. They pick up their relief checks from wooden mailboxes stacked behind the front desk. Once again it's too late in the day to cash them at the bank. The desk clerk says no for the hundredth time, ignores an offer of a sexual favor, and gets back to marking his notebook. The queens shrug, scrounge for a cigarette. Start to think about coffee and . . . *then what?*

On Tenth Street, a brownstone built in 1880 is for sale for $30,000. In the middle of the block. But who has $30,000? The Italians, the painters, Mrs. O'Reilly, Joe, the hotel residents in their outré laissez-faire allure, Rubin the deli guy, Romanoff the white Russian pharmacist, the tailor, and our friend Bette all shake their heads. *Who has that kind of money?* they wonder. And this thought unites them, although they do not realize why. The art dealer's secret friend *could* buy it, of course, but she already has a townhouse of her own, in the east Fifties. Only Bette knows that the building in question figured prominently in a novel by the great Edith Wharton, as did the Grace Episcopal Church, whose bells have now completed their ringing. Bette realized this midpage and ran outside so quickly to take a peek that the book fell to the floor. She stood on the sidewalk and stared at the grand home, its great windows, sweeping stairs, and copper face. It was true, she knew, that she lived in a novel right here in New York. They all did. And a painting. And a factory. And a dreamland. That is to say, a film.

The young writer clerking the Albert Hotel's night shift studies at City College to become a teacher so that he can earn a real living instead of writing his books from behind the hotel's front desk. This boy, named Sam, has also read the same Edith Wharton novel. But he never put two and two together. And he never would.

11

Chapter 2

On April 4, 1928, Bette arrived by bus to Manhattan Island. For a whole month she avoided the trolleys, double-deckers, and elevated trains as she could not imagine how to approach them. Instead, young Bette stayed in her rooming house on West Twenty-Fifth Street and walked to every destination, finding a counter job at an all-night diner on Sixty-Second and Eighth Avenue. Coming home too late through the Irish slum of Hell's Kitchen, she wondered about her safety and how to assess it. The cook from the diner, a Negro boy named Earl, also a tender twenty years of age, kindly escorted her and started to explain what then became obvious. In New York City there were all sides of the track on the same block. And that's the key to how the machine churned.

"When you walk into a place, you say, 'Hi, how're you doing?'" Earl instructed. "And then you go to the other side of the room."

"Well, what good is that?"

"It's a world of good." Earl knew. That was clear. "You show them that you see who they are, you show respect, honor them with a greeting, and then move to a corner so they don't worry that you want something more."

"You establish," Bette summarized.

"Exactly."

And so their understanding was born.

Turned out the apartment next to Earl's had long stood empty, and so on a hot August afternoon, she moved in. It didn't take but one trip up the stairs, everything Bette owned was in her arms.

"That's what makes New Yorkers tough," Earl realized, watching her sweat from so little labor. "It's not the crime or whatnot. I'm telling you, it's the weather. The winter is too cold, the summer is too hot, and spring lasts a week and a half."

Winter *was* too cold. Not colder than Ohio of course, but several months of three or four feet of snow in a city that just can't rest is a lot of work. That's for sure.

For the next thirty years, Bette and Earl discussed the length of each New York spring.

"This one is three whole weeks!" Bette would say with joy, when it applied.

"Like I said," Earl repeated when necessary. "Spring in New York only lasts a week and a half."

Earl lived there with a white boy named Anthony, who was a real cut-up and a distant good looker. Anthony had the place originally and then invited Earl to share it with him. But when things soured between the boys, Anthony was decent enough to not inform the landlord, and let Earl keep the apartment. Eventually the original owner died and when his son came to inspect the place, Earl's tenancy was a "fait accompli."

"What's that mean?"

"It means," Earl said, "that it's yesterday's news."

A lonely breeze swept through Anthony's absence, until the night he just reappeared and suddenly everything was back to normal.

It was clear to Bette from the start that there was no romantic future between herself and Earl or herself and Anthony. Or really herself and anyone. What had happened back home was still burning inside, it was still alive and growing and it was going to take more than some nice-looking fellows. It was like she'd been whipped and never able to get hold of some balm. The sores kept opening, opening, crusting and cracking. She'd see a couple with their child walking down the street, not questioning their bond, and this pain of absence would crawl up her throat and beat at the backs of her eyes until they bled. She felt the venal drip, too thick for tears. But by the time she'd made it to a mirror, it was always gone.

So, one night when Anthony casually draped his arm around Earl's shoulder, she understood that that was the way it was and a kind of joy exploded in Bette's chest. She would never have to explain *herself*. She would never be the most endangered. She would love Earl and Anthony and they would love her, and that's all there was to it. No worry. That precise night she relaxed. That was the most relaxing night of her life. That was the moment she first told anyone about Frederick.

She entranced Earl and Anthony for hours with

her own secret catalog of detail. After half the night had passed, the men went out for a bucket of beer and returned right away, having thought a great deal about her story and wanting to hear more. The compassion. The three sipped that sweet beer and the sparrows' wings fluttered in the night. Even after the graveyard-shift workers stumbled back from the docks and the streetlights came on again, the three of them talked. The boys asked the right thoughtful questions and they cared about the answers. They nodded and commented with recognition. Earl took her hand and said, "I understand."

No one in Bette's life had understood or even said that they did, and now she had both gifts in one person. Now she could burn, bleed, and talk about what that was like, and there would be no problem. As she spoke, Bette started to see her own self more clearly. She started to discover things that silence had camouflaged. Bette found herself recalling details and attributing meaning to those details that all the internal repetition in her mind had kept under wraps. From this day forward Bette lived her life by thinking and then discussing her thoughts with Earl. It was the only combination that worked. In a way, she realized that this was why she had come to New York after all, to find someone to talk to. Now that she'd found him, her life would make sense. Bette was reassured.

At first there was an ice box, gas light, and a coal-burning furnace in the cellar. The ice man's horse brayed for oats, snapping its heels on the cobblestoned streets. Knickers and caps were the style for young men, and Earl kept that going for a while. Anthony brought home fashion magazines from the printing factory from time to time, and Bette glanced at them but never really tried to be a flapper. It was only after the triumph of registering to vote that she stepped out on her own and appeared at dinner suddenly with a bob. Both Bette and Earl were staunch Democrats, but Anthony just didn't care much and took his vote for granted. As time passed, her short hair became more convenient than meaningful, and she'd dressed accordingly ever since. Long legs, short skirts, strands of beads over flat chests were never to be Bette's natural encasement. So when fuller dresses came back, she felt more at home and was relieved. A modest skirt and sweater really worked for Bette. It gave her privacy to feel.

Of course she drank illegal whiskey, they all did. The Fronton Club on Washington Place was a special treat. Earl pointed out Edna St. Vincent Millay drinking alone and this impressed Bette. Both that he recognized her and that Millay did whatever she cared to do. Charlie's Place was where Earl and Anthony could camp, as there were plenty of male couples and women making love to each other all around them. Bette looked at it all blankly. Romance held no appeal. She was still torn to pieces by Frederick's cruelty. She simply could not see how a person made the decision to behave that way. Until she understood, she would not be interested in men again. Chumley's was the most romantic of the illegal spots. From the outside, Bette couldn't perceive a thing, not a stir, voice, or sway until they passed through a sleepy courtyard as the bouncer watched from a gated peephole in the old wooden door.

Suddenly, when Anthony, Earl, and Bette were understood to be, of all things, desirable, he swung open the thick wooden portal, beckoning them into the deafening roar. That's why it was called the *Roaring* Twenties, she realized some decades later. Because those hidden places were capsules of explosive sounds of joy.

These speakeasies were the grand places where the three friends planned their futures, and so did all the city dwellers. Whiskey was a hope machine, and if one used it to be emboldened, dreams could certainly come true. Earl made up his mind one drunken night to be an actor, and the next day started going uptown to play small parts in basements and to midtown once in a while to play a spear-carrier. Bette and Anthony and Earl went out to see plays together and then read the scripts out loud at home. Bette had already started her secretarial courses and took off her waitress uniform for good when she got a job at Tibbs Advertising Incorporated as a stenographer. It was a big debate between the three of them as to whether she should save her white-collared server's dress and apron *just in case*, but she just decided to burn the thing. So, one night at 2:00 a.m., the three comrades went to Washington Square Park and set it on fire in a trash can while doing a wild dance.

The market crashed in 1929, but they didn't really feel it until 1932 when Anthony got fired from the printing plant. Bette held on to her job, but Earl had to start hacking slabs of beef in the meatpacking district where a lot of Negroes ended up. Prohibition was soon repealed to give the unemployed some way to eat up their pain, but no one could afford to go out for drinks anyway. Being on the skids financially affected Anthony terribly. Normally, Earl would leave the house at four in the morning, Bette at seven thirty, and Anthony at eight. So traditionally she and Anthony would share a cup of coffee before they both began their day. Now, she'd leave him in the mornings with his wifebeater and cigarette, where he remained until her return. The only thing that had changed was his beard. Anthony suffered, and so did their neighbors. Evictions took place with regularity, and Bette found herself on the street with a crying neighbor, helpless and unknowing how to comfort or correct. She lacked so much knowledge for soothing others. It was startling. How pointless she both felt and was. How useless. Anthony suffered for three more years, and they lived off of pieces of discarded meat that Earl could bring home from the slaughterhouses. Finally, Anthony decided to go to see his parents and learn if it was true that they would never help him out no matter how bad it had gotten and how deep his need.

That first night was a strange night. Anthony had been expected home from the Bronx for dinner, and Earl and Bette waited without any discussion. They silently agreed. But by ten, it was clear something had happened, and they devoured the overfried potatoes and beef pieces. The next day he returned, shaved and with a new shirt that was too big on him, as if he had shrunk. He couldn't look either of them in the eye, and in his private time with Earl something terrible passed between them. The next day Anthony sat at Bette's table smoking a cigarette and then lurched suddenly and ran into his place next door. She heard him rummaging, opening and slamming drawers, and then watched him take his belongings in Earl's suitcase, wearing Earl's old newsboy cap. He was gone.

Eventually, Earl learned that Anthony had returned to his father with the promise to get married, and that in 1937 he had gotten married. In 1939, when Earl saw him across the room in a bar for men, Earl begged him to return home, offering every possible promise, but the problem at the core of the negotiation was that Earl had not done anything wrong. So there was really nothing he could fix. The day after Pearl Harbor, Anthony signed up, and like so many with nothing to live for and so many with every hope in their breast pocket, he was killed in the Pacific. His wife became his widow, with all titles and benefits.

These events altered Earl and Bette. They switched places. At first when Anthony disappeared, Earl was stunned into silence. Then he tried to brush it off. This went on for years, they barely mentioned it. While a kind of forced normalcy took the place of grief, the resuming of regular activities seemed empty and uneventful. But once Earl encountered Anthony in that bar, once he had begged his love and been denied, then everything was out on the table.

Anthony looked at Earl as though from within a fog. His face was slack, his eyes were unfocused, his mouth was flat.

"I'm not in love with you, and I'm not attracted to you," Anthony lied.

"You just want to be married and have men on the side so your father will love you," Earl said, and then regretted it. Perhaps if he had lied to Anthony as well, he would have eventually come home.

This is what plagued Earl forever after. If he had lied to the liar, perhaps he could have had him back. But instead he'd told him the truth. It was his fault. Earl sat in Bette's apartment night after night and cried. He repeated his feelings, did not know how to change them. She understood this, of course, and now Bette was the experienced one. She knew what unjustified abandonment was like. She knew what betrayal meant. She knew. Frederick. Frederick. And so, somehow Bette and Earl became equals in knowledge. This is when their mutual understanding deepened. This is when their friendship turned as permanent as the ocean, as mysterious, as unquestioned, as wild, clean, and as endless. There had now been cycles of reliability, of compassion, of each one pulling the other's weight. It was all proven now. All clear. Earl found other men, but they never carried the same density, his interests were never as carefree. Everything was fraught. And even when Anthony died pointlessly, that pattern got worse. If Anthony had survived, he would have found his wife unbearable. But because Earl had told him the truth, he had fled into the arms of the enemy. Dead on a beach, barely making it to shore.

Over time, Earl and Bette came to the understanding that they shared a fatal flaw, one that set them apart from other people. They could both love completely, only once. It was a curse and yet a fact, and this is what had brought them to each other, this recognition. The one grace bestowed. In this particular emotional state, neither of them would ever be alone.

Now, it is 1958, and Bette's apartment's decor is more a product of the thirties and forties than this moment. Having come with nothing, every single object had to be acquired. Nothing was handed down and few belongings arrived as gifts. For the most part, her possessions were selectively and carefully purchased or appeared by accident as neighbors moved or sold petty items out of desperation. An old crocheted lace doily sat underneath a crystal candy dish. The dish had represented a whim for occasional caramels, but now it held sewing needles and thread. A metal washbasin stored neatly underneath the sink, behind a light green curtain she replaced every few years. This basin was crucial as she used it daily to soak underwear and sore feet. Toes in the tub, sewing in her lap, she'd lean back into her rocking chair and rest. That chair came from a church sale on Carmine Street, and she'd carried it home herself even though it felt ridiculous to haul furniture through the neighborhood. Men did that, she well knew, but Earl was at work and she would not ask a stranger. She had arms, after all.

When the load got to be too much, she'd set the chair upright and rock for a few minutes on the sidewalk—first at Ninth Street by Trude Heller's nightclub advertising Carmen McRae, and then a block later in front of the New School for Social Research where refugee intellectuals from Europe tried to figure out what had gone wrong. Each task had its place. There was a quiet but eccentric pleasure in rocking one's self outside on the sidewalk. Passersby would smile or ignore as they had other tasks before them. This was her city, after all. And she could be as singular as the lot of them.

Supper was always important for Bette and Earl, a sign of civility and reliance. She used linen napkins every day and always set the table with love. Bette looked at the clock again. Eight o'clock! Both pillows were askew on Earl's waiting chair, so she prepared them for his arrival. Plumped quietly. Smiled. Normally it was quiet in Bette's apartment and very light. But not at this moment because it was finally night.

Earl was uncharacteristically late. Of course he was a freewheeler and often had adventures coming home. He'd stop off someplace for relief of some kind or be moody and sit out overlooking the river. He'd have a drink alone or with others or just walk off all the frustration of his day. But sooner or later he would show up for supper, and he would always appreciate that it was there. This night, however, the realm of the unusual had come to bear. The stars were coming out, others were completing their dinners and crawling into the evening's embrace. Bette looked, paced, rearranged, turned the radio on and off. She even sat and stared out the window at the street light's yellowed glow, how it cast shadows on a young fellow waiting for the bus. He had changed his clothes and seemed to bounce with anticipation. Was he headed uptown for a look or a meal or a walk or to visit a friend? Was he going to Times Square for a show, or to play Skee-Ball and eat at the Automat or Yorkville for a goulash, or did he have a dance hall or movie in mind? The bus would take him anywhere he wanted to be. So, what did he want? What was he thinking? What song was he singing? The green bus rolled up, illuminated from within, and the boy swung on, tossing his nickel into the basket, and slid onto a yellow seat of woven straw. Now it was the moment for Bette to imagine that something had gone wrong.

Just then, a reversal occurred in which the key

turned suddenly in the lock. That is the most comforting sound in a person's life, isn't it? When the other uses his own key to finally come home. Behind this happiness was Earl himself, a bottle of cold beer wrapped in newspaper, tucked under his arm. He dropped the curative keys into his worn cloth jacket pocket and threw it onto the hook, the one he had installed for this very purpose. He was exhausted. This wasn't the renewed expression of a postwork recovery, Bette saw right away. Instead, Earl's long-nosed, still handsome, but sunken face fronted a tired, depleted fifty-year-old man who had come directly home from working with animal carcasses without a chance to breathe or grieve over what kind of day after day fate had handed him. And how he could not imagine a way for that to change.

Chapter 3

Earl watched Bette's concern.

"They kept you until seven thirty," she said, getting it.

He saw Bette take his jacket kindly off the hook and drape it on a wooden hanger, to take better care of it, of him, this particular evening, knowing both he and his poor jacket needed special attention. *They* were the Lazio brothers, the hardworking, hard-driving owners of the meatpacking plant on Washington and Gansevoort where Earl spent his life. Those blocks were greased with animal fat, innards dripping from metal waste drums as hooked carcasses swung in and out of freezer rooms onto smelly, wormy streets. The guys hacked away at pig corpses, sides of cows, and gutted lambs, the human chests and legs splattered with animal muscle and blood as though their days were blades of grass in a field of slaughter, faces coated with the slick, stinking refuse of death. They had to not notice if they wanted to get by, not notice the similarities between the sheeps' intestines and their own flesh, fading and wasted by boring, brutal labor. They had to go through that mess with their eyes wide shut.

"The best thing I can say is that another day is over," Earl almost cried. Only those Lazio brothers had enough power to disrupt their supper, and every time they wielded it, Earl almost gave up. He had no other way to react but despair that these men decided when he would eat.

Earl shrugged it off temporarily, placing Bette's mail on the old maple side table, where her new telephone now sat. CAnal 8-0151. The phone and the mail belonged side by side, a neat containment of messages from the outside world in case of emergency. For years there had been an outdated wooden box on the wall of Romanoff's Pharmacy that everyone shared. But now they each had their own. It was like an individual work of art, those table phones, like the Brancusis they had seen at the Museum of Modern Art. Sculpture and appliance becoming one. This concept had tickled Earl and moved him toward his own phone as well, ORegon 7-5676. The awaiting comfort of plumped pillows on a beckoning chair waved to him, and the man settled back into it where he belonged. Ah!

Earl and Bette had long ago agreed that the only reason for him to work in a slaughterhouse, besides the fact that it was close enough to walk, was to have flexible hours. But whenever he came back from doing a play, the Lazios made him stay late. Who did he think he was anyway? An actor? NO! They had to remind him. He was a pig slaughterer. Every time. Punishment! Earl's soul. He wished. Sorting intestines. She brought him a glass for his ice-cold beer, soon he would relax.

He took a sip. Then he remembered.

"There's a letter for you."

"Really?" She sounded vague, computing how the words *a letter for you* could have anything to do with her.

"From Ohio." Earl glanced across the brim of his glass, waiting for some kind of reaction.

"Oh," she said. Not a flutter.

"Okay." Earl drank his beer. If Bette were really upset, she would let him know. No need to guess. But she could handle anything, including being upset. It was remarkable. She had perspective and that's what he needed, what he counted on her to provide. Suddenly the bitterness of the brew set in. That refreshing adult sour. Earl leaned back. He was home. And he wished again that there was some way he could make his life better.

Bette served them both a chicken fricassee dish she'd learned from a neighbor, Zelda Glukowsky, twenty years before. It had become a family recipe. Their family, he and Bette.

"I'm painting my place," she said, spooning out the potatoes.

"Good idea, it's been ten years."

"Eight."

"Oh yeah," Earl remembered. "You had to stay with me."

That was the week Earl had discovered his mother was gone. They'd packed up all of Bette's belongings into cartons from the liquor store and hauled them

26

across the hall to his place. And, eight years younger, they were standing on stepladders, ceiling paint dripping on their faces. That's when the postcard came. Into the middle of all that mess. Not even a telegram. And one year after the fact. A three-cent stamp from North Carolina.

> *Mama died last spring. Your sinful ways*
> *shamed her through to her final day on earth.*

From his sister. "Sister" in quotes. She didn't act like a sister. Too ashamed of him to take up her sisterly responsibilities. That's when they'd begun the conversation about buying private telephones. To save themselves from the humiliations of postcards coming at the wrong time. They'd discussed it for years. A person could always hang up a phone midsentence and not have to hear the bad news. With a card, that was not an option.

"I'm proud of you," Bette said, casually eating. Like being proud of him was as normal as a piece of chicken.

"I know." He was being honest. "You're my family. Eight years? Needs paint."

They started to talk it over. Should they hire someone this time? They were both older, both worked all day. In fact, they were both starting to *feel* a little older, less gung ho. But Bette hated to spend. Earl offered to help. Did either of them really want to paint at this age? No.

"You know what?" Earl announced. "I just realized that I don't want to go back to work."

Bette stopped, sat back, and looked at him. She

knew it was important and would listen completely.

Words swirled around inside Earl's heart. They became pictures, weather, sentiments, scraps of paper. They became those new kinds of paintings or some windstorm gone wild. They became the storming sky, the cloudy sky, the sun breaking through, the sun disappearing. They went here and there. They walked, they ran, they ran out of breath, they gasped for air and fell face down in the mud. But now he had created the moment to be listened to. He had created a friend who listened. He had told her he had something to say. He had done it all, and the event was taking place. He had forced himself to admit the truth.

He just said it. "Leon."

Bette's face registered the severity of the situation. She was disappointed *for* him, *with* him. But not *in* him. She wanted things to go his way and took his side. So, it was clear from her reaction that there would be trouble. That Earl would have to pay. They had different kinds of struggles in this world, these two. He desired to love and she didn't. She did not want to be alone in painting her apartment, and he was there to help. He needed a man to love him, and she was there when the man did not. They both wanted someone trustworthy to talk things over, to have each other's keys, and to eat those precious meals. Nothing worse than eating alone, and that would never happen again. But Earl and Bette let the world in differently, and so each one experienced the world's cruelties and pleasures on diverse planes. The other could only look on helplessly and listen. And yet in some fundamental way, the other could still really, really know.

"I'm sorry," Bette said. She was listening.

Leon had still not forgiven him. And yet, Earl also felt that he, himself, had not done anything wrong and didn't need to be forgiven. Yet, it was this offering of love to Leon that was the crime and Earl was willing to *be forgiven* if that would bring them together.

"Even though there is nothing to forgive." He would just do it. That's how much he cared. "How do you handle that?" he asked. "When someone is angry and you didn't do anything wrong? It's crazy making. More than that, it's actually crazy. The truth is . . ."

Earl stopped and was still. His beer beckoned to him as a diversion but he did not touch the glass.

"The truth is that Leon hates me. Leon walks away when I come near. Leon makes me eat my lunch alone. I'm so angry," he said. "I'm so angry that I'm in this spot again. Why did Leon have to ruin everything? And how exactly did it get so bad so fast? It's just one blind-side after another. The boy is a tease. That's a fact. Since the day Leon came to work for the Lazios he has done *everything*, I mean *everything,* that a randy young fella would do to show interest. He was not *innocent.* He could have wrote that book. The *I want you* book."

Earl counted transgressions on his fingers.

"Leon stripped in front of me in the locker room every goddamn day. Leon invited me out for beers. He patted me on the back. *Patted.* Many more times than were necessary."

Bette and Earl had planned it for months. The seduction.

They had worked so hard.

True, Bette expressed concern about Leon's young

age. Twenty-two. And her fears grew after the night that he'd come for supper. He was lovely as a palomino. But . . . when they'd shown the boy that framed photograph of Earl with Eugene O'Neill. He didn't know. He hadn't heard. Didn't know who Eugene O'Neill was. O'Neill!

"O'Neill!" Earl said.

Bette nodded.

Leon did not know the word *understudy*.

"Understudy."

Bette nodded.

Earl could not impress him with having understudied because Leon had never heard of *The Emperor Jones*. How could a black man not know about that? So what if he was young, he still should know. Now, the boy couldn't appreciate Earl's value. That he was deserving of kindness and respect.

Bette and Earl had been so disappointed, they cried.

Earl should have accepted it back then. The truth. That if Leon had known anything that mattered about this life at all, it might have worked out better. The three of them. A family. Leon for pleasure and Bette, Earl's friend. It would have been perfect. Someone to watch grow. To love. His beauty.

"So, why the hell did he give me *two* photographs of himself?" Earl could not figure that one out.

"I mean," Bette said.

"I mean, come on."

"Come on," Bette said.

Earl took some more chicken.

Leon was dishonest. That was the thing. Wanting it and pretending he didn't. Just like Anthony. Just like

Frederick, what Frederick had done to Bette. Feeling it and then pretending. Yes, that's what they did. Bette had grown to recognize lies a mile away. Why couldn't Earl figure that one out? Earl loved that chicken fricassee.

"Hey." He had a thought. "Do you think that letter could be from Frederick?"

Bette rose immediately from the table. It was instinct, she didn't have to think. She went to the telephone and picked up the solitary letter lying on the small tray behind the new copy of the *Saturday Review*. She examined the envelope with some critical tenderness, knowing it could be what she had been waiting for, and yet of course it easily might not.

"No, it's a woman's handwriting."

Bette softly tucked the letter back behind the magazine, sat down, and finished her meal. But she did glance up at the solitary photograph on her sideboard. Frederick's haircut, fresh from the barber.

"I wonder what he looks like now," Earl said, offering her the last wing.

"I'm sure he's still handsome." She shook her head no, wrapped up her napkin, and laid it on the table. "Those are looks for life."

They both knew, for a fact, that Bette would see Frederick again. He wasn't decomposed, like Anthony. He breathed and so what was wrong still could be made right. Not like poor Anthony, whose wrongs could never be corrected. Every day that a person is alive, they can wake up and do what's right. Earl and Bette agreed.

"Leon is a beauty," Earl sighed, finishing up the last

piece. The beer was finally working.

"I'm sorry," Bette said. "But he's out. Draw a line through his name. Next!"

"I know," Earl sighed. He knew the score. "So, who do we hire?"

"For what?"

"To paint your apartment." Then he grinned. "Ohhhh, I know. I should hire me a man."

"Don't you do that." Bette was afraid. She swept the crumbs off the table with one hand into the other and poured them on her plate. "Hiring a man is risky. Anyone who would sell himself that way is too dangerous. You're valuable. Your life matters."

"Who could be more dangerous to me than I am to myself?" That was the truth. The bottle emptied, he stacked the plates. "Are you going to read that letter? Someone could have died."

She thought it over for a minute.

"I don't think it would make a difference," she decided as he carried the plates to the kitchen sink. "Even if some paltry sum was involved, I don't want it. What would I buy? A new plate? There's no place to put it."

"I'd love to open up my own theater," Earl said.

"I would like that too."

"What would you do if you got rich?"

"Give you a theater."

The last time a letter had arrived from Ohio, they'd both stared at it for a week. Finally Bette read him the note from the neighbor down the road reporting that Bette's mother had passed. That was fourteen, fifteen years now. Her pain was not so much that Mother had died but that she hated to be reminded that she was alone. When Earl's mother died, he ached for the loss of her, the loss he had already been grieving for twenty-three years. Now it was official. That was the difference between them. They both felt things deeply, but Bette was not sentimental and Earl was.

"You are not alone," he said. Now it was Earl's turn to read minds.

"I'm so happy you're home," she smiled.

When a person has to put down and pick up their own plate, cook alone and eat alone and wash up alone, then stare at an empty chair, well, there is no breath. Earl and Bette both breathed. Those sighs of relief required relief. Now for dessert.

"The world is the world of others," he said. "That's what it's all about."

"Should we paint your apartment too?"

"You know I need it."

"Listen!" she cocked her head mischievously. "I can hear the sound of paint chips falling off your walls next door."

They listened, and then they laughed.

"As soon as things calm down at work, I'll find someone to paint us both." Outside the window there was a siren blasting and wailing for attention as it screeched around the corner and then faded down the lane. Detective movie. Some cars honked their horns, showing off that they could. There was action and danger on the street. One person's tragedy was another person's underscore. Someone was bouncing a rubber ball against the building in the dark. Like a heartbeat. Earl took out the tea bags. Turned on the water to boil.

"Yeah, what's happening there?" he asked.

"So many changes at work."

"Still?" He took out two cups and saucers.

"Yes," she said. "It's over my head."

"You just don't care. You just don't care about that job."

She didn't and he knew it. When the old boss, Mr. Tibbs, died, his son, Hector, inherited the business. Tibbs had long confided his doubts to Bette about his son's abilities, but when Earl and Bette talked it over they both agreed the old man had no other choice.

"You can't control from the grave," Mr. Tibbs had told Bette, "only from the earth." Then he'd sighed. "Even if Hector runs my business into the ground, it would be better than rejecting my own son. That would be a terrible pain for him to bear. Why be cruel?" The old man had some mercy.

Earl had followed every episode of Tibbs's deliberations, and the phrase "from the grave" had become a common refrain between him and Bette. Although not so much since the old man had passed and his incompetent son's reign on Bette's life had become reality. Bette was now young Hector's confidante, as he had no idea of how to run a company or even how to shine his own shoes. That the old man remembered Bette as well as sealed her duty. In fact, she found the kindness somewhat embarrassing. He'd left her 25 percent of the worthless company, which she knew was payment for caretaking Hector. Babysitter's wages, to be exact. But still it was the first time anyone had ever thought about her for the long term, and the gesture was deeply moving to Bette. In fact, it was so rare she found it upsetting to even consider. Hector admitted immediately how stunned he'd been when the business landed in his lap, as he'd been preparing emotionally all his life to be left bereft without it. But now that his father had outwitted his disappointment, he was entirely unready to act. And Bette knew it was her role, now, to guide.

"So, in the end," Earl had pointed out, "the old man did control from the grave. By giving the boy more than he could chew. And landing you with an extra set of teeth."

There was a lesson there, of course. That loving someone too much can hurt them terribly. Trusting them when they are untrustworthy can ultimately destroy. Earl did an imitation of Hector, scared silly, clutching the armrests of the commuter train, a ghastly gray, trembling at the thought of all that responsibility. But Earl and Bette both imagined that the other Connecticut scions probably weren't very different from him, and could provide Hector with some helpful insider's tips on how to do what he was destined to do. In fact, their prediction did come true. Night after night, in the club car on the way back to Greenwich, Hector heard interesting schemes from his fellow heirs and started scratching around for a way that he, too, could have a *new* idea. One day Bette finally reported at dinner that Hector had made an announcement: *Some changes need to be made around here.*

That became the catch phrase on Tenth Street for a while. Whenever Earl got fed up with life, he would announce, "Some changes need to be made around here," and then laugh because he was in no position for those changes to be made. What Hector lacked in execution, Earl lacked in resources.

But Earl and Bette had stopped laughing when one Wednesday morning the young boss bounced into his office announcing that he didn't want to do print advertising anymore. He wanted to branch out.

"To radio?" Earl had guessed.

She'd nodded. *"And beyond."*

From then on Hector talked and talked, and Bette had to take every word down in shorthand and then type it all up.

Whistle. The tea was ready for drinking. Civilizing, a cup of tea.

"Like I said," Earl repeated dreamily. "You don't care about that job." He wondered where the hooligans at the Albert Hotel were headed to have fun that night. "Young is good," Earl said, knowing it belonged to someone else, like Leon or Hector. Youth. He could accept that.

"But Hector is *too* young," Bette said. "In all ways. And some young people get too excited. They think they're going to get rich."

"I want to get rich." Earl cut two pieces of cake.

"Well, Earl, buy a television set."

"To get rich? Why? Is that what's on there?"

"I'm telling you." Bette took a bite. "Something is up with those televisions. It was all Hector talked about today. Television advertising. He said it was the *new thing.*"

"The *new thing!*"

"Hey," she jumped with excitement, "they're going to need actors!"

Earl did not have to think. "White ones."

"You never know," Bette said.

He shook his head with that familiar no. "No but-lers. No ooga-booga cannibals." He waved his fork. "No chauffeurs. No shufflers. Wouldn't play them. No *yowser, yowser*. Nope. No way. Not. Never. No. No."

"Okay."

"Now, *Othello*! That is worth reaching for." And he held his fork royally before him, high and mighty as a sword.

"You'd play a king," Bette beamed.

"That," he resumed eating, "is worth reaching for."

And they were back into trying to figure it all out, feeling once again that there *had to be some way*. Some way for Earl to have the right life, the one he was meant to have, the one whose absence stalked him, chased him, haunted him, kicked his ass.

"Maybe if you got them some tickets the next time. The Lazio brothers."

But they both knew that there really was nothing to be gained by having two old meat cutters watch Earl play a spear-carrier. Of course, if he were to perform *The Emperor Jones*, for example. Now, that would be a different story. Or *Porgy and Bess*. He would definitely invite the Lazios to P and B.

"*Porgy, I's your woman now. I is. I is,*" they sang together for a while.

Then it was quiet. Dinner was concluded. Every-thing important had been touched upon. The cake was eaten, the tea was drunk.

"Oh well." Earl leaned back. The dreaming was over. "You will never read that letter."

"Probably not."

"Yeah."

"But you already knew that."

Yes. It was true. He already knew.

Chapter 4

The next morning Earl left the house at four thirty. He hadn't had to be at work until seven for a couple of years but had been leaving at four thirty for so long that it was impossible to stay in an empty bed for another hour. He liked starting out in the dark, preferring the empty streets as he walked west past all the sleepers, the dreamers. Every night Earl had the same kind of dream. He dreamed that his dreams had come true. Every night someone he loved and missed terribly, who had been cruel for no reason, would come to him and be kind. It could be Anthony, or his mother, or his sister, or Leon, or any of the men in between. In the dream they would just forget about it and come hold him, have fun together. Then he would wake up and say a few things out loud, as part of that half waking. He would say, "Help." And he would say, "I am so lonely." And sometimes he would say, "I hate my life." At that point stepping out into the dark town was something to look forward to, something motivating.

By the time he'd made it far west, the other guys would start to appear, converging from uptown, Brooklyn, the Lower East Side. They'd all started out alone and ended up together.

Earl would shoulder his way into the crowded twenty-four-hour greasy spoon on Gansevoort, filled with unwashed men at the counter drinking coffee, eating steamy bowls of hot oatmeal, and smoking, shoulders hunched. Black, Spanish, and white. It was gorgeous. The way they'd talk out of the sides of their mouths, gesture with their cigarettes, or ruminate deep into those cups. Everyone came to work dirty and waited until the end of the shift to shower and soap up. They'd wash together and go home sparkling clean in the evening, but start off dirty in the morning. They had their ways, these guys. Pans of greasy eggs, pans of fried potatoes dripping in grease. Tired men with big hands and lives of filth. Everyone else was in bed, but they were already dirty.

Propped up by camaraderie, Earl went across the street to the Lazios' and checked in to the locker room. He took off his shirt, his regular pants, and put on the gray cotton pants, shirt, and black rubber apron. He stepped into the black rubber boots. He pulled on his work cap. Soon they would all be covered in entrails. Earl turned to move out into the cutting room, and there was Leon, just showing up. That boy was never early, never made enough space to just let something happen. Possibility scared that boy.

"Good morning, Leon," Earl said.

He hadn't thought about it, really. The words had simply come out of his mouth. It was normal, after all. Two people know each other. They see each other. They say good morning. It's not even something to consider. He looked at Leon and smiled politely. But the boy flashed eyes of rage and turned his back. He cut him dead. Would not even say hello.

The pain Leon caused felt unbearable. And yet Earl would have to bear it. Now he would be in pain for the entire day. He would suffer. *That's why they call it "cutting dead,"* he thought. Here he was, fifty years old and his heart hung over his belt. The boy had wanted him and had become afraid of his own feelings. Wasn't that bad enough? Did he have to shun him now, too?

Earl watched Leon do this all day long, refuse to look at him. Refuse to speak to him. Not stand beside him, not offer a hand. All day long! The whole fucking day.

He's a professional, Earl thought. *Wish I could learn that, pretend another man doesn't exist, just because we touched.*

Did Earl really wish that? No. Yes, in fact. Well, no, not really. Well, yes.

That was his crime, wasn't it? Being desired. They'd been walking along Gansevoort that night after Leon had come to supper. It was a strange destination. Instead of going out to a bar or strolling Little Italy, they'd come right back to their place of employ. Right back to the stinking meat and the emptiness, to the sidewalks still slick with fat. They belonged there, he'd guessed. Out of sight. Someplace secret and disgusting. And while this thought crossed his mind, Leon reached over, slipped his arm around Earl, and leaned his head on Earl's shoulder. Beautiful brown boy. Hair, sweet against Earl's cheek. Alone on the cobblestones. Not a footstep in the distance. Earl turned to this young pony and kissed him with all the love he'd been saving inside. The two men kissed in the streetlight and then Earl, naturally, without thinking, ran his hands down the young boy's ass. Hell, they were face to face, cock to cock, pressed against each other. *It was natural*, being that close, to wrap his hands around the young man's ass. What was he supposed to do? Hold his arms out like wings and become a dickless angel, just there for the kiss, and then flap his way back up to ball-less heaven? He wasn't thinking. He wasn't thinking. And Leon jumped.

"Get your hands off my behind," he snapped, stepping back. Like Earl had felt him up on a crowded subway. Like Leon had had nothing to do with it. Like he was innocent. And Leon stared at Earl with an expression of complete shock. As though his favorite uncle had betrayed him. Had violated him. As if Earl was the criminal here, and Leon didn't exist. "Don't you touch me," he said. And Leon turned and fled, literally ran down the street, his boots the sound of gunshots. And that was it. Done. Now Earl had to work all fucking day with someone pretending he was not a person. It just hurt, that's all. It just hurt so bad. That pretty young brother running away from him. Like it was all Earl's fault.

What would happen if someday Earl actually did something wrong to someone? They'd probably kill him. *No*, he realized. Then he'd be the Emperor Jones. *"Dere's little stealin' like you does, and dere's big stealin' like I does. For de little stealin' dey gits you in jail soon or late. For de big stealin' dey makes you Emperor and puts you in de Hall o' Fame when you croaks.*" O'Neill, O'Neill.

The day was long and sad. No surprise. Little acts of cruelty make life hell. Don't other people realize that? Earl stumbled out at the end of the shift, clean, with hell in his head. He walked down West Street, watched the longshoremen unloading mysterious crates. Stood still, looking at them heave-ho. Shit, he was too old for that job now. Where were those boxes coming from? Someplace . . . like . . . who knows . . . *Venezuela.* Earl wasn't exactly sure where that was. Near Brazil probably. Or maybe it was a haul of sardines in the tin from Portugal or Alaska, or jade from China with a stopover in some other out-of-the-way unknown . . . *Guam* or whatever. Bananas? Some kind of shiny ebony wood from his ancestors? Oil don't come in crates. It comes in tankers. Music? Perfume? A gorgeous new feather-bed with a handmade quilt from France? An accordion? Potbelly stove? Waffle iron? Phonographs?

"Where's that ship in from?" he asked an old-timer.

"Utica," the guy mumbled. He had lost his bottom teeth. That meant someone punched him in the face, hard. Or else he fell down dead drunk, flat forward. Either way, the fella had made at least one bad decision.

"What's in there?"

"Scrap."

That's what I should do, Earl realized. *Jump ship!*

What he meant was jump *earth.* Leave the ground behind. No more streets. No more breakfast specials. No more shoulder to shoulder with the passersby. No more Leon.

43

"I should get me on one of those ships," he spat out.

"Ever been to Utica?" the bone mouth asked. And then he started whistling. Yep, he could whistle without any bottom teeth. At least the man could do something. The tune was the melody that went along with the words of an old song.

> Got me a mule, her name is Sal
> Fifteen miles on the Erie Canal.
> She's a good old worker and a good old pal
> Fifteen miles on the Erie Canal.

Earl imagined spending the rest of his days sailing from Buffalo to Albany and back again, with a little shack in Utica, running on the steam of a broken heart. These kinds of cities were awfully quiet. *Nothing around you matters.* That was the problem staying here in New York, *everything* around him mattered. Leon matters. Emperor Jones matters. It's all within sight. He could never go numb because it was all so damn fascinating. And he had never perfected thinking about other things without thinking about himself. Maybe if there were nothing else to look at, he would stop looking at all his own fuck ups. Day in, day out. When does that ever stop? Desire? The wish, the disappointment? When does a man ever grow out of that? This is what Earl wanted to know. He wasn't getting on no damn boat.

Earl walked east and a little south, and soon he was on Bleecker and Carmine where the Village Italians had their main drag. Rabbits hanging in the butcher's window with fur still decorating their ankles.

Here's what Earl noticed that day about his devil home:

(1) It's a city of laundry. Everyone else knows exactly what each other's got because it's *all* hanging out of windows, across rooftops, lying over every available iron grate. It's intimate. It's a fact. Eight million undies on display. When a woman wants to put on something sexy for her man, she has to dry it before he gets home. No point watching it flapping from a clothesline before he sees it draped over his lover's voluptuous body.

(2) Children are the kings of New York. Yeah, back home he could go fishing or swim naked and no one would bother him. But so what? Here, the kids run free in the royal realm. Everywhere there's a pack of them with a clear-cut leader in rolled pants and some scheme in the making: jumping on and off the backs of buses, racing around corners, hanging on each other's stoops, being cruel or loving. Even the loners could do as they pleased. He saw boys eight, ten years old and curled up in a corner in a dream or weeping, making plans about how to get some friends someday. No adult knew exactly where they were or what they were up to, as long as they appeared for supper. The kids saw everything that happened in the neighborhood and it showed on their faces. The joyous responsibility of catching the drift.

He kept going down Bleecker, past the funeral home, and that new leather shop where the beatnik kids were buying sandals. They loved them sandals. He didn't quite get it. What was so happening about sandals? On both sides of the street, tired, dirty Italian men trudged home from construction jobs. They lived on Mulberry, Sullivan, and MacDougal. Bleecker had a lot of cafés those days. Some were still Italian, but some were for the poets. Or they switched, depending on the time of night. But the side streets belonged to the working people. Grandfathers, fathers, uncles all hired on the same site. Earl never had dust on his shoes at the end of the day. That was a sign of pride. But these slum kings stomped home dirty and presided at rickety kitchen tables, grit still under their nails. *I'm telling you*, he said to no one. *Some of those Sicilians are black.* Was he the only one who could see how African they were? And the women? If they cut their hair a little differently it would all be clear as day. *Who are they kidding?*

In '54 Earl had gone to see a theater acquaintance sing an opera set on this block. *The Saint of Bleecker Street*. It was about a girl named Annina blessed with the wounds of Jesus Christ. She heard voices and saw visions of the angels. Her brother, however, was an atheist. That's where the story got interesting. He thought she needed to do some time in the loony bin, but all the neighbors bought that she was a saint. They were very old-school. Maybe Leon was an angel sent by God to teach Earl a lesson. But, what could that lesson be?

You're never gonna make it, he thought, and then said one word out loud.

"Never."

46

By the time he got to Sullivan, he'd seen a lot, and had taken in a couple of lessons. The street kids were playing in the wading pool at the Children's Aid Society. Most of them had never seen a lake. Most of them had never worn a bathing suit. But they didn't know and they didn't care. They could still have fun and cool off.

Learn from the urchins. He laughed.

At the southwest corner of Washington Square Park, a gang of brothers and other cats were ensconced on the cement tables, playing chess. There were always some black guys hanging out here. A weird mixture of out-of-work beboppers, local philosophers, hard workers on their way home from fixing something for a living, hauling something, serving somebody. Next to them, the eternally unemployed drinking on the sly. A handful of Negro students from that hovering university were exhausted by the burden of constant uplift. Missing their hardworking fathers back home, they'd sit on the edges, little eggheads, soaking up the camaraderie. Earl slid beside Jerome, an older fellow who always stopped off for a game of chess before heading back to his house in Saint Albans, Queens. Earl liked him, but did not share his tastes. Just because a person was black, did not mean that J. J. Johnson had to be *your man.*

"J. J. Johnson is my man," Jerome had said so often, Earl smirked undercover each time, imagining what would happen if that could ever be true.

"It's bebop slide," Jerome promised over and over again like it was a miracle at Lourdes. "That J. J. Johnson. Now, he my man."

Earl was an actor first and foremost. He loved the classics. *Hamlet. Othello,* of course. Musical innovations always eluded him. But he had been made curious through Jerome's braying about *jazz trombone, I tell you, trombone!* So, he did take the recommendation and sat one night alone at the bar to give the notorious Mr. Johnson a chance. Later J. J. pulled up beside him for a beer between sets. They had a nice chat. J. J. was a blueprint inspector at a Sperry plant on Long Island and could only get off work to play music one night a week. Earl was impressed by the gleam of that trombone and what kind of depth it took to make it swing. But the truth was that Earl liked stories and this music was too abstract. He was glad he'd seen J. J. before the man lost his cabaret card, but really he'd rather spend his hard earned money on a play.

That was his fate somehow, Earl. To go out alone. Sidle up to someone at a bar or on a bench by a loading dock and try to strike up a relationship. They'd talk for a while and then the other would be on his way. Earl missing him already, while 'for the one he'd trapped into a chat, it was a throwaway. Unless they were both up for sex, and then it would be behind a building or, if he got lucky, in one of their apartments for a few hours that he could never get to stretch into a night. He liked to be in bed with a man, but most of them shied away. Whenever Earl would see some potential, he'd clean his place, change the sheets. Set up the two pillows in clean cases. He'd have four bottles of beer in the Frigidaire, a pack of smokes. Whatever a fellow might need. But it would be years in between the nights anyone else climbed between those sheets. Sometimes Bette was his only real conversation of the day. He'd go the whole twenty-four hours without interchanging with another soul for real. Being lonely is a bad habit, like dope. Don't start or it will run your life. That's the advice Earl would have offered Leon, if he'd ever had the opportunity. *Don't make loneliness work for you.*

He saw a small brown-skinned boy shyly standing apart from the adults. The kid was fascinated, could not take his eyes off the men but could not approach them either.

Get yourself some friends, boy! Earl wanted to shout out. *Before it's too late and you don't know how.*

On the northeast corner of the park, Earl stopped at the Chock Full o'Nuts. This was the only store in the neighborhood with an all-Negro staff besides Mary Raye's Pink Tea Cup on Grove where the NAACP would meet. Village Chapter. That's why the great Jackie Robinson had gone to work for Chock Full o'Nuts as director of personnel. He knew where to go to help his people. Earl did not know where to go. And he wasn't sure exactly who *his people* were. He stepped into that place every once in a while to exchange smiles with Sheila and Nancy and the other young ladies in yellow uniforms who worked the counters. There were no tables, no plates. They served the doughnuts on wax paper. Sometimes he'd order one of those cream-cheese-and-date nut bread sandwiches. Chock Full o'Nuts brand coffee. Everybody sat alone. He had that freeing feeling when he stepped in, like it was *his* place. Where else was he going to be treated that nice? A lonely black man looking for a cup of joe. Like how he felt when he was in a theater when he was acting in a play. When he could walk through the stage door and old Pops would greet him.

"Good evening, Mr. Coleman."

"Hi, Pops."

"Have a great show."

"Thanks."

Earl bought two doughnuts for dessert, one plain for him and one powdered for Bette, and started the final stretch from Chock Full.o'Nuts up University Place.

At the corner of Tenth, he bought his nightly bottle of beer at Rubin's Deli. Then he saw the strange beige Bentley Bette had mentioned parked for a second time in front of one of them galleries. It was such a beaut, he stood quietly with appreciation. Admired the thing, its grace. There's something about excess beauty that makes both energetic children and tired old men stop suddenly and stare with admiration. They just can't help it. The shine is paralyzing, that otherworldly spark. It's an affirmation that someone he did not know, somewhere he would never be, was living high on the hog. The whole pig.

Earl couldn't help himself, he was pulled toward its gleaming chassis, and only then did he see the equally beautiful black man in front of the chariot's carriage, daintily smoking a cigarette. Handsome man, handsome car.

The guy had a good physique and carried off the uniform with panache. He wasn't buried by it, he surpassed it. Matching beige uniform, cap tipped rakishly to the side.

Then the guy looked up and caught Earl's eye. There was kindness at first, followed by a swelling recognition.

"Frankie?" Earl called out. "Frankie, is that you?"

Big smile, beautiful open face. Now, this was the good news, and not of the churchgoing kind.

"Earl, baby, what you doing around here?"

"I live here, man, right across the street."

Frankie was a fellow actor, from the old days. He and Earl had worked together in *On Strivers Row*, could that be fifteen years back?

"You mean *eighteen*, Earl, dontcha?"

"Already?"

"Yessir. Eighteen years back."

Standing there, Earl melted inside with the joyful surprise, the realization that he could still love. He was still cursed and blessed with a fucking open heart. Here this darling guy had crossed his path. *Frank.* Just when Earl had been so low, scraping the sidewalk down, that's when Frankie appeared with his sweet smile, saying something friendly, showing some sort of kindness. Earl was filled with a terrible joy. Just being remembered brought it out in him. Frankie placed his hand casually on Earl's shoulder and left a scar. Earl got a whiff of his neck, a sign of his languid wrist, his strong hands. Earl could see the whole thing, how easily it would unfold. If the other would only agree, they could make themselves happy, together forever. Every pain that had come before would be no matter. Life would begin anew. Instead of waiting for death, Earl would want to live, to live longer and longer to have another lifetime with his man. His man, Frankie. Frankie's dreams in his hands. Someone to roll over and talk to in the morning light. Like it had been with Anthony, now dead for fourteen long, hard years. Silent widower, ghost mourner, man with no marker, no title. That hell could finally end. Morning. That was the key to happiness. Someone in the morning. You wake up and he's not a dream. Coffee together at the table. Shirts hanging side by side in the closet. T-shirts in the drawer. Two towels. Frankie's specialties in the kitchen, in the bedroom, his books, his musical tastes, his friends, his family. The way he looked at things, those phrases. More light. More hope. Salvation. Frankie. Salvation. Frankie. *Bring it to me. Bring it to me.*

Seeing the potential before him brought out the truth of how his life was so paltry. After dinner with Bette, Earl never knew what to do with himself. Go out and get in trouble or lie down on his beat-up sofa and read the paper until he fell asleep. He knew not to get in bed too early or it would be a painful night. Lonely, empty, remembering, can't shake it. He'd learned to lie on that sofa until the paper fell from his hand. Sleep off the first three hours and then groggily transfer to the bed, already hoping not to awaken. It was the only way that worked. There were times though when he just couldn't make it and would recite *Othello* until the longing made even that unbearable.

> Think, my lord!
> By heaven, he echoes me,
> As if there were some monster in his thought
> Too hideous to be shown. Thou dost mean
>   something:
> I heard thee say even now, thou likedst not that,
> When Cassio left my wife: what didst not like?
> And when I told thee he was of my counsel

In my whole course of wooing, thou criedst
    "Indeed!"
And didst contract and purse thy brow together,
As if thou then hadst shut up in thy brain
Some horrible conceit: if thou dost love me,
Show me thy thought.

Earl looked at Frank, joking, warm. It all made
sense. This darling guy. He was a beauty. Earl smiled.
Show thy thought. Frank smiled back. There was hope.

Just at that moment a svelte woman in pants and
dark glasses came storming through the gallery's
doors. Earl saw her barreling like a submarine tor-
pedo and jumped to the side to get out of her way. The
lady gallery owner, Miss Parsons, chased after her
half-heartedly, knowing it would not resolve, and followed her into the back of the sedan.

"Gotta go," Frank said, stubbing out his smoke.
"Hey, you free tonight?"

"Yeah, I'm free."

"This is your lucky day."

"Every day is my lucky day." Earl was so happy.

Frank handed him a ticket and replaced his chauffeur's cap neatly on his graying head. "It'll be a special
night," Frank winked, and slid back behind the driver's seat.

The kids on the block who had gathered for a return communion with the Bentley stepped away to let
her depart. With a deepened respect that came from
repeated discussion and inspection, they admired her
silent roll uptown.

"Who was that?" Margaret O'Reilly asked on the way to Teddy's Butcher Shop, clutching her mama's grocery list. One half-pound sliced bologna.

"That was Frank," Earl answered, fingering his ticket.

"That wasn't Frank," one of the queens from the Albert Hotel corrected. "Honey, that was Greta Garbo."

"Oh yeah?" Earl couldn't care less.

"Yeah," she said, wrapping her sweater expertly into a veil over her hair. "*Dat vas Ninotchka.*"

Earl did not care. He was riveted by the black words on the small red slip in his hand. First he saw the raised letters spell out the name "Carnegie Hall." Then he saw the title "An Evening with Paul Robeson."

This was it.

He was being handed his one true last chance on earth for happiness. Last opportunity to be cared for, to be seen, to be recognized. Acknowledged, held, loved, and heard. To be valued. To never sleep alone again. To be cut slack, to be forgiven, to be given a break and defended. Last gasp of loyalty, honor, respect, and, again, love, love, l-o-v-e. No more shit. It would all be over now, just things going his way, just finally at this late date everything being set finally, finally right.

That night at supper Earl and Bette talked through every detail.

"Did Frank have on a wedding ring?"

Earl wasn't sure.

"Did he wear one back in 1940?"

Definitely not. Earl remembered checking backstage all those years ago and filing away that hope for later. Well, later had arrived. Amazing how long he could carry a tender wish born in one moment of noticing that there was no wedding band. No girl.

"It looks good," Bette concluded. And they both agreed.

Earl sat back in his chair stunned. He couldn't move. Bette cleared the plates, boiled the water, and got out the tea bags, because he was immobilized. He was paralyzed by happiness. His eyes were wet. His hands tingled. His dick had weight. His chest glowed proud from under his best shirt. Paul Robeson! Othello! Emperor Jones! And Frank. Paul and Frank. Paul and Frank. Sitting next to Frank and watching Paul, together. *Together.* Two mature black men, both still good-looking. Two actors with the same dream and knowledge behind them. And the fellow on the stage, the actor who'd made it, made them think it was possible. Paul Robeson who had gotten that dream right. It was an omen. Tonight. Tonight, Earl's whole life finally made sense. It was all going to click, to come together, and come true. At Carnegie Hall. Carnegie Hall! Frank. Frank. Beautiful Frank. I love you, Frankie. You're my man. Mr. Robeson. Mr. Robeson. Othello!

"Whatever happens . . ." Bette trailed off.

He saw the love and fear in her eyes. She was being realistic, but she wanted it all to work out.

He could not be realistic. Hope was not realistic. Love was not realistic. Salvation for Earl Coleman was not realistic.

"Hey!" Earl almost forgot.

"What?" Bette poured the boiling water into their cups.

"Guess who was in that Bentley?"

"Who?"

Earl unfolded the linen napkin and draped it alluringly around his head. *"Dat vas Ninotchka,"* he said.

"Well, well," Bette marveled. "Now that is truly something." A bona fide star had made a cameo appearance in her movie. "You don't say."

After this night, Bette would never have to watch him be humiliated again. He would never cause her that pain. He would sail on through life. He would have everything. This was it. This was his night. Finally. A king.

Chapter 5

Earl sat, proud in his suit, in the balcony at Carnegie Hall, overlooking the crowd below. He did belong somewhere, after all, and that somewhere was here. This was his world, and it was Frankie who had brought it literally to his feet. A theater, his people, his man, his suit. It was sold out, but he had a ticket. Smiling as he soared past those on line with no chance of getting in. Stride! Everyone seated before him in the red-curtained and wood-paneled hall had a ticket too, the price of admission. Some were there for the moment, some for the music, some for the movement, some for the meaning.

"Excuse me."

Earl stood happily to let an attractive young woman pass by him in the aisle. She had class and so did he. There were rituals and decorum and elegance in this world, and he fit in perfectly.

"Earl?"

"Yes?"

How did she know him? He scanned his memory. Was she a dancer? Did she work at the Chock Full o'Nuts? Someone he'd met at a show? Nothing clicked.

"I'm Lynette Carter."

"How are you, Lynette?"

He couldn't place her. Must be early thirties. Stunning. Dark-skinned, lovely demeanor. Fashionable style of the sophisticated young. Not churchy, modern. Not uplift, *arrived*. Black skirt, black turtleneck, black stockings. She crossed many worlds, that was clear.

"Frank's daughter." The lights dimmed. She slid into the seat next to him and crossed her legs. "I grew up with Robeson's records," she whispered. "So excited to finally see the man."

"Daughter?" Earl bleeted, knowing he had to internalize something terrible very quickly.

He could smell her perfume. She was being seductive. The audience hushed as the piano accompanist appeared, took his seat. Hands, poised in midair, ready to go. The crowd could not contain their joy, murmuring happiness even at simple anticipation of something wonderful.

"He sends his best," she whispered again. Her voice was full, smoky.

"How's your mother?" He still held out one last straw. *Oh, my parents divorced years ago. That marriage was a mistake . . . well, you know.*

"She's doing fine. They're having a dinner party tonight. Thirty years of marriage. It's a blessing. There he is!" Already Lynette was contented and absorbed.

Who am I? Earl trembled.

At that terrible moment, the chasm within Earl's soul split open. He could feel the rotten liquid oozing through his chest, dripping out of his ears. Simultaneously, Robeson appeared. The room embraced him in cheers.

The star was sixty. His kidneys were hurting. The US government still would not give him back his passport. He was up against more than he would ever be able to handle. But Earl did not take any of that in. He crumpled his program and seethed. He melted. Devil reality forced its evil self back onto the throne.

> *Every time I feel the spirit moving in my heart,*
>   *I'm free.*
> *Every time I feel the spirit moving in my heart,*
>   *I'm free.*

Earl stared at the stage. Where was he? He trembled. His soul had fallen to the floor, rolled down the aisle, and leapt from the balcony, crashing into the lives of the people below. Causing tragedy. Ruining everything. Ruining everyone else's night. Ruining Paul Robeson's big moment. That was how Earl felt. What did he do about how he felt? The same thing he always did. Diminished silently. Lost life. If ever, anywhere, there were a group of guys all walking in Earl's specific shoes, trying to do something about the pain, well . . . the news had not reached him. The loss was always, always, always his own personal, singular, queer, old loss. And it was always the taking away of connection, keeping it ever impossible to simply have.

And then the Holy Spirit revives my soul again.
There is a balm in Gilead to make the wounded
  whole.

Lynette turned to him and smiled. He smiled back. Applause. Now, Robeson was singing something in Russian. How did a black man know Russian? Earl had met plenty of Communists in his day, but they didn't speak goddamn Russian. He was burning now, Earl. He was enraged. Why didn't Frankie tell him he had a family? Earl replayed the scene in his mind four times.

"Hey, you free tonight?"
"Yeah, I'm free."
"This is your lucky day."

Goddamn that boy, Frankie never said *he* was gonna be there. What a sly devil that one was. How could Earl be so sloppy? Bette always said they had to pay attention to *everything*. Every detail. But he didn't. He wasn't attentive. *Fool. Fool.* Frankie was passing Earl off onto his own daughter. Pimp. He must want her himself. Putting her on a date with a man almost her father's age.

I grows weary, and sick of trying.
I'm tired of living, and scared of dying.
It just keeps rolling. It keeps on rolling.
It just keeps rolling along.

Lynette kept glancing sideways at Earl, smiling. Then she would look ahead at the program. She wanted to know what would happen next. She was grinning at him, having made up her mind. Like they were in on something together. Earl did not want to be in on anything with her. She was just like her father. Fucking charming. Nice. She saw conspiracies on her own behalf when there were none. Lynette pointed to the program. Earl smiled back at her. He was blind with rage. What was this woman grinning about? He knew. He knew what she was thinking. What she wanted. She assessed that Earl was everything her father had built him up to be. How much wronger could a person get?

The audience burst into applause, jumping out of their seats. They went on and on, clapping and moaning. They could not believe their own luck. This night would become a story their grandchildren would tell. That was for sure. The lights focused onstage and the audience got the message. *Calm down. Let the man sing!* That was one thing Earl knew plenty about. How audiences do what the lights instruct. It was uncanny. They don't understand why they're doing it, but they obey.

Being in an audience intensified Earl's feelings. It had been that way for as long as he could remember. A stage provided the opportunity to be in the world of others, to be listened to, engaged with. Doing a play meant that the other person had to answer, they couldn't just walk away and pretend. They were forced to stay and follow the script to its denouement. They had to face him. Resolution guaranteed. But being in the audience was the opposite. Earl watched someone else get all the validation. Here he was, in the wrong spot again. Everything was out of touch with everything else.

And then he felt calm. This was so familiar after all. Being disappointed. It was a blanket he knew well. It was the most normal feeling of his life. He knew how to be disappointed, but he didn't know how to have hope. Hope turned him into an idiot. He couldn't handle hope and that now was clear. One glimpse of a chance and he immediately went overboard. Nothing was going to be up to him. He had to go with it, one more time. He had to go with loss. That was his path. *Okay, listen to Robeson, you fool. Let him give you something. Don't come out of this with nothing.* Listen. Listen.

> Soft you; a word or two before you go.
> I have done the state some service, and they
> know't.

Something grabbed at Earl, like he'd been lassoed by a chain.

> No more of that. I pray you, in your letters,

His heart recognized something, breaking through his isolation.

> When you shall these unlucky deeds relate,
> Speak of me as I am; nothing extenuate,

It was happening on stage. What was it? What was

it? Earl saw Robeson, his face, the resolution of a man playing a role from his soul. Othello! Robeson was reciting Othello!

> Nor set down aught in malice: then must you
> speak
> Of one that loved not wisely but too well;
> Of one not easily jealous, but being wrought
> Perplex'd in the extreme; of one whose hand,
> Like the base Indian, threw a pearl away
> Richer than all his tribe; of one whose subdued
> eyes,
> Albeit unused to the melting mood,
> Drop tears as fast as the Arabian trees
> Their medicinal gum. Set you down this;
> And say besides, that in Aleppo once,
> Where a malignant and a turban'd Turk
> Beat a Venetian and traduced the state,
> I took by the throat the circumcised dog,
> And smote him, thus.

The audience exploded, and Earl found himself propelled from his seat, reaching for the sky. Clapping, cheering, jumping, opening his heart like a country woman with no place but church to be herself, nothing better to look forward to than the preacher's gold on Sunday. It happened too quickly to pass over. Joy was a truck coming on full force into his same lane. Collision. He was happy, happy!

That was it. Pretending made Earl happy. He told himself bluntly to just forget life. *It is not available.* And then he felt something soft and warm reach out to him and saw his hand being held by a young woman's hand. When he looked over, she was beaming, and Earl realized that he was beaming. And they were united, Earl Coleman and Lynette Carter. They were united in *Othello*, holding hands in the balcony. He was not alone. He had Paul Robeson.

Before Othello stabs himself, he asks the others to listen to him for a moment. And they do, because of his service to the state. Because he is somebody. He already knows that he's going to die but is worried about how he will be remembered. This problem was so different from Earl's own problem. Earl didn't give a rat's ass about what could happen after he died. His worry was about the rest of his life. Right now. How was he going to make it through? How was he going to survive this minute? Becoming Othello removed that problem, the problem of the everyday. Earl was lonely every day. Not Othello. Othello asks the others to see him as he *actually* is, no better or no worse. Earl couldn't even get that far in the conversation. Othello loves "not wisely but too well." Earl never got a chance to love. Not since Anthony.

For the rest of the concert, Lynette held his hand and smiled at him. Earl smiled back and thought about the man he didn't have. His boyfriend. That's how it was going to have to be. Earl's lover would have to take other forms. He would have to be roles and celebrities and images from the street. Earl would have to conjure the person up in his mind, like his own personal genie, and carry him around in his pocket. Tell himself, *my man is waiting for me at home.* Or, *I'm going to meet my man.* And then going home would be happy and walking to his destination would be happy. So what that no one was home and no one was meeting him anywhere? He'd just defer. Place the man around the very next corner. *That's how it would have to be*, Earl settled on it. Since he still lived, he would have to pretend.

What was happening? The audience was cheering. The concert was over. Earl had somehow missed the rest of it. There was a stunning beauty to the night, sweet with the earliest promise of spring to come, as Lynette led him out onto Fifty-Seventh Street. The sidewalks were full, everyone living life in front of each other, creating each other's worlds.

"I'm going to a party. Want to join me?"

"Sure," Earl said. Why did he say that?

On the subway he was still asking himself that question. Lynette talked and talked, which gave him some time to think. She was newly divorced. She talked primarily about her ex-husband and the key facts of the situation, the ones that bothered her the most. She was annoyed now about how great he had looked in his army uniform when they'd first met. But then, after the war, back from Berlin, he hung with his old friends from the neighborhood and never took his responsibilities seriously. It all got very old. She was tired of being his mama, always asking him to keep his promises. She was clear about what she wanted. Lynette Carter was looking for someone more mature, more adult. Like her father. She wanted a man who understood the importance of stability. She was finishing her master's in social work at Adelphi and doing her fieldwork at Kings County Hospital in Brooklyn. It was a long commute from her parents' place in Harlem, and she knew it was only a matter of time before she got her own apartment again. She had dated a Jewish psychiatrist she'd met at Kings County, but he still lived with his parents in Elizabeth, New Jersey, and was a big baby. She'd already had a black adult baby, why get a white one too? No, Lynette Champagne Carter wanted a grown-up black man to live with in Brooklyn or a Puerto Rican neighborhood like Chelsea, someplace friendly. A lot of her friends from City College became artists, intellectuals, teachers. They were a happening crowd. Earl would understand them, being an actor like her father. He would really like their scene.

Earl came to the answer to his own question. He'd said yes because he had nothing else to do. Even if he'd pretended that his man was waiting for him at home. It wouldn't be very long before he got there and was alone. That's why he'd said, "Sure." So now he had to do it. Go to this goddamn party.

At the Union Square exit of the RR train, Earl stepped into the quiet of a phone booth to call his service. He closed the door and sat on the wooden seat, trying to recover while dropping nickels into the slot. It was an unusual choice, since he knew that no calls had come in. No auditions, no spear-carriers, no understudies, no one-liners sweeping up in janitorial uniforms. But he had to try. It was one last chance for the universe to rescue him from leading this woman on any further. He'd made a deal with fate. If only one good thing happened, he would free her and go home. But there was nothing. He was torn because he only lived four blocks away. He'd be home in five minutes, and miserable, escaping from the night into his apartment.

But then where would he go to escape from himself?

"Okay," he smiled. "Let's go."

When they got to the party on West Eleventh Street, it was packed. Folks lining the walls and crowding the stairs. It wasn't a home, really, more like a rehearsal room, but someone who didn't know much about carpentry had thrown up a couple of sheets of drywall and created cubicles where a few people seemed to be living. Each section represented a room with a bed and belongings, but there were no windows, and in some cases the drywall did not reach the ceiling. Doors were openings with curtains, hiding piles of books, clothes, fashionable Mexican blankets, drawings tacked on the walls, typewriters, notebooks, Chianti bottles covered in melted wax. Each one had been set up for the party with drinks, beers, remnants of food long gone. Guests had to poke around the tenants' belongings to find an opener for the beer. A number of the girls had unopened beer bottles that the men were cracking on the backs of chairs, showing off their manhood. Some good-looking guys, white girls with their hair piled high on their heads. Black girls outshining them at every turn. But the white guys could be hot in their dopey out-of-it-ness. They could act like they didn't want it, when they did. Or that they didn't know how much they wanted it, what was causing that rise in their pants. That was sexy.

He followed Lynette into the huge central area that was packed with young kids. Even younger than she was. Basically, it was a white kids' party with some black folks. Who did she know here? Didn't look like doctors. She gazed at him and raised her eyebrows.

He could tell this wasn't what she'd expected. She wanted a poetry reading or some shit like that. Some hip cats. Some weed, some drums. She wanted to show him how cool she was, but she wasn't. She was just a hardworking, good-looking woman who needed a man. He understood that. She had a fleeting fantasy that this man would be an artist or whatnot, but that was just whimsy. It would only give her more problems. Artists never make it, even if they should, and that's hard to understand and live with. No, she needed a tax accountant or a teacher. Someone solid who knew how to hand back the papers on time and wore a tie. She didn't belong at this party, and neither did he. It wasn't for them. That was one of the things he loved about being in a play, the camaraderie. Going out for drinks and ending up at someone's place with a handful of folks talking out their hearts. He loved that.

"I gotta go to the bathroom," he said.

Lynette smiled, nodding her head to the music some guys were making in the corner. Their sound was okay.

Earl pushed his way to the bathroom line. It was long and slow. Lots of girls ahead of him, smoking, laughing. Women take a long time in the bathroom. They have to look at themselves, prolonged inspection. It was a swirl of other people's dreams, their self-images, imaginations.

"What do you do?" a sharp-tongued white girl asked him. She was bold, he could see that. She had energy. She laughed and her eyes gleamed.

"I'm an actor. What about you?"

"I'm writing a novel," she said.

"Oh, yeah, how do you do that?"

"Well," she said. "It's hard to explain."

Earl looked over her head. Lynette was talking to another woman, still swaying to the music, waiting for his return so she could pull him onto the dance floor. He needed to tell her. He needed to let her know that this wasn't going to happen. The charade was already too elaborate, had gone on for too long. Every minute more that he lied to her was a bigger waste of her life. He didn't want to do that, create disappointment for others. He had to stop this game now.

"Excuse me," Earl said, and determinedly pushed his way through the guests, turned the corner, and without making the decision, simply fled down the four flights of stairs, and burst out into the night. He ran like someone mean was chasing him, and then, when he got to the corner, he was filled with indecision. Should he go upstairs to his apartment where everything was known? All the cracks, the dust, the sounds that entomb? Or walk around some more looking for something that wasn't going to happen?

Then Earl remembered his boyfriend, the one in his imagination. But where was the guy? He wasn't upstairs. He wasn't around the corner. He wasn't waiting in a bar or killing time in the park. Earl leaned against his building. The rough, cold bricks held his face. The concrete base scratched his palms. The support felt so good. He'd been tense all night. The mortar scratched his aching back. He turned and pressed his body full against 21 East Tenth Street. His toes, his thighs, his cock and balls, stomach, chest, his lips caressing her. He licked her. Buildings are "shes" like cities and boats. But his building was a flamer. She camped. She was a queen, whose drag name was Mary or Helen. The bricks drank his tears. It was so comforting. His building was his boyfriend, that was all there was to it. That's how it was going to be.

Chapter 6

Earl's joy carried Bette through the evening. The potential for his suffering to end would be so freeing to both of them, a great relief that she very much wanted to feel. She looked forward to the loss of an ongoing worry that he was always endangered.

A new chapter.

Just imagining the change unleashed other passions in Bette. Her mind floated and then lingered on faraway forgotten things, elements of the past like the smell of honeysuckle by the road behind her girlhood home. That had never happened before. She cut open an orange and brought it to her nose. Ah, delicious. Frank would do that for Earl. With kindness. She knew he could.

What is love?

Bette had wondered for most of her life. Her conclusion?

When both see the other as real.

What is real?

When both understand the feelings and perceptions and desires that the other holds, as precious, pungent, and meaningful as one's own. Their realizations are as powerful, and their deprivations are as grievous. To notice. To care. That he is listening, and she is listening. That one is not more important than the other.

What is listening?

What you say to each other is a promise, which becomes remembered, and then enacted. The spoken is transformed into the lived, deliberately. And the mechanism for this is cooperation. That is to say, the relationship.

What is a relationship?

To be awakened to the other, as though leaving a dream.

What do we want from life?

We wish the responsibilities, opportunities, and realities of the new day to be more delightful and enticing than the escape of sleep.

This is what she wished for Earl.

As for Bette, herself, she was quite a different type.

Bette loved her chair. She loved her cup. She loved the plant growing tall in the corner and the freedom of the evening before her. Everything had come through her labor, her imagination, her commitment, and now it was all in place. She loved the records standing strong on the shelf and the chance to both own and choose music without impediment. She was balanced, she had Earl to care for, and she had a job that didn't mean a thing. So she had feeling and relief from feeling.

After some thought, Bette selected the recording of *The Threepenny Opera* that Earl had gotten as a gift from Marc, the show's translator. They'd met at one of those actors' parties where the exalted and their subordinates drink the same beer. Earl said Marc "had a thing for Negro men." There had been a tryst in the man's apartment, but he would not let Earl stay the night. Too intimate. Instead, he'd signed a copy: *To Earle, Yours, Marc Blitzstein*, misspelling Earl's name and thereby nipping any potential romance in the bud. Earl felt that a person should take the time to learn another person's name. And he was firm on that matter. Bette had spent her early life being called "Betty." But, ever since *Of Human Bondage* made Bette Davis a star, citizens of every country and in every walk of life had known how to pronounce it.

Bette and Earl had gone to the Theater de Lys on Christopher Street to see the production of *The Three-penny Opera*, and both loved it. It was so sophisticated. The story was about the poor and their own version of society, rich in passion, deceit, and dreams, just like the rich. But making dreams come true when one is a prostitute or petty thief is hard because they don't really know how things work, and live in illusions that something might go their way. That it might all be about luck, when actually most fates are predetermined, she knew, just by where and how one is born. The music was dreamy, eerie and evocative. Like the sound of mist. And they both loved the words, which were deadpan and deep and frighteningly true. It kind of summed up the historic moment: complexity explained with words that anyone could understand. Bette's favorite lyrics came from Mack the Knife's pronouncement that the play's lovers were caught in an illusion of faith. That they were trapped in a false wish over which they had no control.

> *They've got that . . . moon on a dark street.*
> *They've got that . . . I feel my heart beating true.*
> *They've got that . . . anywhere you go, I will*
>   *go with you.*

It is a kind of disease. Like pneumonia. Love fills a woman's lungs with fluid and then she drowns. Bette knew.

Earl's favorite song was performed by an actor he'd met named John Astin, singing about joining the army. Earl had gotten his draft notice after Pearl Harbor and barely discussed it. Hanging in the air were thoughts about Anthony, who was still alive in the Philippines or Iwo Jima, somewhere hot, dangerous, and buggy. Earl, at that point thirty-two years old, had gone off to the physical and came back with a big H stamped on his card. Bette knew he had caused that, decided not to go, that much was clear. Exactly why or how was not something he'd cared to share. To die looking in the swamp for Anthony seemed to Bette not enough of a motive. *Freedom* was a qualified word. Certainly fighting Hitler was right and many black men were signing up to do just that. But she knew Earl had his reasons, and, after all, this was a decision that Bette would never have to make for herself.

For the next two years, Earl tried to find out the details of his love's whereabouts, but the guys coming back had no news, until one showed up at the Lazios' in uniform looking for a job, and gently reported Anthony dead. On that beach. That's when Earl had stumbled home, in tears, and finally explained to Bette that he just didn't want to go through it. He didn't want to go through segregated units and cleaning white men's latrines, and being excluded and worse for being a fag, and eating substandard segregated rations and sleeping in segregated mosquito tents, and coming back to nothing. It just wasn't what he wanted to do. So, he'd told them the truth and they'd let him go home. That's why his favorite song from *The Threepenny Opera* was "The Army Song."

> *Let's all go barmy, live off the Army*
> *See the world we never saw.*
> *If we get feeling down, we wander into town*
> *And if the population should greet us with*
> *   indignation*
> *We chop 'em to bits because we like our*
> *   hamburgers raw.*

Together, the song that Earl and Bette both found themselves humming was "The Useless Song" because it said more than two things at once, and they both enjoyed that sort of intelligence.

> *If at first you don't succeed, then try and try*
> *   again*
> *And if you don't succeed again, just try and try*
> *   and try.*
> *Useless, it's useless, our kind of life's too tough.*
> *Take it from me it's useless. Trying ain't enough.*

*Since people ain't much good. Just hit them on
the hood.
And though you hit them good and hard, they're
never out for good.
Useless, it's useless, even when you're playing
rough.
Take it from me it's useless. You're never rough
enough.*

When the record was over, darkness had muffled
public life. Commerce, routine, the actions of measured
time that occurred by day were over. Night was when
the free self emerged, when passion was expressed,
and when people made grand mistakes. Murder took
place at night, and sexual pleasures and violations and
combinations thereof. Lies were told at night because
"it's getting late" meant the clock was ticking and what
a person must have, had to be. These were the hours
that Bette saved for a good book.

Tonight she would conclude a novel that had carried her through the last three evenings. Some more
hours were passed thusly and then the final pages
were turned, conclusions artfully revealed. Bette liked
a novel whose insights into the human mind were not
predictable and yet, upon revelation, were stunningly
and obviously true. *People are not as we wish ourselves
to be. And yet facing the truth is what makes us fully
alive.* In this novel, the hero deserved praise after all,
and Bette was relieved about its ending. In her nightgown, she asked herself, *What do I remember most?* and
then enjoyed recalling the mountaintop scene. When
the hero looked out over the countryside and realized

that the entire world was one living thing, as energetic and filled with beauty as the horse by his side, as himself, well . . . Bette sighed, and held the volume to her chest in an appreciative embrace. The gift.

Then, outside her door, she heard the sounds of two laughing, flirting drunken men passing by. She could hear Earl slurring.

"Here we are."

Then she heard the other fellow. That must be Frank.

"Come on, Mary, you can do it." He seemed happy and also drunk. "Okay, you're too stewed. Give *me* the key."

Then she heard Earl's lock turn across the hall, she knew the particular way that it clicked and scraped, the familiar whine as his door creaked open.

"Nice place," the visitor laughed.

Was he being sarcastic or truthful? The answer would reveal his position in the world. If he had nothing, Earl's place would look grand. If he had everything, it would feel impossibly poor. If he had just enough, Frank would understand that it was waiting for him to make it a real home. The door slammed shut.

Bette picked up a new book of poems she had been saving for last. She'd admired it repeatedly at the Eighth Street Bookshop, which was her test. No matter how much a book beckoned to her in the store, she had to step away, and then be pulled back. That was the sign, when she didn't want to leave it. To spend her evening with that volume in hand, and have it join her home, was an investment. Every time she looked at the binding of a book she loved, she remembered its treasures with a shiver. The contents of that object could never be known with a glance and brief assessment. It had to be delved into, opened, held, and respected for the relationship to take hold. This particular book was called *North and South* by Elizabeth Bishop. Eli at the store had recommended it. And all the bookshops lining Fourth Avenue from Fourteenth to Eighth seemed to carry it. Bette returned to the poem she had loved the night before, "Casabianca," and read it out loud again.

> Love's the boy stood on the burning deck
> trying to recite "The boy stood on
> the burning deck."

There was the sound of sex from next door. The bed was banging against the wall and there were moans.

> Love's the son
> stood stammering elocution
> while the poor ship in flames went down.

Bette listened. She put down the book. And then she stood, without thinking, and was propelled, as if by motor, toward the telephone table by the entrance. She picked up the letter from Ohio, still unopened. Stared at the return address. It was a familiar but lost memory.

"Oh God," Earl gasped.

Bette put back the envelope, turning it face down, and walked to the radio, which she kept by her bed, yet could play loud enough to be heard in the living room and barely in the kitchen. Someday she would have a second radio placed over the stove, but not yet. Turning it on and off was often her final engagement of the day, and then again the first one to greet the morning. She liked to hear a voice. Normally she would have read more poetry before going to the radio, but she wanted to give Earl the privacy he deserved.

There were not many stations on at this time of night. Her habit was to listen to the news or a commentator, the quiet murmuring of his voice in the dark. Tonight, however, his soft voice did not create the insulation she desired, and since the moment called for music, the options were even more limited. There were bad recordings of classical symphonies, which she couldn't stomach. She would only listen to the Bach cello suites on record, never on a radio. There was no dimension. The only other possibilities were static or rock and roll. She could not decide. Static? Rock and roll? Static? Rock and roll? Defeated, she turned off the machine and listened for a moment, still standing. Something was wrong.

"Hey!" she heard Earl yelp. It was an unusual tone of voice for him, nervous surprise. "What are you doing?"

"Shut up," the other man yelled. He no longer sounded drunk.

"Give me my wallet!" That was Earl.

"Shut up!"

The bad one was not Frank, Bette was sure. This hostile voice was much too young.

"Hey!" Earl tried to yell.

There were sounds of violence. A gurgle, gasping

for air, a violation that was inarticulable. A lamp got smashed.

"Asshole," she heard the bad fellow say. Then there was a terrifying thud of someone being hit, his body falling to the ground. Which one was it? Which man had been damaged?

"HEY," she shouted through the wall. "HEY! What is going on over there?"

She paused for a moment, and then threw open her apartment door, boldly yelling down the hall. "STOP IT!"

A young man, he was really a boy, burst out of Earl's apartment. He lunged for the staircase and ran right into Bette, almost knocking her over. She was pushed back against the hallway wall, and for one second they both froze. He was an amateur, and Bette had the nerves of a lion. She stared him down, memorizing that face, defiantly. He might have been twenty-two. White. Dark. Devilishly handsome. Eyes like a burning deck. Though still afraid and somewhat awed by his own violence, he was clearly on the way to abandoning conscience entirely. She could tell.

Being so young, he was the one who panicked, unsettled by seeing someone care so fearlessly as she did. Earl's door slammed suddenly behind them. Bette knew it was the broken hinge, but the boy looked back, looked forward.

"I am calling the police," she said, as if she were the police.

Finally, he got ahold of himself and bolted. Scampered past her, vermin that he was, sliding down the stairs. Earl's wallet clutched in his fist. Bette turned, regaining composure to move forward, not knowing what she would find in Earl's place. Was he dead? Or worse? Resolved to calm, she walked quietly toward his apartment and was met by his staggering appearance—confused, frightened, with a string of blood crawling down his face. But clearly and completely alive, having managed the humanizing decorum of pulling on a pair of pants. She put her arm around his bare shoulder and turned him into her open doorway, closing the door quietly behind them.

Only then, did she allow herself to feel.

"Oh my God, Earl." She locked the door in case that monster ever tried to return.

"I was robbed."

He looked down at the floor almost in shame. Or was it deep regret? Almost like a liar who doesn't know how to get out of it. His demeanor was so sunken, it belonged to someone else. Someone Bette might pass on the street and think, *Poor fellow, now there is a person ashamed of himself.* He had the torso of a workingman. Certain muscles, hugely developed, and the rest slack and tired. In that moment, Earl Coleman was the saddest, most alone man who ever lived on Tenth Street. And Bette realized, right then, that if he needed to feel alone, that's what he needed to feel. She would tell him the truth, that he was not alone. But she wouldn't insist on it. It didn't matter if he recognized her devotion right then. The important thing was to listen.

"Come on, honey, careful. That's it." She guided him to his big armchair, where he always sat when they listened to records and talked. "Let me take care of you."

She went back into the kitchen, put on some water for tea, and wet a clean dish towel. Kneeling before him, she wiped away the blood. He didn't notice. He was finished.

"You're all right now."

Bette went to her sewing drawer where she kept emergency medicinals and cut a strip of gauze from a sterilized roll. Then she cut two pieces of adhesive tape.

"I'm boiling water for tea," she said.

Still nothing.

"Then I'll phone the police."

"No," he whispered, barely able to make a sound. "Don't call the police."

"He robbed you," she said, placing the folded gauze over his wound. She stated the facts. "He hurt you."

Earl gnashed his teeth. "Do not call them."

Is that what he's worried about? The police did not have to know what really went on. "I won't tell."

"DON'T CALL THE POLICE!" He screamed at her. He was furious. Like she was the one who had done all of this.

Bette thought for a minute. He was not of his right mind. Something had gone wrong with Frank and then this scoundrel was the second punishment of the night. On top of Leon's cruelty earlier the very same day, which they had reviewed at supper. Here it was almost time for Earl to go back to his morning shift. He was exhausted by disappointment and not in a place to make good decisions. And yet he had to have some remnant of control. It had to be up to him. No matter what. Something had to be his choice.

"You do not deserve to be treated this way," she said. This was how Bette showed compassion. Stating the obvious, simply. It showed the other person that she knew they were real. That things happened in their lives, unfixable things, just as had happened in her life. She made it clear that she realized this and would always take it into account.

Earl was not thinking about Bette, she could tell. He was barely thinking. Inside, his mind was whirling with pain before vision, and cloud before memory. He was trembling. The kettle whistled. She went to set up their cups and two tea bags, wondering about doctors and stitches. She brought out the steaming cups and placed one by his side, where he liked it, on the arm of his favorite chair. Bette touched his wrist. She brought him a shawl and wrapped it around his shoulders. She took his fingers in hers. He responded, gripped back.

"Something is wrong," he said. He was weak. He looked up at her from a place she had never seen.

"How can I help you?"

"Something is wrong and it's really big. I'm missing . . . my life. My life . . . it's unbearable."

"You're safe now. It's over."

His face was contorted and he surprised her by being loud, insistent and rude. "I am *not* safe."

Bette was surprised that Earl seemed so mad at her. What was she not understanding?

"My whole life is a sham," he said. It was an accusation, as if it was her doing. The pain of his precious life.

"That's not true." Bette was worried. She didn't understand. He was experiencing something whose dimensions she could not grasp. What should she do?

Something didn't make sense.

He looked at her through watery eyes. Like he just couldn't believe she would be so stupid. Like he was shocked. "What is true?" He blistered and then snarled. He bled and wondered.

"I know you," she told him. "And you are loved for the real you." That was her truth.

Earl looked at the floor in disgust, made no effort to hide his disappointment. She had not said the right thing. What was the right thing?

"Tell me what you need," she said.

"First I was a little boy in my mother's house," he began. "Imitating the voices on the radio. Then one day I didn't have any mother. I didn't have any cousins. Because one day *they* caught me doing whatever with whomever's son. And from that second on, I did not have any people. I did not belong to anyone. I could not run home because there was no home. You know . . . you know. Somehow I lived. Somehow I got on some bus. Somehow I met Anthony, and he saved me and I moved into this place. And I got a second dream, of being on the stage. My first dream had come true. I had my man. I was set. Then I was waiting for the second dream to happen. But somehow Anthony was gone and then he was married and then he was dead. Why did he have to do that? From then on I have loved this one and that one. Waiting, waiting, any second now there would be this new world. And somehow now I'm old. And I am still in that same apartment. And somehow they won't let me on their stage. And somehow the world did not change."

"I see," she said. "What can we do?"

Earl paid no attention. As if her voice was just traffic.

"I want the truth to not be true," he whimpered.

Her heart broke. Who has the power to grant that wish?

Chapter 7

Bette dreamed she was lying on the beach. The sand, cool and smooth beneath her, lovingly covered her shoulders. The sun was cool. The birds sang beyond. There was Frederick. He was the sand. He was the sun. She looked up and she was lying in his arms. He was peaceful, smiling. He told her he understood. He knew why he had lied. He was wrong, and he regretted it.

"Why did you lie?" she asked.

"I did it because I lacked integrity," he told her. "I was so overwhelmed by the potential approval of my father, his money, that I did not recognize the corruption of his approval, that it was dependent on treating you dishonorably. I did not realize one equaled the other. I was so tiny. I barely existed. I had no soul. And yet, despite that, you have always loved me, because you could imagine me becoming myself and I never could."

Bette was so overwhelmed with joy she forgot to say, "I forgive you." But it wasn't necessary, was it? He was grateful that they had both lived to see this moment of reunion. This was why they had lived and how they had lived. She snuggled into his chest and closed her eyes again. The water came to her feet, retreated.

"I love you, Bette," he said. "Now, everything will be right."

She opened her eyes and heard the birds outside her window. Living in the weedy tree. They were talking, discussing, their voices were deep, sonant, they listened and they responded. Sing, sing, now it's spring. The breeze, delicious through the window. Inside and outside were the same temperature, she turned between the sheets. They were clean because she had washed them. The bed made because she had made it. The pillows were plumped, the floor was swept, the milk was delivered in its shiny glass bottle. She had taken care of herself one more day. Frederick would come.

Pulling on her robe and slippers, Bette stepped out into the hallway and knocked on Earl's door. No answer. *Good.* He had gone to work. If ever the sun rose and Earl could not work, she would help him, that was certain. But thankfully today was not to be that day.

In fact, for the next week, their routine appeared to be unchanged. Bette made the decision not to pry and simply carried on loving, friending, caring, and listening. Earl was tense but then seemed to calm down. Like he had figured something out. She wasn't sure if he'd decided to keep this news in his pocket, or if he'd really found a way to get back to routine. But she let that be his secret. After two weeks had passed, he got an audition. So there was toasting and dreaming at the dinner table, but then no callback and life moved on.

At Tibbs Incorporated, Hector was perpetually in turmoil.

"A dynasty," he kept saying. "Build a dynasty."

Bette kept her head down and took care of her petty responsibilities. Hector ran around the office in a panic, wanting this strange thing and having no idea of how to get it. It was becoming a distraction, his grasping. Bette tried to understand what "a dynasty" meant in terms of television advertising. She ate her egg salad sandwich brought from home and organized the paper clips. As long as she didn't care what happened at the office, everything would be fine.

After three weeks, Bette suspected that the crisis with Earl was in the past. He seemed calm and able to continue. As a result, she worried less, and spent more time thinking about the books she was reading, the lives of the people in her neighborhood, the beauty of the city, and the faces on the street. One day, at ten after five to be precise, Bette walked the three blocks from her office and stood at the bus stop on Fifth Avenue at the corner of Forty-Second. The steps of the public library were full of young people romancing, and the lonely ones with books, leaning up against the stone lions. *Couldn't two people in love read together?* Bette thought. *Now that would be perfection.* The lions were distinctly American. They appeared to be young, as all Americans seemed to be, and were neither religious nor overly ornamented.

Bette had long been aware that her city was punctuated with monuments and each one had a different place in its heart. For example, Grant's Tomb was something most people overlooked and felt indifferent toward. No one had an opinion about it, or about Grant for that matter. The Empire State Building, on the other hand, reflected the collective greatness that this family of neighbors could only experience in association with one other. It defined the power of their unity. The Statue of Liberty stood in for the poignant, recent past and ever-looming future of refugees begging for a chance. And the arch at Washington Square Park reminded those old enough of the Great War, cheering the soldiers back from France. For the younger set, the arch was a place to arrange to meet a friend and then wander among the bongo players and folk singers, understanding the real possibility of a better world ahead. These library lions, though, were personal. New Yorkers climbed on them, scratched their ears, and leaned against their mighty trunks. Only a city dweller could eat a sandwich nonchalantly at the feet of the king of the jungle, while preparing for battle, sometimes by reading books.

The diesel fuel from the bus awakened Bette from her reverie. She climbed the steps and threw her nickel in the basket. She smiled at the driver, hanging on to the leather straps, moving along until she twirled into an empty rattan-weave seat. She loved their scratchy exterior and soft stuffing, the unique feel of shellacked straw under her fingers. Sailing down the avenue, passing through the Garment Center, she watched others come off work, go on to their second shifts shepherding racks of new clothing back and forth from factory to store. Some were made in sweatshops, others by the International Ladies' Garment Workers' Union. "Look for the Union Label" was their motto, and she did. But there were always enough new immigrants to man the sweats. They were visible from the subway in Chinatown at night, rows of women bent over machines or hand sewing, surrounded by scraps.

By the time the bus hit the Twenties, there was a quiet stretch. Not much defining those blocks besides some townhouses belonging to old New York families, like the Roosevelts, yet looking a bit dingy and alone. The side streets were for manufacturing and tended to be deserted after five. Some mornings she would walk to work and thereby pass through the bustling Flower Market, stepping on a carpet of stems, leaves, and petals lining her path. Flowers had no second shift, so by this time of day, it was all swept up and only the old Cubans, hand-rolling cigars, were still busy at work.

The bus passed Madison Park, surrounded by insurance buildings, and headed straight onto the Flatiron, sitting on Twenty-Third and dividing Fifth Avenue from Broadway. This is where Broadway changed from West Side to East, having been an old Indian footpath that traversed the island, already in place when Manhattan was divided into a grid. Every evening, on the way home from work, Bette took an admiring look at the Flatiron. It showed audacity, certainly. Daring, with a singular penchant to stand out. But was it really beautiful? Did it sit right on its lot, or did that slight misplacement convey an eerie knowledge? Strangely, the building expressed more character in the rain than in the sun. Its gray-brown, three-sided facade shone slick when wet, but could not animate and command in the sun's glare. Each of these constructions was like its people: stringent, bland, grand, original, repeti-

90

tive, one of a kind. Outlandish, overbearing, inspiring, useless, devoted. They each lived in public, in front of each other, and brought their people into relationships of passion both ecstatic and crushing. A building displays itself, after all. That's what it's for: to serve and be considered. To be used. Publicly. To be useful and still mysterious. Tamed and wild. An outdoor museum, with no guard. No admission.

Normally, Bette descended at the Tenth Street stop, but this day she felt freed by her engagement and so rode all the way through the Washington Square Arch, to the bus turnaround that circled the park's central fountain. There was Salvatore playing with a gang of kids, his pants rolled and his air triumphant. The bus then paused, and she could see the Good Humor man, venturing out in the brisk spring air. Mothers rocked their baby carriages in the playground, and kids slid down, seesawed up, filled empty Martinson's cans with sand, and climbed the concrete stepping blocks to grab a drink of water. The bus started again, on the reapproach to the uptown lane of the avenue, so she rode one stop, and got off at the corner of Fifth Avenue and Tenth.

The block was filled with the early evening duties of her neighbors. Handball, stoop and chair sitters, reading the sports page, having a smoke, catching their breath. Radios could be heard outside through windows. They had each once been a stranger and now they all belonged.

Much later, Bette would barely recall a wispy image of a young woman, in a dress from a faraway place, suitcase in hand, staring at a crumpled piece of paper.

A newcomer, looking at the buildings and then back at the paper. But at the time, Bette, overwhelmed with the enjoyment of her ride, proceeded to Teddy's Butcher Shop to buy four lamb chops and then new potatoes and onions and peppers from the greengrocery down the street. It was only on the way back, shopping in hand, that Bette consciously focused on this out-of-place young lady, waiting for something or someone to set her straight. Late with supper, having wasted so much of the early evening daydreaming, Bette bypassed the stranger, barely registering her even a second time, and hurried into her building, up the stairs, to get ready for Earl.

Turning on the radio, taking off her coat, putting her hat neatly on the shelf, her handbag by its side, Bette changed out of her office clothes into a light cotton dress and then added a soft wool sweater. She began chopping the vegetables and listening to the six o'clock news. Bette felt happy. Her life was right. Earl was feeling better, and she had not let the office dominate her soul. She enjoyed her city, her block, her habits and rhythms. She could honestly say that her life suited her and that everything would be all right.

And then, only then, did she become aware of the timid knocking at her door.

Chapter 8

"**B**ut I wrote you!"

Bette had never opened the letter. She did not think it would matter.

And this, perhaps, is what happens when one refuses knowledge. A kind of chaos ensues. Now, as a consequence of her own avoidance, Bette found a young woman named Hortense at her threshold. This young woman had anguished for weeks about her youthful fate, and then one night, when everyone else was asleep, had written in secret to a hidden, forbidden address, asking for a place to stay when she ran away to New York. She'd waited futilely for a response, with daily anxiety. Intercepting postmen. Finally, deciding that the only possible explanation for Bette's silence was a well-intentioned response waylaid into a dead letter office someplace east of the Mississippi, Hortense acquired a suitcase and hid it in the woods. Realizing she had to take that chance, she bought the bus ticket.

Hortense's arrival in New York City occurred that

very day. And Bette had denied herself the right to say yes or no by avoiding the facts of the matter—that *someone* was trying to get her attention. So, despite her knowledge of the dangers posed by others, Bette listened to her better self, the one who had a very active interest in the ways of the human mind and a general curiosity about how people experience the world. Besides, such a particular request had never come her way before.

"I thought that . . . usually . . . when people . . . decline, they say *no*."

"That's true," Bette conceded, recognizing, with some concern, how far she had stepped from common convention.

The girl before her had a small nose, blue eyes, long brown hair streaked with blonde. A foreigner.

"Why would you want to stay with me?"

"Well," the girl squeaked, somewhat endearingly for her obvious lack of sophistication, her heartland manner, Midwestern accent, and the simple fact of being new. Then she stopped, embarrassed, not knowing if she should say more. But having that thin kind of Caucasian skin that Bette herself had once possessed, Hortense's hesitancy showed itself immediately as a blush swept over her pink little ears. Bette remembered, suddenly, that *back home* this was considered "cute." But here it provoked a flat response of waiting, waiting for the person to change into someone to be taken seriously. It's not that city life changed one's biology enough to impede blushing, but rather that embarrassment was less and less of a common reaction to events.

"Well?" Bette asked.

"All my life I've heard . . ."

Oh. Bette felt pain. *They still slandered, habitually.* Having to picture *them*, the banal and powerful who had driven her from her home. They were still so closed? They hadn't adjusted their views after thirty years? She'd almost forgotten but not quite. They were so small. All this time later and they still pointed to her as the bad example. For new generations! The one to be avoided. No better object of blame had come along to take her place.

Bette thought about her cousin's triumph, her parents' condemnation, her brother passively smoking in the corner as she packed and left. She remembered them almost in black and white. More like sepia. Like a photo portrait from her parents' time instead of the contemporary snapshot. Frozen. Formal. Distinctly ill at ease. They led their petty lives filled with lies and deceit, and they dared to condemn her. She had long ago come to understand, with Earl's help, that her expulsion by the family was the most determining act of their lives, as well as hers. It made them who they are. Just as their cruelty had created her it had also created them. *That's why I never opened the letter*, she realized. She'd ceased to believe that her actions could have consequences on others, since it was these others who had always had consequences on her. That was a breach, Bette knew, of decency. She must always be responsible for her actions. Therefore she owed this girl her full consideration.

"Bette! I'm so sorry."

Sorry? Bette looked up to discover Hortense's expression of recognition. She saw Bette's hurt! She acknowledged it. And she was feeling regret at having caused it. The girl was so clean, all this showed in her face. She cared. But why?

"Yes?"

"Cousin Bette, don't let it . . . don't let them . . . they condemn people like us just for . . ."

"Like *us?*"

There was only one *us* in Bette's life. A black homosexual actor who lived next door. She had never heard another human being compare themself to her. Of course Hector *tried* to implicate her into his responsibilities at the firm. "We," "the team!" and other kinds of gung ho. But she would have none of that. Here, this young girl . . . it was . . . destabilizing, in the desire it provoked. Bette could not deny the longing to belong, and how quickly it had come upon her. After all this time, literally decades, the mere mention of ancient transgressions propelled her into a whirlwind of lack and confusion. And she suddenly, desperately wanted to be loved by more than one other person on this earth. She wanted this. When had she last wanted something she couldn't have? A family. How could it still be so open? This wound?

"Yes!" Hortense insisted enthusiastically. "Women who want to live differently. As *we* do. Who have bodies and minds to be used for other things than marrying off into ignorance and staying there, recreating themselves in tiny ignorant babies and some dull man. When instead *we* can have . . ."

"What can *we* have?"

"Adventures!" Hortense found the word.

Bette looked at her with interest. This young Hortense was more what, in the old days, would have been called the flapper or suffragist type. The kind who could have been found in the speakeasies *and* registering to vote. Somewhat the way Bette, herself, had begun. Hortense was ahead. And certainly she had an accurate picture of the fate that awaited her in Ohio. But . . . Frederick . . .

"Your father?"

"Yes?" Hortense was shy now.

"Does your father condemn . . . this . . . too? Still?"

"Father has a woman," Hortense blurted out, seemingly in spite of a resolve to caution.

Ah. Bette felt calmed. Hortense was important. She had information. And she also had a fury to her words. Hortense was offended. But *why?* Did she identify with her mother's claims and the order of propriety? Or was it lying in any form that provoked her outrage?

"He has a mistress!" Hortense blurted out again, like a truck backfiring diesel fuel. Then she looked secure, as though she understood the social terrain of apartment 2E. "And yet he condemns *you* for offering yourself to him."

"*Offering?*" HYPOCRITE. *Still.* "Still."

Bette backed off from the face to face. She was exhausted. Like rushing to work through a terrible snowstorm, it took all of one's determination to carry on, but impossible to go back. The only alternative was to sit on the snowy curb and freeze to death. This was more intimate interaction with a stranger than she had had in decades. Perhaps ever. She walked to her window for a brief escape. Back to the world she knew so well, from the perch she preferred: *observer*, instead of *participant*.

Outside, it was all there waiting for her. Relief. She saw a young Negro boy selling newspapers and an older Negro man carrying his shine box home from work at the shoe repair. Would one grow into the other? Or would the child heal the violations endured by the adult? Were they father and son? Friends? Did they share their workday together, give each other someone to talk to? Side by side, telling their stories about what it was all like? Did the older reassure the younger, was he proud? Did he respect him? Understand? With that kind of love, was having dreams possible? Bette had built a life for herself, without dreams. Oh, she wanted the best for Earl, but for herself? It was too lonely, a goal. If she were to reach for anything, she would surely be disappointed. No motive could outweigh the potential for pain.

Bette knew she had to step back into the room. She couldn't just do what she wanted to do, sit in her chair and watch the world. She had a responsibility to respond. Slowly, she turned around and was slightly dizzy to discover that Hortense had not moved. The girl was waiting. Waiting for Bette. For Bette to decide. Bette looked right at her, as someone in authority would. Summing her up.

There were two things about Hortense that stood out boldly: her flawless skin and her hope. Hope to escape the fate of Ashtabula, Ohio. None of the biblical prophesies of retribution for evil acts had come to pass for these oh-so-righteous relatives. They just lied on and on, apparently. On and on and on. In grace.

Apparently.

"Does your mother know? That Frederick has a woman?"

"No. Mother does not know."

Only then did Bette see that Hortense was still standing in the doorway. That the door was still open and that Hortense was still holding her suitcase. That's how much Bette was in charge here. The girl made no assumptions. How odd. How fresh.

"You can put down your suitcase."

"Thank you, Cousin Bette."

Bette noted that this interaction felt reasonable. It felt manageable. It felt good.

"So, he has a woman."

"His mistress lives only a mile from our house. Downtown. Her name is Mildred Tolan."

This name, it was buried somewhere in Bette's psyche. "Not Patricia Tolan's daughter?" That was it! How had she remembered that nonentity from fourth grade?

"Her *grand*daughter."

Hortense's eyes lit up. How preposterous. And Bette felt the same way. They agreed, it was clear. Frederick was ridiculous.

"Oh, Hortense." Now, this was the advantage of living long. One survives to see the cruel, the misguided, the deranged show themselves again and again. *Patience, Bette. Patience.* Knowing witnesses were accumulating now, standing by the road, waiting for the parade to finally appear.

"My father is destroying our family over a girl my age."

"You're sure your mother doesn't know?"

"Yes."

"And tell me, Hortense. What do you think about that?"

"That is the life that they wish for me. And so I know I am not loved. For a parent who truly loved would wish better than deception and petty passions, and would fight with everything they had to give their child another path."

Hortense did not feel loved, because Hortense somehow knew what love truly was. And she knew that her parents did not hold those capabilities. Bette smiled. Frederick had once known real love. She was the witness. That he'd never found it again was no surprise. Bette was enjoying this enormously. Her horrible cousin, Crevelle, successfully deceived in front of her own child! She felt no pity for Crevelle, and she was glad to know that Frederick was unhappy. Foolish. A squanderer, still. Certainly this would all lead to his transformation somehow. She dared to think it could.

It had finally come. What all books and plays and films promised. The reversal. Bette had long ago dismissed these manufactured literary devices as unhealthy as frozen vegetables. But here it was before her. On her doorstep. A reversal. After all this time of yearning, yearning, missing Frederick, her family, her life—after all this, it had come to her. On a cross-country bus. Today. The change was before her.

Bette had to be wise. She could not slam her door now, now that the heavens were singing. But she had to also see Hortense as her own real person, with her own character. Not just a messenger.

Sizing her up again, Bette discovered an arrogance

that she appreciated. Clearly Hortense had gotten on the Greyhound already expecting Bette to give in to her request, to invite her to unpack, and to stay. And now Hortense had achieved this goal. Without making Bette feel pressured. She had learned well at those etiquette classes. In church. And every other place where facade was installed. If the family had remained prosperous, then most people in that little girl's life had opened the door for her, until the moment she'd rebelled. But by then, of course, it was too late. She was a conceited, healthy female looking for equals to respect and resonate with. And this had made her leave the known and be alone. That showed far more than entitlement. It was a wishful pluck and courage from which good things could come.

On the other hand, Hortense had no picture of the horrors that awaited her if Bette were to say no. After all, it was Bette who had been forced to walk up and down the avenues, dragging her belongings, looking for boarding houses, and settling into the wrong ones. It was Bette, with no one to help her, who had spent frightened, sleepless, freezing nights with insects and worse, enduring the terrifying sounds from men and women in alarming states of despair and disintegration. She was the one who had lived on old bread and coffee for an entire year and had to save for two more years to buy a real bed. Now, this pretty girl before her wanted the short cut. In fact, she expected it. She wanted heat and locked doors, cups with saucers and matching forks. She wanted sheets, lamps, a soft couch, and Bette's precious radio. She wanted tea.

"I have an allowance," Hortense said into the silence. "I can contribute."

Oh. "I see," Bette answered quietly. This was a more civilized separation from family than she had assumed. No horrendous ejection with her father's back turned and her mother's teeth bared. No crawling on the floor, crying, begging her brother to *say something, do something, help me. Help me.* No door flung open, threats to phone the police, a one-way ticket to Cleveland thrown at her feet, and Bette having to grovel and grab it, having no other resource. Then pawning it and her locket and books and glasses for a bus ticket to New York and arriving hungry. None of that for Hortense. This departure was arranged, monthly allowance waiting at the Western Union. Hortense was less damaged than Bette. She was not as deprived. She did not carry the blame for someone else's failings, only for the price of her own ambitions. *Yes*, Bette realized. Hortense was a different animal. One who had not been beaten.

"It is substantial."

Chapter 9

So, the textile business was ever booming, and Hortense would not be a burden. Knowing the girl could easily afford a furnished room, and all her meals in luncheonettes or better, intrigued Bette. It wasn't desperation that brought Hortense to her door. She had a higher purpose. Maybe . . . maybe the girl was telling the truth after all. Maybe . . . maybe somewhere out there existed people who actually did tell the truth because they knew no better. Maybe not *everyone* was so dangerously corrupt. Maybe Hortense was . . . a blessing. Finally. The good of Bette's life would actually come to roost. Perhaps Hortense was, after all, not like *them*. Could it be that she was like . . . *us*?

"So, it was a choice to leave your family behind? You were not expelled."

"I could not breathe in Ohio."

This was a distinctly admirable response, Bette noted, and then took in that the girl was still standing.

"Please, take a seat."

Hortense smiled, let go, soared, sweeping into the

apartment, past Bette, to a perch on the windowsill. She didn't choose the chair, so carefully positioned, but the sill itself, so she was pressed against the glass. But instead of looking out, she leaned back into the frame and kicked off her shoes. She smiled, stretched, relaxed. She was pretty and plain like they are in America. Like Bette's people.

"My older brother is married and dull. My sister is about to do the same. And I just cannot go down that path of Ashtabula society luncheons."

The streetlight came on. Evening was now upon them.

That was the moment when Bette saw it. In the light of the night, illuminating the photo on her mantel and the girl's face. Hortense looked quite a bit like young Frederick. She had that sincerity. That compelling charm and open heart. Perhaps Hortense was more a mixture of Bette and Frederick than of anything else. What Frederick could have been if he had had the courage Hortense displayed. What he could still be.

"I don't want to be *her* child," Hortense said, unveiling her uncanny instinct to say the perfect thing in the perfect moment. "I want to be yours. Be like you. You're brave and you have escaped. You've been gone for . . ."

"Thirty years."

"And here I am, come in your footsteps."

Bette assessed. There were crucial points of agreement between the two of them:

(1) Ashtabula, Ohio, is boring. Not worth it. Even thirty years later, everything there was known.
(2) New York is not that way.

Bette watched Hortense. *Who would she become here?*

The natives, those who were born in the city, learned to crawl on sidewalks. Their palms were callused, and concrete their natural habitat. They thrived. There were the refugees from Europe, China, and the descendants of slaves, brought in chains. These people had nowhere to return to. They had to make things work. Then there were the exiles from America's own provinces, a problematic breed. She had seen many come and go. Some, like Bette, had been thrown away by their own people. But others were in a more ambiguous spot. There was that tenant in apartment 3B who realized he would rather be a big shot in Kalamazoo than one of many on the island of Manhattan. Then there was the girl, Maryanne, they had hired at Tibbs Incorporated to tutor young Hector in English literature. It became clear to Bette, immediately, that Maryanne only wanted to be with people who were exactly like her. Who had all the same holidays. So she took the bus home to Tampa and never looked back. There was the young counterman who worked briefly at Rubin's Deli slicing lox. He missed the sun and the beach and his mother's loving attention. Ultimately he could not find a reason to live without those things and so returned to somewhere near San Diego. And then that fellow who had come to Tenth Street to be a painter but really only wanted the easy life. He was gone in a year, to someplace where . . . she'd forgotten. These were the benign ones. They arrived, did no damage, faced facts, and then went back home with stories to last a lifetime. About all the *characters* they'd met.

The problem, as Bette and Earl had often discussed, was the newcomers who visited "recklessly." They wandered without restraint, buoyed by an intoxicating imagined safety ever awaiting them at home. *Back there*, eternally somewhere, they pictured *real* people with feelings and needs, deserving of respect, with faith and recognition. While *here* it was a carnival, where no one mattered and all were interchangeable, serving only one purpose: catharsis. These types would then cause havoc on New Yorkers just to see what that felt like, for the experience of acting out on another person. They thought this was freedom. The illusion was that when all the people before them were used up, the perpetrator would simply return to where life mattered. And never look back.

"They never realized," Earl had said, "that us darker, more solitary types also have hearts."

Over and over he and Bette watched the newcomers like a spectator sport. When the damage they'd caused had started to accumulate and the mound of consequence had grown unmanageable, the destroyer tried to jump on the Greyhound like a black-hatted cowboy onto his waiting white steed. But, SURPRISE! There was no more sunset to ride off into. There was no one on the other end willing to wire the ticket. The precious, protected home phone number had been disconnected. The others back home had their own problems and ultimately didn't care. In fact, *they* had been counting on *him* to bail them out with some big city fortune, not the other way around. His girl had married someone else. His mother had drunk up every penny he'd sent her. The factory or mine or mill had finally shut down so there was no work to be had at all. Everyone died. Everyone forgot. No one even liked him in the first place. They'd found Jesus Christ.

Now, the bad fellow was himself stuck forever, face to face with all the pain he had casually created for others, who also had nowhere else to go. Their agony became the rest of his life.

"I don't have a return ticket," Hortense murmured dreamily. Bette saw that the girl had a guard, and she easily let it down. She felt sure that Bette had accepted her. She was used to talking honestly and had stopped strategizing.

"Why is that?"

"Because, Cousin Bette, I am going to break every rule ever written in Ashtabula to ensure that I can never, ever return."

"It was true for me," Bette whispered.

And then the story of Hortense's voyage unfolded. She was a good storyteller. Alert. Walking from the bus terminal that late afternoon, Hortense had felt that everyone she passed on the city street knew the same secrets. But she did not know. This excited and frustrated her. She wanted to be an insider.

"The sidewalks were so crowded, and I continuously bumped into people. It was *so* embarrassing. I apologized and apologized, but it kept happening. Yet they never bumped into each other. Why?"

"Because," Bette said, remembering that cold night three decades before when twenty-year-old Earl Coleman walked her home from the diner and explained the world. "Because New Yorkers have a special way of moving. They advance ever forward. By gliding. Little sailboats catching the wind."

Feeling free and knowledgeable and having *fun*, Bette threaded around her apartment, *gliding* like a swami on his flying carpet, arms akimbo, her feet barely touching the ground. Hortense laughed, and joined her then, the two of them twining around the furniture like fairies on dust. Dancing, really. Playing.

"If you stand on the street like an ox and cart," Bette stopped still, legs heavy and solid, taking up more space than any city dweller would want or need. She squared her shoulders, an overbuilt wrestler prepared for assault. "Like you are staking your claim. Well, Hortense, you will never get to your destination. We have to share, be aware. We're all on that sidewalk together. This, dear Hortense, is important to know."

She heard herself say *dear*.

"I want to know."

What else?

"And look people in the eye." That also mattered. "But not like you're giving your heart away. Not like, 'Howdy, neighbor' in an Ashtabula cornfield."

How strange to use that as a point of reference. Bette had forgotten she'd ever had a childhood landscape. She'd had a life after all, hadn't she?

"Look them in the eye," she repeated. "Show that you are noticing."

Again Bette and Hortense flew around the apartment, but this time their eyes were in sync with each other, and again Hortense, a quick learner, never faltered.

"Good girl!"

"I understand!"

"Now you are just one of many human beings and each has a face. No one is a blur. You are acknowledging that face." Bette stopped, and flopped back into her chair. "It is not intrusive. In fact, recognition is very polite here. People have names that are hard to pronounce."

Hortense stopped gliding.

"Pronounce them."

And so the second lesson began. This one unfolded as a Pygmalionesque elocution class on how to finesse the names Shallowitz, Signora Gambetta, Marianna Colón and her son José. With an *s*, not a *z*. How to speak all varieties of English. How to eat grand food. Eat lox, salami, Chianti.

"*Key Auntie*? What's that?"

"It's gorgeous."

Bette could see the future. Hortense and Bette and Earl drinking Chianti, walking to Chinatown, buying crabs from their markets for supper. Sculptural green vegetables whose names they would never know. Fresh spaghetti hanging in ropes from the ceilings of Italian shops. Round Jewish rolls, called *bagels,* chewy and warm from the boiling vats. Earl pointing and explaining, Bette smiling in the sun. She could imagine this suddenly, now that it was real and before her. She could imagine. Three.

"They must be so happy to be in our country," Hortense cried out with pride.

Here the romance stopped dead. Bette's face fell. She'd forgotten that arrogance, those misconceptions.

She became stern and separate. That attitude could not be allowed to fester.

"No, Hortense." Bette's voice was unforgiving. "Ohio is *your* country. You've left your homeland behind. This is *their* country. *You* are the refugee. Hortense, you are the one who will have to adjust."

"To what?"

Bette thought for a moment.

"To the quiet."

"Quiet? But it is so noisy here."

Bette said nothing. She knew from many years of solitude that it was very, very quiet on Tenth Street. For years there could be no sound but one's own breath. Until one day, a strange girl knocked on one's door.

Then, a new sound came into Hortense's life as a key scraped in the lock and the door slowly opened.

Hortense looked up and gasped.

As Hortense's life changed second by second, she had still not been prepared, never imagined, that she would participate in an event like the one that was suddenly before her. No member of her family or community had ever considered in all their years of fantasy, fear, and resistance that Hortense would one day witness an adult Negro man open the front door of her mother's cousin's apartment, with his very own key.

And so, she screamed.

Yes, Earl was home from work.

Earl barely flinched. Of course he saw that terrified white face, so familiar and so banal, so wounding if he let it be, and so he never let it be. What did he care about those idiots? He just smiled with superiority, underlining her lack of worth and his immunity.

"Hello, Bette."

"Hello, Earl."

Bette took his jacket off the hook where he had just placed it and hung it on his wooden hanger. She took his bottle of beer and went to get a glass. Leaving Hortense to muddle through this moment on her own and to transform.

Earl smiled at her again. She was nothing.

"Hello, *you*," he said, bringing her to shame.

Bette returned with the bottle opened and a glass of froth, and handed it to Earl, because he was the king.

"She's from Ohio," Bette said calmly. "The letter."

"Ohhhh," he laughed. "That explains it." And he drank a rewarding dose of beer.

Before their eyes, Hortense adjusted. She visibly realized that this was a test and that she had to meet the moment. She had to let go of all the stupid rules she had been raised with. The ones designed to confine and control, with no purpose but pain.

"Pleased to meet you. My name is Hortense. I am Bette's cousin."

White people had white families, a sad fact Earl had learned long ago. Whenever he'd had a white person in his life, he'd wound up having to deal with their ignorant relatives. Look at Anthony. At what happened. There is a lot of baggage that comes along with white people, like the inevitable rest of their race.

Earl looked over at the suitcase by the side of the door. He observed her backward clothing, her bland features, her silly hair.

"Moving to New York?" he said with innuendo. *Another one. You'll never last.*

"Yes," Hortense smiled, despite her uncertainty.

Was he right about her implied unavoidable failure? *No,* she decided. *He was wrong.* And then she faltered. Was she supposed to say *Yes sir?* Or would *yes* be sufficient. Did real New Yorkers call each other *sir?* She guessed that they did not.

"I've got some lamb chops to cook," Bette announced, and disappeared back into the kitchen.

Earl put down his glass professorially, scratched his chin and walked around the privileged urchin with an air of species investigation.

"Let's see," he played the guessing game. "Hmmm. You moved to New York with . . . two dresses . . . three pairs of panties . . . a diary . . . two pairs of socks . . . a nightie." He paused, knowing he was missing something. Then snapped his fingers. "And a book!"

Bette was in the back chopping onions. They could both hear the knife hitting the cutting board. They were alone in this moment together, Hortense and Earl. And it was Hortense's responsibility to make it work.

The fact was that Hortense had never had a full conversation with a Negro. She had certainly never heard a Negro man say the word *panties.* It seemed audacious, and then she knew that it could no longer be so. It had to be regular. *Equal.* In this house, people said whatever words they wanted to each other and it was a gift, of candor and honesty. The world cracked open with possibility. Now Hortense could never go back. She had already learned too much.

"What book?" she asked, gamely, coquettishly, showing her gumption for the spar, a willingness to play. Her ability to be the same . . . with anyone.

Earl examined her closely. She was a rube, but she

had a mind. Few influences, but depth. What would someone with those abilities select as their one and only book? He made his choice.

"The Bible."

Then he guffawed, triumphant. He had her number.

"Yes," she answered. "The bible. *An Actor Prepares* by Konstantin Stanislavski."

Earl laughed out loud. The lamb chops were sizzling in the background. He had to admit he was impressed. She'd outwitted him. That little pink one.

Chapter 10

From that day on there was new life on Tenth Street. Earl slept in, until the latest possible moment, and would give a wake-up knock on *his ladies'* front door as he started out for work. Five syncopated beats. *Shave-and-a-haircut* . . .

Then he would wait in the hallway, until a sleepy Hortense, in her nightgown, hair askew, opened the door and smiled.

"*Two-bits,*" they would sing in unison, and crack up. She'd wave goodbye and then watch his trip down the stairs as the sun rose, joining the other silent, sleepy workers in the morning's gorgeous blue-gray shadow.

Hortense would then run to the window, throw it open, lean out, and wave goodbye. And Earl would turn up from the corner below and smile.

This new energy at the beginning of the day allowed him to start off looking at the other fellows on the streets a bit differently. He saw them dreaming and scheming with their hands in their pockets, watching the sun's flakes drip down the sides of the buildings sheltering their collective journey to the job. Weirdly, from time to time, he found he appreciated their beauty without the devastating pain of not being able to share it. What was that? What was that shift? It set his day in motion differently than it had been all those years when he rolled out of bed on his own. But by the time he'd get to the West Side and had been alone with his thoughts in the dawn, his countenance would move more to gray and become starker and more familiar. Perhaps the truth was that losing his family had kept Earl away from young people. Maybe that was why he'd cared so deeply for Leon. The energy. Or, was it just Leon's ass, sweet lips, and seductive promise? Or was it both? Was it about being young and beautiful, or was it about being a different force? That was it really, what Earl had been trying to get for so long, a different kind of light—a new person, on a daily basis, with their own new information and perspective. That's one reason he so badly wanted a boyfriend: he just needed a friend. Not the guys bantering by the chess tables in the park. They were sweet, but had their own families to go home to. He wanted more input. More surprises. Even at six in the morning. He liked being recognized. It allowed a new kind of comfort in that secret chill of dawn, and was worth foregoing a long, full breakfast for some quick toast and a steamy cup of coffee with other similarly situated men at the diner across from the meatpacking plant. How was Earl going to get a lover? How? Every effort ended in disaster and despair, ended in cataclysm. If only Hortense were a boy. He needed a man! He needed a friend to hold and talk to, someone in bed, a man in his bed, every single goddamn day. Where was he? He was just nowhere to be found, that guy. Nowhere. Nowhere.

It had finally happened. Earl had grown up into an old, lonely fag with no way out. With too much pain and too much hurt and absolutely no clue how to turn that around. He'd seen those types his whole life, and now he was one. Sitting on the edge of life. A person who always shows up alone. Who sets off alone and tries to get in. The guy filled with stories to tell that no one wanted to hear. Realistically, that was the truth. It was time to just enjoy what he could and mourn in private over the rest. There was no way he was going to discuss this feeling with Bette or anyone else. With Hortense in the room, they couldn't discuss his feelings in the same manner as before, and in a way it was a relief. He was sick of others knowing how bad he felt. No way. It was too terrible. It was embarrassing. Too irrefutable. Too impossible to change. *Accept it,* he'd begged. *Accept it.* But he didn't want to. He just couldn't do that to himself.

At the same 7:00 a.m. moment that Earl finished his cup and suited up to hack gristle, Hortense was completing her toilette. She made Bette's morning coffee, and the two of them would chat, chat, chat. Then they'd bustle around the table, buttering each other's toast. Within a very short time, Bette felt comfortable leaving the plates undone and setting off to work, assured they would be washed, the table crumbed, and everything in place waiting for her when she returned in time to make supper. Clearly all would be cared for. It was new, this experience of not having to engage *all* the mundane details. Brand new. Truly knowing that another person was going to clean in her absence opened up a cavernous space in Bette to do, to rest, to think—indeed, to feel.

Once Bette was on her way, Hortense did indeed clear and rinse. She'd leave for her nine o'clock acting class, reciting lines to herself and studying the people she passed on the street on her way. So many of these faces and gestures would come in handy, later, as character studies. For example, that young mother's stride, like a man, but with such a pretty, soft face. Her body betrayed her responsibilities and her eyes held her true soul. The woman's story was evident. She had the burden of the family's finances, and this was an unexpected obligation. And so she had to simultaneously harden, physically, while holding a place of love and vulnerability for her child. Hortense could capture that! She was sure. And for the rest of the walk up to Twenty-Third Street, she tried on different pairings of smiles and strides, finding the right one. And spent the last few blocks perfecting it until she felt natural in her role.

This new arrangement also transformed Bette's approach to *her* job. Now, instead of reading a book or daydreaming about a piece of music heard alone the night before, she would wait for the bus across the street with a kind of energetic glow. She always got a seat because her stop was at the beginning of the line, and from that perch, she'd comfortably watch out the window as the bus crawled up Madison Avenue. Looking at the people around her and starting to wonder what their reaction would be to *television advertising*.

Not that she really knew what that was, but this was the subject now discussed in the office all day long, five days a week, and there was no point in pretending it wasn't happening. Why not at least try to understand? She had nothing to lose and it could be interesting. Change.

Newer riders came on board the bus, and by the north side of Union Square there were never any seats left. She saw their expressions of disappointment, realizing they would have to stand. How, even though they'd already known when they woke up that there would be no seat, they were upset about it. No one wants to stand on their way to work. People have desires, needs that don't meet their realities. And yet those wishes do not disappear. She had made her wishes disappear. Now she wanted to rediscover what they actually were.

Every day was a surprise with Hortense. And every day was a surprise at Tibbs Advertising. It was exciting. In fact, it was fun. The value of a day was entirely different, Bette noted. It was not something to be endured, but instead to be enjoyed. *That's what change can bring*, she thought. And laughed to herself out loud. The man reading the *New York Post* in the next seat stubbed out his cigarette. He looked at her and smiled. *People are moved by happiness.* She felt moved herself when she realized that happiness is more than getting through without pain.

This morning, when she entered the office, Hector was in his usual frenzy of worry. He was doing so much, but he had no idea what he was doing. Lately, Bette had been more willing to try to help him. That was the thing about healing. It only happened when something was made right. If nothing was ever made right, there was only so much that one could do. But with Hortense's appearance and Bette's chance to have relatives finally—well, that mattered. It wasn't just willpower, it was substantial. And it made her feel better toward Hector. Someone was fair to her and so she had more to give. That's how it worked. A person just could not do it all on their own. It was a proven fact. Bette was almost ready to say that she and Hector were in there *together*, after all. But she still didn't grasp exactly how. All that was clear was that Hector was in over his head, and she felt a new kind of sympathy. An interest. This particular morning he was already pacing before she'd even hung up her sweater.

"Bette, I need you to take shorthand."

"Right away."

She could not bring herself to call him *Mr. Tibbs* after a lifetime of calling him Hector. So for the moment, she refrained from calling him anything at all.

"It's important."

"Be right over."

She draped her sweater casually over her chair and grabbed her steno book and a pencil, always kept sharpened in its holder.

The important subject so badly in need of immediate documentation was indeed something momentous. Accepting that he could never forge this new pathway alone, Hector had been advised by a friend on the New Haven Line commuter club car to hire a consultant. This was a new kind of job emerging in American business, and Hector's friend encouraged him to "get on board." Three Canadian Club and sodas later, Hector was convinced that experts were now available for all to engage, instead of being secreted away in the most powerful corners of the Pentagon. So, for a fee, even a small guy like him could take advantage of their "know-how."

This morning he was interviewing his first consultant, a very lively, young, bright, and, well, brassy brunette named Valerie Korie, who had beaten both him and Bette to the office by a good fifteen minutes.

Prompt, that one, Bette noted.

Valerie was the smart, independent type, there to offer the service of her mind. She was an expert at having ideas, imagining things, and making them come true. She was hired to think, to think of things no one else could come up with, to put seemingly unrelated themes together and to make them *click*. Her clothing confirmed these talents. Not necessarily the A-line skirt, but the bag and shoes of different colors and the seemingly masculine watch, prominently displayed on her wrist instead of a bracelet.

"Like it?" Valerie asked, noticing Bette's gaze.

"Why . . . yes."

"It's waterproof and shockproof. Omega."

"The last letter of the Greek alphabet," Bette answered, surprising herself.

"Exactly! The be-all and end-all of . . . time."

Hector took his place behind his desk, Valerie had the visitor's chair. Black leather, soft and pliant. Bette sat in her usual hardback, best for taking notes.

"Listen up, Hector," Valerie snapped, not giving him a moment to take the reins.

Bette looked over at his reaction. Valerie's big smile,

red lips, and matching tight red sweater were very effective. He seemed grateful to not have to be in charge.

Although trying to remain professionally skeptical, Bette immediately saw the girl's appeal. Valerie was the 1958 version of the 1920s woman. What Hortense seemed to be aspiring to. This was a type that hadn't been around for, well, decades. With the Depression and the war effort, the independent gal who used to be a regular part of daily life had seemed to disappear. And Bette hadn't noticed, until just this second. But here she was, coming back into style, and it was refreshing. Perhaps that had happened to Bette herself, without even understanding it. American women had become reticent, and she'd lost some of her own pizzazz. Luckily, these young ones were reinvigorating the mold. Of course there would be adjustments for the modern age. This crop were not radicals, they were *professionals*. But the last crew had won the right to vote, so Bette felt excited to see what a different, grand revolution Valerie's kind would achieve. The 1958 model was sleek, slick, bright scarf, sharp heels. *Looks*, Bette reflected, *are a big part of it*. She meant business.

"I mean business, Hector. And business, as every American knows, means power."

Business means power, Bette wrote on her steno pad.

"Bring me in as a consultant for your firm, and I will expand Tibbs Incorporated into a vibrant, competitive advertising agency so that you can 'Market Tomorrow to America Today.'"

She speaks in slogans, Bette noted. *Convenient for shorthand.*

"Great!"

That was Hector. Whatever Valerie said was fine with him. His goals had proved beyond his grasp, so as long as someone could think of something he wouldn't have to do it. He smiled, and then crinkled his brow.

"But, how?"

"Good question. This requires . . ." She leaned in as though to whisper the answer, but then laughed, flipped her hair back, and trumpeted. "HARD SELL."

Bette wrote the words *hard sell* and then added three exclamation points.

"As opposed to . . . ?" Hector leaned in so close that he was practically lying on his desk, grasping for the answer.

"Guess," Valerie cooed.

"Soft?"

She nodded. He was learning. Bette was too, and so far, so good.

As Valerie explained it, *marketing* was what they needed to move into television. This corresponded strongly to what Hector had suspected, but what marketing actually was remained a bit of a mystery. It was different from advertising because of the element of subtlety. Advertising, as far as Hector was concerned, had always meant encouraging people to buy something. But marketing had to do with making people *feel* differently. So that they would then be better predisposed toward purchasing the thing. Toward wanting it. More. Marketing was some kind of modern science that involved how people think, and their desires. It was deeper, speaking to more human truths. A new realm of understanding that could not be overlooked.

"Television will reach EVERYONE!" Valerie proclaimed.

How? Bette wondered.

"We want ALL of America to understand our ads," Valerie said. "It's DEMOCRATIC!"

This further intrigued Bette. How could all the people understand the same thing? Was marketing the way to get her family to understand that her life mattered? For the men who ran the theaters to understand that Earl needed a part? Could marketing erase inequality, and let all people's feelings be seen on an elevated plane?

"How?" asked Hector.

"Ask your secretary."

Suddenly all eyes were on Bette. This had never happened before. She had never once been called upon in a meeting to give an official opinion. All her guidance had been sought by the Tibbs men privately, in quiet conversation. When Hector was a boy playing under the desks, she'd put bandages on his knees and helped him when he lost his glasses. Yet, she had never considered actually participating in conversations like this one. Of actually having a voice.

"You're an emblematic American," Valerie bestowed, as though this were a good thing.

"I'm not sure," Bette said.

"We'll see."

Valerie turned to face Bette entirely. Like they were having a romantic tête-à-tête in the Russian Tea Room, and no one else in the world existed. She shone her light on Bette. And the rest of the world was obscured.

"Now, Bette. Tell me. What values do you look for when choosing something?"

That was a bigger question than Bette had anticipated, and she started thinking about what the true
answer might be.

"Or . . . ," Valerie cooed. "Some*one*."

This follow-up was so insinuating, it carried the
weight of its own frisson. Bette was actually flustered.
The idea that she would choose someone spoke to
something forbidden, unseeable. And yet this woman
saw that it was there. *Potential.*

"So?"

"Yes?"

"So, tell me, Bette. When you go to the market to do
your grocery shopping, what kind of soap do you buy?"

That was easy.

"The least expensive."

Valerie came a bit closer. Bette could inhale her perfume, Promising, like an unripe apricot. Bette could
see the hint of her cleavage. It was all a tease, wasn't
it? Suggestions of something more. That was Valerie's
lure.

"So!" Valerie eureka'd. Her enjoyment was infectious. What had once been a dreary day at the office
had become a huge romp in the snow. A free-for-all of
fun. "You let THEM decide for YOU?"

Now, here was yet another thing that Bette had
never considered.

"You let THE PEOPLE WHO SET THE PRICES determine what you will hold in your hand every single
morning? What will touch your face?"

Bette had truly never thought about things this
way, and she was intrigued to examine her own habits.
In fact, she wanted to. She wanted to know herself better as much as she wished to understand her own time,

this historic moment—where was the society headed? She realized she'd like to know.

Valerie explained carefully that the ways that "things" were going were called *trends.* And that these trends no longer happened by chance or because of huge global events like wars and floods. They now were dreamed up in offices, just like this one, and then *marketed* to the rest of the world. A new sector was in charge, and governments would realize this and have to follow. Basically, Valerie explained, from now on people would only buy things on purpose, instead of by accident. And people like Valerie and Hector—if he was lucky—would be the ones to decide what others would own. For a handsome fee, of course.

"Wake up!" Valerie sang, like Mary Martin in *South Pacific.* "You have the RIGHT to CHOOSE your own soap! The same way you have the RIGHT to CHOOSE your own man. It's YOUR world! TIDE or ALL!"

At first Bette thought that *tide* referred to the natural rhythm of waves, and *all* was eternity, but then she realized that Valerie was referencing the two boxes of laundry detergent that sat side by side at the Daitch Shopwell on University Place.

"That's what hard sell does, Bette." Valerie looked at her with an expression of reluctant truth, conveyed out of loyalty, for her own good. "It lets *you* decide."

"I see," Bette said. And then, remembering to take notes, wrote down the words *I decide.*

"I see," Hector said.

Bette had forgotten he was there.

"Now, Bette," Valerie led her to the next moment. "What if you could have any brand of soap that you wanted, regardless of price? What brand name most appeals to you?"

This time the answer just slid out. A thought she had never previously entertained became so obvious and on the top of her consciousness.

"Truthfully," Bette said. "I have always liked the name LUX."

Again Valerie rewarded her with a grateful smile, those big brown eyes, an expression of contentment bordering on the obscene.

"You see, Hector?" She spun around on her chair, reaffirming that this entire exhibition had been for his benefit so he could feel addressed and serviced. "Hard sell! LUXXURRRYYY. *Luxury,*" she purred. "Persuading people to imitate the habits of the idle rich."

Hector literally leapt from his seat with enthusiasm, then felt perplexed about where to go next, and so flopped back down again. Then he leaned back and assumed, for the first time since he had come into ownership of Tibbs Incorporated, an air of empowerment.

"She likes LUX," he pointed out, delighted at having a perception. "But she doesn't buy it."

"Americans dream of being rich," Valerie retorted on the beat, with a gravitas previously reserved for the United Nations. "But they are NOT rich. This is a very important insight when you try to sell them something."

"But the rich don't wash dishes." Bette was practical at heart, and there had to be a place for that. Even though she, herself, no longer washed dishes. Now that Hortense was in her house.

"RIGHT! And they don't do their own shopping."

Bette had to admit that she still did her own shopping and wouldn't want it any other way.

"So," Valerie let out some more rope. "Wouldn't you rather *feel* rich while doing what poor people *have* to do?"

Yes, she would. The answer was obvious, even though Bette wasn't poor, but she understood the logic. She had a secretarial job. That meant she could pay her rent, buy groceries, go to the doctor, see plays on Broadway, buy all the books she wanted, give something to charity, and count on a stable pension in her old age. Yet, Valerie's argument was illuminating, it was the *feeling* of being free that Valerie was after. And so another door was opened. Once Bette let herself buy LUX, she would keep buying it. The way she had come to the same job day after day. It would become known, stable. It would make her feel safe. And then someday an innovative personality in another office somewhere would come up with a marketing breakthrough that would make Bette feel strangely bold. On an impulse that had been fabricated, but would feel organic, she would try something new. Something she'd never even noticed before but had seen *advertised on television.* She searched her memory, scanning a picture of the supermarket shelves, settling on something previously invisible but subconsciously planted. Cutex. It sounded like LUX but it was hard to say why. Cutex. Was it the Texan? Or was he just Cute?

"What is Cutex?" she asked.

"Nail polish remover," Valerie answered, fanning her red-tipped fingers.

"Oh," Bette laughed. "First you would have to sell me the polish."

"NOW YOU GET IT!" Valerie was in love with Bette. Or at least that's how it *felt*. "STRATEGY! I could sell you anything if I had to. I could sell you fake nails, nail files, nail polish remover, and then I could sell you a salve to soothe your aching nails. If I need to sell it more than you need to buy it, you will buy it."

That, Bette came to understand, was the essence of hard sell. She looked up at her child boss. He was lost in Valerie's web. And so was Bette. Hector didn't have to worry any longer. Someone else would solve all the problems. He reached his decision without a moment's hesitation.

Hector put his hand out over the desk and rose to the occasion.

"Sold," he said.

And the deed was done.

Chapter 11

Hortense was thinking:
Discovery itself is freedom.

Earl was thinking:
Sex is filled with gratitude, but then back to real life like it never happened.

Bette was thinking:
I am capable of more.

Earl realized:
I am capable of more.

Bette realized:
I love Earl, Hortense, and in its own way, I love Valerie.

Hortense realized:
Discovery is endless. Therefore freedom is endless.

All three were mistaken. And yet, two were also right. Tragic, isn't it?

Bringing their family back to three, just like the old days with Anthony, rejuvenated some lost pleasures for Earl and Bette. They retained the nightly listening of music, talking over the day, reading poetry and sitting, united by the radio, as they always had. This elevated all of them, especially as Bette and Earl were able to instruct young Hortense with their ardently hard-won knowledge. The presence of three made possible again the reading of plays, which corresponded to the needs of Hortense's acting class scene preparation. So now, when Earl returned home from the nightly bloodbath, he entered an apartment that combined the steaming scent of dinner with the studying of scripts.

This one evening a succulent pot roast with pars-nips, carrots, and a can of tomatoes was simmering under cover. Hortense's presence at home some after-noons allowed for more thoughtful and slow cooking dishes, as she and Bette could cooperate on the nour-ishment of them all. Bette sat at the already set table, spectacles positioned, book in hand, as Hortense re-cited from memory. Bette, of course, had performed this very service for Earl for years, helping him learn his lines. And so she was well versed in the role—not to prompt unless called upon but not to lag either. Her job was to help, not to have an ego, and as far as acting went, better left to others more emotionally expressive than she.

Hortense stood in the living room, ethereal yet royal. She recited.

> My lord, I have remembrances of yours,
> That I have longed long to re-deliver;
> I pray you, now receive them.

Bette knew, of course, that there was a problem

with the way Hortense understood the line. But she had no idea of how to correct it. Hortense seemed to be a bit bouncy. She didn't grasp where the pauses were. And the wrong words seemed to be emphasized. But Bette was not knowledgeable enough to help in that way. So, she simply stuck to the task of memorization and hoped that the rest would follow.

"No, not I," read Bette. She needed stronger glasses. Age had come upon her. "I never gave you aught."

> My honor'd lord, you know right well you did;
> And, with them, words of so sweet breath
>   composed
> As made the things more rich: their perfume
>   lost,
> Take these again; for to the noble mind
> Rich gifts wax poor when givers prove unkind.

Earl's key scratched hello in the lock.

Bette heard the sound and felt joy.

Hortense did not hear, but looked up and smiled when she saw his face.

He walked in on his two ladies, waiting, in the court of Denmark. Hortense curtsied him a welcome.

"There, my lord."

Bette gave her best stage laugh. *"Ha, ha!"* She wasn't above acting from time to time, after all. "Are you honest?"

Now, Hortense's Ophelia joined Bette's challenge, but with a more girlish yearning finding its way into the question. "My lord?"

"Are you fair?" read Bette. She definitely had

to go visit the ophthalmologist and strengthen her prescription.

Hortense gave Earl a hard look, in character of course. "What means your lordship?" She was full throttle into Ophelia's seductive invitation.

Now Earl, like all actors, had memorized *Hamlet* many years before, alone in his apartment. Often, after too many drinks too early and with a long, lonely night before him, he'd recite the play, lying in his bed as the room spun. But this evening Earl was in his princely glory, turning his workingman's jacket into a royal cape and his bottle of beer into a saber.

"That if you be honest and fair," he said, "your honesty should admit no discourse to your beauty."

Earl felt, at that moment, that he could still play Hamlet someday. It wasn't all over.

Hortense twirled her skirt. "Could beauty, my lord, have better commerce than with honesty?"

"Aye." Earl was sweeping across the room. Flying. "Truly . . ."

Ophelia was his now, she was entirely his. With his dignity, his grace, his boyish good looks, still. It wasn't all gray yet. He could still play a prince.

Then, for one minute, he thought of Leon. Remembered the boy, softening a bit at work. That very day Leon had changed his shirt in front of Earl, rather than hiding in a corner. He gave the gift of his glistening chest. It was a form of apology, perhaps. There is a sweetness, an undeniable pleasure, when an older man sees the beauty of a younger one. There is a knowledge there that the young can never grasp. Of course that is a longing, but there is also a wisdom.

". . . for the power of beauty will sooner transform honesty from what it is to a bawd than the force of honesty can translate beauty into his likeness."

Earl was over Leon. No, he wasn't. His feelings ricocheted from corner to corner. He felt this and then he felt that. Leon was weak, but someday he could be strong. Leon was shallow, but someday he could have depth. Earl had been strong and had been deep, and so it was all doomed—that was the truth. That was the problem. That was it. An equal. If he expected equality, he would never be happy. It was Leon's potential that was so crushing. Earl had to ignore those who *could* do the right thing but did not. He had to be able to accept a man with half his character and do whatever that guy wanted. *It's my fucking standards*, he thought. *They're killing me. Forget about them and stop living in heartbreak.* Earl was unsettled at how much better that felt. That unfamiliar consideration of taking less just to get something. Much, much less.

He looked into Ophelia's blue eyes. She didn't have Leon's beauty, but at least she was game to play. She would try to have a better life.

"This was sometime a paradox, but now the time gives it proof. I did love you once."

That was it. It was as if, right there, Earl had told Leon that he had loved him, *once*. Earl had just said it, admitted it out loud in apartment 2E, with Leon on his mind. He was healed. What a heartbreaker. What a relief. What a loss. How sad. But now it was over.

They were all three satisfied. They were all three at their best. This was it, what everyone else had: their own crowd, their own team, their own built-in set of

133

hands. This, Earl, Hortense and Bette discovered, was the secret world of home. Here everyone had a playmate, and it was a little bit safer, a little bit more secure. Each could imagine a new possibility. Each could take on a new feeling. There was always a witness and there was always a friend.

"Now, Hortense," Earl hung up his jacket directly onto the wooden hanger. "Let me help you with that."

Hortense was relieved. She knew she had talent, she could tell. She looked in the mirror each day and saw the life force circling her soul. Others spotted it on her in the street, *charm*. She saw the smiles as they noticed her. It was pleasurable, watching her. She had *it*, but she lacked craft. If she was honest with herself, clearly inexperience was her problem. Earl had a special situation. He couldn't be judged by his lack of success. This she had come to understand. It wasn't fair out there for Negroes, and gifted people had to suffer. But she, she didn't have those obstacles, so, if he would offer to help . . . well, that might make all the difference. She'd been hinting, and now here it was. The moment that could change her life.

"Thank you."

In particular, the more Hortense heard Earl discuss theater, tell stories, analyze performances, and layer motivations, the more she understood that when it came to most plays, she did not know how to say it. And he did. Once he laid it out, she'd be able to show off at scene class, and they'd be stunned by her improvement. And would be able to see her potential as well. Everybody would.

Putting the most important things in life first, Bette

turned off the pot roast, as the family decided to postpone dinner until Hortense grasped at least one of the basics.

"Stop *pronouncing* it," Earl said, slowly. He wanted her to understand by example so she would see what was to be avoided. "Just speak it," he said, simply.

"Okay," she almost whimpered. It was embarrassing, but she wanted to learn.

"Just talk it."

"Okay." Brave smile. "Here goes. 'Could beauty, my lord, have better commerce than with honesty?'"

"Could it?"

"What?"

Earl went soft and slow, as was necessary when instructing most young actors. The central lesson of the evening was being imparted. Hortense had to know what the line meant in order to really ask the question.

Earl liked Hortense, she was fun, that was the truth. But would he ever be able to respect her? This question had circulated in his mind for a while now. And truth be told, the moment at hand was a test. Could she learn from him? Could she see what he knew? Could she accept her own limitations and follow his instructions? Could she see his value? If she could not, he wouldn't care. But if she could, she would have a better time of it in scene class. He wasn't invested in her class, but generally everyone benefited when some reality was on the table. He watched her take in the challenge to understand, to understand what in the hell she was saying. It wasn't just actors who had this problem. Most people don't listen to themselves half the time. They say things that they are trying out in their mouths, sliding around the sounds, but they don't mean them. An actor can choose for his character to not mean the lines of the script, but he has to understand what his shadow does not.

On Hortense's count, she got the gravity of the moment. Yes, she had been stupid not to consider the meaning, to focus on the sound. But now that Earl had caught her, it could only help. How else are people supposed to learn unless someone knowledgeable explains it to them? Earl was kind. He wanted her to do her best. Just what he wanted for himself. That was a gift. She knew that. She stared back at the page. She concentrated. Hortense looked at those words as she had never looked at any words before. She mumbled them to herself, trying to decipher the puzzle.

"Could beauty have a better business partner than truth? Is that what it means?"

Bette went back into the kitchen and turned the flame on low. This was best left to professionals. Besides, she could see that progress was getting made and dinner would soon begin.

Earl crossed his arms. The maestro! Every actor had to find his own solution. Make his own choice. No one should tell him. Unless it was hopeless.

"Well? Hortense?"

Hortense was confused. "Aren't they the same thing?"

Bette returned from the kitchen with a sealed casserole between two beloved frayed potholders.

"Cousin Bette?"

"Yes, dear?"

"Cousin Bette," Hortense asked with a newly found

intensity, as if this were the singularly most important question of her life. And perhaps it was. "Aren't they the same thing?"

"What, dear? I'm sorry, I didn't hear you."

"Cousin Bette! Are truth and beauty the same thing?"

Bette and Earl laughed so loud and so long. And it united them. Of course they had always laughed together, but each of the two had had the responsibility for initiating it. Once Anthony was gone, they'd never been both relaxed and then moved to joyful guffaws by the comments of a third party. It was normalizing. Easy. Warm. This adorable girl. She brought love all around.

"Truth and beauty are *not* the same thing," Earl explained with the kindness of really knowing.

"What's the difference?" She really wanted him to tell her the answer. If he didn't, she would have no way of ever finding out.

"Well," he paused sagely. "How much is your allowance?"

"Enough to live on."

Enough to not say so, he thought. *Ah, the discretion of the rich.* But he also realized that he and Bette had never discussed the matter. He didn't even know if Bette was aware of the figure. And that felt unusual. That something such a part of their lives would go unspoken. Or more importantly, that he no longer knew every thought in Bette's head. He felt somewhat angry about this. But then noticed his own feeling and felt all right. He looked from Bette to Hortense. Who was smarter? Hortense was reaching for something. Bette was not. She had been more animated of late. They both had. But she was still not ambitious. Hortense was. At that moment, Earl realized that Bette did not, in fact, know the amount of Hortense's allowance.

"Well then," Earl said out loud. "Truth and beauty can look very much alike. When you have the dough. But, without the cash, they're two entirely different things."

Bette felt a stark honesty coming from her own heart. "Hortense, my dear. You have both. Earl and I have only one."

"Which one do you two have?"

Bette and Earl looked at each other with all the tenderness and understanding they had earned together.

"Truth," they announced with one voice. And laughed.

Dinner was served.

This was the prelude to a special night of laughing. Of Bette bringing out a box of assorted chocolates she'd bought at Barton's on a lark on the way back home from work. Then Earl brought out a bottle of brandy he had saved for so long that he'd never imagined actually drinking it. He had been waiting for a happy occasion. He had been hoping that Leon would be the one. *Someone to celebrate with.* But now he knew that was never going to happen, so no point in not drinking it.

On an actor's impulse, Hortense asked for her first taste of brandy.

"I want to lose my head," she said.

Both Bette and Earl imagined that was a line from some movie, but they too were losing their heads. They were happy. They were all happy. They didn't have much, their next accomplishments were all before them, all unknown, and yet they felt good in the moment, enjoyed the ride. It wasn't all about wishing for something that would never come and then enduring that fact. Life could have a moment of gaiety and cracking open the ten-year-old brandy bottle.

Silly girl, thought Earl, bringing youthful energy into their lives. And he had a strange feeling. As she was singing now, singing a song from that new show *West Side Story*.

> *Tonight, tonight,*
> *Won't be just any night,*
> *Tonight there will be no morning star.*

He started thinking about Leon, listening to Hortense's sweet voice. He drank some more brandy, and felt . . . Earl felt . . . he really wanted something . . . he wanted . . . want.

> *Tonight, tonight, I'll see my love tonight.*
> *And for us, stars will stop where they are.*

She stopped singing. It was late. He could see that Bette was exhausted. Earl was the guest here, he was keeping them up. Old folks have to turn in. But he didn't want to. He wanted to keep singing.

"Oh well," Bette yawned. "Time for sleep."

Earl caught Hortense's eye. She didn't want to sleep either. She wanted to stay up. With him.

The end of the evening was now inevitable, and yet Earl and Hortense had communicated to each other, silently, that there could be more fun. If only they had been allowed to stay up longer. But they could not. Because Bette needed to sleep.

At the door, Earl held out his hand. Hortense took it, and they shook good-night. But when it came to Bette, impulsively, he leaned over and kissed her on the cheek.

"Oh my," Bette said.

It was unusual. The gesture.

When the door was closed after him, Bette and Hortense exchanged a smile. A great feeling had been shared between them. The two women started to tidy up, push back the table, as they now did together every night, in order to pull out the sofa bed. Hortense was so practiced at this transformation that she knew to take the pillow out of the hall closet and to pile the cushions on the old sofa. This was her task now. This was how she lay down to rest at the end of her day. There was no more yellow canopy bed in Hortense's life. No more wallpaper. No more matching bureau. No more ribbons in her hair. There was no more old toy chest filled with the dolls of her youth. Everything was blank, starting from scratch. Her mother would never buy her another thing. It was all Hortense's job to make it happen, her life. She had to start thinking that way. This was permanent now. Nothing at her service. If she wanted more, she had to plan. Decide. Opportunity was all that awaited Hortense. And it was her turn to leap.

Chapter 12

Hortense was possessed by an overwhelming knowledge. As her cousin bustled about with the night's final preparations, Hortense could not move to help her. Something enormous had occurred. She had become . . . a woman. And it was nothing she had imagined back in her yellow bedroom, in the flowered fields, or even on the bus rolling across the farms of Pennsylvania hurtling east. She had never really understood what adulthood would entail, but now she did. Passion. Not imagining, wanting, or yearning for something better. But instead, a depth of commitment to what truly existed in her life *right now*, and the fierce, vicious loyalty it required to make it inseparable, unloseable, permanent.

Hortense turned toward the window. Suddenly, she could see *it*, the thing that kept Bette herself staring for hours in the way that relatives repeatedly flocked to church or an astronomer chose the stars over earth. Hortense understood that the living cinema, the human theater outside that window was now *her* world. It no longer belonged to Bette alone. These were the streets where her life would take place, under the old wrought iron gaslight transformed for electric, whose eerie glow had no parallel in nature. This was her Act One, and the climax and intermission were soon approaching. She opened the window wider and brought her body to the night.

A silent bicycle passed through the shadows below. A man lit a cigarette, a dog whimpered. She could hear the whoosh of his match. Then the dog, comforted somehow, was silent. Any moment now, a bevy of dancing girls would tap out onto the avenue, followed by chorus boys dressed as toughs. It reminded her of the set of *Guys and Dolls*, which she had seen on Broadway for four dollars, and made her yearn even more for the new movie version that was not yet released. This was her life now. Hortense Marybelle Webb. Riding the subway was not a rocket ship to Hollywood, it was Hollywood. Turns out Busby Berkeley was a kitchen-sink realist compared to everyday life on the island of Manhattan. And New Yorkers naturally conversed in that snappy dialogue overflowing with wisecracks and comebacks that sounded written, but were in fact expertly improvised on the smooth.

"He had a voice like rancid butter."

The short kid in her scene class had actually uttered that line as part of lunchtime banter.

Hortense was a star, having her star turn. This was her moment. This, she knew, was her cue. This was *it*.

"Bette?"

"Yes?"

"I want you to stop."

If ever a human being had spoken to Bette that way, given her an order like an old dairy farmwife or an Ashtabula school marm assuming the role of God, well, if anyone had even tried this approach over the last thirty years, Bette could not recall it happening. After all, a reasonable person must be reasoned with, not commanded. The sharp rebuke was so unfamiliar an occurrence that Bette felt nothing but curiosity. Too preposterous for anger, only a genuine question seemed right.

"Stop what?"

Now, on the third line, Hortense turned from the window to face Bette fully. Only now that she had turned could Bette see the tears in her eyes. Background music, please.

"Stop treating me like a child." Hortense paused, brought her vocal tone down to room temperature. "There is no need."

Truth be told, Bette did wonder, at first, if the girl was performing a scene from a play. But then she saw Hortense's expression of determination, one that could be accessed but never imitated. She saw that it was both willful and childish. Reminiscent of Shirley Temple singing "On the Good Ship Lollipop." Lips pursed, cheeks puffed, imitating authority in a manner that had no authority. Trying it on for size.

"I agree," Bette said. "There is absolutely no reason for me to treat you like a child. Are you worried that you might be acting like a child?"

"I know," Hortense barreled forth, losing her nerve

and then grabbing it again. "I know that you and Earl are lovers."

There. She'd done it.

"You do?" Bette almost laughed.

"Yes. The passion between you is palpable."

Bette considered. Then decided.

"It is?"

"Yes."

Hortense was in full swing now. She started coming toward Bette. *Downstage cross.* It was the action that began her monologue.

"Bette."

Pause.

"Bette, I want you to know for sure that there is no need to abide by the hypocritical conventions of Christian chastity for my sake."

"I agree." Bette tried not to laugh.

"Christian chastity" was a phrase she had not heard uttered since her childhood. But more importantly, it was an idea she had not heard considered. It was on the garbage heap of history along with *outhouse* and *Satan.* Concepts that modern man no longer regarded as worthy of consideration. It was outdated, part of a benign nostalgia for rural times gone by. Bette would never see that world again. She added to the list of things forgotten: *pigs' feet, ice cream churn, dandelion greens, quilting.* Oh yes, also *stable boy* and the song "Bringing in the Sheaves." Actually, no. Bette and Earl had sung "Bringing in the Sheaves" when he got the postcard saying that his mother had died. But never again since that day.

"Because," Hortense continued, "after all, Bette, we are both grown women."

"I have been one for some time," Bette concurred, at least about herself.

Bette looked at her young cousin. She could see her flaws and her strengths. She was fun, engaged, hopeful, lively, and had commitments. This was marvelous. But she was also unaware of what others were thinking. That was a significant flaw. Of course, Bette knew, one could never be a mind reader, but at minimum it was important to factor into one's imagination that others *were* thinking and that the content of these thoughts was always in question. Hortense did not seem to know this to be true.

The matter at stake here, Bette noted, was that if Hortense did not know that others had their own considerations, she could not understand who they really were. That would apply to Earl as well as to herself. It was almost strange, to be that oblivious. But the recognition made Bette want to help the girl to change. Bette wanted to watch Hortense as she grew.

"I mean," Hortense took Bette's hand in hers, "you, Cousin Bette. You have desires, dreams, deep loves. And like all women who have walked their own path, you also have a soul mate. And I understand that true soul mates are chosen by God, they cannot be replaced or denied. So, I truly understand . . ." Here Hortense opened her eyes so wide, they devoured her face. "So I truly understand that soul mates do not need a piece of paper from city hall, as long as they have their lives intertwined as they wish."

"I see." Bette was taken aback by the God talk. She

145

had long put those promises aside and wondered if Hortense actually believed these things. That Jesus Christ was the Son of God, born of a virgin. And that he had died for their sins and rose again. It seemed impossible for Hortense to be the kind of person to take this seriously, so the invocation of God could only be a bad habit. At the same time, she did feel partially pleased that Hortense recognized the primacy of her commitment with Earl. Yes, they were soul mates of a sort. They were friends for life. That was true. And it was very precious. A treasure. But Hortense's histrionics around their friendship seemed a bit silly. It was the racial element, Bette knew, that had brought this to a fever pitch.

"True," Hortense continued. "You two could never marry."

"Why not?"

"Isn't it illegal?" Hortense seemed suddenly unsure as to the factual basis of her deep concern.

"Not illegal in New York," Bette answered with pride. It then occurred to her that marriage between blacks and whites might still be illegal in Ohio, and she resolved to stop at the library and look that up. This had never crossed her mind before because she had never considered marriage under any circumstance, and neither had Earl. It simply did not come up, except in relation to poor Anthony and how the power of the thing sucked him away.

Hortense fell back to the windowsill, glanced out. There it was again! The play's next scene had begun. Someone was making his entrance, coming home late. He was staggering, whistling. Where was he headed?

Another bar? A tenement walk-up to an angry put-upon wife and child, whose rent money he had just drunk down? A posh elevator building filled with martinis and evening gowns? *Oh my*, he was whistling a song from *Guys and Dolls*.

> *Luck be a lady tonight.*
> *Luck if you've ever been a lady to begin with.*
> *Luck be a lady tonight.*

Bette looked at Hortense's back, her long hair, and felt amused. Yet, she did not know how to respond. The truth about Earl was out of the question. It would be many years before Hortense would be able to understand the homosexual way. It would take experience and the recognition that she, herself, was not superior. And even then Earl would have to start the conversation in his own time. His own fashion. Unless, of course, he found a new love, then it would all be presented, matter-of-factly, and she'd have to jump on board. But, meanwhile Bette had enjoyed being imagined, by another person, in that silly, dreamy way. Of course, Hortense did not fully understand about Frederick. He was her father. She claimed to see through him, but there could still be sentimentality residing there, enough to keep her from being able to internalize the full truth. Was Bette ready to risk it? She had been patient, waiting to see if there was a moment when Hortense would be able to understand. Perhaps that moment was upon them. After all, Bette had also been twenty when his initial cruelty had unfolded. Perhaps she could empathize with that other young girl Bette had been so long before.

"I just want to be sure that you know," Hortense added, a bit lost somehow, "that I understand, Cousin Bette. And that . . ."

"Yes, dear?"

"That I love you."

"You love me?"

Oh.

A door opened then. For them both.

Appropriately a bird soared by. City birds don't fly at night, unless a certain freedom of spirit takes hold of their hearts. So the swoop of their glide means joy and the whimsy to take a chance. Or it could mean that a New Jersey gas tank had exploded into flames.

Bette felt as though she wished to cry, and yet she did not cry. Someone who she was related to loved her. This person saw her, somewhat self-centeredly, but with good intentions nonetheless. And this young girl was kind. Bette had not thought about, considered, imagined, or wished for such an experience for many, many years. That ancient hope had only brought dismembering pain and had to be pushed aside. And yet, somehow, miraculously, it had come to her. It had knocked at her door, and it had delivered.

"I don't want you to hide anything from me," Hortense said.

"I can try," Bette answered.

"My father and my mother live in a state of one lie following the other. Lying is the structure upon which they lean." She spoke to Bette as an equal, invested in the same thought. "They don't tell each other anything that matters, and they certainly don't tell me. I swear they no longer know what is actually taking place. The scramble to strategize through lies has become a way of life."

Just as I feared. Bette felt confirmed and therefore free to be sad that these people, so important to her fate, had made the wrong choices. And now everyone was suffering. Bette, the least.

"I don't want that to be my life," Hortense said. "I want to know the truth and I want you to know the truth."

All these years Bette had worked hard to keep the facts straight. She recited them regularly when she was alone, memorized them, like lists. She did this as an investment in the future, so that one day, if ever the opportunity should arise, the facts could be easily recited and honestly conveyed. So that others could be made to know and understand.

(1) Frederick lied.
(2) I was punished as a consequence of his lie.
(3) Et cetera.

And now that day had come.

"Do you understand?" Hortense was finished, it seemed. Waiting for a response.

"Yes," Bette said quietly. "I do understand."

For some strange reason having to do with time, luck, coincidence, fate, and justice, on this strange Tuesday night, in her nightgown, that long longed for moment had come to pass. This was finally the place for those facts, that story, to be recited. Out loud.

"Your father," Bette began haltingly. Those were difficult words to form, as his daughter had never been her imagined audience. So strange to yield now to feelings large and unwieldy. Bette had not told this story since that one full recitation to Anthony and Earl when they were all so young. Anthony, still living, poor thing.

"Your father is my one great true love. Your father."

"What did he do?"

Bette spoke slowly, but she was steady. She picked her way from rock to rock over the swirling dangers of the swollen river.

"Your father seduced me by the banks of the Ashtabula River."

The breeze.

"The next day, my family, that is to say *yours*, my mother, my father, my smoking brother back from the war, my cousins, my aunts and uncles, Frederick's parents, his sisters. Our neighbors, our world. We were all summoned to the parlor of his father's—your grandfather's—home. Paid for by the labor of the workers at his mill. Now your father's, I suppose."

Hortense nodded.

"We were served punch, out of a cut-glass bowl. And I still had the scent of Frederick's love on my skin. I was so pure, so calm, the right thing had happened in my life. I had found my calling."

Hortense was absorbed. Bette could see. She had lost the artifice.

"His father, your grandfather . . . is he still living?"

"No, long passed. I only knew him as a feeble, help-less mass, sitting silently under a shawl in a corner chair."

"Of course. Well, at that time he was one of the most powerful men in the county. He stood tall, with a glass of punch in his hand, and announced that your father would soon marry my cousin. Crevelle. Your mother. And the room was filled with cheers."

"Oh, Bette."

"My tears are their cheers. It would always be that way."

"I understand."

"Something came over me then. The discord between their joy and the lie at the base of it. The world would divide into two at that second forever. For all time, at the same time. There would be the world of falsity and the world of reality, coexisting, ever in conflict, ever in struggle. I looked at the cross around your mother's heaving breast. I called out."

Bette stopped here. She did not know why.

"What did you say?"

"*Stop*."

That was what she'd said after all. In fact, she'd said it twice. And Bette stood erect, in her apartment, just as she had done in that room full of tyrants, and held out the same hand, now wrinkled, and called out, "*Stop*. This is not the truth."

Everyone had turned to her. Innocently. Wonder-ing. But not Frederick. He knew what she would do.

"The truth is," Bette returned to that critical mo-ment, raising her head with the same primitive defiance. "That Frederick seduced me last night. By

151

the banks of the Ashtabula River. He pledged his love to me, and I to him. He cannot marry my cousin. He cannot."

"Oh my," Hortense gasped.

Bette looked into the young woman's eyes. Hortense finally understood her own legacy. She finally saw the real Bette. She saw her strength.

"That is not true," Frederick lurched. His spilled punch.

"Yes, it is," Bette told him, told them all. "Yes, it is the truth."

Bette felt weak. She backed up a few steps and collapsed into her chair. Hortense saw this but knew better than to move. The two of them lived together in the silence, while Bette regained some direction. She soothed herself by reviewing the facts, internally. Reviewing the memorized list of facts. This brought her back to the crucial moment of the story. The moment when Frederick chose a life of lies and Bette had to forever pay his price.

"Frederick said, 'That is not true. You offered yourself to me, but I told you my heart belonged to Crevelle. You would not accept my truth, and here you are again, weaving a web of lies.'"

"Father," Hortense spoke. But this time there was no gasp. She recognized the man that she knew in that story. She understood that this was exactly what had taken place. "I see."

"Do you understand?" Bette asked.

"I am not surprised," Hortense said.

Bette nodded her head. "He claimed that the truth was a lie, and so he attempted to eclipse all the joy that had existed between us. But I would not cooperate with that eclipse. It was only the sun passing behind a cloud. Eventually it would reappear. As it always does. As you arriving on my doorstep has confirmed."

"What did your parents do?"

"My family had more to gain by believing him. After all, I was claiming to have committed a sexual transgression, and this was not a reasonable claim in their minds. It was not something that could be defended. Crevelle was my cousin, the daughter of my father's sister. Frederick's father owned half the town. My parents would do nothing but lose if they took my side. There was no honor in the truth for them, for it was shrouded in social niceties and material realities, and for my family those superseded love. Believing me, supporting their daughter, would have cost too high a price."

"What price?"

"A decent marriage, an upstanding citizen. As a sacrifice to those things, I was vilified and forced from my home. My father gave me a one-way ticket to Cleveland. I begged my brother to intervene, but he just stood in the corner and smoked."

"I see."

"Because of your father's cruelty, I lost my home. Because of his cruelty, I lost everything I knew. And yet, he is still in the center of my heart."

"Why? Cousin Bette, why do you feel this way?"

The answer to Hortense's short question was the most hard-won revelation in Bette's long life. She had worked toward an understanding for decades. The feeling of love persisted, that was undeniable, but why did it persist? This was the most central mystery in her struggle to understand, to be aware, to acknowledge that *yes*, in fact, she still loved Frederick. Even if she wasn't supposed to, even if it made no sense. But because she had done the labor of understanding, she had finally come to realize why.

"Because I saw him be good and tender, so I know that he can be."

That was the knowledge she had found within.

"All right," Hortense said. "I understand."

Bette had made the right choice. Hortense's lack of protest showed that she was capable of recognizing the obvious. All of Bette's life the obvious had been denied. She was smarter than Hector, but he owned the company. Earl was a brilliant actor with the soul of an angel, but petty prejudice kept him in the slaughterhouse. If Anthony had owned the love that he felt, he would be alive today. These clefts between truth and power pervaded. But now there was a third party who could take this in. Accept it. Not pretend it wasn't so. Hortense had fulfilled that need.

"I saw him receive grace, so I know that he can."

"You witnessed his true self."

"Yes, my dear," Bette's heart broke with gratitude. "I did."

They were both feeling the weight.

"All of these years he has *chosen* to be one kind of person. A liar. But because I *witnessed* him be truthful and good, I know he can choose that again. Goodness will eternally live on as a possibility within him because it was part of him once. The body remembers. That potential is never lost. Once a person is kind, they always have the option to be kind again. They know what it feels like."

Hortense's head was cocked to one side. The pose had long ago been discarded.

"You see, Hortense, Frederick caused me to lose my family and my home. I know in my heart—actually I knew it that moment when he denounced me in your grandfather's parlor . . ." Then she realized. "I suppose that is now *your* parlor, after all."

"Yes, it is," Hortense answered flatly.

"In that moment, something inside me became broken. I am not . . . I am not . . ." *Tell the truth.* "I am not a hero. I am regular. And I have been . . . affected. Because of him, I came to New York. And I made a new home. And now, Hortense, you and Earl have given me a new family. You too have come to New York *because of him*. I know that I will never lose you. It is all now as it always should have been."

"What do you want from Frederick?"

Bette extended her hand to Hortense who took it without question. This conversation had gone far better than Bette could have ever imagined. Now she would offer this dear girl the greatest treasure of Bette's life, her insight, the product of all her effort. The gift that all that loneliness and suffering had borne.

"After thinking about this for so many years, Hortense. I have come to realize that I believe in . . . the duty of repair."

She watched.

Had Hortense fully comprehended that phrase? That long sought-after phrase that Earl had helped her discover?

"I know there is cruelty in life," Bette said. "But I believe that it can be followed by reconciliation. In order for this pain that remains in me to heal, Frederick must see the healing. That is what I want from him. To make peace with me, in person. I know this can be done."

Hortense nodded.

"And Earl?" Hortense asked, her heart racing.

"Earl?" Bette felt peace. "Earl will never betray me. Earl will never lie."

"So, you're not lovers then?"

"No," Bette said. "Earl is the most important person in my life." Bette was exhausted now. She was ready for bed. "He has my keys."

"I see," Hortense murmured, waiting another half hour before stepping out into the hall.

Chapter 13

The truth being revealed, everything in Bette's life had become exciting, something to look forward to. She now hurried to Union Square to catch the IRT to the office because it was so much faster than the bus. She'd pass the old D.W. Griffith studio, then Lüchow's German beer garden, to jump on the subway in front of Klein's department store next to Hammer's Dairy Restaurant. There was a passion in her gait, a connection.

Running up to Union Square each day also provoked her imagination. In the past there had been labor gatherings in the square, Communists and people wishing for great change parading around with banners, signs, and hope. But the last few years had quieted down somewhat. Perhaps due to Senator McCarthy and his ilk. The park was getting a bit shabby, unsure of its new social role. Too preoccupied with new activities to make a sandwich, she'd buy a pretzel off an ancient wooden stick from the old lady with a basket full of them on the corner and nibble all through the day. Warm and chewy with huge crystals of thick salt, a full lunch hour seemed frivolous. Too much going on.

At Tibbs Advertising, a cyclone had hit. Hector hired Valerie Korie to come in one day a week on a consultancy basis, yet she seemed to be there for five. Plus, Bette suspected, she stopped in on Sundays. Valerie couldn't stay away. Her enthusiasm brought an excitement to the place, which made them all take their new tasks very seriously. As though, suddenly, advertising really mattered. As if it were world peace, wash-and-wear clothing, and a man in space rolled into one. Hector and Bette got in earlier but still tried to gesture toward old-fashioned hours: arriving punctually at eight and leaving precisely at five. Valerie's hours had more flare to them: unpredictable, a kind of reflection of an unimaginable way of life. She'd saunter in at nine or ten, which implied late nights filled with lascivious enterprises and rides home in empty subway cars. Or some days they'd arrive at work and she would be just finishing some mysterious task, having acted impulsively all night on a new idea. At other times, she'd hover in the office long after Hector ran off to the commuter train, which implied to Bette that Valerie had no one expecting her and certainly no one waiting on her for supper. All that freedom made Valerie increasingly intangible and a bit wild, and therefore far more trustworthy as a source of information about the future and culture's edge.

Bette and Hector both loved this. But for different reasons. Hector, having spent his entire youth and manhood in Connecticut, could not, for the life of him, imagine where she went, what she did, and with whom. Bette, who had seen and heard a great deal, without having to go through too much of it herself, had a clearer idea of what was involved. The known and the unknown had equal pull. Valerie emerged as a curious, interested person who had apparently found joy in the discovery of all things. She loved solving problems, finding solutions, and constructing ways to persuade others of these very conclusions. Her brown hair was full and she tossed it like a presiding mare. Her fingers were garnished with rings. Her neck was exposed so that everyone guessed what lay just a few inches below. Her arms were teasingly garbed, then revealed. It was all a promise, Valerie's package. She loved having ideas, and she loved carrying them through. And, as all love truly is infectious, hers caused an epidemic. Bette was a perfect candidate, since she had always been a reliable person who fulfilled her assigned tasks, but they were rarely amusing. Now, the office was a strange new fun house, one that would rival Coney Island even without the fried clams. But instead of the mindless distraction of a tunnel of love, Tibbs Advertising was becoming a laboratory where the future was being born. And therefore . . . anything could happen.

The first thing Valerie did was rearrange the desks. She preferred to have the staff together in one room, talking to each other constantly throughout the day. Then she painted the whole place a new color called *teal*, or at least she persuaded some muscular, dark-haired man in a T-shirt to do it for her. She brought in mirrors and flowers and—of all things—a cigarette machine, which no one used but her. Valerie would light a cigarette, perch on the end of Bette's desk from time to time, and ask her advice about very important matters: about packaging and phraseology and what Bette was aware of and what had eluded her consciousness. Questions about singers and products and automobiles, about beer and hats and cosmetics. As far as Bette could assess, not knowing was as important as knowing, and whatever answer she gave seemed to be taken very, very seriously. Bette found the new organization to somewhat parallel the important changes unfolding at home. More cozy. More intimate. A lot more conversation. Valerie believed that this was good for business and allowed them all to be "liberated" from the drudgery of the old-style "office drone" setup, permitting them to think together and most importantly, "act on impulse."

The general enchantment was so consuming that Hector became like Dorothy, asleep in Oz's poppy field, only to dreamily awake one morning, two months later, and decide, almost haphazardly, in the commuter train on the ride home, to examine the budget. What he found there was so alarming that for the first time in his life, Hector had a fourth cocktail. In fact, he was so disturbed that he actually ordered something he'd never had before, a Rob Roy. One half Scotch, one half sweet vermouth, a dash of bitters, and a maraschino cherry. It went down like cough syrup mixed with moonshine and required an extra helping of ice. By the time the evil concoction had completed its slide along his throat, Hector faced facts. It was time to panic. The costs Valerie anticipated and had started to happily accrue were so unimaginably enormous that all he could envision was his house seized for lack of tax payments, the office closed down for lack of rent checks, and the impossibility of ever purchasing the new automobile of his dreams. One that Valerie had pointed out to him in a magazine. The 1958 Lancia Aurelia.

Hector had been spending as much time thinking about the car as he had thinking about Valerie. One had come to symbolize the other. If he could have a car of that quality, he could certainly have a woman of the same caliber. Yes, it's true, Hector had been having forbidden thoughts about his new consultant but was dutifully channeling them into a desire for this car. The more research he did, the more Hector felt driven to own the Lancia Aurelia. When the maker, Vincenzo Lancia, had been born in 1881, his father already had decided that the boy would become a lawyer. This paralleled Hector's own fate. And like Hector, Vincenzo was not suited for his appointed task. Instead of hitting the books, young Vincenzo defied his father and hung out at bike shops, becoming a mechanic, eventually going to work for Fiat, and then starting his own company. The Aurelia had the world's first V6 engine. Hector wasn't quite sure what that meant exactly, but it was the first. More importantly, Valerie thought it was *elegant,* and that's what Hector wished to become.

This drunken reverie on the sports car he would now never be able to drive came to an end as the train pulled into the Greenwich station, and Hector had to face facts. She was breaking him. She would destroy everything his father had amassed and leave poor Hector penniless. Did they still have debtors' prison? Because that's where he was going. Most immediately, Hector would have to explain to Sue that the olive-green Frigidaire she was dying to install was just going to have to wait. And the braces for Stevie and Sally's ballet lessons. Who was the devil who'd invented colored kitchen appliances that every housewife in Connecticut simply had to possess? Who? *Who?* Now the whole house had to be redone. It was just the kind of thing Valerie would have come up with. An expenditure that served no purpose and fit no need but for some emotional reason everyone had to have it. Olive-green refrigerators. If only Valerie could do that for Tibbs Advertising. Come up with something preposterous that everyone with a spare dollar felt they had to own. That's what she was promising, after all. The mysteries of desire and consumption. And when wanting the best, one has to pay, but . . .

The next morning Hector and Bette got in on time and waited for Valerie to appear. Bette did her weekly books, calculating, balancing, adding, and subtracting, making deposits and signing checks. Hector paced endlessly, anxiously clutching Valerie's budget and waiting for the clock to strike nine. Then ten. It was excruciating. He practiced his speech over and over again. *Of course I've always known that television would be an expensive proposition. That's why the profits were so inviting.* But this budget of Valerie's was just . . . *over the top.* He hoped she had a simple explanation and would not be revealed as a fantasist, living in a wax-paper world made out of other people's money. Finally, unable to contain himself any longer, he thrust the documents under Bette's nose, and she adjusted her reading glasses to have a better look.

By ten fifteen, Bette had seen what she needed to see and had come to a conclusion about the situation. She was simultaneously intrigued and uncomfortable with Valerie's level of risk. But that had been the draw all along. It was personally challenging, and Bette liked that. After all, for most of her life she had usually wished for things to remain the way they were. Surprise had never served her, and this budget was very surprising. Yet, Bette had a strong instinctive confidence that Valerie knew what she was doing. That she knew more about how things worked than Bette or Hector did, and discovering how much one does not understand can be very frightening. It was time Bette and Hector committed to facing the music, learning what needed to be learned, and stepping up to the challenges of the unknown. Bette found this prospect thrilling, and that desire to change overrode her traditional hesitancies about spending.

After all, Hortense had excavated a whole new arena of trust in today's youth, and Bette was realizing that being born *after* the Great Depression and growing up *after* the Big War seemed to make this new crop of young people a lot more open minded, bolder, and more inventive than their frightened predecessors. In fact, she had to admit that this get-up-and-go that Hortense and Valerie exhibited was more *adult* than Bette herself had ever been. It wasn't about keeping to one's self to stay out of the line of fire, but instead reaching to be the person who gave the command: *Ready . . . Aim.* There was a new line of attack in the hearts and minds of this fresh crop of young ladies, and Bette found all the strategizing involved to be energetic. In fact, she found it inspiring.

"Well?" Hector asked, trembling.

"We have to hear what she has to say." There was nothing to do but wait.

Finally, at ten seventeen, Valerie, the leopard, pounced into the office. She was sleek, lethal, lovely, and ready to win. Hector paced before her, sweating, nervously stating his case.

"We can't . . . the budget . . . impossible . . . risk . . . risk . . . risk."

Valerie stayed calm, friendly, and in a poised place of supremacy over all the financial and psychological nooks and crannies of the situation. Bette noticed the way Valerie took in and assessed the evidence before her: Hector's expressions of worry, the stammer in his speech. Bette knew as Valerie appeared to listen with sincerity and respect that she was actually preparing her comeback. Valerie's mind was on two tracks simultaneously, like the Sarnoff stereo systems being advertised in the magazines she left around the office. Bass and treble. She could engage in the present and plan for the future at the same moment.

To be a winner in this world, one had to be able to think about a few different things at the same time, Bette noted. And she resolved to try this out for herself. *It's the only way to get ahead of the game.*

Bette noticed her own thinking in terms of *the game* and laughed. What game? She wasn't playing any game. This was all Hector's problem, but it couldn't hurt to learn how to play, could it? It might someday come in handy, somewhere. If she ever really wanted something so badly she couldn't live without it. In that case, it would be good to know how to get it. *Wouldn't it?*

Back to the workplace action, Hector was finally winding down his long-winded frightened soliloquy, and the second he landed, Valerie actually leapt off her perch and launched into what Bette could now identify as *hard sell*.

"It's a new world," Valerie smiled, opening her arms and reaching for the sky. That was the kind of gesture that won people over right away. A shapely, attractive seductress, casting all pose aside to move as freely as a child in an open field is supposed to move, but rarely does. The image evoked a liberty that might have never been, and in that case was evocative and compelling, provoking desire in those watching her for a better childhood, and marvel that someone else could have one now. Valerie twirled around the office like Leslie Caron in *An American in Paris* and looked to the heavens above. When Hector and Bette followed her gaze, all they saw was a dirty pressed-tin ceiling that had escaped the new paint job. They both recognized it immediately as something that needed to be renovated into a surface more modern and sleek, using materials they could barely pronounce, like *asbestos* or that new . . . *fiberfill*.

"Look," Valerie laughed, pointing at the dirty patch of ceiling. "Soon we'll have a man in space."

She had a beautiful smile, and Bette looked closer, transporting through the water stains to imagined trails of rocket ships to Mars, and this tickled her greatly.

"Do you really think so?"

Being lost in Valerie's dream was a lot more fun than being lost in Hector's worries. Bette was getting the hang of this, what Valerie had called *positive thinking*.

"I know so." Valerie grabbed Bette's gaze and seized it. "Do you have any children?"

"I have a young cousin, Hortense."

"Imagine," Valerie said. "When she is your age, she will be able to shuttle to the moon, the way you take the 6 train to work. Every single person in the world will speak the same language: ESPERANTO! And Hortense will travel to China . . . by jet pack!"

"Really?"

"THE FUTURE IS COMING!" Valerie laughingly threatened and promised. "That's a guarantee. And all of its ideas will have to be sold."

The imminence of the future seemed reasonable to Hector and to Bette, something they could understand and get behind with ease.

"Here!" Valerie slurped, reeling them in like trout in a stocked pond. "I will teach you how to sell the future. I will let you in on all my techniques. On one condition."

"What?" Hector and Bette gasped in unison, hypnotized by possibility once again.

"On the condition that . . . if you are persuaded . . . you will make me partner."

It was silent in the ring.

"Partner?" Hector squeaked. He'd never counted on sharing with anyone, but somehow the seduction of pure curiosity kept him lapping at the bait.

Bette waited for Valerie's snappy comeback, but she said nothing. Why did she do that? It was so unusual. Bette waited and waited. What was Valerie's strategy?

What game was she playing now? Finally, Bette realized. Valerie's silence allowed Hector to wilt on his own. He didn't need any help losing.

"Okay," he choked, and collapsed into his chair, exhausted.

Now that the overture had earned a standing ovation, Valerie swooped into the opening number.

"Let's say"—she was being coy, pouting her bright red lips like Clara Bow would have done, if she had been in color instead of black and white—"just for argument's sake, imagine that *I* am the product." She indicated her own shapely form as though she were the Lancia Aurelia. "What are my selling points?"

"Well," Bette said, jumping into the game, willing to learn. "You are fast. And that means modern."

"And attractive," Hector blurted out. Then he noticed he had just been impulsive and thought, *What the heck?* Truth was, it felt good. "And awfully complicated. So psychological."

Valerie had them now because this was where Freud came into the picture, and that was her strongest suit. She had been psychoanalyzed and strongly recommended it for business.

Freud, as Valerie explained to a spellbound Bette and Hector, *of course* had discovered the conflict between the conscious and the unconscious. Bette had not realized that there was such a conflict and wondered how something so intangible could be recognized. She imagined him staring at himself in the mirror with a magnifying glass and Sherlock Holmes cap. The more she thought about it, the more this idea of psychology appealed to her. It had involved noticing one's own feelings. Mr. Freud probably had observed himself doing one thing but feeling another, and realized the two were in contradiction. Everyone had the same experience, but he had been smart enough to call it something, a *conflict*. Once it had a name, others could refer to it as something more than a weird feeling creeping inside. And the word *conflict* allowed others to see what he was talking about and then they could think about that too. Finding the right word was a big part of it, Bette was sure. And Valerie agreed, describing that process as "branding."

"Freud discovered," Valerie enticed further, "that if a person is not aware of what they *truly* want, they will become . . . fragmented."

Another great word, Bette thought. She understood exactly what Freud was referring to. That experience of being torn apart by outside forces and one's own inner spirit.

"This applies to marketing," Valerie assured. "Once the customers' secret desires have been revealed, they will act on them. After all, there are two kinds of people in this world. Some want to *be* Marilyn Monroe, and some want to *have* Marilyn Monroe."

Bette was stunned. She had never had a single thought about Marilyn Monroe. Either way. Or was it a metaphor?

"If . . . ," Valerie neared conclusion, "if advertising could let these people act out their fantasies through the products they buy, people would be happier, not hurting those around them out of unexpressed anxieties. So, marketing is good. For America. And that's why brand names are so important."

"Can you give an example?" Bette was still stuck on Marilyn Monroe.

"For example," Valerie gleamed, "people, blindfolded, cannot recognize the taste of their own brand of cigarette." She took her own silver case out of her purse and held it open under Hector's nose. "Cigarette?"

"Yes, thank you."

Valerie struck the match, waited. Hector inhaled, took in its flavor, exhaled with an expressive sound of relief. "Ahhhh."

"Yes, *ahhhh*. The universal testimonial of a good smoke." Valerie smiled reassuringly but suddenly bared her saber. "Brand?"

Bette yelled out the answer, "Lucky!"

"Yes, you are." Valerie had her now.

Bette had never won before. She'd never shouted anything out, and she'd never been the one who was right. And most importantly? It felt great. If this was the new world Valerie was offering, Bette was ready to sign on the dotted line.

"How did you know?" Hector was flabbergasted. Bette had leapt ahead of him. She'd never been the one who was so publicly knowing before. That was disconcertingly strange but also somehow comforting, because he would never have to make decisions all alone.

"She chose it by assessing *me*," Valerie explained to Hector like he was very, very young. "Not the taste of the cigarette. She instinctively knew that I am a LUCKY girl, and therefore would choose a brand name that defined my best attribute. Right?"

Bette blushed.

"Now, Hector? Bette? You have both learned beautifully. And here is the reward for all of your hard work." She put her fingers to her lips and tooted an invisible horn. "Our First Television Product!"

The shift in focus made the room spin. How could Valerie have planned this unveiling at such a perfect juncture all along? How could she know them *that* well?

As Bette and Hector contemplated these questions, Valerie had already advanced. She whipped out a veiled model on a small wooden tabletop pedestal that had been successfully hidden underneath her desk in anticipation of this inevitable conversation. Which explained why she was always lounging across that desk and never sitting at it. *Voilà*, she tore off its shroud.

"ROCOCO!"

What was revealed was a glistening jar of liquid as rich as Texas oil and as enticing as the heavenly nectar of the gods.

"Rococo?" Bette asked. "Isn't that some kind of pottery?"

"NO!" Valerie was at full blast. "RO-CO-CO. AMERICA'S FAVORITE CHOCOLATE DRINK."

Hector and Bette were overwhelmed. Both believed, instantaneously, that all they'd ever wanted was a rich, cool, fulfilling chocolate drink. Thicker than an egg cream but even more refreshing. No need to create a mess by *adding* the Fox's U-Bet syrup. This drink was already custom made in its own individual serving. Fresh always. And always just enough.

The fact was, Valerie could have sold them Edsel and Doomsday and Estes Kefauver for President and cod liver oil. Valerie was so far ahead of them, relationally, it was like being converted to a religion one never knew existed. Like growing up in Iowa, only to discover the Buddha's lair one blistery night from a traveling carnival acrobat. It was incongruous and yet undeniable. All this time, Valerie had pretended they were on the same page, but secretly she was the one writing the book. Before eight in the morning and after six at night, she was developing chocolate juice and designing the jar.

"How does it taste?" asked Bette, managing to integrate her former practicality with this newfound awareness of desire and its role in marketing.

"Oh, that doesn't matter."

"It doesn't?"

"No." Valerie seemed offended.

"Why not? Isn't chocolate supposed to be good?"

Valerie gazed at Bette through a gauze of disapproval, and it stung so hard, Bette resolved automatically to learn all of the new rules as quickly as possible.

"Bette. *Dear*," Valerie lovingly condescended. "Let me explain. And you, too, Hector. Pay attention."

"Okay."

"How something tastes in *your* mouth can never be known by another person. Therefore it has no status."

They both nodded. That made sense.

"The more important question is . . . WHO CAN WE GET?"

"Get?" Hector was lost.

"To endorse it, silly."

Ohhhhhhhhhhhh.

Hector and Bette relaxed. See, everything was all

171

right. It all linked together into one intense, dynamic apparatus of a logic system, one orderly new way.

"Soooo," Valerie coooed. "Who do you suggest?"

Bette was still thinking about Marilyn Monroe and the question of being versus having. But Hector's hand was waving.

"Yes, Hector?"

"Konrad Adenaur," he tried lamely, but knew it was wrong before the name of the new leader of Germany even escaped his lips. Germany was trying to live down its bad reputation and wouldn't be a good product enhancer.

"No."

"Jayne Mansfield!" Bette was on a roll.

"Better. But too trashy."

Then the three of them paced the office like Groucho, Harpo, and Chico in *A Night at the Opera*, looking for the brilliant, crazy scheme that would make everything be okay.

"We need someone dark," said Valerie, who was, herself, quite dark. "Regal." That too could describe her. "Mysterious."

"You?" Hector tried.

"No," she dismissed him. "I know! The Queen of Rumania!"

"Great idea," Hector guffawed.

"Yes. Then the buying public will think that our chocolate comes from the land of the Gypsies, instead of Central Pennsylvania."

Her brow furrowed.

"But, Bette, is there still a Queen of Rumania? Or do they have a Stalinist look-alike?"

172

Bette made a note to go to the library on her lunch break.

"There must be a queen somewhere," Valerie seemed to be in despair. "Maybe in exile in the Bronx. But the bigger point of all this is to give people what they secretly want. POWER! MONEY! GLAMOUR! Or at least the suggestion of all that, so that they will give us back PROFITS. To achieve this, we must convey our message subliminally, so that the consumer doesn't have to take . . ."

"Responsibility?" Bette guessed.

"Brava, diva," Valerie applauded.

So much had happened. Tibbs Advertising had its own product, developed precisely in order to build an ad campaign. Bette noted this with gravitas. The object was not important in and of itself. Aside from world peace and food for the hungry, there were few new inventions that would ever really make a difference. Maybe a robot that would do all the work, raise the food, and fix the subway system, but beyond that, the only reason to invent a new product was to make money. What mattered most was how people were made to feel about themselves, after all. And Valerie had made Bette and Hector feel so much. She had excited them, made them participate and imagine new ways. She had made wildness acceptable, and in turn let Bette feel a bit wild. A bit able to, well, manipulate. Do what it takes to have things go her own way instead of staying out of the fray as she had done all her life. And there was a physical element, the beauty of the thing, the imagination of its taste, the design of the jar. There was more here than simple function. Not *too* much more, but enough that a regular person could afford from time to time to make things feel more special than they were. To enjoy, really. To love.

Other people have so much power. They can destroy and they can build. Other people can change Bette, at whim, they can make her life bearable or they can strip her bare. Other people are the world, aren't they? Their whims, their strengths, their callous impulses, their depth or lack of spirit. Bette felt that this new knowledge unleashed a kind of dangerous excitement. Almost atomic. What could she do to them? What could she do *for* them?

And then it occurred to her . . . Earl! Was there anything she could concoct that could help Earl get a role? One that he deserved?

The suddenness of this potential overwhelmed her, and she leaned back into the depth of possibility. What would have to happen for Earl to be treated fairly, and what could Bette do to accomplish this?

Bette knew she was in a realm over which she had little understanding. Earl's problem was that he was black. Nothing else stood in his way. Would a change in his fate have to be tied to the forward motion of the entire Negro race, or would it be possible for him to become an exception? Paul Robeson had accomplished an awful lot, but he had such special circumstances, so many simultaneous varieties of approach. He had great degrees from prestigious universities. Earl had not finished high school. Robeson was masculine, a football hero, of all things. Earl? Well. No. Earl had none of that. Could something else compensate?

Then there was Earl himself. He had high standards. He wanted to play a king. Well, that had worked for Robeson. Earl was not a Communist so that was one check in his column. Would there be a way to *market* Earl to be more than fate would allow?

Bette resolved to think about this more. And knew better than to bring it up to him unless she could first develop a realistic plan. He did not need to be further disappointed.

Would Valerie help her?

That seemed to be unknown. Valerie loved a challenge, but content was her weak point. Marketing justice? Would she even know what that meant? Bette wasn't sure. Valerie knew everything about current events but held no opinions. She was somehow above investment in any outcome but sales, and yet enjoyed the fray. Would she use her skills to help Negroes? Bette weighed the odds. *If the price was right*, of course. But what if the project was just . . . interesting? Bette felt Valerie would agree to something if it were fun. And that would be Bette's task. She'd have to watch and wait. Wait and see. See how much she could learn and toward what end. Then she would decide when all the facts were in and try to come up with something grand.

Bette awoke from her reverie and saw Hector's libidinous sparkle. One that clearly had not been ignited in many moons. She noted it cautiously, for one second considering jealousy, but then replacing that with concern for the etiquette of the workplace.

Valerie, too, was not blind. She held out her hand to him.

"Partner?"

He clasped it.

"Partner!"

They shook hands.

"Okay, chums." Valerie had had her way with them, and now victorious, was done. She turned her back. On to the next challenge. "Let's get back to work."

Chapter 14

The long, quiet nights of reading and radio had disappeared from Bette's life. The complexity lay outside her now, instead of within. And this signaled a great change. So great, in fact, that it provoked daily revelations, hurtling like meteors splintering off of newly discovered planets. There were, she now knew from experience, two worlds. The world of those who must generate their own urgent understanding versus the world of those to whom meaning arrives on a silver tray. She was transitioning from the former to the latter.

Being alone means doing all the work: the thinking, the feeling, the fetching, the creating of events and activities, the understanding of those events and activities. The cleaning up afterward. There are no mechanisms of avoidance. All is stark, and so the lonely are very, *very* well informed. But when one has the diversions of family, of young people fretting over their hair, or three-way conversations at home *and* in the office—well, so much, so very much, is easily avoided that it now takes an enormous effort to actually confront what used to be entirely inescapable. What one can't avoid when alone is the truth of the matter, which becomes barely noticeable when distracted by others.

In Bette's case, the habit of loneliness had made her merciful because she so desired the mercy of others. This new apparatus of engagement did not automatically make her cruel, but mercy was no longer the first thing on her mind. It wasn't mercy alone that had passed into a forgotten place. So, too, had the crash of one teacup slamming the base of its saucer. The resonating groan of a rocking chair. The cacophonous click of the light switch following the resounding thwack of a closed book. Lost from her life were the hours spent on a page of words, taking in the author's intentions and unintentional gifts, carefully, slowly noticing their order, as one can only do in solitude and quiet. Lost too were the other hours spent before the window, thinking about human beings known and unknown, marveling in their beauty, their singularity, their struggles, gestures, tears, hopes, and fates. They had been so important, those strangers. They had been her world. Disappeared was the momentous meaning of a singular step taken on the street by each sole survivor. Newly lost from Bette's life were the sounds that had long befriended her: the milkman clinking bottles, the street sweepers who scratched the skin of the avenue, the night bus drivers and their quiet, lonesome riders. These ghosts had been replaced by Earl and Hortense and Valerie and even Hector. An army of people who knew her and knew her name and, in fact, belonged to her. Who were accountable to her, and who were tangible. Being alone, whenever she was, by chance, alone these days, had an entirely different meaning than it had in the past. It meant temporary respite from others who would surely soon reappear, instead of the central substance of her breath.

The fact was that Bette had quickly shifted to thinking about herself in an entirely different way. The divide between who she was *before* and who she would from now on truly be, well . . . it was a cavernous revelation. The crypt, so to speak, was sealed on the old. She had loved Frederick. She had loved her brother. She had loved her mother. She had loved her father. And those loves had proved to be fatal errors. As a result, she had since loved only Earl. This choice, between Earl and loneliness, that had lasted thirty years, had lived quite actively as a threat.

For example, if Earl was in a play and had all his evenings absorbed, then the devil peeked through the surface of her life. The devil was pain. She would come home to no one and nothing. Have no one to shop for or cook for. No one to urge on, to listen to, to comfort, and hope for. She walked the streets with no one to talk it over with later, and no one stood by her side. Bette and Earl knew no pretense. They even talked openly about death. They discussed watching each other get old. The responsibility. And then the decline and final absence of one or the other. She knew they were friends for life. But only *now* could she see how much she had lived in the shadow of that final loss.

How would she have ever borne it?

She just had not faced that really, the impossibility

of life without him. Or he without her. But now, the survivor would have Hortense and all her friends and ideas, and her new whims and decorations, her songs, her passions, and all her information and will. Knowing this made Bette more able to recognize how bereft existence would have been on her own. Now that it was no longer to be. The relief of that potential pain, its removal from the realm of the possible. It let her see. It let her see how difficult her life had been. What she had had to endure, and that she had survived it, to this new moment . . . well, that was just a miracle. A miracle. She would never have to go back there again.

Most people have someone to go visit, and that was a fact they take for granted. Somewhere they could relax and another person did the cooking. Most people received Christmas cookies or birthday cards. Most people were considered into Thanksgiving plans and had Sundays organized around their pleasures. Most people had others who knew what they liked or needed and so could present the right book or the perfect slice of pie. What kind of sweater they preferred. Earl gave Bette a sweater for her fiftieth birthday that was V-neck with buttons and pockets. He knew. How? Because he looked and saw what she had chosen for herself. If he had given her snowflake designs across the chest with a tight pullover scoop neck, she would have had to bear that she was not seen, and her feelings about herself were still a secret. Most people have someone who knows what they like. They do not view these things as privileges. They see them as natural. A right. Like freedom of the press. And Bette, too, had felt that way about Earl.

Now that she had more, she realized how paltry their gift to each other had been in comparison. And therefore how much more precious. When others imagine people sitting at home alone on Christmas, they think of beggars in rags standing around a flaming oil drum by the Fulton Fish Market or in a gaggle somewhere passing the rum bottle, and even then there is a crowd of them. The lonely. Or Scrooge counting his gold. Or the man in an overcoat, hat pulled down over his tears stirring, stirring, stirring that sweetened cup of tea, trying to make it last. But the cared for don't realize that on their daily path of neighbors, workmates, and faces on the streets there are those, like Bette once was, who sit quietly looking out the window at other people's holiday lights, listening to other people's laughter, and finding the makings of other people's eggnog waiting in the morning trash.

From time to time Bette and Earl had found a stranger in their paths, one with even less than they. With not even that *one* door to knock on, that one person to say "Happy Birthday," that one other glass to clink. And they would invite this person over for a drink of whiskey and piece of chicken, since a whole turkey was too much work, too big, and just didn't make sense, in the end. Actually, one year they had made the turkey, the stuffing, the macaroni and cheese from Earl's mother's kitchen. They had made the cranberries and the creamed onions from Ohio. But it had brought a great sadness to the both of them. All that food, some candles, and that stray fellow from Washington Square Park, the student Earl had befriended, who didn't have the bus fare back to South Carolina for the holidays. The boy was not buoyed by all the trimmings bereft of voices. He couldn't hide how depressing he found it, the emptiness. And so, they decided to not try that one again. They decided they didn't need it.

They had these moments together.

They had not had to endure them alone.

Occasionally Bette had wished that Old Mr. Tibbs would invite her to Christmas dinner or Easter Sunday. She wanted the taste of lamb. She could barely remember leg of lamb or mint jelly and knew that one bite would bring it all back to life. But the invitation never came. From time to time Earl spent Christmas or Thanksgiving at a bar, or if he had a "boyfriend" at the bar, perhaps at some queer party uptown or a theater party downtown, and he'd get drunk and try to get laid, or had gotten laid but wanted love. He always wanted love. Poor Earl. He always wanted it. Always. Poor Earl. And when it didn't come, he'd knock on her door because, after all, human beings must have someone to speak to. They must, in the end, ultimately speak.

Now, though, at the age of fifty, Bette was starting to believe in the intangibles of life, like luck and providence. *There was nothing like joy*, she noted, *to make people believe in the inevitability and preordination of good fortune.* Perhaps she was not ready to attribute her current state of true happiness to God's will, but she couldn't help the creeping feeling that this was meant to be. That Bette was meant to have a context. There was a certain arrogance about those who received multiple birthday cards. But now, with her sudden change of fortune, she could see how others were so easily persuaded into thinking that their luck was natural. That it did not even exist at all, it was just so inevitable. Their luck. Attention, she had come to find, was disarming. It made life into an unconscious blur. The only reason, in fact, that she continued the practice of trying to understand her own meaning was out of habit, really. She simply did not know what else to do when riding the bus. She did not know where other people put their minds when the truth was not so pressing.

Tonight, like every one of these new nights, *after dinner* was a magical time of enrichment and success. Not a deep and festering wound looking for some temporary relief. This was the shift from a life of occasional joy in the magic of small things to overwhelming, sustaining joy. To the regular. It invited her to blindness about the other sufferers she'd left behind. The world was less of an organism. It just was. Others mattered less and became less real because she had her own company. In a way she felt crueler and more selfish. She could feel her happiness creating a wall between "us" and "them." Bette knew, for a fact, that that far-off summer when her birthday next appeared, her fifty-first birthday, there would be more than Earl's bouquet of flowers. Earl's card. His gift. There would also be Hortense planning ahead, and maybe even Valerie would offer her a drink. Maybe Valerie would whisper in Hector's ear and a bonus envelope would appear, or a card. Another card! That was a family. She and Earl didn't have to do everything themselves.

In the future, perhaps Hortense would marry. Bette and Earl could be the elderly relations and get invited habitually to the new couple's home for Thanksgiving. For Christmas and for Easter. She'd bring the pie but someone else would make the lamb. She could taste it. That lamb. She and Earl could play with the babies and then escape them. Come home early, maybe to have a drink with Valerie and her kind. From one crowd to another. Invite them all to see Earl on the stage and then go out for a table filled with friends. Real friends, the kind Earl always yearned for. The kind that stick around. And when they could no longer work, Hortense's children would come to the house with hot soup in a jar, and stories about what the teacher said, or who was the best Yankee, which song was the new thing. And all of that.

Chapter 15

Bette came home with three gorgeous filets of flounder from Joe's Fish Market, and some mushrooms and a pound of broccoli plus three large potatoes for baking. But when she walked in, the kitchen was occupied by Hortense, arms up to her elbows in ingredients, nose in, of all things, a cookbook. There was no special reason why Bette had never used a cookbook. She relied on hand-scrawled recipes from neighbors and the advice of shopkeepers for her recipes. And every now and again she'd try something from her imagination or that she'd noticed advertised at Romanoff's, like grilled cheese with tomato. Or cream cheese and olives on pumpernickel bread.

Hortense was making dessert. A nine-inch square Betty Crocker instant chocolate cake, from a box. Made extra special with a topping of broiled marshmallow frosting.

"It says *cream* three tablespoons Parkay margarine. Bette, what does *cream* mean? Add cream to the margarine?"

Bette had never even tasted margarine. Since the war, Oleo had to stand in because no one ever had real butter. It reminded her of hard times and of poor Anthony.

"It means to soften the margarine, make it creamy."

"Okay. But how?"

"With a wooden spoon? Perhaps a fork."

"Thanks, Bette. Wait, the recipe calls for two table-spoons of cream."

"I guess they mean for you to add it then."

Bette knew better than to get involved. This was Hortense's way of growing up. Of doing her part but asserting her own point of view about what constituted an appropriate food for the dinner table.

"Half cup chopped walnuts. One cup Kraft minia-ture marshmallows. Mix lightly."

Truth be told, Bette had also never eaten a marsh-mallow. Well, so be it. They each bring what they have to give. Suddenly a scene came to Bette's mind from a novel she had read called *A Tree Grows in Brooklyn*. There was a poor family living in Brooklyn. So poor that sometimes they didn't have enough to eat. But the mother made sure that no matter the deprivation, no one's dignity would be undermined. One morning there was nothing for breakfast but three cups of cof-fee, and so the mother set one for each person. Herself, her husband, and their daughter. Starving, the father devoured his cup, watching the mother slowly sipping hers. Then he turned his attention to their child, who used the hot drink to warm her hands but never tasted a drop.

"You're wasting it," the father lapped lasciviously, looking for a way to get that coffee into his exhausted soul.

"It's her cup," the mother insisted. "It's hers to do with as she likes."

Bette had always been moved by that scene, the right of every family member to their own way of doing what they needed to do. That's what love is, really. The recognition of that simple fact.

"It looks great," she said to Hortense. "I can't wait to try it."

Soon Earl arrived home, tipsy, and happy about it.

"I had a glass of wine and a bottle of wine," he said, laughing, and then produced two more bottles of real Italian Chianti, each encased in a straw basket good for hanging in someone's cellar, awaiting special occasions. Clearly this was a special occasion, Bette noted. A joyful celebration simply of being together. And her heart was so open. This was her life now.

Three hours later, marshmallow cake devoured, Bette and Earl were sitting next to each other on the couch, smiles larger than their own faces, hands over their own eyes as Hortense had instructed, waiting as told to do, and warned absolutely not to peek.

"Okay," Hortense called out from the darkness. "Now!"

Earl and Bette slowly opened their eyes to a seemingly empty apartment. Then they could see Hortense's arm slither from behind the front door to place the needle on the Victrola's spinning disc. She landed it expertly and the music began to fill the room. A scratchy recording of Aaron Copland's *Appalachian Spring* came into their lives. The front door swung open, and Hortense leapt over the threshold, hovered and loomed, in black leotard and black tights, assuming the stance and gestures she had learned by watching Martha Graham's dancers, the junior company members, and students who earned some nickels by teaching "movement" at the New Dance Group. She strode barefoot, squared her arms, becoming an ancient Greek column, a temple, and a vase. She stomped, at one with history. She held and folded at the waist, a living hieroglyphic. And finally, in what Hortense had come to understand to be a "modern" flourish, she ran barefoot, dipped, held, and crumpled . . . into death.

Bette and Earl waited until they were both sure that it was over and then clapped wildly. Earl was the most enthusiastic. Bette, unsure, trusted his lead.

"That was fantastic," he said. "That was so . . . artful." He clapped and clapped. "You're really on to something."

"My," Bette said, also clapping strongly, but still a little bit confused. She had been to the ballet many times. And seen Agnes de Mille, of course. But this?

Earl touched her arm. "That's the future, Bette."

"Really?"

More future. More future. That's all anyone talked about, wasn't it? First television, now this. And then Bette wondered if she could get a slogan out of that. Something to bring to Valerie the following morning.

Everyone thinks they know what's coming. Was that enough? Okay, she realized, she was open to change. That was now true. The past had certainly not worked out for someone like her. The future was the place. She could invest in that.

Earl was still clapping.

Earl seemed so happy. She enjoyed it. He usually didn't get this drunk until he'd gone out into the night, but she didn't mind. She was glad he'd stayed around. He seemed so playful. He had a kind of parental pride for Hortense. Like Daddy sitting at the side of a Little League game marveling that his girl could hold a bat. *Do girls play Little League?* They probably did not. *What is Little League?* It was one of those terms bandied about, but truthfully Bette wasn't sure of what it meant exactly. Children playing baseball, wearing uniforms like Babe Ruth and Lou Gehrig, on sandlots in those new housing developments on Long Island the GIs had bought into. She'd never seen one and didn't care to. There was no good reason to move out of the city, no matter what people said about *s*chools. It was better for children to be free than enslaved, and growing up in New York City was schooling enough to make up for not having Little League. Anyway, Earl certainly was laughing himself silly. Like it was some private little joke that kept cracking him up but nobody else could understand. Then Bette felt silly too and started laughing just because he was laughing. She was so thankful that they had a family that valued art, not batting averages. Bette was thankful that Hortense was an actress and a *modern dancer* instead

189

of a housewife out there. Bette noticed herself being *grateful* and wondered sincerely if religion would soon follow. She was curious to watch herself and had no idea where it would all go. All this happiness. Where would it lead?

"This is really exciting," Earl said.

"Yes," Bette laughed, wiping tears from her eyes. "But why? I don't have a clue as to what is so funny."

"Tell her, Earl." That was Hortense.

"Tell me, Earl." Bette was having so much fun.

"Tell her about the architecture," Hortense said, placing the record back in its sleeve.

"It's like architecture," Earl said.

"How?" Bette asked.

"It's like buildings," Earl said, slowing down a bit. "New shapes for the modern age." He stopped laughing.

Bette thought about what he'd said. The city was changing, true. There were buildings going up everywhere, and most of them were for business purposes. Walking down the street had a different feeling when her shoulders grazed sleek glass and steel instead of ornate mortar and decorative iron. Both were beautiful, but they had different meanings. One night Bette had hugged a building. She'd told Earl about it and he admitted to the same thing. They'd both, of their own accord, pressed face and full body, open arms against its flank. She could see how buildings could influence humans, instead of only the other way around. It was natural. People and their creations constantly interact, transform each other. Always reflecting, influencing, reflecting.

"I understand," she said.

"Yeah," Earl sighed, somewhat relieved. "There is change."

But one thing perplexed Bette. How did Earl know so much about this, when she had never heard a thing?

"The body in space," Hortense prompted. The girl was standing still now. In the middle of the room.

"The body," Earl said, turning toward Bette but not really engaging her. He seemed to be figuring it all out right then. "Is different. The body is different." He wasn't sure of where he was going, what his point was. It ellipsed away. Something vague . . .

"What do you mean?"

"The body," he tried again, "is different in different spaces."

Bette felt confused. She started to become a bit muted. "Space?" She remembered Valerie and the promise of jetpacks. "Do you mean like Mars?"

"*Yeessss*," Earl said strangely, like he'd changed his accent. He had a weird expression on his face. She wasn't sure what he wanted to convey.

"I don't get it."

"Look," he said and then stopped, changed his tone. "Like coming from Mars but living on Earth."

She waited for it all to coalesce. His point.

"Look," Earl said again. His brow was tight. "When it is not your world, the body has to twist."

Bette was surprised to find herself thinking, for the very first time, that maybe this *was* her world. And then she thought that if that were so, it would come between her and Earl, because it could never be his world. His exclusion was too large. What would she do in that case? This had never been a consideration before. Whatever would she do if the world was letting her in and continuing to keep him out? Her impulse was to stay with Earl, no matter what. The loss of Earl would be greater than the loss of her new purpose or engagement or excitement or goal, her connection to others, her cousin, her job. The loss of Earl would be greater. Why was she thinking this way? It was silly, really. Nothing had happened. Why was she thinking like this?

Bette looked around her. Earl and Hortense were frozen. She felt a strange heaviness in the apartment. Like there was no air. But the windows were open, there was in fact air.

"Why?" she asked. This shouldn't be so hard to explain. She should be able to comprehend this.

"The body has to twist," he said again. He was looking right at her now. There was so much that was strained in his face, she barely recognized him.

"What do you mean?"

"There is too much punishment."

He seemed ashy. Like he was going to faint.

"Feelings!" That was Hortense's voice. Where was she? In the background somewhere.

Bette felt a kind of fog circling around her like she had felt once when she'd swooned in the middle of Macy's. Hortense's voice seemed to be coming at her as if through a megaphone or across the sea.

"Tell her, Earl!" That was Hortense again.

Earl looked terrified. He scowled at Bette. "Well you see . . ."

"Tell me what?" Something was wrong. Was he dying?

Earl looked down. Bette was aware of Hortense's

rigid body somewhere in the swirl. The world was shifting, the floor was sinking, maybe the apartment was on fire.

"You see, Bette . . ."

"No, I don't see." Bette felt wrong. She had done something wrong. A terrible thing was happening. Earl looked like a coward, how was that possible?

Hortense took a step toward them.

"Bette," she squeaked. "Earl and I are in love."

Earl grimaced. He never would have put it that way.

"In love?"

"Wait a minute . . ." He looked like a pile of ashes. "I wouldn't say . . ."

"Isn't it romantic?" Hortense rushed in on them.

Bette could feel Hortense's devouring flame leap out to grab her and Earl, sizzling their skin so that the fat dripped onto the burning carpet. The world was being consumed.

"Isn't it, Bette? Isn't it so, so romantic?" Hortense whirled around like girls do in movies. "That just at the beginning of my life, I have had the fortune to meet my true soul mate and so my path through the world will be one of love and devotion. My parents will object, of course, but that doesn't matter because Earl and I have found a deep love. One that defies all convention."

Bette, as she had been, ceased to exist.

"In love?" She looked into Earl's frightened eyes. He had no soul. "What do you mean *in love?*"

Hortense threw herself at Bette's feet, her arms strewn across Bette's lap and Earl's as well. "I know I can speak openly with you, Cousin."

Bette looked at this thing. Hortense was some kind of crow. The sound of her voice was a threat to crops.

Hortense was smiling. How can anyone smile?

"Earl and I are lovers," she destroyed. "I have given him my virginity, and now we are soul mates forever. Like you and my father."

"Lovers?"

"I thought you loved him. But when I found out that you didn't, that you're just friends, I knew we could all be happy together. A family. There has to be a couple for there to be a true family. You know that, Cousin Bette. There has to be . . . that bond."

"But Earl and I are not *friends*."

Hortense was stopped for a moment. Something did not fit into her categories of knowledge. There was a thud. The Chianti bottle had fallen over.

Earl snapped at Bette. "Stop that."

"Earl and I are *friends for life*."

Earl was disgusted. "Bette!" He reached for the bottle, and for a moment grabbed it like a truncheon, not knowing what he was defending. His own right to do or say whatever he damned pleased whenever he damned pleased to say and do it, that's what. It wasn't his job to make sense. The world didn't make sense. That wasn't his fault, don't blame him. He wasn't taking the blame for every single thing. That was for damn sure.

Bette stared at him clutching the bottle. He could commit mass murder and put them all out of their misery. But he put the bottle back onto the table and felt disappointed.

Earl realized that he had somehow, in some unarticulated way, expected Bette to just go along with everything. He hadn't thought it through, everything was happening so fast. He didn't have a backup plan.

"Shut up," he said to the silence. And it obeyed.

Bette did not understand why Earl was being cruel to her. Why was he punishing her? His actions. His reactions. His treatment of her. None of that made sense.

"Cousin Bette! Cousin Bette!" Hortense wanted her attention now. But Hortense did not deserve her attention. "Cousin Bette! Say something."

Hortense lifted herself from her knees and brought her face into Bette's line of vision.

"Cousin Bette? Cousin Bette? Say something. Your face. You look so ugly. Why won't you say anything? Cousin Bette. Say something!"

Bette could not.

It was that kind of moment. One person destroys another one's life but does not expect a reaction. When the reaction comes, even if it is the first gasp of shocked silence, the reaction itself is dehumanized. Hortense and Earl seemed outraged that she didn't know what to say. Didn't they imagine that this was shocking? Only if she wasn't real could they falsely construe her reaction as will.

"Bette," Earl said blandly. "She's innocent."

"Cousin Bette!" Hortense shrieked. "This is better than my dreams."

Bette's neck snapped. "*Your* dreams?"

Under other circumstances Bette might have said, "What do *you* know about dreams?" But this was beyond response. How does one reason with an arsonist?

Chapter 16

Wait! What happened here?

In order to understand the proper sequence of events, consider going back forty-eight hours in time.

Let us return to not the day before the night in question but *two days* before. The end of that shift where once again Earl worked a hard, gross, painful, boring day at the Lazio Brothers' Slaughterhouse and finished it off, as usual, by taking a long shower, putting on dry clothes, and dusting off his street shoes. Back to, as he briefly reminisced in Chapter 11, those few moments of transition in the locker room when Earl had noted a kind of "softening" on the part of young Leon.

That day, instead of glaring at Earl like the daddy who'd taken away his supper, instead of purposefully stomping over to the far corner of the locker room and dressing furtively as though needing to be very, very careful, instead of all that rigmarole, Leon stood casually by the next bench over and slowly took off his dirty, bloodstained workshirt, put his street pants over his arm, walked demurely into the shower. Returned glistening wet, overly dressed for locker-room etiquette with his clean trousers already belted, but still shirtless, and took his merry time finding and putting on that slow-buttoning, long-sleeved shirt. Both the excessive modesty and the excessive display were clearly for Earl's benefit. And that double message signified the poor boy's conflicts. How operative they were.

Well, well, Earl thought to himself. *I guess that's Leon's way of saying, "I'm sorry, now can you suck my cock?"* Then Earl laughed out loud.

"What's so funny?" Luis asked, stark naked like most of the guys.

"Life," Earl said, putting on his soft jacket.

"What else is new?"

And all the walk home, Earl tried to calculate how many days it would be before Leon hit on him in some way, some crazy-ass, duplicitous way that would probably lead to something very, very hot and then for sure another blowup as that guy, that cat, that sleek young thing, that *boy* was not reliable to act right. *Ah, Leon.*

Earl remembered Bette saying, *"I'm sorry, but he's out. Draw a line through his name. Next!"*

"Next," Earl said to himself, coming upon the guys playing chess. "Next, next, next."

"Earl, baby, what's happening?" That was Jerome, waving him over. "You got time for a game of chess?"

"Don't you have to be home for supper?"

Jerome sat longingly before the table, chess board laid into the concrete, pieces tantalizingly already in place and ready to go.

"My wife has her club night. Dinner is waiting for

me in a chafing dish, so I can eat it any old time I want to. Besides, my wife doesn't make me come home for supper. I go home for supper because I want to."

"Glad I got that straight."

They both started laughing.

"Don't you believe a word," Jerome whispered and twinkled his eye. "Come on, Earl, let's play a game."

"You know I don't play chess."

"I know that yesterday you did not play. But this is today. You can never imagine what may transpire over night."

Earl flashed on Leon's chest.

"Now that's the truth."

How come Earl never really hung with these guys? With Jerome? They liked him. They were good men, kind. Family guys, some of them, okay, but others had question marks around them. He could make some friends here, in the park. He knew that. Earl surveyed the crew. There was George. Now George had a wife, but that was a joke. Whatever makes fairies go out and get wives? Of course, Earl knew exactly why they did that. They had to. Didn't want to live on the edge of everything like Earl did. He, of all people, could understand that. From all the married guys he'd had sex with or romanced through the years, Earl had come to the conclusion that black, white, or indifferent, most queer guys were married. Or was it that most married guys were queer? Or that most guys were queer? Or was just everybody queer? Well then, if everyone is queer then everyone is whatever . . . so that explains how George pulls it off. But a man could not pull the wool over every set of female eyes, that's for sure. Like that Lynette Carter. She was a nice person. They could have been friends. Earl finally admitted to himself that he felt terrible about how he'd treated her and that he, in fact, owed her an apology. That was it, he resolved to apologize. Just as soon as he got home from Washington Square Park, he would call on his telephone. Shit, the only calls he ever made on that thing were to his actor's service. Time he started using it to . . . apologize. Maybe call Leon. Now that was a bad idea.

Truth was, he could marry a Lynette Carter as far as the companionship side of things went. She had her own life going on and was smart and wanted a family; that would occupy her, too. But the problem would be in the bedroom, of course. There was no way Miss Lynette Carter was letting Mr. Earl Coleman get away with not having a clue as to what he was doing, not one clue. It just wouldn't pass. She'd notice right away, and then she'd track those wistful gazes at all her male cousins and her strapping handsome father. And within two nights and a day, she'd be annulling his ass. And then another black woman would have been used by some man, and all the problems of the race would be replicated by Earl, and once again everything would be his fault. All he was trying to do was get out of the line of fire so he could have a moment to breathe and figure out how to live. That's all he was trying to do. So how does George pull it off? *How does that faggot do it?*

"Hey, George?"

"Yeah, Earl, what's happening?"

"Oh, not much. How's the family, George?"

"They good. Thanks for asking. My son is going to City College in the fall, did I tell you that?"

"No, congratulations. That's huge."

"Yep. We're so proud."

"I'm sure you are. How's your wife?"

"Sarah's good. She's taking classes at night now to become a home nurse. Inspired by our boy."

"Night classes, gives you a lot of empty evenings, hey George?"

George looked scared for a second, and then he got a lascivious look. "Why?" George's voice got all smoky. "You got some empty nights?"

Earl watched the switch. Frightened to turned-on in under a second. That must be the key, after all. George got turned-on by being scared, scared of the truth. What could be sexier than that? Wow. Everything! Earl was not turned-on by being scared. He just wasn't. He wanted relations with men to be smooth and loving and on the up and up. Why was that so fucking hard?

"It's okay, George. Don't worry," Earl said. He was feeling kind right then. He was feeling benevolent toward George. "It's okay." He was feeling sad, all of a sudden. "See you later, George. Congratulations on your boy." And Earl slowly stood up off the bench and waved the fellows goodbye. *Not everyone gets a way out*, he thought.

He stopped in the Chock Full o'Nuts to buy three doughnuts from Sheila.

"Why three?" she asked, smiling with that edge that Sheila had. She was a smart one and good-looking. Always nice to customers, always doing her job. *Was she married?* He looked at her ring finger. *Yes, she was.* Suddenly Earl was flummoxed, he didn't know how to answer that question. He was buying three doughnuts so that the two white women he had dinner with every night could each have one and he could have one too. Why was he going home to two white women when neither of them were *his* woman and he didn't even want a woman, anyway? At least if he was going home to a woman, she should be *his*. The situation was just too hard to explain. *I'd rather be going home to Leon, believe you me. If Leon was my man, I'd be bringing home a dozen doughnuts.* But the most that Leon was ever going to be was a blow job and a punch in the jaw. Earl's jaw ached already, not from the blow job, but from the punch. Poor boy. Leon was a mess.

Earl knew how he'd gotten here, but it was too hard to explain. Sheila just wouldn't really understand.

Coming out of Rubin's Deli with his beer bottle wrapped in a sheet of newspaper, Earl noticed immediately that the neighborhood kids' attention was focused across the street. *Shit.* That fucking Greta Garbo and her goddamn luxury sedan parked again in front of Betty Parson's gallery. *What were those two ladies up to anyway? Bumping in the Bentley? Goddammit.* Earl knew he had to go talk to Frankie. Give him some kind of explanation. So, doughnuts in hand and beer under his arm, Earl crossed the avenue, doing one of those things that good people always have to do—apologize for being wrong when the world itself is the problem. Not make excuses when there are a million legitimate ones to make. The problem was, as Earl knew all too well, that it was somehow *unreasonable* to expect normal people to think that someone they knew might be a fruit, to take that into consideration. One could argue drunkenly on the corner of a corner bar that they *should*, but they were just not going to do it. So then what? *You can't expect . . . well, you just can't expect a thing. Not a fucking thing.*

"Hey, Frank."

Frank was looking beautiful, standing at attention in his suit and tie, his matching cap, shined shoes, smoking a cigarette. He was a beautiful brother, and that was the truth.

"Frank!"

Lost in thought, the man looked up, and the expression of disgust on his face caught Earl entirely off guard. Frank hated him.

"I don't want to hear it," Frank said and turned his back.

Just like Leon. Turning their backs on Earl when it is all a lot more complicated than that. Okay, okay, Earl shouldn't have run out on that girl. It was wrong. He should have walked her home to Chelsea—and then what? Then-the-fuck what? Made some excuse? What kind?

"Sorry sweetheart, I thought your father wanted to bone me, love me, and move into my bed and be my man. I guess there was some kind of misunderstanding."

He just couldn't say that, and everyone else would agree.

"Look, Frank, I'm sorry."

"Get away from me."

Frank tightened his shoulders. Earl found himself looking. He looked at the nape of Frank's neck. Why was this happening? Wasn't there any way out? Any way at all?

Was there any way out?

And that's when Earl turned and just floated back into his apartment building on a cloud of no solutions, on a cloud of *that's my fate*, in a kind of existentialist state like those cats in Paris. And on automatic he climbed the stairs, turned the key, and walked in on Bette and Hortense reading out loud from Hamlet.

As you may or may not recall, the night of *Hamlet* ended like this:

The end of the evening was now inevitable, and yet Earl and Hortense had communicated to each other, silently, that there could be more fun. If only they had been allowed to stay up longer. But they could not. Because Bette needed to sleep.

At the door, Earl held out his hand. Hortense took it, and they shook good-night. But when it came to Bette, impulsively, he leaned over and kissed her on the cheek.

"Oh my," Bette said.

It was unusual. The gesture.

Then, thirty seconds later . . .

Earl staggered back from Bette's to his apartment, reciting Hamlet, holding the brandy bottle, and setting it up to be finished by his bed. He hated his apartment and yet he loved it. It was always there and had seen it all.

Thank you, walls.

He pulled himself up off of the bed and kissed the walls.

Thank you, floors.

He placed his cheek against the wood.

Then, stiff, he crawled back onto the bed and took

a sip of brandy. Comforting himself, dick in hand, he leaned back and took a drink.

Leon, he should call Leon.

Earl reached over and grabbed the phone. Receiver tucked under his chin, he was half-hearted about his own cock but excited at the possibility of talking to Leon. He dialed zero.

"Operator."

"Hey, Operator, how you doing?"

"All right."

"Can you give me the number for Leon Waters? In Brooklyn?"

"One second, please."

He reached for another drink.

"I have two Leon Waters in Brooklyn. What is the address?"

"Oh no," Earl was sad. "I don't know his address."

"Well, hold on, we'll figure it out," she said, Brooklyn accent, that New York mix of Italian and Irish that can't be found anywhere else on the planet.

"Okay. Thanks."

"One Leon Waters is in Park Slope and one is in Bushwick. Which do you think it would be?"

"My friend is a Negro."

"Well then he ain't in Park Slope," she said.

"Bushwick, then."

"Here's the number, Fulton 9-7669"

"Thanks," Earl's heart was racing. "I'd vote for you for Miss Subways."

"No problem."

Earl was bouncing on his knees on his bed now, like

a teenager—that was it, he was still a kid. *Oh well.*
F-U-9-7-6-6-9.

Busy signal.

Fuck. He hung up and dialed again.

Busy signal.

Who was Leon talking to at two o'clock in the morning? Who the hell was he chatting up? His mother in Chattanooga? His auntie in Chattahoochee? *Get off the phone, chat boy.*

That's when he heard the knock at the door.

What the hell?

"Earl?"

"Who is that?" He zipped his pants, put the phone on the sideboard. "Who's there?"

"Let me in, it's cold out here."

"Hortense?"

He opened the door and she jumped into his arms, hands around his neck, and kissed him on the lips. She barely knew how to kiss, but she was wearing a thin nightgown and no underwear, the feel of her lithe, horny body, the free access, the smooth skin, her breasts pressing against his chest, *strange and in the way.* The way she went wild, pressing her crotch against every part of him, rubbing on his leg—she wanted to get some, but she didn't know how. Kissing, kissing.

"Open your mouth," he said. Cock still hard, he ground into her, now on the bed, her pressing and pressing, slithering up and down his body, trying to rub her thing, not knowing how, and then she reached down for his.

"Oh, you are a good girl," he said, excited. But how

was he going to get off, she didn't know how to do nothing. And he couldn't get a girl pregnant. No way.

"I want you," she said.

Wow, what movies has she been watching?

Earl turned off the light.

"It's more romantic this way. Here baby, take it in your hand. You've never done this before, right?"

"I love you," she said.

Oh boy. "We'll talk about that later. There you go, hold it. See? See, I like you. That's how you know a man likes you, when his thing is strong like that. Now move your hand with mine. There you go. You must kind of squeeze, and trade up fingers and your whole hand. You'll get it. "

This was it, the biggest night of her life. The first time he had done it was heaven, but by the tenth time his mother caught him and that was it. That was the end of Earl Coleman as a loved person.

He looked at Hortense through the filter of night and her eyes were open. He closed his eyes and moved her hand up and down with his. Left her to try on her own while he played with his balls a bit. For the first time he wondered if straight people touch themselves in front of each other. And realized he had no idea how or why they did anything at all. But, she wouldn't know either.

"I want you," she said again, pouting, opening her legs and bringing his dick right to her little bush.

"Are you sure?" He was jerking himself now, she'd abandoned ship.

"I want you."

"Okay," he said. "Let's do this together. Now, show

me exactly where you want me." Really, if he'd had a flashlight he would have taken a good look at whatever it was she had down there. He knew there was some kind of hole, but she wasn't going to be any help. *Jesus Christ be my guide.*

He started poking his cock down there, looking for a way in. It was slimy and the pathway not evident. Wait, there appeared to be some kind of entryway, he tried to move forward, still poking, trying to find the road in.

There. There. He knew from being alive that a man's supposed to go slow on a girl's first time. How did he know that? Whoa, there it was. Wow, this thing of hers did not want his prick. There was no room.

"That's it," she said.

He tried to go in slowly.

"Ouch."

"I'm sorry, baby. Do you want me to stop?" *Do straight people use grease?* he wondered. *If they don't, they sure as hell should.*

"No, I want you to take me."

"All right, well, let's work together."

"Okay."

She was a brave little soldier, that Hortense, but something had turned in the whole operation. What started out hot and horny had become some kind of job, getting his dick into this girl was the goal. He tried thrusting it in, maybe that was the way, just break it open or something.

She lurched, but he couldn't tell if it was good or bad.

"Okay?"

"It's okay," she said, clutching his arms, seemingly more from surprise at all the discomfort than from the passion she had begun with. Her motives had shifted.

"Here we go, Hortense."

He tried saying her name as he started pumping. Very slowly. He was afraid to go as fast as he would have liked. The apparatus just wasn't opening for him, the walls weren't moving apart the way he would have preferred.

"Hortense." Half thrust. "Hortense." Push forward. "Hortense, here we go baby, all the way in. There you go. We made it."

They were lodged together, finally, having reached their goal. She wrapped her legs around him tightly, holding him inside her. But he couldn't help feeling a bit of concern that this tight grip was also intended to postpone the inevitable return to thrusting at what must be getting kind of sore. He'd had big daddies who didn't care about his ass and how much they hurt him. Earl knew what that was like. But no one was supposed to get fucked in the ass, it was a skill queens acquired with pride, through hard work and determination, and when they learned how to make it work, they deserved whatever they could get out of it. But pussy? Pussy was supposed to come naturally. Look at this mess, the girl had come into his room with a big hard-on for him, and now she was stuck with his cock inside her and no way for either of them to get off that way.

"There you go," he said, like he had said many a day to other men taking it for the first time. "You're a brave little bo—girl. You're a beauty."

That was his standard line, *You're a beauty.*

And slowly he pulled out of her place and started rubbing his dick, kissing her, and holding her. She seemed all right.

"Baby, you turned me on," he said. Another classic line when he needed to jerk off after fucking.

"I did?" She was so proud.

"Did you get what you needed?" he asked, sheepishly, hoping the answer was yes, because if it was no, they were both out of luck.

"I got exactly what I needed," she said, smiling.

"Then, this is for you."

He closed his eyes and thought about Leon and Frankie, and the guy who he'd fucked on the pier that lonely Thanksgiving night and the boy who sucked his cock behind the parking lot, the married man with the wedding ring who jerked him off at the Paramount and that piece of street trash who'd stolen his wallet and started all this downward spiral, that punk, he was hot though, he was the last man who had fucked Earl, who had held him in this bed, a thug, and then Anthony and Anthony and Anthony and Anthony and Leon and Anthony and Anthony and *Anthony*.

"I made you do that?" came the little squeak from the other side of the bed.

"Oh yeah, baby, you're the best."

It was over.

He was exhausted. He had to go to work. Shit, now what?

Earl turned on the light. She was smiling, she was sweating. She looked pretty enough. She was happy. He'd made her happy and she didn't even get anything, whatever it was that women get.

"I'm so excited about my new dance class," she said.

Oh no, she wants to talk.

"It's about movement in space and architecture of the body. New movement for a new era."

"Wow," Earl said. "That's so interesting." He put on an exceedingly soft and gentle tone. "I think you'd better go home now," he said.

"I love you," she said. And they kissed. "You're a great actor, Earl. I know I can learn so much from you."

"Thank you," he said, truly touched. No one had ever said that to him before.

"You're a great artist."

Earl was so exhausted he could barely see her to the door. But he did manage to turn the knob, pat her ass, and lock it tightly behind her.

She's not the worst I've ever had, he thought. *She's smart and she's got money and I could help her with a lot of things.* And most importantly, she wouldn't have his number. Not for a long, long time.

Earl knew that there was no God, but there was fate, and it worked in very strange ways. There was no way that he'd sought this out. Fate put it in his lap. He had nothing else going on. Nothing else at all. No one cared about him. No one was watching. He wasn't going any other place. He wasn't going any other place at all.

Strangely, instead of falling asleep, Earl just lay there for a while, kind of blank. He was wide awake, everything swirling around him. Finally he jumped from the bed to the dusty bottom drawer of his bureau. There he found a pencil and a pad of paper and a small pile of envelopes he'd kept for years for special occasions that never seemed to arise.

Dear Lynette,

I owe you an apology and an explanation. I am a homosexual and I did not have the grace to tell you so. You will make a great wife for a great man who can appreciate your gifts. I am very sorry for the pain I have caused.

Yours sincerely,
Earl

Chapter 17

The next day was the day that Earl drank "a glass of wine and a bottle of wine," coming home with two more bottles of Chianti to get him through the evening. That was the day that Hortense made a marshmallow cake and the night that she showed her modern dance, and then Hortense and Earl came clean to Bette. And that night they slept together again in Earl's apartment. Spending more time talking and analyzing, planning and scrambling, than making love, although there was another somewhat similar—but less surprising—penetration. Earl expected her to be more open now that she'd been broken. Like a rock through a plate glass window. But they were both bewildered to learn that it didn't seem to work that way, it wasn't automatic. Apparently this accommodation took time. Who knew? They decided that she would go see a doctor, or whomever women talked to about that sort of thing as well as pregnancy. Or perhaps he would try to use rubbers. He nodded *of course*, like they were a lifetime habit, although Earl had significant doubts that he could get used to them at this stage of the game. For something that was supposed to be "natural," this sex between men and women was sure a whole lot of trouble.

When the morning light came in through the window, all appeared to be right in Gotham City. The milkman's metal cage rattled its glass bottles. This milkman's father had also been a milkman, but with a horse-drawn wooden cart not a white truck and cute white uniform. Son loved that uniform as much as he had loved his father's horse, named King, but his father hated it. He hated being told what to wear. To be completely truthful, Father *somewhat* admired the crisp cap that came with the pleated white trousers and the embroidered nameplate on the white button-down shirt. But Father also saw the conformity this created—although he did not know the word *conformity*—and longed for the old days when he ran his own business and hadn't had to sell out to Borden's.

Like other mornings, the bus groaned its approach and spat exhaust. Romanoff started a pot of Maxwell House Coffee for the first arrivals at his pharmacy's soda fountain. Joe drove up with the day's haul from Fulton Fish Market and parked the truck right in front of his shop. Piles of the day's *Sun*, *Herald Tribune*, *World Telegram*, *Mirror*, *Post* and *Times* sat bundled before Readers Stationery Store. Salvatore was reading a Superman comic book in bed before his mother woke him to go to school. Margaret O'Reilly was lying awake, staring at the ceiling, wondering when her father was coming home. Her mother hadn't gotten out of bed in three days, and Margaret hadn't even tried to get to school. She knew she wasn't allowed to go by herself. But now that every scrap in the house had been eaten, her stomach was growling and she had started to think about a solution. Trying to avoid using the toilet because of the filth of her mother's vomit on the tiled floor.

Across the street, Mike Mitchell of Flat Rock, North Carolina, now known as Cookie, and Archie Cantwell, of Paris, Tennessee, now known as Theresa, were staggering home from an all-night party, talking about love. Then, they found themselves locked out of the Hotel Albert for failure to pay their rent. It was inevitable, really, and yet they were surprised. Solomon Liebling, the tailor, took off his outside hat and put on his inside hat, turned on the lights, and uncovered his sewing machine. Sam, the clerk at the Hotel Albert, decided that the title of his novel would be "The Healing." And then he was unsure. And then he thought it should be "The Haunting." And then he thought he might name it after that Elizabeth Bishop poem and call it "The Burning Deck." And then he considered "The Twist." And then he looked for a title without the word *the* in it. He liked the title "Cookie," but none of his characters were named Cookie.

A painter slept happily with his arms around his lover. A painter slept happily with his arms around his wife. A painter slept happily alone. A painter barely slept for a broken heart. A painter slept. A sculptor slept in dirty sheets. A sculptor was up all night with a terrible cough. Salvatore's mother was already cooking. His father was shaving, dreaming of the beautiful painter girl down the block whose boyfriend beat the hell out of her. He wanted to save the girl and have her save him. Señora Colón read her Bible. Her son, José, studied his medical textbooks. Mrs. Shallowitz snored obliviously. The new residents of the townhouse in the middle of the block were a collective of painters opening a club for exhibitions and conversations. Six of them would sleep upstairs. The lawyer brother of one of the artists had signed the deed as a favor. If the kids couldn't keep up the payments, he'd just buy them out at cost. Yes, everything was as it was, as it had to be, and as it could only be. All except for apartment 2E. There, something had gone terribly, terribly wrong.

By sunrise, Bette was still sitting in her chair. Her napkin was still on her lap. The dishes were unmoved. She was still thinking about how much she hated Hortense.

An hour later there was a knock at the door.

"Bette?"

She ran to that voice. It was where she belonged.

"Why do you knock?" she cried. That knock assaulted her, it intensified her grieving, having to talk through a sheet of wood. "Why do you knock?"

"I can't just walk in anymore."

She pulled open the door so hard it rattled the wall. Bette saw her friend before her. She was so happy to see him. She wanted to see him, to see his face. This is where she belonged. Face to face with Earl.

"I want you to let yourself in," she said, gathering herself with care. "As you always do."

There. She felt human again. Here he was, asking for a kind of forgiveness, and she would grant it without question.

"I can't." He lingered awkwardly in the doorway.

"Of course you can." She showed her love.

Bette, of course, had not known anything that had transpired. Nor had she been privy to the inner workings of Earl's heart ever since the day he was beaten by that predator. She did not know about Lynette, about married George, about the smiling glance from Leon. About the confrontation with Frank or that Earl stood back from Jerome and Sheila and other black people for fear. She really did not know how deep the fear. And she really did not understand what it meant to so badly, so badly, *so badly* want to feel loved. Not just as a friend, as Bette loved him, but by someone with affection, who thought he was the best. To need that physical closeness, that contact. How devastating it was to him that he was not going to have a boyfriend. Not anymore. She really could never know him, after all. She could never understand how sad he was that no man wanted him. She could not know.

"Of course you can. Do it. Do it now. Make it well." Smiling at last, she gently pressed him back into the hall and closed the door. She returned to her seat and waited. It could all be undone. He could take out his key and turn the lock. Then the pain would be healed.

The next bus pulled up to its stop on the corner. It had the usual low rumble. She could feel the bus rock as it waited for customers to board. Listening, she recalled the cradling feeling of riding that bus. The safety of all those people together, shoulder to shoulder, keeping each other warm. She waited. Earl was taking too long. Had he gone back to get the key?

One of the things that hurt Bette was how unacknowledging Earl was being. What was wrong with

216

him? It was a basic principle of human understanding: When you do something hurtful, you have to allow the other person to be hurt. To feel hurt and to act hurt and to say and show that they are hurt. You have to give them their moment. The recognition. People can't live without it. He had to give her something. Bette felt fear. How long would he make her wait?

Then, she heard the key turn in her lock. At that sound, her courage returned. Someone else knew, for a fact, that she was a person.

"See," she said out loud. Bette felt happy. The right thing is so small and easy to do. Just choose it. Let the good return. Choose the kind act of recognition. It makes everything whole.

"Bette . . ."

"Thank God," she said holding Earl's face in her hands. "Thank you, God!" And Bette burst into tears because she had never before needed God and then been answered. Never. She was so filled with gratitude, love, and feeling. She was human. She looked into Earl's watery eyes. "You've changed your mind," she said to him. "My friend, my life. I forgive you. Now, let's clean up last night's supper." She picked up a plate.

Earl did not move. He was enraged. Bette did not understand, she would never understand, and it would be a waste of his heart to try to explain it all to her. He was sick of having to explain himself. All those years of telling her everything, talking everything over. What right did she have to all that information about him? None. It had all been a big mistake, a huge, huge mistake because now she thought he owed her.

She thought she owned him. That was more the truth. She thought she could give him orders about when and how to use a key. He was a fifty-year-old man. No one ordered him around like a stable boy.

"There is nothing about me that needs forgiveness," he said, steely as he had ever been. "I do what I want to do. I don't have to explain anything to anyone, including you."

"All right," she said. Bette felt, in that moment, that it was fine to give in when you love someone. "We'll never speak of it again. Once that cow goes back to where she belongs."

"Don't tell me what I am going to speak about."

Bette was surprised at the depth of this. He was acting in a way that guaranteed her to be wrong no matter what. It was a game.

"All right," she said.

She would give in to him now, and later he could meet her. She would recognize what he needed now, and later he would do that for her. She would just have to wait. She could wait. She could do it.

Bette took in, right then, the degree of her own surprise. The proper thing would be for him to allow her to have her pain, then for the two of them to sit down and figure out the truth, together. But instead, she felt strangely and unfamiliarly that he was trying to control her. To stop her from speaking. Why would he do that? Perhaps Earl was embarrassed that he had been so thoughtless, that he had overlooked her humanity. Her feelings. The two should have discussed this privately. That was obvious. But, this was one of those occasions where people had to give each other multiple chances. They had to be flexible with each other so that there could be peace.

"She's moving in with me," he said. "No matter what you say." He shifted menacingly, as though Bette were a stranger and Earl, endangered.

"Why are you doing this?"

He hated how much she expected him to answer.

The only choice Bette could make was to love Earl. She chose to believe that he could tell the truth.

What's wrong with her, he thought. She felt free to ask him anything. It wasn't that way anymore. Didn't she see that? Didn't she see?

"Are you actually in love with her?"

"That's not the point." *Dammit,* he did not have to answer her. *Stop talking,* he told himself.

"I don't understand," she said.

Earl's face opened up like an iron mine whose heart imploded underground and suddenly the surface of the earth's crust cracks.

"Don't you want to feel loved, even once?"

She looked at him strangely. What was this?

"Regardless of how flawed or imperfect the lover is. Don't you want to feel it again in your whole fucking life?"

The pain in his voice was some kind of vindication for Bette. They still told each other the truth. He hadn't been able to deny that. Even if he was having a delusional relationship with a subordinate, his relationship with Bette was still real. That would never change. She could see that now.

"Don't you?" He was shaking. "If you had a chance to have a real life, wouldn't you . . ." He grasped and grasped and found a phrase he had never, ever uttered. "Wouldn't you get married?"

Bette thought honestly about his question. "No." She knew right away that her answer was true. "I believe that you and I will always find a way to help each other. I promise."

"Really?" he snarled. It was a curled, bitter bite that she had never seen from him before. "And how would you protect me from a life of throat-slashing rent boys? Can you give me a normal life? Can you? No, you cannot. Well, she can."

"Oh, Earl. This can't possibly end well."

He didn't want to waste too much more time on this. It was futile. She wasn't listening. "What about my acting career?"

"I believe in you as an actor, you know that."

"But do you believe that I can get a lead role?"

"I hope you can," she said.

"Hortense knows that I can. She's taking classes, she sees the pulse among the young. She thinks I can do it."

Bette sank. Was that what all this was about? He was sacrificing her because she couldn't sit around and pretend?

"I can escape from myself," he said. "Watch me."

"Earl."

He was tired and he had to get to work. "You are not going to go along with this, are you?" Her time was almost up.

"Earl," she said with all her heart. "You are not being honest. You are lying."

"That's what I thought. You don't believe in me. You pretend that you do, but you don't. I've come to give you back your keys."

There was a knock at the door. Both Bette and Earl feared it might be Hortense. But there was a man's voice.

"Delivery. Delivery. Hello? Delivery."

Bette walked to the door, plate still in hand. She opened it for no reason, being unable to make decisions or even to take in what was happening around her. Two young white deliverymen in matching blue coveralls entered carrying a huge box. They glanced at each other, having caught a white woman and a black man in the middle of something going very wrong.

"We got a delivery here. Where do you want it? We were told to deliver before you left for work."

Despite the fact that they strained visibly under the weight, Bette was silent. Not as a matter of will.

"It's sent over from . . ." The man in charge shifted his burden and checked out the clipboard stuffed under his arm. "Tibbs Advertising Incorporated," he read out loud. "Miss Valerie Korie." Shifting again, he held on to the end of the massive crate with one burly arm and with the other handed Bette a note. She opened the envelope and read to the room:

Dear Bette,

Here is the future. You can beat the world at its own game.

Yours, Valerie

Defeated by the etiquette of waiting for permission, the guys lowered the future onto the rug. Taking crowbars out of their tool belts, they pried the boards apart and removed the casing, revealing a large-size television set.

Relieved, the headman asked, "Where do you want it?"

Bette did not care. "Anywhere."

"You have to tell me where."

"Right here is fine." She wanted this to be over.

"Right here? In the center of the room?"

"Fine."

"Most people have it against a wall."

"I don't care."

"Don't you want it to be facing a chair?"

"No."

"Okay," he'd had it. "Sign here."

She signed.

"Enjoy," he laughed. The two men looked over Earl one more time. Something abnormal was going on, that was for sure. Then they went back out to the truck.

Bette put her plate down on top of the television set. She glanced back at Valerie's note.

Beat the world.

"Earl, you called that girl *innocent*? The most cunning people are always excused."

He held her eyes.

"Earl, please. Don't you see that my family has come all this way to destroy me once again? Ever since I was old enough to feel, I've been sacrificed to her mother, my cousin. They smacked me and caressed her. I fled, abandoned, while she married my love. And now I, the

222

poor relation, have found one single lamb that is my joy, and they, with whole flocks, covet my one friend and steal you from me. Hortense is robbing me of my simple happiness. Robbing me. Robbing *me*. I cannot let this happen."

Earl's eyes dried up. They became cracked and flaked to the floor. He reached into his pocket, pulled out her keys, and dropped them onto the rug. He did not say he was sorry. But he did storm out, as though he was the one who had been wronged. He closed the door and left her, standing there, alone.

"Somebody," she said to nobody. "Somebody has to have my key."

Then Bette said the word *no*.

Then she said, "*You.*"

But there was no one there to hear.

Intermission

∽ ACT TWO ∽

Chapter 18

Crevelle Truscott Webb had never, ever considered—even once as a nightmarish flight of fancy—that she would someday take a night train to New York City and then a taxi to the Astor Hotel, to sleep alone in a room that cost the same nightly rate a textile worker in one of her husband's three mills earned in a month. Never. And even if, in the deepest sleep and most disturbing dream, such a fantastical occurrence had made a gesture of an appearance, it would never, ever, ever be so that she could arrive the next day at this "home" or rather pathetic "apartment" on a dreary street to speak *on purpose* to her cow of a cousin, Bette.

And yet, here she was.

It was a dark afternoon, but all afternoons were apparently such. How could this shanty ever get light with enormous buildings surrounding it in fortressed isolation from the sky? The apartment was noisy, dirty, entirely exposed to the petty details of strangers' lives. It had no charm. The contents were ancient, not antique, and more like other people's castaways. There was no order, no color coordination—in fact, no color. And no coordination. Everything inside was relentless: overbearing stacks of books, overbearing rows of music. Each chair established for reading and none for social intercourse. There wasn't a welcoming spot. Furthermore, it was very uncomfortable. The seats were old and stained. The stuffing threadbare or gone altogether. It was absolutely *not* a home. More like a Salvation Army storeroom.

Crevelle had never been east before. Had never traveled alone before, and had never, ever been to a city larger than Cleveland. And she hoped to never have to do any of that again. She felt displaced as well as put-upon. Bette had served her a shabby pot of tea laid out on top of—of all things—a television set, standing in the middle of the room like it was a Louis Quinze on public display. The candy dish had pins in it. There were a handful of dry, disgusting, supposedly "Italian" cookies that Bette called *biscotti*. They were stale and strange. Crevelle noted immediately upon being served these *biscotti* that Bette needed a new plate.

Crevelle knew from the start that the crisis to which she had been beckoned was actually a conspiracy masterminded by the sinister General Bette. Bette was the only truly evil person in the family, and as long as evil lives, it weaves its destructive web. She and Frederick had discussed for years their deeply held belief that Bette would one day return to get her revenge. And so they were not at all calmed when she ignored her inheritance by refusing to respond to a carefully orchestrated letter from a neighbor announcing her mother's death. They knew it was a ruse. She was a panther lying in wait until the opportunity presented itself to pounce and devour the gazelle. For this reason, they warned their children, almost from birth, to protect them from her evil influence. Evil. There was no other word for it. Anything less would be a dangerously palatable euphemism. Bette was a cancer, untreated. It was inevitable that her malice had finally escalated to such a level that the family was forced to respond. They were now obliged to pay her the attention she so desperately craved because she had kidnapped their child. Who knew how many years she had planned this disaster, how she had lured Hortense, with what promises? For, like all witches, Bette could never have her own child, and so sooner or later she would come to take theirs. And now it was sooner than anyone had expected. She had stolen their beloved daughter with the most grotesque of intents and then she had fed her to the wolves.

"You will have to trust me," Bette said, dunking the stale biscuit into a cloudy cup of tea.

"Trust you?" Crevelle could not believe the gall. "It is *because* of you that my daughter is marrying a darky savage three times her age." Crevelle knew better than to drink from that cup. The porcelain was cracked and had probably never been washed.

It had been over thirty years since Bette had heard the phrase "darky savage." In fact, she had forgotten that it even existed within the realm of human vocabulary. What a strange sound to come from a person's lips. Over time she had forgotten a lot of the details of that life, what *they* believed in, fought for, how they characterized the world. She'd retained a basic repulsion, but its many precise causes had, truthfully, somewhat faded. This meeting brought a great number of them back to mind in sharp relief. Implicit here was the fact that, as usual, Bette had told her cousin the truth. Repeatedly. Not about Earl's nature, of course, but about everything else. Her hope had been that Crevelle would come to face reality, and then the two of them could work together and ultimately reconcile. This had always been Bette's wish, that she and her adversaries could have experiences together in which the truth would be revealed. But that was precisely why they shunned her, wasn't it? To repress the truth. And here, Bette saw Crevelle repeat her age-old dilemma. If Bette is evil then she is not to be believed, but if she is human—with feelings and a heart—then what would Crevelle do? This situation was strangely ideal to start the path toward truth and healing because Crevelle needed something. Therefore, she was being forced by fate to face the dangerous precipice of the false tale she'd been hovering over all of her life.

Bette tried again. "No, Cousin," she said calmly. "You are wrong. I *share* your anger. I am not the cause of it."

"A darky," Crevelle fluttered. This was just more than she could take. "A black who cannot put food on the table?" Contrasting this fact with Bette's calm demeanor only amplified one thing: Bette hated them so much that there was no conceiving how low this monster would crawl. "After all these years . . ." Crevelle rocked her head in dismay. "After *decades*! You still have nothing better to do than spend your time hating us. Trying to destroy us. Just because I have Frederick's love."

After each of Crevelle's statements, Bette refound her strength. She had to. It took an enormous amount of courage, but after each blow she paused and located it again. No matter what anyone else did, Bette had to rely on what was true.

"Wait! Crevelle," Bette softened and came closer. "You are not seeing the person in front of you. You have invented another Bette. More convenient for your purposes but not me. Listen to my words. Hear my feelings. *I do not want them to get married.*"

"Liar!"

Bette had to think. How could she help this idiot listen?

Lightning cracked.

Bette turned, out of habitual pleasure, and watched the bolt's charge find its way through the buildings' secret spaces, illuminating their souls.

Crevelle, too, had a reflective thought. She noted that in Ohio, a tree would have split in two, but in this God-awful cesspool, nature had no place, no role.

"More tea, Cousin?"

The curtains whipped as Bette poured tea into her own empty cup and left Crevelle's untouched. Then she went to close the window and used the opportunity to stare out into the flashing gray. Tenth Street was smothered in black rain.

The outside world is dark and true, she remembered. And she needed it to get her friend back.

Bette had given Crevelle an opportunity to love. And Crevelle had thrown that opportunity away. Ever since this nightmare had begun, Bette felt that certain things inside her had changed. Again. Certain internal aspects shifted in place. It was as if a blood vessel snapped and her spine was slowly filling with it. Something terrible and unknown was on its way, unstoppable and organic. It was as though she'd grown a third lung and an extra oxygen supply. Something was destroyed and something superhuman replaced it. There was essential change. And it was accumulating by the day, by the hour. With each insult hurled by Crevelle, Bette transformed. After all, resistance can only be impervious for so long. How many opportunities could she give everyone to tell the truth? How many times could she hope before something great was terribly lost? Yet a new kind of blinding strength was required to be able to continue to give.

Suddenly, Valerie's face appeared before her, like the man in the moon. A vision. A rejuvenation. At the same time, a kind of haunting and a healing. And with it came Valerie's brash lips, forming a word . . . *psychological.*

"Crevelle," she said, simply turning. "I've found it more *psychological* to not oppose Hortense. It makes more sense to keep her trust and then become available to her as the relationship with that man inevitably collapses."

Her cousin was unable to understand. *Psychology* had not yet come to Ashtabula.

Instead, Crevelle had her own vocabulary for crisis, and it was rooted in attack. "Do you know why no one loves you?"

Bette, it so happens, had long wanted to know the answer to this question.

"Why?"

"Because," Crevelle said. "You have no generosity."

"But . . . I just offered you . . ." Bette had offered her cousin so many important things, but she selected the most effective one. "Your child."

Crevelle's nerves were frayed. How had she been plunged into this nightmare? It was not her hell. It was someone else's. She reached into her purse for her cigarette case.

Bette also had a cigarette case. A newly purchased prop, bought on instinct at Romanoff's from his display of penknives, lighters, watches, and other accoutrements of social negotiation, for exactly this occasion. She'd practiced swiping it off the mantel, and then enacted the gesture as if it were a daily routine. Reach, swoosh. Reach, swoosh. Bette intercepted Crevelle's stretch and, locking her cousin's eyes, snapped open the silver locket.

"Lucky," Bette said softly.

"Yes, I smoke Luckies." Crevelle was confused, but took the cigarette and waited obediently for a light.

It worked.

"You have beautiful hands, Cousin," Bette said through the match's glow. "You are still beautiful enough to inspire passion."

Crevelle inhaled, posed, and then released gratefully into her smoke.

"I'd fall in love with you myself," Bette lit her own. "If I were a man."

The two watched each other smoke. Something they never would have done as girls. It was forbidden, and they weren't the kind. *Strange* to realize now, of course. Especially since Bette had made love without marriage

233

and Crevelle had not. Only Bette knew this was true. Crevelle pretended it was false. It was the first time Bette realized that she had had illicit sex while refusing to touch a cigarette. *This is what being near family does*, she thought. *Unearths forgotten facts.*

They listened to the rain, the horns, the wheels, the sky.

"You missed your mother's funeral," Crevelle said. "The grave had been dug too narrow. The coffin would not go in. The gravediggers pushed and pulled, turning it in every direction. They even used a pick and crowbar."

"My brother?"

"I don't recall if he did much about it. Not the type, you know. Well, perhaps you don't know what he's like."

"Was he smoking?"

"Does he smoke? I wasn't aware."

Bette had always hoped that her brother would someday do the right thing. But so far he had not, since she had never heard a word of apology.

"Crevelle," Bette flicked the ash. "You understand the ways of love far better than I. You know that once Hortense betrays him, she will never come back here. She will leave him destroyed, forever, never wanting to face the consequences of her actions on another human being. That is why she *must* betray him."

Crevelle actually laughed. "How can an old maid know that?"

"Her father," Bette answered, quieted by rage. "Your husband."

Crevelle, newly relaxed, was shocked at Bette's audacity. The timing was so abrupt, she couldn't even react with appropriate outrage. There had been no chance to build.

"I was dangerous to Frederick." Bette spoke matter-of-factly, as if discussing how the coffeepot worked.

"Why?"

"I was dangerous because he had violated me. I became a witness to his darker self. And so, he shunned me. He did it because he, himself, had been cruel."

Crevelle winced, knowing she should seethe instead.

"This we must instill in Hortense. She will be proud to have destroyed another person. She'll carry it all her life like a crown, that she had a choice." *Like Tide or All.*

"My husband did no such thing," Crevelle recovered the required outrage.

Bette watched her. This woman would rather lie than save her daughter.

Crevelle turned away abruptly, and then from her new vantage point spotted the ancient photograph of Frederick on Bette's side table. It took her aback. This was a picture of her husband that she had never seen. The idea that it presided over another woman's life, these many years, brought Crevelle to her senses. Bette would never be swayed by argument. Conversation was pointless.

"You are insane," Crevelle confirmed, putting out the cigarette. She was fed up now. The newness of these surroundings had been replaced by her innate sense of superiority. "Tragically, I am dependent on you, since Hortense will not open the door of her apartment. This is, after all, your swamp. So you know its brutal rules and understand how to save my daughter from your own brand of slime."

"I do know how to save your daughter."

"All right then. No more niceties. I am willing to pay a lot of money to have Hortense returned."

This was how Crevelle regained her confidence. She had money and Bette did not. Nothing would ever change that. Crevelle boldly surveyed the dingy set of rooms where her cousin sewed and read. Listened to the record player. The pathos of that miserable life.

"All right," Bette said. "Pay it to her, then."

"To support *his* pleasures?"

"No, no. I know this man. He is good."

There it was, the truth. Earl was good. Bette knew this to be supremely true. The cruelty he was exhibiting was a temporary insanity. Bette had come to understand that it was the humiliation of having been robbed by that young thug who had pretended to like him that had driven Earl to this desperate place. The shunning by Leon, the loving wish for Frank. She understood what had happened. The exclusion from his true field, the stage. The pain of his family's prejudices. There was so much working against Earl, but she had mercy. It could all be healed. It could all be faced and healed. After all, the truth was that Bette had faith. She believed in him.

"Her advantages," Bette was sure, "will become a greater and greater insult in his life. So, send her money, Crevelle. Flood her with it." Bette sat back, reflecting on this new strategy. She believed that it would work. "It will bring him shame."

"He has that much character?"

"Yes."

"And you have even less than I thought." Crevelle was pleased with herself now. She had the situation under control. Obviously Bette was a half-wit. She was quickly ready to use her worst instincts on Crevelle's behalf, and she didn't even want cash. Bette's lack of taste for money could work to Crevelle's advantage. Yes, that was the key, after all. Crevelle now finally came to understand the situation with some clarity. She realized that Bette still loved Frederick so much that she wanted to save his daughter. Well, whatever delusion was motivating the shrew, Crevelle would get her girl returned. Then she would put an end to this relationship forever. No one in the family would ever speak Bette's name again.

"All right, Cousin Bette. I will cut her off and send *you* Hortense's allowance. Feed all indulgences until the man is ashamed. But keep control of it in case your plan fails. All ten thousand."

"Ten thousand dollars?" Bette had known they were very rich but . . .

Crevelle took advantage of the moment to make a show of looking around the apartment. "You are too frugal to be foolish. This way the darky savage cannot steal my daughter *and* her fortune."

Bette sat back calmly, but her mind was racing. "I will do my best." She had to make every turn bring her closer to her goal. Every tiny little thing.

Crevelle stood, gathering her belongings. Her provincial coat, hat, shoes, and bag, all the same matching navy blue. She looked at herself in the mirror, it needed a dusting.

"I'm back to the hotel awaiting your report." She paused at the door, fully in control. Writing checks was something that she did well, and the role that enhanced her greatest strengths. Bette's hair had never known a beauty parlor, her skin had never seen a facial. She had no colorist, no tailor, her hands had never passed a manicure. Now all of that neglect lay clearly on her sagging skin and pale, limp hair. "You've aged, Cousin." Crevelle clicked her tongue and shook her head.

"We haven't seen each other in thirty years."

"Surely retirement approaches," Crevelle deigned. "You must look forward to sleeping late, collecting social security, and watching the television."

"What should I watch?" Bette asked. It had occurred to her that someday she might wish to turn the thing on.

"Oh, I prefer Milton Berle. He's quite nice."

"Why do you like him?"

"He's funny."

And with that, Crevelle was off.

Chapter 19

When Crevelle departed, she left behind a strange silence. Bette listened to it for a while, displaced awkwardly by its lack of familiarity. There she found a whole new dimension of dread, impossible to assimilate into some kind of intimate balance. She soon understood that this was the deathly quiet of suffocation. This silence could be Bette's fate. If she did not act boldly and with command on her own behalf, she would perish and yet still live. That was the fear, that this terrible nonlife could go on forever until the end. Thus the challenge that her beloved Earl had brought into her lap, the problem that he had created for her to solve. He had made the decision—even if it was impulsive and not thought through—a decision nonetheless, to place her in this teetering position where she had no choice. He had taken away her choice.

How strange. Desperation had made him blind, perhaps, but oppression has consequences on people's emotional lives, and now he, so uncharacteristically, had become the perpetrator, as—suddenly—he saw only himself. Just like *they* do.

Bette took in her situation. There are many different kinds of love. True, novels and cinema, the work of culture and commerce, have prepared all to believe that only two really matter: the romantic pairing of a man and woman, and the love between parent and child. Every message trumpets these as everlasting, of central importance, and beyond evaluation or reproach. But in Bette's experience, neither claim was true. Yet all forces around her repeated constantly that they were. How could it be that every amplified voice reinforced a claim that anyone with eyes could see was preposterous? Herein lay her basic problem, the cause of her separation from most people. They believed these foundations to be stone, and she saw them to be sand.

One of the many precious lessons Bette had learned from Earl was how to assess a situation. This was specific to the treatment he endured as a Negro. She saw, almost immediately, that if she evaluated people, situations, and institutions only by how they treated white people, she would have a distorted and untrue understanding of their nature. But if she listened closely to how these same powers treated *him*, she would uncover their true meaning. For how they treated *him* was the measure that counted. It was the reveal. Therefore, Bette learned that who someone really was depended not only on her personal interaction with them but on how they treated others. Refracting this information, Bette came to understand that she, herself, was also a kind of measure. A conscious person could see the real value of romantic love between men and women or familial bonding by similarly examining how they impacted *her*. She, too, was the example of the "other," the failure who brought into relief the flaws of the whole system. She, too, was the one who should be considered.

At this point, truthfully, it had all become very difficult to grasp. Why did Crevelle think that she *loved* Hortense? Because she was trying to reclaim her for the white race? What made Hortense think she *loved* Earl? Because she wanted to scandalize her family and create an image of herself as brave? At least Earl didn't feign love for Hortense. That was the crumb of hope.

"Love," in these examples, was an enactment of value. It was an assertion of place in the social order. It meant everything on the outside and little within.

Bette looked inside herself and knew for a fact that the love she had for Earl and he for her—the years of loyalty, the time, the confiding, the rooting for, the thinking of, and now her unfaltering faith that he could ultimately do the right thing, the acceptance of conflict, and the refusal to shun him—that all this was more powerful than the twisting and discarding that took place between blood relations. Than the deceptions that transpired between lovers. She knew that this love should be the center of novels and poems and plays, operas and such, but it couldn't be. Because then all the falsity would be exposed in comparison—to love when you are not supposed to is so much deeper than to love as instructed to do. They are two different animals. One is imposed, the other discovered. One is preordained, the other improvised. One brings reward, the other must survive despite punishment. Really, these two opposing experiences should not be called by the same word, *love*. Perhaps in the future, poets would resolve this. Bette could only hope.

So, the stakes were clear. The goal, clear. But still to be grappled with was the painfully weird impracticality of Earl himself. Ignoring the consequences of his actions on her life would not help him reach his goal. Kindness would have been better. More effective. But he had taken the other path. *It was dumb*, she thought plainly. *D-U-M-B, dumb*. She wished, for both their sakes, that he had been more humane. But he had not. Now, he forced her to save them both herself.

One of the many painful aspects of all this was that Earl was violating his own principles. He was exploiting her lack of power. The fact was that Bette could not give Earl what was being kept from him, any of it—money, sexual attention, confidence in his future as an actor—she held none of that social sway. And so he had discarded her. That was very wrong. All along he had claimed to see what really mattered between friends. And yet here he had made a shallow choice. Love alone, Bette came to understand, would not meet this with equal measure. She too would have to look at her own palette. What access did she have? What could she actually control? How could she equalize the situation and force him to negotiate? They had to negotiate. She could not live like this.

From then on, each new day, Bette spent her mornings listening for the sounds of life from next door. As she accumulated clues, she developed each step of her plan. And then she put the plan into effect. Its development was ongoing. And flexible. It had to be if she was to get her friend back. It would require all of her resources: creativity, bold action, fearlessness, daring. She would have to scare herself to find the strength to turn back this tide, as so many forces opposed her in her quest.

Bette's motives were sharpened dramatically by the pain of this unnatural separation, needing it to end. The sudden disappearance of all that she loved was happening for no discernible reason rooted in her own behavior, as far as she could see. It was being imposed on her in compensation for the deficiencies of the world. If Earl would just sit down with her and tell her what she had to do so that they could be friends again, no matter how bizarre, she would do it. But he wouldn't communicate. Why?

He expected her to be plunged into darkness: no friend, no one to see, to hear, to speak to, to share with. He had found a new process to engage in, clearly, and Bette was sure that its complexities created a very convenient distraction from the loss of her, but she had no such distraction. All she had was nothing. All she had was an absence that she did not deserve and could not live with. And he would not understand how strongly that motivated her to seek change. His game was over-kill and that forced her to respond. If he would bring it down to human scale, she could accept a great deal of loss. But something had to make sense. There are always ways for two people to make things better. But they have to talk. Annihilation is a bad strategy, it gives the other nothing to lose.

Finally, after a week of suffering, preparation, and

long hours of internal deliberation, finally all was in place to begin her plan to bring back her real life. Her life. To bring back her friend.

Day one of the campaign started as always. Hortense went off to her class, but the audition had begun before leaving the house, Bette could hear the theatricality in her voice.

"I love you," Hortense sang out like she was Deanna Durbin or someone more contemporary but equally false and despicable. "I left today's cash on the table." Then, as soon as Earl's door clicked shut, Hortense snuck to Bette's apartment.

Bette had offered her a secret meeting, and the young girl had arrogantly accepted. It would never occur to her that her own cruelties would be met in kind. She expected only service from poor old Cousin Bette. This agreement reinforced Bette's suspicions that Hortense held a secret life of doubt that she hid from Earl. Just as he hid his from her. Hortense had not learned enough about the reality of her parents' marriage, their daily practice of lies and deceit. No, she ignored reality and imitated movies instead. Like Earl, she vainly assumed that only *her* heart was complex.

Bette heard the girl's footsteps approach and then the timid, secret knock. As she silently, slowly, opened the door.

Hortense quickly slid into the apartment, watching to be sure that she was not observed. Secured, the young girl gazed at her older cousin with an effective expression of empathy and pity that she had picked up in some class. Hortense thought that she, herself, was in command, as she had come to bring bad news. And, of course, only she knew how bad the news actually was. Taking her old place in her old chair at the table, she reached for her cousin's hand and held it between both palms, in sympathy. Slowly, with care, she picked over her words.

"No matter how many times I tried to raise the subject with Earl, he simply refused to discuss it. He is not open to any reconciliation, nor negotiation. He would not even consider it. He said that you are . . . that you are . . ."

"He said that I'm what?"

"Evil."

Earl had called her *evil*? She knew he had chosen that word deliberately, not because of any proximity to truth, but because he instinctively knew that of all the words in the lexicon this was the one that would most hurt her. It was as she had suspected. Earl had focused all his rage at her. The world's erasure was too big and overpowering. The self-satisfied racism of the theater, men who couldn't love each other fully with intelligence, white people and their endless arrogance, other Negroes who didn't understand his desires, keeping open his heart, all this had become too much to hold. And so he had decided to hate her. It was so much easier. And of course she cared, when so many around him simply did not. He could affect her.

"It's the power of suggestion," she said to Hortense. "He is imitating your family."

Bette became even more convinced that nothing would change this spiral until she and Earl could speak. Alone. Like last time, it was hard, but they had told each other what was true. They needed to do that again. To remind each other of this gift between them. That is not evil. It is the opposite. That is love. Recognizing the mistake and forgiving it. Facing it. Together. That is a true friend.

"I'm sorry, Bette. I told him he was wrong."

"What did he say?"

"He said that I am under your influence."

Bette was reeling. He was pulling out all the stops. He was playing that bitter game, where the offender pretends that he's the one who has been hurt as a device to avoid being accountable. Certainly he'd been on the other side of that often enough to know exactly how it worked. Now she had a new level to contend with. Earl was using the enemy's tricks. She knew that she had to adjust to meet him. But in her heart, she was falling without moving.

"Are you?"

"I think we can all get along," Hortense said. "Like a family."

That word. *Family*. Hortense was the only person in this scenario who had one, so maybe she should know. It pained Bette through and through. Her second family was turning out to be just like her first. She was being accused of things that had never happened while someone else lied. Just as with Frederick. But the stakes were so much higher this time around. The fact was that now Bette could not pack up and move somewhere else. She could not start all over again. This was Bette's final life. Things had to be made right *now*. She would not have a third chance.

"He said," Hortense quivered. "That you would never be friends again."

"Did he say why?"

"No, he won't tell me why."

That weapon of undeserved silence. It would crush her if she could not rally. How to get relief?

"And Bette, I have to tell you . . . you know how much I love you. But I have to tell you one more thing and this is very hard to say. Bette . . ." Hortense looked at the floor. "I have to tell you that we are moving."

"Moving?"

"Yes. We've taken a place on Thirteenth Street. Earl insisted."

"But you have no money."

"Well," Hortense sighed. And Bette noticed a slightly more adult air about her this time. "There is the three months free rent that they give you for signing the lease. And Earl believes that my family will come around and reinstate my allowance so that we'll be able to pay the rent by then. Fifteen dollars a week. If it wasn't for your secret generosity, we would starve."

So Earl was counting chickens. This was important information to assimilate. He thought, somehow, this girl would elevate him into the world of *them*. That this girl would get him out of the slaughterhouse. Bette's heart broke at his desperation but recognized that hers matched it. Perhaps there was a way that Bette could earn more money so that she could help him on his way and he wouldn't be needing . . . How could Bette earn more money? This was something to bring up with Valerie. Not yet, but . . . eventually. Yes, if Bette had more money this could be a very different situation . . .

Bette knew something that Earl did not. That family would never accept a Negro. That was that. She knew them better than he did. And all these years when she had spoken about them, well, apparently he hadn't been listening. That was sobering news as well. He thought he could *handle* them, did he? The idea that he could ever access Hortense's advantages was pure illusion. Bette wondered if every liar in Hollywood felt the same way.

As with each phase of this horror, at first Bette was shocked. Then she adjusted. The difficulty was that Earl kept adjusting as well. Every time she assimilated his next act of aggression and caught up to his new layer of cruelty, he escalated once again. He was power mad. But what he did not realize was that she could not give up. She had to make him negotiate. And he knew very well that if he moved away he could avoid ever speaking to her again. He could lie forever. And she could not let that happen.

"Which building?" she asked calmly. Remembering that she needed all information. Every piece of it.

"The brown brick. On the corner, next to Mr. Moon's Hand Laundry. I spoke to the landlord. Earl says they are always willing to rent to a white woman. After I sign the lease, he'll just move in. That's how it's done."

Bette knew that was how it was done.

"Maybe," and Hortense turned very, very sweet. So charmingly soft and endearing. "Maybe, if you could help us get some more money, he would be grateful." Hortense tried to look blasé, but her desperation was behind the wheel.

Ah, Bette was gratified to note. *Hortense and I have the same instincts in this regard. A good sign.* Bette had to be able to think like . . . *them.*

It was alarming and yet necessary. Bette knew that if she and Earl could just speak to each other, everything would be all right. Even in their last awful conversation he had admitted that he did not love Hortense. If he spoke to Bette again, if they had a series of conversations until all was resolved, well, he would remember what it was like to be real with an equal. To be loved for himself. For his soul. Not out of envy for his talent or to be used for shock value. For him. As soon as this insanity stopped she would forgive him, immediately. It would take five minutes. She would just tell him honestly how much pain he had caused her, and then it would all be over. After all, Earl was her dearest friend, and she was his. She deserved to be heard.

Bette saw Hortense to the door and listened as she walked down the stairs. Then Bette stepped to the window and watched Hortense cross the street. At that point, she opened her own door and took the seven steps to Earl's apartment.

"Earl?"

"Go away," he yelled through the door.

"This is not humane," she said. "You are my dearest friend."

"Was."

How does he think of these things? His instinct was so destructive it was stunning. How can someone be that terrible so easily for no reason? Did he read about it in a play? If Bette were ever to decide to treat someone like that, there would have to be a reason. She would need to plan ahead.

"Earl, don't talk to me that way, please. Can't there be some healing between us?"

"Nothing about me needs to be healed. I'm sorry I ever trusted you."

He did it again. Escalated. She asked for reason and kindness, and instead he eviscerated her.

"Don't say that," she crumpled. "I beg you."

It would be hard for Bette to refuse any human being who said, "I beg you." Even a hobo in an alley. Certainly not someone she knew.

She waited. Then Bette heard him stomp up to the door, stand there, and refuse to open it. *Sigh.* He didn't want to be bothered. She heard him put on the chain, implying that she would break in. Kick the door down. He was ridiculous. He was recreating her as his own monster.

"What you are doing," he screamed at her through the wood. "What you are doing to me is *worse* than anything they've ever done to me." His mouth must have been directly on the peephole. "It's worse than my family throwing me out. It's worse than the racism on the stage. It's worse than those lying boys who broke my heart or beat my head. You are worse than every animal I ever slaughtered. You, Bette, are the worst!"

"Why?"

"Because you are using my confidences against me."

The truth exists. She knew that. The truth can't be unknown. To speak it is not to *use* it. To speak it is to defeat the lie. To speak it is the responsibility of those who know and love. To pretend is not to love. Not after this.

This was all so difficult, so hard to handle. Bette was lost inside, but she had to find a way. Earl was creating a false logic system. A smoke screen. What was the "worst" was not the cruelty he had experienced at the hand of others. Or that she loved him in the face of them. Or that they had spoken honestly about these forces and about his desires. But the great crime, in the mind of Earl, was that she would not agree to let him destroy her life. She would not agree to an inauthentic relationship. She would not suddenly play along.

"Earl," she said. Her cheek up against the door. "Don't shout at the world through me. I can't take it." This was the truth. "If you deepen the wound, I too will deepen. I don't want to. Don't make me. Speak to me instead. If we work together we can both shift and a solution will appear."

The door opened then with the force of the tornado that took Dorothy Gale to Oz, and there Earl stood, enormous in its frame. She was so happy to see him. To see his face. She loved him. She missed him all the time. Here he was, everything could be all right.

"All my life," he said, shaking. "I have been the person that no one wants to be."

"So have I," said Bette.

"Well, I'm not going to be like you anymore," Earl sneered. He was filled with hate. There wasn't a molecule of light. "You don't matter."

Then the door slammed shut.

Chapter 20

By midnight Bette had established her goal. She had to keep Earl in the building at all costs. *If he moved, it was over.*

She heard sirens, police cars or ambulances pulling up to her corner, the swirling red glare illuminating her hands in rotation.

She would live in silence forever, she would live in the unbearable state of being unjustly shunned, and she could not let that be so. He had to stay next door so that they could talk.

There were voices in the hall and heavy steps.

Only if they spoke could the healing process begin. Now she had to determine her first course of action.

There was a heavy, authoritative knock.

"Police department."

Bette opened her front door to a trio of police officers, ambulance drivers, and a nurse.

"What's the matter, officer?"

"Did you hear anything strange going on at the

O'Reilly residence?"

"No."

The young cop, already fat, already disconnected, had already been through too much with no way to process it, and he was only at the beginning.

"When was the last time you saw the mother or the child?"

"I usually see them every day . . . out the window. We both lean on the windowsill at the same time. 6:00 p.m."

"Every day?"

Two medical technicians carried out a stretcher with a large body bag.

"Usually. I mean, lately I . . . I haven't been looking out the window."

Bette glanced up as a nurse emerged holding a creature in her arms. Not a girl, not a person, but a shrunken, trembling, staring, starving . . . not an animal . . . not an alien . . . but something between death and hell. Too weak to walk, protest, or register her own experience.

"Miss, how long has it been since you last looked out the window?"

"Two weeks. No, longer. Three weeks. Maybe a month? Perhaps two."

"And why is that?"

"I've been . . . busy."

"And you didn't hear a child crying next door."

"No. If she had cried, I would have heard her."

"All right."

"Margaret's not a crier."

"Well, if she lives, she'd better learn," the cop said.

"'Cause she's got a damn good reason to cry."

Bette looked at Earl's door, but no one was stirring. Those two weren't going to acknowledge that something grave had taken place. Jarred from her own dilemmas, Bette stood in the hallway until the parties dispersed, and then slowly backed into her foyer and locked the door. There she crumpled. She had no idea. She didn't see. That poor little girl. If only Bette had remembered other people instead of having to be the object of all of Earl's rage. Bette sobbed, she felt her limbs tingle. That girl suffered because no one was watching. The person who should have been watching was Bette, and yet she had been too absorbed. In her own happiness. In her own sorrow. Bette cried from regret for this other person's pain. Her helplessness. It was so unnecessary to be helpless. It was a state of mind. Beyond being a child. It was being a defeated child. Defeated by your own home and the inability to escape. To not see that someone else's trouble is taking your life away.

Bette stumbled to the bathroom and took off her sweater. Her dress. Her underpants and brassiere. Her slip and her stockings. Garters. She took off her glasses and stepped into the shower. It was cold or it was hot. That was up to her. She had control. She had running water. She didn't need someone else to feed her. She had a body. She had arms and muscles and a belly made of steel. She had two soft breasts that she held in her hands. She had a neck to carry her busy, busy mind. She could do it. She could find the right course of action that would bring this chapter to a positive resolution. She would not be Margaret O'Reilly.

Bette would not be the victim of someone else's pain.

And then it all came upon her. She comprehended exactly what to do.

Bette arrived at the office at seven forty-five, knowing she had to make the call first thing after eight. It could not wait until lunch. She would have to sound crisp, businesslike, corporate. Sitting in the office, receiver in hand, she felt shaken to her bones. Terrified. She was a novice mountain climber swinging alone from peak to peak. It was dangerous, she knew, to be this bold. But many others played chess with people's lives. Most players opened with the pawn, carefully developing the center of the board. And there were many staunch advocates of this approach, in theory. Careful development of the blockade, protecting the power center at all cost. Now that he was at the helm, Earl led with his queen. Risky, threatening, exposed. So she was forced to endanger her own queen, just to stay in play. Bette reached to dial and felt a contortion so deep that her feet clenched, gripping her shoes. Earl had underestimated her, he had left no thread of decorum. She dialed and listened to the heralding ring.

" . . . Yes, Mister. So you understand, he . . ." She thought back to Anthony. How his pale skin made it possible for Earl to have that apartment. "The man in question . . . he is . . ."

"He is what?"

"He is not . . ." Suddenly she changed her path. "They are not legally married. . ."

"I see."

She waited. She had hedged. Was that a flaw?

"I don't want that in my building."

Her heart opened. "Yes, of course you don't want that in your building . . . Yes, of course."

She hung up, exhausted. The universe buzzed around her and then the panic set in. She was so excited her bones ached. Was it *panic,* after all? No, it was a kind of breathless thrill. It was the sheer energy of daring to exist. She could exist. She did not have to be blamed for everyone else's weakness. That was not the purpose of her life. If Earl and she could talk, none of this would be necessary, but he made it necessary. He expected her to disappear, but she could not because she was a living being. She had rights. The right to not be blamed—again. She could respond. Actively. Doing something to defend one's place. To improve one's life. To take control. It was going to the edge of her capacity. Soaring.

The office door swung open and Hector strolled in. So, she had to rally a pretense of the ordinary, quickly, in preparation for the next chapter of achieving her daunting task.

"Good morning, Bette."

"Good morning, Hector."

Determination gathering, she took a deep breath and began practicing her lines for Step Two.

Darky savage. Darky savage.

Bette had a secret life.

As he hung his hat, Hector looked at her with little boy eyes, the way he had run to her as a child coming to visit his daddy in the office. When old Mr. Tibbs realized that his only son was not the brightest bulb in the shop, he mercifully lost interest rather than try to humiliate the child into improvement. But a sidebar to the benevolent ignorance was that he noticed almost nothing more about his son beyond the boy's limitations. Ever. Including when he was hungry. The mother rarely made an appearance and was never mentioned. For all Bette knew she was in a lunatic asylum or on an international bridge tour indefinitely. So, more than once, Bette had rescued the tiny growling stomach of little Hector with half her sandwich brought from home or half a homemade sugar cookie. More than once she had listened to some question or tale normally relayed to a parent.

"Beth," he'd lisped at the age of four. "If the dinosaurs come back to earth, are we all gonna get thwashthed?"

"No, Hector. We won't get squashed because the dinosaurs are extinct. That means they are never coming back, because they no longer exist."

"Okay."

Here he was now, before her, a man. And yet he carried that same wounded expression of simply and utterly having no idea what to do. Ever worried about getting squashed, but now not knowing for sure, by whom.

"Bette?"

"Yes, Hector?"

"Has Valerie come in yet?"

Bette looked at the clock. It was eight twenty-five. "No."

"Bette?" Something was troubling him.

"What is it, Hector?"

"I like her."

"I like her too." Then Bette thought a bit. "I also admire her."

"So do I," Hector said, a bit overenthusiastic. "I love her. I mean, I'm in love with her."

There it was.

"What about Sue?"

"I know!"

Hector Tibbs, who had never broken a rule on purpose in his entire life, was not only harboring adulterous feelings but was confessing them to the one person alive who had known him the longest. His dead father's secretary. Obviously, the situation had reached a state of emergency.

The fact was that Hector, though married since the age of twenty-three, was finally, for the first time in his life, truly and passionately in love. He'd steadily experienced Sue as a conveyor belt of domesticity and had realized long ago that if they ever stopped discussing details and arrangements, they would have nothing left at all to say. One day he even tried to not participate in any conversation about pickups, drop-offs, dates, times, menus, tasks, errands, money, or decisions. And he quickly discovered that the only other material between him and his wife were reports of each of their activities. Sue would report on her conversation with her mother, what Sally did, what Stevie did, what the neighbor said, and what the gardener billed. Hector, in turn, would describe the new events at work, Valerie's new ideas, the new paint on the office walls, and Sue would give an opinion, an evaluative statement or advice even though she knew *absolutely nothing about any of it.* She didn't ask questions, so she couldn't understand, and whatever it was that was in her soul or her head, she either couldn't bring it to her lips or was as unaware of her own interior life as he was. Twice now, he had almost just come out and announced, "I'm in love with Valerie," really just to give them something meaningful to talk about, but he wouldn't dare. What would she do with that? And more importantly, what would he?

Hector had found Valerie to be the most delightfully, willfully, and singularly charming woman he had ever encountered. Of course, he didn't get out much. Besides Bette, waitresses, and the other society wives in Connecticut, he hardly met any women at all. He spoke to his colleagues' secretaries and receptionists, but there were so few women in any position of authority or autonomy that he really had not been this close to one before. And he found her a marvel. If that's where women were going, he was all for it. Alive, engaged, displayed, and at the helm of every craft. If only women were allowed to be as good as they could be, well then, chaps like Hector would be allowed to take second place, which is really where he knew he belonged. It would be better all the way around, and he hoped other men would hurry and wise up, so he could take off that damn tie and be able to stop having to make decisions he would never be equipped to make.

Valerie was changing his life on a daily basis. For the better. But that was the problem. Alimony, too, would change his life on a daily basis. All this talk about *marketing* had made Hector realize that there was a better life out there, waiting to be grabbed. But for a price. There, he'd finally admitted it. His happiness boiled down, like everything, to the price of the ticket. Was there any way out?

Bette listened to these confessions. Truthfully, she could empathize. Valerie had changed her life as well, it was undeniable. How else would she have been able to begin to grab the reins, to try to have some say in how her own time was spent? Stop being acted upon and start being part of the action? Well, without Valerie it never would have been. She could see why Hector wanted to be closer to her. Bette felt the same. Strangely, Hector and Bette, who all their lives had been on the opposite side of every social, cultural, and characterological divide, were suddenly united by marketing. They were both at a crossroads. They were both deciding not to be what others wanted them to be but to brand themselves for the world to see. To do their own packaging, so to speak, and to direct their powers to their specific target audiences. Instead of being doormats for the rest of time, they had both decided to become themselves. *LUX.*

And yet, Bette was intelligent and Hector was not.

"Hector," she warned. "Be careful. You do not yet know how Valerie feels about you. Don't you dare make a pass at her unless you're sure. It will jeopardize the business."

That was practical advice. And it dovetailed with the one significant doubt that Hector had been carrying around for weeks. It was the sneaking awareness that his sweet Valerie not only had no interest in the likes of him but actually had a taste for street toughs.

"I think she prefers convicts to regular working stiffs."

"Why?" Bette asked.

"Well," Hector stammered. "This realization came to me one evening about a month ago."

"What happened?"

Valerie had persuaded him that part of his job was to go out for drinks with clients. There was more business to be done over dinner than there was in the club car of the commuter train, and Hector had better get used to both the camaraderie and picking up the check.

Hector had found it excruciating. He didn't know what to order, didn't know what to talk about, and rarely seemed to laugh on cue. After shaking hands, convinced that he'd done more harm than good, Valerie had suggested that the two go out together for one more drink.

"Just to *postmortem*," she'd said with a wink.

Of course he was secretly delighted, but also fearful that she would tear him to shreds for his miserable performance. Valerie chose a bar on Christopher Street, a side street he had never seen or heard mentioned. After arriving at the dive, which was called Julius's, Hector excused himself to go to the men's room. Well, the back of the bar around the urinals was filled with some very unsavory characters. Hector did not know exactly what was going on, but whatever it was it did not feel legal.

By the time he returned to the bar, Valerie was being overly friendly with some sort of gang kid.

"What kind of gang?"

"You know, James Dean haircut, extra tight T-shirt. Pants two sizes too small. Boots."

"What were they talking about?"

"She was asking him what kind of pomade he used. Some kind of market survey. Like we're going to sell products expressly to criminals. What next? Designer work boots? Luxury blue jeans? Brand-name men's underpants?"

Everyone buys something, Bette realized. *Was anything beyond hard sell?* "Then what?"

"Well, at this point I took in that the place was rather dangerous. There were hardly any other women there. And one of them had a tattoo!"

"I see."

"It had a rough-and-tumble atmosphere. And it was in the Village."

"I live in the Village," Bette said.

"Really?" And something turned inside Hector. For the first time he felt a bit . . . curious. For the first time he had the thought that Bette lived somewhere. And this tremendous knowledge made the truth lurch forward. "And that's when I realized that I am in love with her."

"When?" Bette actually wanted to know, because she had fallen in love with Valerie at the first introduction of the word *Lucky*.

Hector's forehead crinkled. His mouth fluttered and a tiny tear appeared in his gray eyes. "When the thing that scared me most was not the thought of being robbed at knifepoint but the realization that I might never be dangerous enough to win her heart."

And with that Hector became so overcome that he had to wipe his eyes on his sleeve and turn away for a moment, to regain the pretense that he relied on to replace his lack of composure.

The truth is that Bette's mind was a machine these days. She wasted no information and no opportunity. Her consciousness was purely associative as she was on survival mode, full time. So all she processed cognitively from this admission and display was: Fear + Danger + Love + Risk = Earl.

"You'll have to make her jealous." It just came out of her mouth, as though her thought and speech were instantly coalesced. Normally this would have been something she would never have said or even considered. But now . . . there was a new kind of *instinct.* There was a new apparatus that had been assembled in her soul, one that wanted to be a master of its own fate. "Take out some other woman. See how she reacts."

"Cheat on Sue? What if I get caught?" Hector had never, ever seen Bette give advice before. And certainly nothing beyond wearing a hat in the rain. He was elated and mortified, attracted and repulsed. He broke out into a rash and mopped his lips and neck.

But in that same moment it all became clear to Bette. What her subconscious had discovered was delivered to the forefront of her thinking.

"Maybe," she said seductively, feeling something she had never felt before. Feeling *sly.* "Maybe someone who is also married."

"Do you think she'll notice?" He was considering it.

"Valerie notices most things."

Then it was exactly nine, and Valerie briskly entered the office in her newly acquired ensemble from B. Altman's.

"Hello, chums."

Bette and Hector looked at each other and smiled.

Chapter 21

"Chums," Valerie jauntily tossed. "Bad news!"

"Oh my God!" Hector panicked. He was so wound up. Was she leaving him? Already?

Valerie laughed that gorgeous laugh, like the wind through the pine trees outside Picasso's window in the South of France. Or something else unimaginable and mythic. She patted Hector on the back, and Bette saw him tremble.

"Don't sweat, Mary. Just a setback." Valerie pulled off her leather gloves, hung her red-and-white woven hat with netting, and swiveled her chair up to her brand new desk. The one she made Hector order fit to size. "The Queen of Rumania is *not* available." And then she sighed and pulled out her lipstick for a quick touch-up before launching into the day's new campaign.

Bette, who did not wear lipstick and would not know how to put it on, even with a mirror, grabbed her steno pad, her tool of war. "Do we need to find a new fallen monarch?"

Hector swiveled awkwardly in his chair toward Valerie's beacon of light. "What about . . . ," he hesitated insecurely, reaching for any way to complete the thought. "Albania?"

"Could be," she considered, and then dismissed. "No, we need to find a new theme." Valerie assumed the pose that equally fascinated both Bette and Hector. It was a lovely, determined stare off into the atmosphere. Her face relaxed, her brown eyes reflecting the office lamps, and her soft brown hair, hanging full and then bouncing off her shoulders. She looked like a painting in the Metropolitan Museum of Art. Something both royal and divine. The way women with power used to be before the glamourless Eleanor Roosevelt, Bess Truman, and Mamie Eisenhower turned high society into a barn dance for the 4-H club.

Bette both enjoyed and observed Valerie's charm. "Something dramatic?"

"Hmmm, perhaps."

"Something dangerous? Risky?"

"Like what?" Hector snapped. He was terrified of himself at that moment. So much so that it overwhelmed his usual terror of the rest of the world.

"Let's see," Valerie intoned from her hypnotic trance. She recited a list of the attributes they were seeking for their ad campaign, as though taking inventory in a looking glass. "Something exotic, sensual, mysterious, dark. Something primal, animal, primitive, and implicating."

There it was. A gift from God or fate or simply coincidence.

"Like . . . ," Bette offered hesitantly, even though she

was perfectly sure. "Like a . . . dark . . . y . . . savage?" Bette spoke with a combination of urgency and precariousness, as though holding a much-too-hot cup of tea for a little too long.

"What?" Valerie broke out into a surprised laughter of surprise. Her face aflame with amusement, illuminated from within. "Why Bette, what in the devil's name is a . . . *darky savage?*"

"You know," Bette answered carefully, quietly, using all her strength to be sure not to falter. "A king of Africa. Like Emperor Jones."

"Drinking hot cocoa?"

At least she's heard of Emperor Jones. So far so good.

"Well," Valerie seemed inspired by the outlandishness of Bette's proposal. "It *is* exotic."

"But . . . but . . ." Hector was now worried about everything. "Who is going to purchase something because a Negro uses it? They are not generally considered to be experts." This was his money after all. Which reminded him again about the ongoing problem of the budget and that made him have to sit down abruptly, and wonder how much more *this* was going to cost.

"No." Bette carefully slipped on his leash. "A. . . white . . ."

"A WHITE MAIDEN!" It was only Valerie who was quick enough and smart enough and single-minded enough to take the bait without hesitation. "And an AFRICAN KING!"

"Like Fay Wray," Bette said calmly, quick-drying the cement. "And King Kong. She can offer him a hot cocoa to soothe the *savage* . . . beast."

"That is our slogan," Valerie leapt out of her chair

like she had the secret to the Vatican Archives in her makeup bag. "ROCOCO, TO SOOTHE THE SAVAGE BEAST!"

"That's good," Bette said, repressing a smile.

"I *LOVE* IT."

"Me too," whimpered Hector, still trying to figure out exactly what the theme was.

Valerie, ecstatic, commanded center stage and began acting out her visions of the commercial. "First, we show the captured white girl offering the beast some chocolate. Once he discovers how delicious it is, he drinks the entire bowl and, satiated, falls asleep as if they had just committed sexual relations."

"On TV?" Hector croaked.

"No, no, no. Implied. Then while he snores, she can escape. Just like in real life."

Some of this was a bit over Bette's head, but having done what she set out to do, she absorbed every word in preparation for the task ahead.

"This is it!" Valerie cheered. "ADVERTISING IS HAPPENING."

"Where to?" Bette asked, writing.

"Where what?"

"Where does she escape to?"

"Good girl," Valerie turned her light on Bette and bestowed her most elevating smile. "Let's see . . . well, she escapes . . . off into the arms of her hunter husband, camped in the jungle waiting for her return." Valerie squinched her nose now, adorably imagining the final moment of her masterpiece. "And then, as the white girl and her hunter husband are sailing away, back to civilization, drinking Rococo on deck, *of course*, the African waves at them from the shore. AND HE'S DRINKING IT TOO! And he is patting his stomach and speaking African."

"Do you speak African?" Hector asked, completely overwhelmed.

"*Ooga-Booga* or whatever," Valerie literally patted him on the head. "And it means YUMMM." She licked her lips. "Which we, the audience, can understand when he smiles and shows his big white teeth. Very nineteen fifties. It fits in with a kind of one world, United Nations sentiment."

Hector, happy at being touched, agreed. "But with America on top of course."

"Of course," Valerie nodded seriously, acknowledging his contribution. "THE WHOLE WORLD LOVES ROCOCO."

Hector had finally taken in that something wonderful was happening but still had key questions. An African and a beautiful maiden? That would make him buy cocoa? How did one lead to the other?

"Um, Valerie?" he asked. "How does an African make people buy cocoa?"

"Wanting a warm cup of cocoa is a situation that anyone can understand. Anyone who has a television set, of course. The comfort of it is universal. Don't you get it, Hector? It is *mass*."

"I see."

Valerie strode over to Bette's chair. Bette could smell her perfume. Like a fresh mountain flower with a cold flowing brook.

"Very good, Bette," she put her hand on Bette's shoulder. It was the first human touch Bette had experienced since Hortense had pitifully embraced her goodbye. The warmth of a powerful hand on a tense, lonely shoulder. "You are learning very quickly."

"I have to," Bette said. And she felt like crying.

And then, of course, the inevitable ensued. The discussion of the need for a Negro actor and how to get one.

For a long time, no one could think of any, and then Hector thought of one.

"Paul Robeson?"

But it was Bette who surprised them all because, *coincidently*, she knew of a Negro actor. A Shakespearean. A noble . . . savage. And, unlike the blacklisted Mr. Robeson, Bette's contact was not besmirched and happened to be available.

You see, dear reader, once Cousin Bette had decided that she had to find a way to compete with Hortense, she assessed a number of factors. The best way for Earl to free himself would be to earn money. The best way for him to earn money would be to have an acting role. The best-paid acting roles were for those who appeared on television commercials. That's why the profits were so, as Hector put it, "inviting." But no television commercial would feature a Negro actor unless the message satiated the insistence of whites on subservient images that made them feel better about themselves. Reinforced in their superiority. Safe. Therefore, she concluded that she needed to create a television campaign with a job for a black actor, one that Hector and Valerie would accept, that she could use to both help Earl step forward toward financial autonomy and self-esteem, while bringing him back into a realm of engagement with her where negotiation was possible. And apparently, she had succeeded. So far. The other option being, of course, that in the face of this offer he would remember his true values, turn it down, and therefore stop shunning Bette. Believing that all human beings deserved respect.

Hector, at first, was choked up by all the sharing and group intimacy. But then came to his senses and was hit in the heart like a coronary by a return to balking at the immense expenses.

Yet again, Valerie knew exactly what to say.

"Are you scared?" she asked. As if it mattered.

So, of course he had to show her that, "Far from it!" he was *confident and fearless.*

This pleased Valerie, for, as she assured her colleagues, if they did something extravagant and pulled it off successfully, they would make their reputations. The investment would be worth it. And then, they would build their empire.

This finally persuaded Hector, but with one remaining complication.

"B-but," Hector blushed.

"Yes?" Valerie asked dreamily, as if that job was done and she needed to replenish her imagination before moving on to the next.

"The cash." He looked at his shoes.

Valerie put on a cinematic pout. "You were not going to pay for this out of pocket?"

"Uhmmm," he mumbled.

"Hector!"

The answer unfortunately was, "Uh . . . yes."

Valerie became very stern. It was clear that Hector

deserved to be spanked. And she was the one to do it. "Hector?"

"Yes?" His voice was very small.

"Listen up. FIND AN INVESTOR. A partner."

"Like who?"

She had to teach him everything. "Someone to come in with seed money. Offer them shares."

"Shares?"

"IN RETURN FOR THEIR INVESTMENT." The situation was becoming grave.

"Oh, I see," he leaked, even though he did not in fact *see*. "Is that how it's done? These days?"

"Great idea, Hector." That was Bette. She was learning quickly and waiting for Hector to think of things himself was taking too long, yet he couldn't just say yes to other people all day. He would feel bad. All her life Bette had observed women giving men credit for ideas that the men had not conceived. But only now did Bette understand why. It was so those ideas would be taken seriously! The world was making sense after all. She was feeling comfortable, in a new way. As though she were an insider who *gets it*. And could finally play by the rules to her own advantage.

Valerie noted acutely how quickly the old maid was catching on. Most people on the planet simply could not conceptualize beyond their task, but Bette could. That would come in handy.

Hector liked getting the approval, finally. He guessed he'd done something right. That felt good. At least. But now the money conversation had to resume again, and he hoped he'd have another revelation as generating of approval as the last. This time, though, it was Bette who offered the best solution. But Hector was fine with that, as he wanted her to not feel left out.

"You know," Bette proposed. The synchronicity of the moment astounded her. Really, she was shocked at how easy all this was, how naturally it all fell into place. How could something so complex come together under her tiny reign? And yet, events were conspiring to offer her opportunities. And now she was finally equipped to exploit them.

"You know . . . ," she continued.

Bette broke the news carefully to both of her collaborators, that, in fact, in addition to knowing a Negro actor, she also knew a potential investor. A financial partner who would definitely be interested and would certainly be good for the money. In fact, this candidate was her own cousin. Her own long-lost cousin. Crevelle. They had only recently been reunited.

"The woman's husband is enormously wealthy," she assured her hungry cohorts. "He's an extremely good-looking man. Even at his age. But my cousin, Crevelle, is very shy about her resources. She will participate, that I can guarantee. But no one must ever be so vulgar as to mention it to her face. You know," Bette added. "The reticent rich."

Valerie nodded with gravitas. She knew all about that from repeated personal experience.

"My cousin needs friends," Bette divulged intimately. "And confuses money with love. So, if Hector would just mix the martinis and never mention who paid for them . . . Well, I will take care of the more uncomfortable parts. Just flirt, Hector, flirt. Even though she is *married.*"

Hector couldn't keep up. She could tell. He wasn't bright enough to take a hint. She would have to S-P-E-L-L it O-U-T for him again.

"Good work," Valerie's soft mouth.

"And Hector," Bette coached, with some very hard looks. "Some flattery and attention from you cannot hurt."

He seemed surprised. "Really?" But then. Suddenly, it all came together inside his swirling, overwhelmed, thick, but existent consciousness, and he remembered Bette's earlier suggestion of how to make Valerie jealous. This perked him up considerably because today's activities had just enhanced his desire to make her jealous at all costs.

"Great," Valerie tossed off in Hector's direction. "Someone's got the ladies covered." Then she pouted. "But don't make me jealous."

"Really?" His heart fluttered.

So, they were settled then. A Negro actor. A young white girl. Sell shares to Bette's cousin. Everything in its place.

Valerie was very, very impressed with her new protégé. "Bette, you can tidy up *my* life anytime you wish."

But Hector wasn't sure what they had all agreed to, in the end. Especially how much it was going to cost. "Bette? Did you get all that down?"

"Oh yes," she said. "I took notes."

"Could you read them back to me?" He mopped his dripping brow.

"Of course," she said, expertly flipping open her steno pad. *Darky savage. Darky savage. Darky savage.*

Chapter 22

There are many men and women of all temperaments and stations in life on this earth who are sleeping with, making love to, and sharing their day with someone who may not be their first choice. Or even their third choice. Someone who really is not the "right person" for them for multitudes of reasons that will never be transformed, and yet, there can be a kind of tenderness there. There can be a relief, perhaps, that they will never be *that* close. That they will never matter *too* much. In a strange way, this arrangement suited Earl. Confiding everything to a man whose beauty slayed him, whose passion filled his heart—well, what had that led to? Anthony crippled by his family and then dying for no reason with everything unresolved? Earl knew he was in the company of millions of others whose mates had died tragically and could never be replaced. Yet they had gotten some recognition and subsequent caring while he only had Bette. He had tried to replace Anthony, day in and day out. There were all the men, so many of all ages and mind-sets, whose beauty moved him to insanity, to wanting and dreaming and craving and internalizing, always leading to heartbreak. To absence. To missing and losing. Always.

Earl did not see a way that this would change. He didn't intend to give up trying, but being with Hortense would allow for that. She would never, ever know what possessed him, and this would, in a sense, free him. He would be freed from his real feelings, distracted by her, and not lying at home alone at night shaking with loneliness. To have something else to fill his time. And Bette? He had tried living out the other half of love, not the body but the sharing of truths and matching of intellects, and where had it gotten him? He'd hoped she'd be some kind of anchor, permitting him to find love again, but instead she was a trap of comfort, keeping him from really living. Now she claimed they needed to *talk*. Well, he absolutely had no intention of ever speaking to her again. There was nothing there for him. And despite her whining, he'd told her so a number of times, clearly. He told her that *something's wrong and it's really big*. She hadn't listened. He told her he wanted to feel loved. He told her he couldn't bear to keep being the person no one else wanted to be. He told her clearly and openly over and over again. Yet she wanted him to change how he felt. She wanted him to come clean with Hortense and therefore return to nothing. Well, *fuck Bette*. Bette's plan was a recipe for loss, and he was staying out of the kitchen. No one was going to tell him how to feel. She didn't have the right, no matter how long they'd known each other.

There were ways that Hortense annoyed him. She didn't know anything, nothing. She had no information. But he liked explaining things to her, watching her eyes widen and then assimilate the newfound facts. She was smart, that one, naturally smart. So what if she couldn't see through the system? He didn't need that from anyone else. He had plenty of reality and insight himself. What he did need was some sweetness, someone who wanted him to be happy, who took care of things, and who built him up. Someone who believed he could do it, instead of spending their time trying to help him face that he couldn't. He liked her naïveté, it worked for him for now, but it didn't have to work forever. He didn't want it to. She was getting something out of it, a sense of independence from the horrible way she was raised. In the end, this would benefit her, he was sure.

Anyway, he deserved a break. He couldn't hunt heartbreak out of desperation forever and then sleep alone anyway. He was too old. It just hurt too much and that was a fact. If some nice guy found *him*, well he was open to that, certainly. But he couldn't get in the kind of trouble anymore that had come to define his life. And besides, there was the family money. Why shouldn't he have a piece of that? He just couldn't cut up animals all the rest of his days. The thought was unbearable. He could not do it. He could not. He'd seen white people with money before. The families hold it over their heads, but in the end they get a taste. Usually, Earl had observed, it worked out that way. It just required patience, and perhaps he could find some of that. If there was something waiting at the end of it.

Even if it was only a brief rest. That would be better than nothing. Okay, Hortense didn't know how to *do* things. She couldn't cook, she couldn't shop, but at least she tried. He didn't care what was for dinner as long as it was there. How she fucked up the Thirteenth Street apartment was beyond him. But, no matter. It didn't matter. He wasn't counting on her, and he didn't expect much. Whatever it was, that's what it would be.

Besides, Earl was feeling quite jaunty this day because he'd gotten the morning off from the Lazios' to go to an audition. It had been a long, long time since he'd been seen for anything or been in anything. Not since the last African walk-on for *Antony and Cleopatra*. He'd been snooping around uptown to see if there were any real parts to be had, but it was a strange in-between time. The American Negro Theater had been gone for some years now, and everyone was waiting, waiting for the next thing. What was it going to be? Some kind of new Negro ensemble starting up in 1958? Sure, that would be great. But couldn't there be more of a breakthrough than that? The movies were letting folks in bit by bit. Poitier, that lucky sucker. But there was more mixing in real life, so when was that going to show up on stage? Either more plays with better roles for black men, or more mixed plays, or more black plays being seen by everyone, or black people creating their own audience big enough to support the artists financially, or something. But it wasn't his arena, solving things that big. His job was to take the page and bring it to life. That's it. The work of writing that page, pulling together the cash, getting the house lit and tickets sold, all of that was not his job. His job was to make it worth their while. The audience. The truth was that, now that he was older, he worked so rarely he sometimes forgot he was an actor. Forgot to think like one. Hortense was bringing that back to him, he had to give her credit. And it had made him a bit more enthusiastic for the whole endeavor. She had no talent, poor thing. But she loved it. And you have to love the theater cause it sure as hell doesn't love you.

Anyway, there he was, 111 East Houston Street. The Rooftop Theater. This house was unfamiliar to him, but more and more crazy theaters were popping up everywhere he walked. Looked like they were in rehearsal for something. Actors hanging out, smoking, reading their scripts. He loved that. *Wait a minute.* Earl knew that girl, what was her name? He'd talked to her once in an audition room. *Anne?* Young girl. Sassy, smart-ass Irish girl.

"Anne?"

"Yeah?" She looked up. "Oh yeah, Earl, hey, how are you doing?"

"Anne Meara, right?"

"Yeah, right?" She had a big smile, young girl just at the beginning of it all.

"I'm here for an audition, what's going on?"

"It's *Ulysses in Nighttown*. Burgess Meredith is directing it."

"*Playboy of the Western World*? I saw that, on Broadway. What's he doing down here?"

Anne looked over her shoulder. "Blacklist," she mouthed. "Finally back to work."

"That's one talented fellow. Whoa, that's lucky for you. Congratulations."

"Yeah," she said, very pleased. "Yeah, his problem

is my break, crazy how that goes. Maybe that's on its way out, who knows?" She rolled her eyes and laughed. "You looking for auditions?"

"Yeah," Earl said.

"Upstairs, in the back."

"Okay, thanks. Hey, congratulations."

"Yeah, you too. In advance."

Earl climbed the stairs, coming upon a long hallway filled with actors waiting to be seen, nervous, hungover, confident, nihilistic. Studying the scripts or taking a nap. He signed in and sat down, waited his turn among the kids filled with energy, the old-timers still holding on, the theater rats—those are the lucky ones, working so much they live in theaters or hotel rooms or smelly, dirty basements, no time to cook a meal, they're on some stage, somewhere, every night. No clean laundry. *Ah, them's the good-old days.* Earl wondered what it would be like to be in a play again, hanging out with a gang. Bonding in dressing rooms, going out for drinks, confiding. The intimacy on stage when the actors connect and the audience connects and they're all living in front of each other at the same time, together. Then, the day the final show comes down it all disappears like it was nothing. A few years later he'd run into some guy he'd poured his heart out to every night, and it would be, "Hey, how are you?" Friendly and whatever, but kind of cold. That's the way it was.

"Earl Coleman."

"Right here."

He stepped into the room, the typical set-up. Three white guys behind a folding table. Glasses, smoking, blasé, blasé, blasé. One had his sleeves rolled up, that meant he was in charge. The director. One was sweating in a suit. Producer. One had thick glasses, that had to be the playwright. A white girl to the side taking notes.

"Morning all," Earl said, smiling. Showing his best self. That he is the one they would want to spend all that time with. All that hanging out and then *doing it*. Make an impression but not too much.

"Hi Earl," the director said, in a repetitive drone. He'd been giving the same speech for hours and knew it wasn't his job to impress. He had the power, after all. The power of selection. "Okay, page 34. Please read the part of Joe."

"Okay."

Director took a puff off his smoke, and, without bothering to put it out, looked down at the script on his table and, in the same careless monotone, read the role of the bright young white boy, Bobby, the hero of this play, which was called *No Heaven Like Earth*. According to the script, Bobby was twenty-two and trying to break out of his working-class Irish family in a small town in Massachusetts. He wanted to become something. But the girl he loved was a neighborhood girl, and she wanted a home, children, and the safety of the block. In this scene, Bobby was working in his parents' store. The train for New York would leave in three hours and he had already bought the one-way ticket.

Enter JOE, *the Negro worker, 50, carrying boxes and loading the shelves.*
BOBBY: What do you think, Joe?
JOE: 'Bout what?

BOBBY: 'Bout leaving behind everything you've ever known. Can it ever pay off?

JOE: Never know God's plan.

BOBBY: But is there a chance?

JOE: Always a chance. As long as you alive. Once you dead, ain't no more chance.

BOBBY: So, you think I should just . . . go for it?

JOE: Not for me to say.

BOBBY: Well, what will happen if I don't?

JOE: You tell me.

BOBBY: We'll be having this same conversation twenty years from now, with me behind the counter and you stocking the shelves, and I'd better be okay with that or it's not going to be a pretty picture.

JOE: Only the Lord knows what's best. It's our job to follow.

"Thank you, Earl," Director stopped him for a moment. "Let's try it one more time. Can you try to make it a little more engaged? Joe has worked for this family for years. He's a religious man, wants Bobby to do what's best. Invest a bit more. Okay, let's take it again."

The window was open, and suddenly the world was filled by a school of manic fire trucks storming the city, sirens hurling through everyone's consciousness, intruding with the news of *emergency, emergency.*

"Excuse me, I was just thinking . . ."

"Yes?"

Some spirit seized Earl—a bold, brash, angel-devil truth-telling machine when no such impulse should be indulged. *Emergency, emergency.*

"Well, I was thinking that some very bad luck has

brought Joe to this one-horse white town and this boring, demeaning job. The script doesn't say how long he's been there, and I prefer to think that it's just a few months. You see, *to me*, Joe is an actor, a Shakespearean actor. And he came up to Massachusetts with a road company production of *Othello* that went belly up when they got to Springfield. He's just doing whatever he can to get the scratch back to NYC, enough to get a new place and start all over. He couldn't care less what this honky-ass does with his life, but Joe doesn't want any trouble. So, he puts on this shuffling, this pretending he has no grammar, this *sho 'nuf* 'cause he knows the kid is on his way out, and Joe's just hoping that's going to mean more hours for him at the store so he can get home sooner rather than later. You know?"

There was a stunned silence. The producer was tapping his feet and shaking his leg, like a cocker spaniel waiting for his Alpo. Waiting for slop.

"No," the writer said.

"Thank you, Earl. Next."

Some mysterious force had come over Earl between sitting in the waiting room and seeing those fools behind the table. What was it? Almost like an alien possession or a dramatic hit of scarlet fever. A force simply larger than his own intentions, thoughts, needs, and plans had taken control of his mind. He didn't regret it, of course. But what was he doing? If he didn't want the part, he shouldn't have agreed to come to the audition. It was like he had outgrown reality. Just surpassed it. He was so ready to live in another time that he had just future hopped, like in those science-fiction stories. Only it's never black guys who travel to the future. They just carry the luggage. Yet that's what had happened in some strange way, Earl had transported through time to a moment yet to come, when things would actually make sense. When a black character in a play would be a real man with a real reason, with a real story, and a real heart. *It could happen.* Sooner or later. He knew it really could.

Shaken at how unshaken he felt, Earl both strode and staggered out of the rehearsal room. He had some decisions to make. And his eyes refocused on the hall filled with waiting actors, all far more willing than he to submit to the idiocy and therefore far more deserving of the roles. He saw another black face and realized that this lucky guy was coming in to read for Joe, and Earl hoped in his heart that the man would get the part. It was only then that Earl realized that the fellow actor in question was Frankie, up for the same role.

"Frank," Earl called out.

Frank got a pained look on his face. But such a distinctly different kind of pain than the last time Earl had seen him that he knew Lynette had showed her dad Earl's letter. It was all out in the open now, and Frank should know better than to still be so angry. Turned off, perhaps. Even disgusted, but certainly not as naive as he once was, and probably relieved that it didn't "work out" between Earl and his daughter.

"Hey," Frank said, looking up from his book. "You reading for Joe?"

"Yeah," Earl said. "But I sabotaged it. So," he laughed sarcastically. "I guess the part is yours."

Frank looked around at the sea of white faces. "Hope so." Then he put on his Stepin Fetchit face. "Once you dead, ain't no mo' chance."

They laughed. It was going to be okay.

"I don't know, Frank. Is it worth it to shuck and jive for the rest of our days? I'm having doubts."

"My point of view is clear," Frank offered, temporarily shutting his book, but keeping the page with his finger, ready to return as soon as he finished having his say. "I'm an actor. Regardless of the role, my job is to bring it as much dimension and humanity as I can. If I want different kinds of parts to be written, I have to be prepared to write them, and I am not prepared to do that. It's not my calling. My calling is to bring words to life. And I believe that part of the history of the black man is that we are exceptional at bringing meaning to nonsense. Do it every day. So, that's how I look at it. That's my job."

"Okay, well said."

"Okay." Frank was done. He wasn't going to be rude to Earl, but he wasn't going to be friendly neither. No cozy warm hugs and kisses by the fire. Just business.

Earl got the message. "Okay."

"Okay." Frank went back to reading his book. *Giovanni's Room* by James Baldwin.

Earl had heard of that one. He expected to read it sometime soon.

Chapter 23

In the past, the *home* and *office* had always been separate spheres for Bette. Home mattered and work did
not. Now there was no home, and work was going to be
the means toward getting hers back. They'd merged
into a single ongoing stream of thought. She realized
how much more one could accomplish when the entire
day was committed to it. How much more one could
plan and take care of details. Dividing the day into two
separate arenas of feeling just wasn't that productive
after all.

Riding home on the bus, trying to keep all her strategies straight was dizzying. The details of her plan had
accumulated with such depth and precision that they
superseded her ability to store them in her mind. She
took out a pencil and started making notes on the inside cover of the paperback book she had been carrying
around but hadn't yet had a chance to read. *Giovanni's
Room* by James Baldwin. It looked good, but who had
the time? At first she just jotted down key words, com-

ponents of the larger scheme. Soon though, she was pulling them into a kind of picture that she then realized was the prototype for a chart or map. When she got home, she took out four pieces of stationery and scotch-taped them together into the size of a placard or subway advertising panel and carefully, in clear block letters, wrote out her guidepost for action. When done, Bette tacked it up to her living room wall for study and inspiration, but, fearing that Hortense might potentially appear to beg two tablespoons of cream for her marshmallow cake, she decided instead to tape the sheet carefully to her window shade and then roll it up, like a treasure map or the plans to assassinate Hitler. All she had to do was pull the string and the shade would spin closed, concealing her meticulous call to action. This also made it easily accessible, available to be revealed with one tug, to be consulted whenever necessary. From then on, at the end of each day, Bette would pull down her window shade, unveil the Plan, and parade the war room, reviewing the list and checking off completed tasks with those pencils that she now pilfered from work and kept sharpened on her kitchen table.

THE PLAN

*1. Bring the power of Tibbs Advertising to my
   cause. Do this by being brilliant, and then
   let the others take credit for my ideas.*

CHECK!

2. Keep Earl living in this building so that he must see me, so that we can talk.

CHECK!

3. Create a humiliating job opportunity for Earl and that hamster that will let him see what she is really made of—how much she wants him to compromise his beliefs.

CHECK!

4. Offer her this job.

Hearing Hortense's footsteps padding down the hall, Bette conveniently rolled up her window shade, feeling like an Allied general analyzing the beachfronts of occupied France. Carefully, Bette placed her ear at the door and listened. Hortense and Earl were arguing. Clearly it had started on the street and carried all the way up the stairs. Good.

Bette could make out Hortense's whining Midwestern twang, the annoying bleat like blowing through a sheep's bladder. The girl was in over her head, Bette was sure. She did not have the skills for whatever subject they were arguing over and had fallen back on her most annoying tactics left over from a childhood she had never actually outgrown. Displayed all the traits that Earl would hate: empty reasoning, repetition, lack of thoughtfulness, shallow inquiry. Children shouldn't have to solve certain kinds of problems ever, such as food, shelter, and paying the bills. If they are burdened at too young an age, they will be doomed in the future, having never known what it is to be carefree. Real children, of course, have the right to cry, blame, or shirk until others complete the required tasks. But adults, Bette had learned, have to do everything themselves.

"Stop criticizing me," Hortense pleaded. "I only had enough money for coffee or milk. I made a choice."

Ah, yes. Bette recognized the dilemma all New Yorkers face at least once in their lives, if not once a day. Having to choose between taking a bus or buying a cup of tea. These are choices that the protected never imagine exist, until the dreary morning that fate makes a personal introduction.

The idea of economic boycott had long been in the American imagination. In the thirties, Jews boycotted stores that sold German goods. Even now, a Negro minister was directing a boycott of buses in Montgomery, Alabama. The goal was to strangle them economically so they would be forced to face facts: that the other party was real and seriously needed to negotiate a change. That this wasn't a joke at all. That was the message boycotts tried to get across. Well, Bette had been looking around with her eyes a bit wider open and had decided to apply this lesson of her time. Make things tight enough for Hortense and Earl that just concessions could be wrangled. Since Hortense had no idea it was Bette who held her allowance, Bette could siphon small amounts to Hortense in the guise of generosity, knowing that it was not near enough to live on. And Bette had rightly assessed that Hortense and Earl did not have the bond that she and Earl and Anthony had had during the Depression. They would not be able to be in it together with compassion, love, and humor. Instead they would grow rancorous and bitter.

And indeed they did.

Hortense squealed, "I could only afford one, so I bought milk. What do you want from me?"

"Can't you do anything right?"

Bette flushed at the sound of Earl's voice. She missed it with all her heart. That familiarity meant everything to her. He had witnessed her entire life and she his. Without each other, there was no past. No one knew. It would be as if none of it had ever taken place. Ever. Of course he wanted his coffee. He was a grown man who gets up and does hard labor all day long. And Bette could tell from his voice that he had obviously been drinking the night before.

"Earl, do not yell at me."

"You just make things worse." Earl slammed the door in her face, leaving Hortense to shiver in the hallway. Bette listened to her whimper. *Interesting,* Bette thought. *That isn't right. Earl shouldn't shut her out of her own house.* This was encouraging news, as far as Bette was concerned. Earl was out of control. He was doing all kinds of terrible things to all kinds of people, not just to Bette. Things that Earl would have condemned in others. He was not of the right mind. No, not at all. This discovery was a great relief. This was a phase, a fit, or an attack of some kind. Not a permanent, dramatic change of character. Only by reminding him in every possible surreptitious way of who he really was would things be brought to a positive conclusion. Of this, Bette was sure.

Expertly preparing her facial expression and grabbing her handbag as a prop to playact *on her way to the market,* Bette opened the door and acted *surprised* to find her young cousin Hortense, weeping in the stairwell.

"My dear, dear girl," Bette soothed. "What are you doing here? What is the matter?" She opened her arms lovingly to welcome the little rodent into her rattrap and patted down her matted gray fur.

"Earl got fired from the Lazios'."

Bette gasped. There was a God. Finally, she was sure. He'd now proved himself three times, so there would be no more doubt. This disaster was a gift directly from Providence. And at that moment, patting the little weasel comfortingly on the back, Bette understood the real reason why God had waited so long to reveal himself to her. Why it had taken fifty years of hard living to finally receive grace. The fact was that despite her guesses to the contrary, Bette had never truly been in need before. She thought she was, but it was never this acute. She would not be able to recover if the situation wasn't transformed. She had to win. The knowledge that she was on the receiving end of Providence's gifts swelled her and propelled her forward. Bette had been prepared to fight every step of this battle for reconciliation on her own. She had never been a lucky person, after all, and had never dared to even hope that fate would step in on her side. But here was an authentic reversal of fortune. An omen, if ever there could be such a thing.

"Why?"

"He won't tell me. All I know is that it had something to do with someone at work named Leon. Someone he would never see again. I don't have any more information than that."

Earl had slipped. He had been unable to conceal his true self, just as Bette suspected. He harmed his own plan for deception, and the question now was if Bette could muster the talent to maximize this moment of opportunity.

"Did you ask?"

"Yes, many times. But he won't explain." Hortense lost focus again and went back to her sobs. "Cousin Bette, how can you live with someone who won't discuss anything that matters?"

"How terrible for you, dear girl," Bette clucked, delighted. "There is nothing in this world more cruel than silence when one is owed an explanation. What are you going to do?"

"He wants me to stop taking classes."

"How awful."

"I know." Hortense took this cue to add a layer of indignity that she'd long held but had no arena in which to express. "He wants me to get a job!"

"NO!" Bette shook her head.

"I can't work a job," Hortense confirmed. "I wouldn't be any good at it." Her outrage at this imposition burned through her pale blue eyes. "I've got to be an actress. I can't serve plates of greasy eggs."

"But Earl is an actor and *he* had a job."

"I know," Hortense acknowledged, and then explained. "That's why he doesn't understand."

Bette nodded in sympathetic recognition. "Of course you can't get a job." She smoothed back the girl's hair, caressed her face, and then offered Hortense the advice that no one in the universe had ever thought to offer to Bette.

"Hold on to your dreams."

Bette was never supposed to have dreams. Only others had dreams. At least that's what Earl believed. Well, he was wrong. And soon he would understand. There was nothing more sabotaging for a person who would never succeed or excel than to encourage them to hold on to delusions that would not come true. It was an act of true destruction for which the recipient would pay and pay and pay. It was a guaranteed sabotage. The opposite of love. It was an act of hate, in fact, to encourage her.

"Thank you." Hortense looked up at Bette with the *trust* that only the most self-involved label other people's debased mirror of approval.

Bette felt that wild passion again. That thrill. The one that had come into her life on the phone with Mr. Swenson, the landlord from Thirteenth Street. Now, Bette realized that there was a reason for her life, and it was larger than being either a scapegoat or a rock. No, there was so much more there. She could be a person in her own right, whose well-being mattered. She could be the agenda setter, a protagonist. The one who wants *and* gets. She could be the instigator, the one who makes things happen and then reaps the rewards. But this transformation would only be fully realized if she, Bette, could focus enough to see how to dominate the system. Others had figured it out. The apparatus. And so could she. She could run the machine. But she had to be smarter than everyone else. Much smarter. Smarter even than her mentor, Valerie. One mistake, and Bette would be destroyed.

"Hortense, my dear," she said with an improvised

calm. "I just now had an idea. It's a small, strange idea. It came to me like an itch or an instinct. Hard to say. But perhaps . . . oh, dare I consider that . . . perhaps this could help you."

"You're always helping me." Little Hortense's eyes were appropriately red now. Her nose was running and her face was swollen. Oh, Bette appreciated the routine. Hortense thought her hysterics would win her . . . what? Not having to have a job while defying the family's standards? Well, whatever made her think that would be possible, it was stupid. And even more ridiculous was Hortense's susceptibility to flattery. She thought that Bette's compliments were true. What an idiot. *People from good families crumble under the least bit of pressure*, Bette concluded.

"Well, I may be speaking out of turn, but there is a possibility . . ." Bette laid on the hesitancy. "That is to say, something has come up at work. It can't be relied on, of course, but please permit me the time to tell you all about it and ask you for some advice."

"Of course."

"Thank you." *What a fool.* How could Hortense even think that Bette would want or need her advice?

Bette then carefully relayed, as if from memory, a conversation she claimed to have overheard in the office but which she entirely concocted out of air. She claimed to have *heard* that there was a vague possibility of some kind of job opening up soon. Perhaps something that might interest both Earl and Hortense.

"What kind of job?" Hortense asked with suspicion, as she definitely did not want to be a secretary like Bette, doing nothing all her life.

"Acting," Bette mentioned, as casually as a blimp crashing into the Empire State Building.

"An acting job?" Hortense abandoned her pose of despair and took on, instantly, that of ecstatic-hyster-ical-female-seized-with-joy, as one would be with an aneurysm of the brain. "For *me*?"

In this moment, Bette had the experience that her opponents had long known but she had just recently come to taste: the experience of saying something false and having the other respond from their deepest place of trust. It was strangely unnerving. Apparently noth-ing and no one could ever be trusted. This was news, and yet she did not mourn, as its knowledge elevated her to new heights of effectiveness.

Bette witnessed and was amazed by this prescient moment in her own life. She watched with wonderment as Hortense responded with such a deep well of feel-ing to something so patently false. It was incredible. The vanity of it. Oh, these false people who respond to falsity. The absolutely rotting excrement of their selfishness. How it showed them to be undeserving of respect. That engaged relationship to artifice.

In her three decades of simply going to work, doing her job, caring for Earl, listening, reading, making din-ner, looking out the window—the simplicity and truth of that life—Bette had never even had a glimpse that this other kind of existence could be so pervasive.

"Oh no," Bette shook her head.

"What's wrong?"

"I was just realizing that Earl . . . well, Earl . . ." Bette sighed. "He is a man of such great gifts. It would be unimaginable to ask him to make a television commercial, like he was a charlatan on the medicine circuit hawking snake tonic to unsuspecting housewives. It's not dignified."

"A TV COMMERCIAL?" Hortense was apoplectic. Her eyes glowed like blood diamonds. "For me? Oh, Bette. This is wonderful!" Her face exploded with hubris. Bette could see Hortense lapping up the milk. This was the greatest moment in Hortense's life, and the moment did not even really exist. How appropriate.

"Yes, of course," Bette said sympathetically. "I can see why *you* are excited."

"Oh God. Oh God. Oh, thank you, Cousin Bette. I will be on television. Television." And she skipped around the room like a little girl learning "Skip to My Lou." "Everyone will see me!"

"Yes," Bette said sadly. "Everyone will see you playing a queen."

"A QUEEN!"

"And everyone will see Earl playing a cannibal."

"Oh." Hortense's face fell in the tragedy of recognition. "He is not going to want to do that."

"I know," Bette said, thrilled to be reassured that Earl still had his standards. Then imitating Valerie's tactic of sealing the deal with silence, Bette waited. She waited for her young charge to take up the task.

"Maybe I can convince him."

Hortense was a greedy little pig, just as Bette had expected her to be.

"Do you think you can?"

"I will have to." Hortense squared her shoulders to the adult responsibility of getting someone else to work against their own best interests so that she could advance. But she was steadfast about it. Noble. As though helping Earl defile himself was an example of good citizenship. "I will have to convince him. We need the money, there is no escaping that. And he's not getting anywhere on his own."

"But if you try to convince him and he still won't . . ." Bette pulled on the guise of anticipatory sadness for Hortense's potential defeat.

" . . . Then I won't get the part either?"

Bette stared into the panic and nodded.

"Well, then. I'll just have to make him," Hortense resolved. "That's all there is to it. I will persuade him tonight."

There was something fascinating about working with a subject both intelligent and malleable. Hortense was quick, but she had no values. Her mind raced ahead, and so Bette could lead her toward particular conclusions. Hortense advanced two steps at a time, but Bette could now handle up to three. This particular chapter of the Plan would be more complex than the previous ones, but no matter. Now that her evenings were free, Bette had the time. It was a matter of commitment, and this, after all, was the most important task of Bette's life. Her devotion was boundless. Hopefully when this was all over and Earl stopped punishing her for the pain in his life, the two of them could apply some of these methods to getting him the production that he craved, of a play he was suited to perform. Why not? Anything seemed possible. They could do it together.

"*Good girl*," Bette borrowed from Valerie, spoken half to Hortense and half to herself. "When Earl sees what you really stand for and how much those values mean to you, then he will come to understand the real you, and only then, my darling Hortense, the truth, as has been said, *will out*."

"I'm going to be on TV." Hortense floated out of the apartment.

Once she was safely gone, Bette turned the lock in the door. She did not want to be disturbed. Solemnly, she stepped to the window, drawn by its magic. This time, however, she was not there to watch the movie of other people's world. No, cravingly, she pulled down the window shade and reviewed her notes.

4. Offer her *this job.*

Bette took out her black pen. The thick one she had bought at Woolworth's expressly for this purpose. Brandishing the marker like the sword of Excalibur, Bette made the long awaited mark of progress.

CHECK!

Chapter 24

Alphonso Lazio came back, after hours, to pick up the bottle of wine he'd purchased for his in-laws' anniversary. He'd made it all the way to the Third Avenue Bridge before remembering the gift was still sitting on his desk back on Gansevoort Street. But he could not show up empty handed. Not since the bad business with his cousin Stevie's house renovations. Everyone was calling Alphonso a "cheapskate," and he couldn't stand to have them think of him that way. So, he drove the forty minutes back downtown and rushed into the office to get the bottle. That's when he walked in on one of the black guys giving another black guy a blow job. Down on his knees, of all things.

"What the fuck?"

The young one, on the receiving end, looked up from his pleasure with an expression of terror, pulled out, zipped up his pants, and ran. But the old guy, who turned out to be that actor fruit, he just sat there on the floor like he couldn't care less. Like he didn't have a thing on his mind except a mouthful of dick. Like nothing could faze him, that guy. If you asked Alphonso, and no one did because whatever made him fire those men was something he did not want to discuss with his brothers, he would have said that the old guy wanted to get caught. That he'd almost had a smile on his face, and it wasn't from the BJ. Like he was happy to be out on his ass.

Walking home, Earl knew he was in trouble. More than usual, but he felt numb. *Money, whatever.* Something would come up. Maybe now he could move to Harlem like he'd always wanted to, didn't have the excuse that he could walk to the job. But as he wandered through those familiar streets of Greenwich Village, Earl also started thinking that something was changing around there. It had to do with his own attitude during the audition. How he didn't even have to think it over before blowing it up, and then Frank's advice to take it easy and be a professional. Was Frank right? Perhaps. Earl had to care a lot to keep ruining everything, didn't he? Was this investment just habitual, or did everything still really matter *oh so much*? Maybe nothing mattered, and he should just obey other people's orders and let it all disappear into air, his wishes. Maybe. The other thing that had hung around in his consciousness since that day was the brief conversation with Anne Meara. When she mouthed "blacklist," like everyone did, and then somehow they both realized it might be on its way out. If Burgess Meredith was directing again. Blacklist, bye-bye? Maybe soon. A new era. What would it be? Now Earl was fired, and he was throwing acting roles out the window. He had a *girlfriend* and was still on his knees. Everything was new now. It was all mixed up. That's the sign of change. Confusion. Stagnancy isn't confusing. Change is. Maybe something real was just about to happen.

Earl turned down Cornelia Street and saw an old dancer he knew named Joe painting a storefront, like he was opening a shop or something. 31 Cornelia.

"Hey, Joey."

"Earl. Long time."

"What's happening?"

"Well, you know, I retired from dancing."

Earl didn't know but wasn't surprised. Joe was too fat to make it as a dancer.

"I didn't know. So what's happening here?"

Joe was an Italian queen, a fag. Dark eyes, dark hair, eternally paunchy. Nice boyfriend named Jon who was an electrician or something.

"Opening a café. Or a theater. Or who knows. Caffe Cino. Two *f*s, the Italian way. Look, we're decorating. Fairy lights, mobiles, glitter dust, and Chinese lanterns. We're gonna put on shows, if I can ever pay off enough cops to get the right license. Come over, hang out."

"You got some good parts for black actors?" A challenge. Earl's mood.

"Just bring whatever you want to do. If your astrological sign lines up, you can put on a show."

Earl looked at Joe. It all made sense, somehow. It was in fact obvious—wasn't it? Some kind of fag theater where the guys could just do what they wanted to do. Some more guys who had come to the same conclusion. *Don't give a fuck* because they have nothing to lose. "Sure," he said. "I'll come by."

300

But as soon as he walked away, it seemed ridiculous. Joe Cino couldn't pull off anything. The place would close before it opened. But Earl would check it out, but . . . maybe. He didn't know what to think. *Leon, Leon, Leon.* He'd never see that boy again. That boy would run home and hide under the bed and get on the next bus to Tennessee, and that was that. Gone.

Earl dreaded going home and explaining all this to Hortense. And then he didn't care. He switched back and forth between hope and anxiety, fear, indifference, and boredom at his catalog of dilemmas. He passed a phone booth and weirdly had the thought to phone Bette and then quickly brushed it off. Then he turned down Eighth Street, looking at the junkies in Nedick's and the new beatnik shops slowly encroaching on the old Chinese restaurant: one from column A and one from column B. He passed the Eighth Street Bookshop, and there in the window was the same paperback that Frank had been reading. *Giovanni's Room* by James Baldwin, who everyone knew was a queen. Earl had three dollars in his pocket. He was broke. The book was ninety-five cents. He went in, purchased it, and then sat down for a couple of hours of slow twenty-five-cent beers at the Pony Stable Inn, surrounded by noisy bulldaggers and some quiet fags. Better there than to go to Julius's where the straight couples were oblivious. *How the hell could straight people be so selfish all the time? How come they never, ever, ever see what's going down?*

Earl opened the book and started to read, and didn't get up to stagger home until he had read the whole damn thing.

Well, Earl thought, crawling back to Tenth Street,

now that *was interesting. Unique,* he could honestly say. Every now and again, he'd remember a passage and open the book up under the streetlight of whatever corner he was on, trying to find the right page.

Like when the dirty, old, queer Frenchman, Jacques, wants to be a kind of wisdom figure for closeted, ashamed David . . . There it was, the passage Earl remembered:

> There are so many ways of being despicable it quite makes one's head spin. But the way to be really despicable is to be contemptuous of other people's pain. You ought to have some apprehension that the man you see before you was once even younger than you are now and arrived at his present wretchedness by imperceptible degrees.

That's where Earl had once lived, but he wasn't there anymore. The book was describing something he knew very well but had left behind. There was just a blank there now. The era of fantasy had run ragged over his will, soul, and desire for so long, and yet, he had to admit, it had dissipated and—poof!—seemed to be gone. He'd humiliated Bette and Hortense. Now he felt better. He felt deader. Better or deader? Hmmm. Sure, Leon got his dick hard, his heart pumping and all of that. He loved Leon. He did. But there was a sadness that was bigger than all of it really. So, what was that sadness going to give him? What was he going to get out of it? Something was going to give, to give in. The world was going to give in or else he was on his way down further. Down so much further. How much further was there left for anyone to fall?

You want to be *clean*. You think you came here covered with soap—and you do not want to *stink*, not even for five minutes, in the meantime. . . . You want to leave Giovanni because he makes you stink. You want to despise Giovanni because he is not afraid of the stink of love. You want to *kill* him in the name of all your lying little moralities. And you—you are *immoral*. You are, by far, the most immoral man I have met in all my life. Look, *look* what you have done to me. Do you think you could have done this if I did not love you? Is *this* what you should do to love?

Nope, that's not me. He knew. It wasn't gonna be that easy.

Chapter 25

It was a short number of long days until the party Bette would give, the denouement of the Plan. But with the newly acquired discipline of her commitment, she imagined, planned, and carried out a perfect evening. Not only had she never thrown a party before, the truth was that she had hardly ever been to any. That is to say, invited to a gathering in a person's home for fun, where they provide everything needed and all one is expected to do is enjoy. It would be going too far to say that she *liked* parties, as a result of this one. But they certainly were demystified greatly in her imagination.

Bette had never bought so many groceries before, and there was no way to get them all home. Fortunately, the young night clerk from the Albert had gotten to work early with nothing to do and had kindly carried the bundles into her apartment.

"I got five rejection letters so far," he sighed, needing to confess his failures to every person on the path.

Each time the manuscript came back he had to re-type the torn or coffee-stained pages, place it in a fresh envelope with a fresh return enclosed, and pray on the way to the post office. Sometimes its pages would be barely ruffled, and Sam's heart would break. *How could they know if they won't take a look?* He had no idea of how any of this really worked. Don't they want the best book, or was it all whim?

"What's the title?" Bette asked, unpacking her bags and calculating all the tasks before her, assured that they would be completed if she would just do and do and do.

"'The Cosmopolitans,'" Sam said, proudly. He enjoyed his title. "I wanted it to sound like a Henry James novel but with an ironic twist. What does it mean to be truly sophisticated in the ways of city life in the modern age? In 1958 it's not society etiquette and the grand tour of Europe, that's for sure. It's a savvy of a very different sort. More barroom than drawing room. More subway than carriage. It's the mix, not the separation, that makes someone *cosmopolitan.* In my view."

"I like Henry James," Bette said absentmindedly, and then realized she had not been listening to the boy, and felt badly because he was discussing his dream after all. "Here," she said, trying to make amends. "Do you want this copy of *Giovanni's Room*? I've been carrying it around for weeks and will never have time to read it." She rummaged in her purse and handed over the paperback. "Oh, I'm sorry, I've scribbled all over it."

"That's okay," he said, mildly interested, jamming the paperback into his jacket pocket, between the four pens he always carried and that tiny notebook filled with observations. "I'll take a look when I get a chance." And he went back across the street to start immediately on a brand new novel, about a girl this time, who meets a young hotel night clerk who holds the keys to her dreams.

Bette began slicing, placing, cleaning, organizing, and doing all the labor of welcoming others. The agenda for this party was a complex one and orderly snacks and drinks would help bring events along to their desired climax. Of course, there is the old adage that one can't control other people. But on the other hand, other people seem endlessly able to control *one*. That's the game, isn't it? Becoming *them*. And the rub. Without intention, their blows are unavoidable while one's own gestures seem to evaporate before given a chance to land. Yet, here Bette was determined to have an impact, and *then* what? In that switch lay the power play. If her plan were to fully succeed, how would it feel to watch others be forced to react to her? Fun for its own sake? Yes, to a degree. Satisfying beyond measure? Absolutely. She could feel huge burdens fall away. With Earl she had never prepared her actions or speech. She was a sap. With this crew, however, our lady was stocked to the gills with the newfound insight of selection. She knew that through awareness came preparation, so all surprises and disappointments created opportunities. To react. For the first time in her life, our Cousin Bette was ready to take the reigns no matter what.

There had never been so many people in apartment 2E. She felt a simple pleasure in that fact alone. It was informative to discover how many could fit comfortably. That actually there was quite a bit of space between the bedroom, kitchen, dining area, and living room. It had felt small, like a cage or a trap, when she sat in there alone, but with others gathered about, it was fine. More than adequate. The distraction of activity was enjoyable, but it was second to the enormous pleasure of watching her play come to life. Just as she'd carefully imagined. And now she had a title for it: "The Cosmopolitans."

Bette took her place on the sofa. She leaned over gracefully and whispered to Crevelle, the way they had before, regularly, when they were girls. Before Frederick lied. Now, because of how Bette was reacting to Earl's cruelty, taking control, she had created the opportunity to return to that very same moment, with the same cousin. She had given herself the chance to *relive*, literally, the delicious feeling of nostalgia. She had forgotten that this alliance ever existed, but once reenacted, it felt natural. It brought back the long-repressed knowledge that her entire life had, in fact, occurred. That she and Crevelle had been friends. Even though it was a conscious deployment now, it was still easy to conspire, gossip, have inside jokes. Bette pantomimed the "natural" intimacies of family. They really could and should have been hers all along, she knew that finally.

Valerie quickly made herself at home, as though apartments like Bette's were her natural habitat. She made no comment about the television in the middle of the living room, now serving as a banquet, covered with a tablecloth and bottles. Valerie easily glided over to the Victrola and flipped through Bette's records, looking for music that fit her mood. There were some that surprised her as being rather fashionable sounds of previous eras. Good music of the past. She realized Bette had known something at some point, about the world she lived in. That in her own weird way, old Bette had at some point been cool.

Hector got busy mixing the third round of martinis. He used a recipe that his father-in-law relied on religiously back in Connecticut, where mixing martinis was a competitive sport. The catalyst for all of life's most important moments. Hector had finally found a practical use for that television set. It was now the bar, a far more effective social role than any Bette could have come up with. She'd found it useful as a drying rack for hand-washed clothes, but beyond that it sat inert, like a piece of sculpture in the middle of her life.

When Crevelle leaned in even closer, Bette smelled her perfume. It was the same scent as the flowers in the fields outside Ashtabula. The freshly succulent, a smell not to be found in New York City except in the Flower Market just after sunrise. Bette remembered it. And then she was uncomfortable, recalling how lovely those fields could be. How soft. The sun roasting her back. A deep longing stabbed her. But she had prepared for that, so now she had the fortitude to wait it out. So what, after all, if she had a bad feeling? That went with the territory when one had larger goals.

"This is my third evening with Hector since I've returned to New York," Crevelle cooed. "My head has turned."

Bette saw how flushed her cousin was. She seemed

drunk with a new kind of freedom, the illusion of expansion of emotion and experience. That was the treasure that the city had always promised. Bette twinkled. Another newcomer to the power of that dream. How ironic.

"Turned and turned," Crevelle giggled. "You and I have made no progress with Hortense, and yet everything in life feels changed."

"Do you like him?" Bette touched her lips to her cousin's ear.

"He loves me."

"How do you know?" She had practiced this too. She focused on each moment with the intensity of a plunging gorge at the base of a shattering waterfall. Finding the right intonation to convey that the details of how beloved Crevelle found herself to be were the most important acts of life.

"He treats me like I am making his future possible," she sighed, amazed.

Crevelle said this in a Midwestern elocution-class sort of way. She was still locked into the buttery, second-rate Victorian manners of the ancient, derivative culture clinging to the bourgeoisie of the central states.

"He treats me," Crevelle slurped, "like I am bringing him closer to the things he needs the most. He sees me as something more than just myself. In Hector's eyes, I am . . . almost . . . a symbol. Yes, he sees me as a symbol of everything he's ever really wanted. The electricity between us is . . . palpable."

That was the same word Hortense had used. *Palpable.*

Bette looked over at Hector. His eyes were on Valerie. Yes, little Hector was finally able to feel passion. It made Bette feel almost warmly toward him. Almost somewhat protective. Both Valerie and Hector were stimulated by Crevelle's influx of cash. They felt more attractive as a result. Hector had propelled this lust toward making Valerie jealous. And so, all of his desire for Valerie was, as Freud would say, *projected* onto Crevelle, the *thing* that could get him what he had to have. He had turned Crevelle into an item, a stapler or a button. Something he needed in order to get something else. *Bravo,* Bette thought. It was amazing what marketing could do when applied to daily life.

"Do you love him?" Bette whispered seductively.

"Bette!" Crevelle blushed. "I am a married woman."

"But," Bette fed her hypocrisy. "Doooo you?"

"Oh," she fluttered. "Bette, I am losing my head. I've never felt so valuable before. So powerful. And just for being me. Me! What am I going to do?"

Bette knew, as she watched her cousin be led down the path to ruin, that there was nothing so informative as seeing people be misled. She had never sought out the falsity of the world before because she had never had to fight falsity. She had been protected. Bette had simply stayed in her honest apartment, done her fair job, and loved her true friend. Now, Earl's turn had thrust her into the world of the terrible others, and there were so many of them. And they were so awful. On one level it was fascinating, the quantity. But suddenly, for one moment, she was overcome by something between nostalgia and clarity, and missed her own life so deeply. As she looked around the party, she took in the full range of her loss. The loss of Earl was the loss of herself. Were she not facing such enormous stakes, she would rather have collapsed into bed and burst into tears. She missed him so much. She was sadder than sad. And here, at this moment, she learned the harsh truth about parties. If the person you love is shunning you, no party will bring joy. One doesn't undo the other, after all. And this knowledge was a surprise. Where was he? Where *was* he?

"Follow your heart, Cousin," she told Crevelle, without betraying a tinge of interior truth. "This is New York. It's a long, long way from Ashtabula, Ohio. You can be yourself here. Or somebody else."

"Yes," Crevelle smiled with the poison of permission. "I can be somebody else."

Hector arrived with the martinis on a tray.

Valerie chose a fairly recent Mel Tormé album and put it on the turntable.

Hector held out his hand in invitation.

"I've got the world on a string," sang Mel.

Crevelle looked at Bette and then stood to take Hector's hand.

As they danced, he surreptitiously turned toward Valerie to gather emotion and then back to Crevelle to deposit it.

Bette sat, lonely on the couch, surprised and pleased to have her sadness interrupted by a visit.

"Can I join you?" Valerie plopped down beside her with an energetic bounce.

It didn't take long for Bette to scan from Valerie's friendly, teasing eyes to the familiar piece of paper she held in one hand. Realizing what it was, Bette twitched with fear, as though shouted out by a ghoul.

311

"I found this under your window shade," Valerie said. She was still smiling, as if she had instead said, "Lovely party." Valerie held Bette's very ornate plan in the clutch of her painted fingertips.

Bette now automatically learned from every move Valerie Korie had ever made. *So, that's how they do it*, Bette thought through her terror. *Smile no matter what.*

"I see," Bette said calmly. Then she smiled.

"Yes, our Rococo campaign is about to launch."

"Yes," Bette grinned.

"The stakes are very high."

"Everything depends on it," Bette said. *Agree*, she remembered. *Agree.*

"I admire how much you care," Valerie said softly. She was very friendly. "About the company."

"Thank you."

"In fact, I admire how much you care about your work. And about the future of television. This checklist of yours is very commendable. It's efficient, systematic, and modern. You are a great employee."

Compliment, Bette noted. *Always compliment.*

"Thank you so much, Valerie. There is something so very exciting about working this way. I've learned a lot from you about thinking ahead and then implementing it. It's so energetic. And personal. It's fun. To care about what comes next."

"We all have personal motives," Valerie said, driving the train.

"I'm glad. What are *your* motives?"

"Ha-haa!" Valerie laughed even though nothing was funny.

Laugh, Bette noted.

Valerie smiled at nothing, looking gorgeous, then sensuously surveyed the room as though decoding and processing everything in her view. She turned back to Bette, bright red lips pursed, and then relaxed into an expression of pure honesty. This was the pose of how one speaks to the only person one has ever truly relied on. The only sure person in one's life. The only person who is real. The only person who matters.

The only one, Bette noted.

"But if I tell you," Valerie seduced. "Then I will lose my allure. You will have power over me, and then I will have to remove you from the scenery. Telling the truth is a momentary impulse with terrible long-term consequences."

Bette was breathless. "I learn so much from you," she said. And it was true. "I listen to everything you say." And that also was true. In fact, this moment was the only authentic interaction Bette had had with another human being since the day Earl admitted that he did not love Hortense. The truth felt so familiar, nourishing, rehumanizing. It was valuable, important, loving, true. Bette felt love and relief.

"Well, look at me," Valerie invited. "I am an Irish girl from Hell's Kitchen. Surprised?"

Bette looked. She had imagined Boston Brahmin or a belle from a plantation in South Carolina. Or a rancher's daughter from west of the Rockies. But now that it was on the table, that Irish girl was in there somewhere.

Valerie spoke in her native tongue, the beer-soaked New York brogue of the dismal West Forties. "My

313

fadda wuz a cop," she said. "My mudda wuz a maid."
Like everything else, this also looked natural on her.
"Do you understand what I just said?" She let the
washerwoman within simply drop away and resumed
her sophisticated, tough-as-nails, free-spirited, entrepreneurial image. It looked natural as well.

"Yes," Bette said. "Your father was a police officer and your mother scrubbed other people's dirty
underpants."

"Yes," Valerie said. "And they wanted the same for
me."

"But you wouldn't let them ruin your life."

"No," Valerie said very calmly. "I would not."

This is what the two of them held in common. Some
profound survival instinct, even with the people they
loved. Bette's losses passed through her. Her family.
Earl. Hortense. The familiarities and kindnesses. The
fun. The irreplaceable knowledge of comfort with another human being. Her belief in Earl. That he could
do the right thing. She still held it. That loss would be
unbearable. It would never leave her.

"Did they ever understand?" Bette asked.

"No."

"Never?"

"No," Valerie smiled.

Always smile.

"They tried to stop me," she said. "Surpassing your
family is a huge commitment. But I did it! I worked
hard and became . . . not a cop, not a maid, but . . . A
TEACHER!"

This came out with an uncharacteristic bitterness.
One she had never let Bette see before. The contempt

in Valerie's voice for herself was startling. It was the first critical moment, this self-disgust for her previous life. How much she mocked it.

"What is wrong with being a teacher?"

"Oh, Bette." Valerie opened Bette's cigarette case, but it was empty. "I naively believed that working inside someone else's system was better than letting my father run my life. But, it was just another version of the same hell."

Bette knew that there was an unopened pack of Luckies in the top kitchen drawer, but she preferred to watch Valerie be uncomfortable.

"Then, one day, I was walking to work, and I passed a display window filled with television sets. Everyone stopped in their tracks, staring. What they were seeing in that display window was more important than dinner, waiting paychecks, or their lover panting in anticipation at home. And the pretty girl standing next to me leaned over and whispered, 'I wish they would watch me like that.' And I thought, *I wish I could make them.*"

"Why?"

"Because I wanted to."

"For what reason?"

"Just to do it."

It had never occurred to Bette that someone would go to all this trouble, all this investment and commitment, that someone would change the way they act and order what they do without a larger goal. Simply to have the power over others. For the *hell* of it.

Literally.

Bette could not imagine going to these lengths without the goal of ending Earl's shunning. How could someone choose this path as a kind of unarticulated sport? Bette hardly knew what to think. Did this make Valerie an even more dangerous figure in Bette's field of action? Or, was she now less threatening for having no motive? Or, was the empty motive actually more compelling than the full one? Was its possessor entirely amoral and therefore lethal? Only time would tell.

Chapter 26

Five minutes later, Bette was still thinking this over.
Why hadn't Valerie asked Bette for her own reasons? Maybe Valerie's feigned acceptance of Bette's
elaborate plan was not feigned at all. She simply didn't
care. It was all the same to Valerie, she assumed that
everyone else was as ruthless as she was. Every deed,
honest or dishonest, moral or corrupt, was assumed to
be a gesture toward a goal. The content of that goal
didn't matter. It was the strategy that mattered. And
she assumed that everyone had one. Valerie had to
understand other people's strategies so that she could
beat them.

Assume, Bette noted.

The doorbell rang a few times before Bette heard it
over her own thoughts and the sounds of Mel Tormé.
But Valerie was still speaking, so Bette let someone
else attend to it.

"I knew you would understand," Valerie told her.
Girl to girl. "After all, Bette, you have your own allure.

I'm intrigued by the next task on your list." She held the chart up to Bette's face, then turned it toward her own and read out loud, "'Tell Crevelle the truth.' About what, I wonder?"

The doorbell rang more insistently. Hector and Crevelle were dipping and turning, they would not respond. So, finally accepting the responsibility of hostess, Bette rose to answer. She wondered if it would be a neighbor complaining about the noise. That was another new experience. Making noise.

"Excuse me," she nodded gracefully to the other partygoers, winding her way to the door, picking up plates and glasses on the way, and nodding happily to the happy guests.

Bette opened to find an angry, middle-aged, balding man. He was slightly overweight, so typical and absolutely defined by his rage. Was he the new tenant who had moved in down the hall? She had noticed the boxes but had yet to meet the inhabitants.

"GET OUT OF MY WAY!" he yelled at Bette, as though being in his way was her only function on this planet. He pushed past her and stormed into the room, casting his eyes about the personnel.

"Can I help you?" Bette asked, futilely.

"Where is my . . . CREVELLE!"

Crevelle was still dancing with Hector, but turned, mortified, mid cha-cha, and she paled with an expression of absolute terror. Her voice jumped from fear.

"Frederick," she gasped.

"So it's true," he spat. "You are a tramp."

Floundering and trapped, Crevelle said whatever meaningless words that happened to come to mind.

"What are you doing here?"

"*WHAT AM I DOING HERE?* You stupid bitch. Look at you. How could you? Idiot!"

At this point everything stopped. Everyone froze. Only the record played.

"What are you doing here?" she repeated, having lost all that remained of her wits, which had been meager in the first place.

Then he slapped her.

"Hey," Hector said, although he made no move forward toward action. In fact, he stepped back and out of the way.

Grabbing Hector by the shoulders, Frederick shouted in his face, "You're that bastard playboy, Hector." Spit landed on Hector's cheek.

Hector, having never been in such a highly frazzled state of risk in his entire life, summoned up a level of emotional indignation also previously unknown.

"Get off me!" he yelled back, and punched Frederick in the jaw, propelling the fellow to the floor. Hector then immediately pivoted and ran to hide behind the couch.

At the thud of Frederick's landed weight, the needle jumped off the record, and the room was suddenly without soundtrack.

In that silence, Crevelle, still three steps behind the action, turned to Hector, crouched beneath the couch cushions. "This is my husband," she said blandly.

"Oh, I'm sorry," said Hector, half rising as though to shake hands but really not. He was suddenly distracted by his new, unfamiliar personality. Dissociated from his own actions, he fell back on his most reliable self, returning to the state of apologetic half-wit who hoped to never do anything wrong. Head between his hands, he wished to disappear.

Finally, gathering what remained of her abilities and relying on years of social training, Crevelle accepted the reality of the present moment. She was a wife. She had certain things that had to be done and said, and so be it. She readjusted. Crevelle ran to her husband and reached for his arm.

"Darling," she said, as if he'd simply slipped. "It's not what you think. This is the man putting our daughter on TV."

"And that's supposed to make it all right?"

"Well, it's . . ."

"It's what?"

"It's fun," Crevelle admitted, hauling up his carcass.

"Fun?"

"People will see her," Crevelle explained.

Frederick felt as though the world had gone insane and lost all its order. This was not ordered. "You sold your virtue to put your child on television? And I am supposed to nod my head and understand? What kind of man do you think I am?"

Crevelle was faced, now, with the reality that she had no way out. She had taken a wrong turn, made the wrong move, and hence she was going to pay. It was irredeemable.

"Darling, I . . . oh my God . . . what have I done? Please forgive me . . . I didn't mean . . ."

"You didn't?" Frederick screamed. He was free to scream as he went about his daily life at home, and this special occasion benefited from that habit. "Well,

320

then, if you didn't *mean it*, how did the entire country become aware of your treachery?"

"I . . ." Crevelle was confused now. As was the rest of the room. There was more to this story than even they knew.

"Thank God," Frederick reached into his breast pocket. "Thank God that someone in this insane world had the decency to send me this letter." He pulled it out and waved the evidence before the mob.

"Letter?"

Crevelle was stymied for the moment. She had a lot to contend with. And now she had to incorporate a letter. Who in the world would write a letter? And then, the world split open and Crevelle realized. She realized the level. The level of deception. She turned to Bette, standing by the door.

"YOU! YOU HORSE! YOU HAVE BETRAYED ME!"

Bette thought of Valerie and smiled.

Frederick stepped forward and grabbed his wife's arm as if it were a raincoat or a golf club, as if she were a person who was under arrest. No will, no agency, no choice. "Blaming your lies on the maid isn't going to help you."

"The maid?" Crevelle had her only laugh. "Yes, yes, she is the maid. The old maid. Oh, Frederick. Yes, the maid. The maid."

Frederick looked at Bette. There was something vaguely, uncomfortably familiar.

"Who are you?"

Bette had waited thirty years for this moment. And now it had come. And strangely, it was Earl who had brought it to her. It was Earl who had woken her up from her happiness and forced her to seize her own fate. Make it happen the way she needed it to happen. Her needs. And here they were. Here it was. Frederick was no longer shunning her. Instead, he was standing in front of her, in her own home, looking at her and speaking to her. Even if he was angry, it was still an interaction, a relationship. There was still a back and forth. Not an erasure but an engagement. Her heart overflowed. She felt a simple peace in just seeing him. At being spoken to. A long-desired satisfaction at having finally made him notice all the pain he had caused surged through her. She felt good. This was the way that things should be. People must face each other and speak honestly. They can't throw the other away as if she doesn't matter. Everyone matters. Everyone deserves acknowledgment. There is no amount of privilege or currency or deception or wish that can keep any individual, in the long run, from that moment of accounting.

"Bette?" he asked.

"Yes, I am Bette."

"You got my daughter into this hell."

She had anticipated the possibility of this degree of weakness. She'd had thirty years to assimilate the extent to which Frederick was a liar. She had done the work to accept that he took no responsibility for his actions. She had faced the level of pain that he was willing to cause. Bette had fully come to terms with the degree to which Frederick would rather destroy someone else's life than tell the truth and make amends. So, the fact that he was blaming her, once again, for something that she did not cause was not a surprise.

She stood there and calculated. Frederick had caused his own carousing. He had caused the alienation of his daughter. He had caused his unloved wife's desperate greed for attention. All of this, he was now blaming on her. That fact did not surprise Bette in the least.

She told him the truth.

"Hortense came to me looking for help and guidance, and I took her in and loved her because she is your daughter."

"Guidance?"

"I feel so happy to see you," she said from her purest heart. "I know that we can solve this by talking, finding forgiveness, and making amends."

This was the moment for him to accept her gift.

"This is all your fault."

Immediately she forgave him again. This time for continuing to lie.

"Don't fall back on your habit, Frederick. Be kind now, and everything will be all right."

"What do you want?" He stared at her like she was a faded mirror refusing to release the promised reflection.

Ah, relief. She felt so happy. He had finally asked her something, something that needed to be asked. The blaming had stopped now. And finally, with this question, the real conversation could begin. Quietly, Bette felt a leap of joy. Something so long buried finally returned to her life. Hope.

With this hope, Bette was fully alive again. She was again the person who mattered, the young girl with a life of love before her. A person to whom others would be accountable. Hope.

"I want you to tell the truth so that there can be a healing."

"The truth?" Frederick looked around shyly. Hector, Crevelle, Valerie, and Bette were watching him. He felt strangely boyish, now. Nervous. Frederick felt naive, almost innocent. It was easy to feel this way. "The truth is . . ." He looked around again. The faces of the others were blank. They seemed to say *go on*. "This is so hard to say." He actually gulped. "The truth is . . ."

"Yes?" Bette was filled with love.

"The truth is that you offered yourself to me, knowing that I was about to marry your cousin. And when I turned you down flat, you pretended that I had been disloyal to Crevelle. I have never been disloyal to Crevelle." There, he'd said it. He'd pulled it off. Everyone was listening, and he'd said the right thing. Frederick felt happy.

Bette's heart fell so low. Lower than it had ever fallen. "That is not the truth."

"Yes, it is."

Bette watched him. His lips twitched. He was vicious. He would not confess.

"Look," Bette said. "It doesn't matter. You don't know how to do right. I forgive *you*. Do you hear? You can't allow anything real to happen, but I can. I am not dependent on you, Frederick. Your life is filled with inauthentic relationships of mutual use. I forgive you. *Now*, you can forgive me so that we can be a family. Frederick, please." This was the third time in Bette's life that she had begged: her brother, Earl, and now this. "Please, choose forgiveness as an act of will."

Would he?

Bette watched him. She saw the young man within the old, the lover within the user, she recognized every good thing that had ever been and could ever be.

"You are insane," he said. "You ruined Hortense's life."

The spell was broken.

It was over. The opportunity. It is amazing what people will throw away.

Then, from somewhere far off came a siren. It was Crevelle, shrieking with the glee of the victorious cruel. "Don't you pretend to be good," Crevelle splattered. "You are not good. You are evil. *Evil*. We are good."

"I am helping you," Bette whispered. "I am helping you become real."

They were all frozen then. It was a climactic moment and everyone knew it. Capitulation hung in the air, a threat that would never be indulged. It was quiet, and then, the moment passed.

Frederick grabbed Crevelle's hand, "Let's go." He dragged her to the door.

As Crevelle attempted to pull off a victorious exit, she knew that a beating was waiting for her on the other side of triumph. Would he berate her in the hall or wait until they got to the street? And then she would have to go back home and face his rage forever.

"Stop!" Bette screamed. *He can't leave now. This is the moment for change.* "Wait!" she yelled. And then she plunged into the strongest impulse she'd ever had. The one she'd always fallen back on, the one that had come to define her more than any corpuscle or cell. The impulse to tell the truth. "Frederick keeps Mildred Tolan in an apartment over the movie theater. And he goes there on Monday and Thursday nights."

"Those are your poker nights." Crevelle's face blanched through her shame.

"Now, wait," Frederick, embarrassed, assessed his audience.

"Don't you see?" Bette said. "I am telling you all the truth."

"I curse you," Crevelle said. But she had no punch. It was just a fact.

"You curse me, Cousin? But everything I tell you is true. It is true that you have no husband. It is true."

"But I do not want to know what is true."

"But I do." Bette finally tired. "The lie serves you, but it destroys me."

Frederick realized that there was nothing further to be gained. He knew from years of crooked, small-town business deals that the current damage was already the result of engaging too long. *When you can't come out ahead, cut and run.* That was his motto and it had worked all his life. If someone is going to be uncomfortable, it's not going to be Fred. Nope. He'd rather eat glass.

"Crevelle," he said with confidence. "What is true does not matter. What matters is who decides. I decide what is true." Then he stepped out into the hall before anyone could dilute his defining last word.

Crevelle glanced in Bette's direction. "I hate you," she said. Then she stole a look at Hector, turned, and followed her mate.

When the door closed behind Crevelle, the rest of

the room lingered in silence. Bette had forgotten the others were there. So rarely was anyone else there, it was a new fact, hard to assimilate. But once she faced it, she felt no shame before them. She did not respect Hector, and so what he saw did not matter. And she knew that Valerie had seen and done much worse in her day, she wouldn't care about anything except for what she, herself, could get out of it.

The only person who mattered was Earl. Bette wished she could see his face. She wished that she could talk to him about what had just happened. Even if he were to marry Hortense, falsely, she still wanted to see him. Bette could be flexible. Earl telling the truth was perhaps not the most important thing. It was more important that she see her friend. That the shunning stop. Bette realized that she would accept any terms if the shunning would stop. She would be their bridesmaid and clean their house if she could talk to Earl and he would be kind. That bitter, terrible, daily, undeserved shunning. If only they could talk.

"Bette," Hector carefully approached her. "Are you okay?"

"Yes."

"I have never seen you like this," he said with some awe.

"Bette has always been like this." Valerie was calmly smiling, unwrapping the pack of Luckies she had discovered in the kitchen drawer. Slamming them against the back of her hand and leaning into Hector for a light. Which, despite his shock, he automatically provided. Some things can never be unlearned, and the symptoms of class are fiercely on the list.

Ahh, Valerie's smile. So sincere and effective. She looked Bette in the eye, invoking their secret sisterhood of the modest transformed. "Tell Crevelle the truth," Valerie said. Then she pointed her finger like it was a pen, and made a mark in the air. "Check."

Everyone stood very still.

Suddenly, Valerie puckered. "The check!"

"What about it?" Bette droned, her mind everywhere else.

"Has Crevelle's final check to the company cleared?"

"Yes," Bette chanted dully. "It cleared."

"Good." Valerie was back to normal. "Good girl."

"Good girl," Bette repeated.

Bette wanted to go to the window. To sit in her chair and look out upon the world, but somehow she could not. She could not move.

"Bette, I wonder what is next on your list." Valerie exhaled, flicking the ash into Crevelle's half-filled cocktail, so expertly chilled it was still sweating.

"Oh God," Hector held his stomach, ready to expel three martinis.

"Are you all right, Hector?" Valerie brought her most feminine concern to his immediate care. "Let me take you outside for some air."

Chapter 27

The apartment was empty now.

Again.

Chairs and cheese askew, Bette teetered in her corner and then prowled her silent cave. In each crevice she revisited a memory. A fawn, she daintily approached the spot on the floor where Hector and Crevelle had danced. Humming to herself, Bette put out her arms to an invisible partner and twirled. Here, by the record rack, Valerie the leopard chose Mel Tormé over Glenn Miller. She wanted to be of her own time and not remind anyone of anything that had come before. This is where the lion Frederick had faced her, bared his teeth, and sprung. Over here, one step to the left, is where he lied about her again.

Bette's pain was so inside her, swimming. The language of this pain burst out through her throat in tiny fragments. A word here. A word spilled out. A phrase exploded. It turned within and any observer would have found it unintelligible. It was only emotionally articulate. Anyway, there were no observers and there would not be any observers. She made more sounds, a joining together of shriek, plead, mumble, the break of heart and thought.

"Earl." That was a word that she spoke.

I forgive you. She felt that.

"I forgive you," she said out loud. It was blurted, uncontainable. She had forgiven Frederick, she had to forgive Earl.

I see your face before me. And the love that I have for you takes over. I am not angry, my dearest friend. I just want this cut-off to end. End it. End it. End.

"This cruelty," she said. "What is in it for you?"

Don't be afraid, she thought. *I know who you are, and I accept you. I accept you. I know you. You are the one doing this to me. My Earl.*

"This lie."

Because you.

"You can't breathe."

And you are pushing your pain, punishing me for your pain. Me for your pain. Me for your pain. Me. Me.

"That's why," she said.

That's why, she felt.

That's why, she knew. *Why you hide behind your locked door. One look at me and who you are, your truth, will emerge. I know you. So, you have to eliminate me.*

"Destroy me."

"Liar."

There was a knock at the door.

This will end.

"Your shunning . . ." *This.*

This will end. This will end. This will end. This will end. This will kill us.

"Both."

Another knock at the door.

"This will kill us both."

Finally, she heard the knock, and Bette, believing that her prayers were being answered, jumped up and ran to the door. She flung it open.

"Earl?"

It was Valerie. She was dripping wet. Only then did Bette realize that days and nights had passed. She had not left the house while the world went on. And that it was now raining outside. That there was an outside. And, there, it rained.

Valerie was wearing a fashionable raincoat. Bette remembered seeing it on Audrey Hepburn in one of those magazines. She had a gay umbrella, lovely rain boots, an endearing hat. Her outfit did a lot of work for her.

"I was down here in the Village," she chirped. "And lost track of the time. Isn't that uncharacteristic?" Valerie took off her hat. "It's rather foolish, really. Not like me. It was too late. And I thought . . ." She unbuttoned her coat. "I thought I'd be in the way of the producers at this point. And I remembered that you were the . . . nearest television. Can we watch it together?" She took off her boots. "Our commercial?"

Robotically, Bette walked Valerie to the center of the room, freezing in front of the television set, still holding an open jar of olives and an empty martini shaker. Each woman stood to a side of it, flanking their mascot. Valerie reached over, stretched out her arm, and for the first time since its arrival, the television set was actually turned on.

At first the image was imperceptible. And this confused Bette. But then, after a bit of warm-up time, a thin gray line started to form at the center of the tube. Once that came to be, the sound began to crackle. Finally, a live drama popped up and emerged into focus.

"Here we go," Valerie said, as though the car she was driving was about to plummet off the bridge and she had accepted it. The destruction. The miracle. Whatever was to come next.

On the television set, there was an actress. Her line was: "But, Daddy. I love him."

This was followed by organ music, as her image disappeared into the commercial break.

In its place came Hortense. Bette's own Hortense! She was sitting on a gray throne wearing a great crown. *Why do they call it black and white*, Bette wondered, *when really everything about it is gray?* This gray, Bette realized, was their commercial.

"Off with their heads," Hortense said, with a put-on British accent, sounding like Edna May Oliver at age twenty-two. She waved her hand as if serving in a round of tennis. *This was supposed to be queenly*, Bette thought. It was a sporty and contemporary gesture. Perhaps she was going for the modern aristocrat.

"Oh, Vincent!" she squealed. "Bring me my cocoa!"

Then Earl walked in front of the camera. He was dressed like a butler, and he carried a tray with one cup of cocoa.

Bette gasped. *"No ooga-booga cannibals,"* he had said. *"No butlers, no shufflers."* But none of that mattered now, did it? The only person who had heard him say those things was Bette. And she no longer existed. Without witnesses, he was free. Free to play a butler. Apparently nothing that anyone says matters. It's just the release of breath. This was the most awful thing she had ever seen in her life.

Hortense reached for the cup and took a sip.

"Mmmmm," Hortense crooned. The chocolate was so wonderful that just one sip made her instantly kinder, and she lost her angry facial expression. "Oh," she shrugged, reconsidering the condemned. "Let them go home."

A man's voice boomed from nowhere. Although he could not be seen, one felt that he was telling the truth. That he really knew. A white man.

"RO-CO-CO," he said. "IT SOOTHES THE SAVAGE BEAST."

Earl stood at attention. He wore white gloves. Hortense smiled and drank her cocoa. The message was subtle. Hortense, the queen, was the beast. Earl's servitude, merely suggestive. Valerie must be some kind of liberal, after all. Organ music resumed and then the screen was replaced, once again, with the actual program featuring that plaintive first actress.

"Daddy?"

Valerie turned off the set.

Again, there was that aftereffect, where the picture reduced to a thin line and the static reduced to silence until the whole screen went dark.

"That's what everybody wants," Bette said.

Valerie nodded. "A good cup of cocoa."

"No. To be seen."

"Do you have any?"

But Bette only had tea. She put on the kettle. "It is such a petty want and so powerful. It drains the heart out of a person."

"Cocoa?"

"No, to be seen." Bette set out two cups on their saucers and placed them on top of the television set. "Those actors," she clucked, nesting a small bowl of sugar snugly between the antennae. "They don't care how foolish, how demeaning. They just want to be seen."

"They want to earn a living."

"Yes, but . . ." No, actually, Bette knew that money was not the only thing that needed to be in place for a man to dress up as a butler with no lines. That this was reliant on other factors. A loss of will, a diminished imagination about what one's life could be. Sustained battle. An emotional abandon. Nothing less.

"*But* what?" Valerie asked. She was being very curious.

"Just that once a person of great quality tastes that kind of diminishment," Bette gestured toward the TV screen. "Once they really know how grotesque it is. Once they live it . . ."

"Then they want more."

"Oh no," Bette stopped her. "Then they realize . . ."

"Realize?"

"Then they realize that this is soul killing, this kind of deceit. That to give and receive love is more important than how much one is seen."

Valerie put her hand for the second time on Bette's shoulder. "No one ever *realizes* something like that. Only in the movies."

"I realize it," Bette said.

Valerie picked out two cubes of sugar and placed them, with anticipation, into her empty cup. "Bette, you never wanted to be seen. You have a different kind of thirst for power."

"I want my friend," Bette said. "I want to eat dinner with him." Bette's voice quivered and her eyes welled up. She was humiliated. This was the first time she had told any human being, except for Earl, what was in her heart. She felt disloyal. Her secrets belonged only to the two of them. "After this commercial," she said, regaining control. "He will want his dignity back. He will want to return to the truth."

"That actor?" Valerie removed her hand. "You think that this great success will leave him repulsed? You are wrong, Bette. Other actors will be jealous, someone will recognize him on the street. He'll be able to say he was on TV. He'll have a story for life."

"But, a butler?"

"Look," Valerie was fed up now. She wanted to move on to other topics. "Success replaces truth. Don't you know that?"

"No."

"Well, it does. There is a joy in working the system that starts to replace daily life."

"Not for me," Bette said.

"Really?"

"Yes."

"You know," Valerie stared at her, like she was a car for sale and either a bargain or a lemon. "You could be a great mind in television. You, Bette, are a very, very smart woman. Too smart to be a secretary."

"It's fine."

"Well, no," Valerie blinked. She had this strange, new expression on her face. It was one of regretful false pity. "I guess not."

"What do you mean?"

"Well, Bette. . ."

"Yes?"

Valerie seemed uncomfortable. How could that be possible? What on earth could ever make her feel ill at ease?

"Hector is the president of the company. I cannot . . . He feels that you have your own agenda. Your own ideas. He feels that you have your own interpretation— ways of understanding things. You seem to be driven . . . by feelings. That's the word, *driven*. And that's the problem. Your feelings. They're intense. There is an intensity about you that is unusual. It makes him uncomfortable. He doesn't have the courage to tell you, so I'm doing it myself. He doesn't like it."

The teakettle whistle blew.

"I'm fired."

"Yes, you're fired. I'm sorry."

"Would you like some tea?" Bette asked.

"All right," Valerie answered, as a sign of mercy. She would drink a cup of tea with this old bag and then move on.

Bette lifted the Swee-Touch-Nee box and her eye caught the packaging. *Flow through tea bag*. She picked one out, swung it by the label. "I guess we should share one."

"All right."

Bette stood, trampled, with the two teacups of hot water before her. Methodically, she dunked the singular tea bag, first in one cup and then in the other. Then the other. Then the other. Then the other. Then the other.

"We realize," Valerie lulled, "that you own one-quarter of the company. And we are prepared to buy out your shares. Which are not worth much. But are starting to be worth something. It should tide you over for a year."

"I own half the company," Bette said.

"No, dear." Valerie's tone both softened and hardened to express her simultaneous authority and generosity. "Hector's father left you one-fourth."

"My cousin."

Valerie did not have time for this. "I'm sure," she said, as condescendingly as she could be without it actually becoming provable. "I'm sure that your cousin will be more than happy to sell us her shares, and I can't see any chance of her giving them to you."

"She doesn't own them," Bette said. She finished the tea-making procedure and wrapped the well-used bag around a spoon. "I do."

"How is that possible?"

"It was my money," Bette explained, squeezing the last burst of flavor out of the bag. "My money produced the television commercial. My money, from my account where my cousin deposited ten thousand dollars for the care of her daughter."

Valerie was as startled as a driver caught on the train tracks at precisely the wrong moment. "But the checks were in her name."

"No, they were in my name. I keep the books. Remember?"

Bette handed her guest the cup of tea. Valerie took it, obediently. And Bette knew that that was a good sign.

"So," Valerie rapidly integrated her new reality. "You own half the company."

"And you and Hector each own one-fourth."

Before her, Bette could see that Valerie was a better actor than Hortense or even Earl. On her own, Valerie stood for nothing. She had no values, and she had nothing worth fighting for except her own empty status. But Valerie's immense gift, ultimately, was that ability to be persuasive on any terms. Inside, she was a moral void. Hortense and Earl had at least minuscule selves. Despite a pervasive lack of conscience, something existed inside each of them that could not be eclipsed. But for Valerie that was not the case. She could fully inhabit any role.

"Well then," Valerie smiled. Entirely recovered and fully adjusted. She sipped her tea. "There is not much cash there. Only potential."

"Then I guess I'm not fired."

"No, I guess not."

"I guess I own the company." Bette smiled.

"I guess so."

"You see much," Bette said. "But not all."

Valerie raised her eyes to her new mistress with the dewy adoration that only a professional sycophant can muster. "I can learn from you, Bette. And I will."

"All right then," Bette drained her cup. "Let's get to work."

There was a knock at the door, and because the moment was so right, and Bette had come to believe in cinematic timing, she hoped after hope that the reversal of fortune would now complete itself. She ran to the door and called out, "My friend?"

"No," Valerie said, over Bette's shoulder. "It is *my* friend."

Valerie stepped through Bette and opened the door as though she, Valerie, were the recently appointed second-in-command to a brand new general. As though she were now Bette's secretary instead of the other way around. The kind of secretary who also serves as bodyguard and confidante, lover and adviser, in all important matters.

Bette returned to her chair and empty cup of tea wondering where all this would take her. She watched as a young, dark-skinned man entered the apartment. He was very handsome. His winning grin and curly hair deflected the menace made evident by his costume, that of a dangerous street tough living in one of the mad undervalleys of life in the city.

"You said *fifteen minutes*," he reproached Valerie with anger, and Bette could see how quickly he arrived at rage. As soon as the man caught her seeing his true self, he switched to a smiling mode, using charm to get away with everything. "But I gave you sixteen," he joked. Kissed her on the cheek.

Bette calculated. Valerie had budgeted fifteen minutes to take away a job Bette had held for thirty years. Thirty seconds per year. And now the time was up. Both of these young people were so efficient. They were a perfect match.

The man smiled brazenly at Bette in a triumphant sort of way. But what was he bragging about? Something about this one was awfully familiar. And the more Bette studied him, the more she acquired a terrible feeling, trying, trying to place him. She had stared at the face once before, under horrible circumstances. What was it? Where?

"Joseph Cadine, this is Bette. The president of the company."

"Hey."

"You!"

She remembered. This was the man who had robbed and beaten Earl on that final night, the one where everything was destroyed. This was the thug who had pushed dear Earl to the place where he could no longer tell the truth. Where the truth was too much to bear. This beast was the conveyor of a punishment so unjust and so unnecessary that it drove Earl from goodness to evil. This was the messenger of oppression so vile that it made Earl vile. This was the perpetrator for whose crimes Bette had paid and paid.

"Hello," he grinned, hiding nothing.

Bette was astounded by his bravado. This boy felt untouchable.

"Do you two know each other?"

"Yeah," Joseph whistled. "We've passed in the night."

Bette was impressed at how quickly Valerie adjusted to the news about company ownership. It was a matter of seconds, really. And now, Bette would learn from her again and follow suit. It was Bette's turn to adjust to this new . . . opportunity. That was the lesson of the void. If nothing matters, every obstacle may have a flaw that, if exploited, can bring you to your goal. Especially if that goal is simply to get there.

"Joseph," Valerie said, with uncharacteristic pride that could only come from erotic reassurance. "Joseph is at the Actors Studio."

"I'm sure he is."

And then it all came to her, so easily she wouldn't even need to draw up a plan. It was natural, now. Bette had been trained. When the strategic opportunity was born, she knew exactly what to do.

"Come in, Joseph," she said, filling the kettle. "Have some tea. The night is cold, and I have some questions to ask you." She smiled. "About acting."

"Sure." Cockily, he took a seat, assured that this old biddy wanted nothing from him but advice.

Chapter 28

Strangely, it had all been quite easy. Dreaming up the money scheme, enacting it slowly. Transferring Crevelle's funds in small amounts, through Bette's own checking account, into the coffers of Tibbs Advertising Incorporated. Making Bette their sole patron and increasingly number-one shareholder. She'd come to the plan as the outcome of many days and nights of intense thinking, intense observation. She'd surmised that both Frederick and Earl had been able to destabilize her because they had both transgressed *suddenly*. Both of their betrayals had been a *surprise*. It was this, the unpredictability, indeed the impossibility of imagining such turnarounds that had, in fact, allowed them to take place. Therefore, learning by example from the people who had successfully hurt *her*, Bette came to understand that she, too, needed to strike in the dark. When no one was looking. When no one would suspect. And where did she have power that was invisible to others? What had they overlooked?

With this revelation in place, she began a systematic mental inventory of every element of the business. She spent hours at home, alone, in her chair. Hours that had previously been devoted to enjoying other people's creations. But now she was only interested in her own creation. She scanned the workday over and over: the steno pads, the cigarette machine, the rolling chairs, the teal walls, the stationery, the ledger books . . . the books! She realized that no one checked the books. Perhaps because they correctly assumed that she would not steal. Perhaps because there were no profits as of yet. Perhaps because all anxieties about the financial records were about staying afloat and none existed about ongoing flow. Perhaps for all these reasons, accompanied by laziness, stupidity, and hubris, the books were Bette's personal terrain. She even tested doing them right under Valerie and Hector's noses, and they never gave it a thought.

Now that she owned the company, it needed to increase in value. Then she would have the resources necessary to be able to share with Earl. To give him a break. In the meantime, she lit a cigarette and relaxed. Bette was trying a new brand, Kent. She'd seen them in the hands of the young couple who'd moved in down the hall. Dave and Gloria. Gloria was pregnant with her first child, and Kents helped her keep some equilibrium between her job as a social worker, taking care of her elderly mother who had moved in upstairs, and shopping, cooking, and cleaning for her husband until the baby was born.

As the next few days passed, Bette's new strategy remained articulate and fresh in her mind. It was beautiful, really. She enjoyed thinking about these last few steps to the climax of her plan, and when she did, there was a gorgeous wellspring of hope that fulfilled her days. Sometimes she forgot that it was a dream and felt a deep satisfaction with life, lived the way that it should be lived. Then she would marvel with gratitude at her own happiness, suddenly remembering that this was just a plan. Not yet real. She no longer listened in the hall for signs of decay from Earl and Hortense. It was implicit. Anyway, she was at the wheel. Whatever falsities they had constructed between them were irrelevant. Their lying days were numbered. 10 . . . 9 . . . 8 . . . 7 . . . 6 . . .

The evening of the denouement arrived, and Bette stood by her front door, listening for Hortense's footsteps to slide down the hall. There was a new weight to the girl's movement. As Hortense's life had grown dimmer, her stride had become flatter. She barely lifted her feet nowadays, it seemed.

There she was, stopping before Bette's door. All would be well.

Bette waited.

The knock.

"Cousin Bette? Cousin Bette? It is Hortense. We agreed to meet this evening at eight, remember?"

Feigning casualness, as though she had other things that were far more pressing, Bette ran to the far side of the room and called out, "Oh yes, wait, I will be right there." Then she stood silently for a few more beats.

"Bette," Hortense whined through the door. "I am in trouble."

She's speaking at a high volume, Bette noted. *There-*

fore Earl must be out living his real life. Bette was happy. She had a rounded sense of well-being.

"Coming," she yelled. Then she stamped her feet from soft to hard, as though to mimic the sound of approaching steps. Finally, she opened the door with arms outstretched. "How can I help you?"

Once safely inside, the girl cried, of course.

"What is it, my dear? Tell me."

"Something wonderful is happening," Hortense bleated through her tears. "And Earl is trying to destroy it."

"What is it?"

"Well," Hortense sniffled. "Miss Korie phoned us from the agency this morning."

"She did?" *Good girl*, Bette thought. *Valerie is a reliable employee.*

"She said that they are considering branching out into producing their own television series."

"My!" Bette brought her hand to her chest, fingering the lace of her blouse, as though it was all too much for her tiny little head to grasp.

"And then she said that they want their first program to be based on our commercial."

"But, that's wonderful, my dear Hortense."

Encouraged by approval, Hortense increased her histrionics. "They want Earl and I to develop a weekly show. It will be called *The Princess and the Cannibal.* It's about a princess who befriends a cannibal in darkest Africa and brings him to Manhattan to be her butler. It is a comedy. Red Buttons would play my father."

"But that is lovely news. *The Princess and the Can-*

nibal. How intriguing a title." Bette was rather proud of having come up with that one. The absurdity of it, the insanity, and how quickly Hortense accepted it as fact. "Why are you crying, my dear? Unless those are tears of happiness?" *That was over the top*, Bette realized. She had to show some restraint or all would be revealed.

"Earl won't do it!" Hortense stamped her foot.

There was a wave of loving that came over Bette. He won't do it. He still exists somewhere.

"Do you want him to do it?"

"Of course," Hortense cried. "It's our big chance."

"Does he have any money?" Bette found her own chest tightening. Earl was so close, she could see his face before her.

"None." Hortense manifested some outrage at this point. "You can't pay the bills with dreams."

"So, he still has dreams."

There was a hope so alive that it sang its own song. It brought its own story. It made its own bed. Her friend. She was right to believe in him through all of this. Underneath the staggering surface of his greed, Earl's essential self remained intact. As did hers. And the two would be joined again, soon, to find rebirth.

"Yes," Hortense nodded tragically.

"What do *you* want him to do?" Bette asked carefully.

Hortense became illuminated by her own vision of a perfect world. The one she felt entitled to. The one that she had been raised to feel should be inevitable.

"I want him . . . to give up all thoughts of *great artistic creations*. To let us move forward into our own age. Television. To be famous. To be rich."

Bette clucked sympathetically. "This is not the man you dreamed of, my poor darling girl. That must be so disappointing."

"It's devastating," Hortense agreed, sucking more and more attention. Wanting more indulgences. More. More.

Bette rose, walked solemnly to her dresser drawer, and pulled out a blue bandanna. Slowly, she undid the knot and opened it to a wad of cash. She counted out singles, slowly. Very, very slowly.

"Hortense, I am giving you twenty-five dollars. I withdrew it from my savings in case of such an emergency. This is from me to you."

Hortense watched, hungrily, as each bill was counted. And once Bette held out the bribe, she grabbed it, then remembered to say, "Thank you."

Bette watched as Hortense recounted the stack. That was a new attribute, something learned from need and deprivation. Hortense counted with a newly acquired knowledge. As each bill passed between her nimble fingers, she knew exactly what it would buy her. Cheap shoes, good shampoo, macaroni, face powder, pay the electric. She looked up at Bette. "How much do we owe you now?"

"That doesn't matter between family," she assured her. "You'll pay it all back when you are able."

"But I want to know."

"One thousand three hundred and eighty," Bette said kindly.

"With interest?"

"Yes, with interest compounded." Bette offered the girl a single cookie, dry and crumbling on the plate.

"Tell me, my dear. Have you heard from your mother?"

"No. You are all I have, Cousin Bette. If Earl doesn't agree to this television program what will become of me?"

This was the moment. The soliloquy. Bette had practiced it in the dark and again in the soft rose light peeking through buildings that announced the coming of the dawn. She had felt it over and over again. So she was prepared to take a deep breath and deliver, to this audience of one, the stark truth.

"If Earl does not agree to this television commercial, Hortense, you will have but one choice."

"What is it?"

"To give birth." A siren blared down the street. Bette remembered that there was a world out there. People were winning and losing every minute. All and nothing.

"What?"

"Be a mother, dear Hortense. Work hard at rearing a child. Put it to bed every night and wake up with it every night and rise to it every morning. Remove its excrement and wipe clean and clean, again and again. Burp it. Watch it grow into a sad person who you cannot control. This will be your masterpiece."

Hortense cowered in fear. "I don't want to." She was panicking.

"You don't?"

"No! Poverty is catching up with us. And Earl has lost interest."

"Lost interest?"

"Yes," Hortense looked to the floor. "In all things." Then the child from the provinces blushed, as they do in Ashtabula, when humanity strikes.

Bette opened her own purse and pulled out a small package. "Hortense, give Earl my extra set of keys, will you? Just in case."

Now, the knock on the door. Bette had timed everything perfectly, down to the most pregnant pause. She'd learned from Valerie's *sixteen minutes*.

"Get that, will you dear?"

Hortense opened the door to a very handsome, dashing, and dangerous young fellow.

"Hello, Joseph. How nice of you to stop by. Let me introduce you to my niece, Hortense. Hortense, this is Joseph Cadine. A . . . friend."

"Hey," he said, T-shirt rolled to reveal chiseled muscle, hair razed at the sides and slicked back on top. Tight jeans, black leather boots. "Hey, Bette's told me all about you." His eyes twinkled, he licked his lips. "She tells me that you're an actress."

Hortense's eyes fluttered. "I've done some television."

"Let me make some supper," Bette sang, and disappeared discreetly into the kitchen.

Chapter 29

Bette gave them exactly one half hour, according to the oven timer, and then reappeared with good food and a nice beer. The two were deep in conversation, and she hovered in the background urging them on, moving back and forth between kitchen and table. She had observed that Hortense had learned to like beer and handled it as familiarly as any adult, not yet needing it but certainly drinking with appreciation.

"As Stanislavski says," Hortense was droning, "'to be right, logical, coherent, to think, strive, feel, and act in unison with your role.'"

"Using *emotional memory*." Joseph, too, had something to prove. That was good to know.

"I can't do that in life," Hortense quivered. Quivering was universal female code for becoming vulnerable and therefore open to being rescued.

"What?" He moved closer. "Poor thing." He reached out his arm to console her and thereby asserted his control. Bette noted his skill at treachery. He really knew how to prepare a victim.

"I can't be in unison with my role." Hortense rested her head on his shoulder. "But I want to. I truly do."

"Hortense," Joseph hummed, "I find that so hard to believe. Just sitting here with you for this short time, I can already feel so much energy and life, such truthful vibrancy and passion coming from you. Whatever is troubling you cannot be *that* bad." He was so good at being adorable. "The obstacles you face today are material for your work onstage tomorrow. It's just another experience to expand your palette."

Once he said openly that she would have work "onstage," Hortense spilled it all. How she had come to New York to have experiences and how she had had them. The really difficult ones. But she was finally reaching her limit. After all these months of hardship, she was waiting for something to pay off. She'd paid her dues and now was ready for the glamour.

Joseph also contributed some confidences from his tiny heart. In a strange way, Bette observed, these two liars were telling the truth. They both had not fulfilled their grandiose goals in short amounts of time. And both felt bad about it. Somewhat ashamed. It was odd to see it from their points of view. They felt that they deserved something without having to invest, and it was fine to use other people to get it because they had to have it. Success! And that was that. It was an interesting moment for Bette. It would have benefited all, if each person had to look at their own goal critically. Which these squirrels were not able to do.

Before launching into the final phase of her campaign, once again Bette subjected herself to the ritual review, which she had come to think of as *self-purification*. Reflecting critically, for the final time, on the parameters of her quest.

Does she really deserve *to be treated with kindness by Earl?*

Yes.

Why?

Because they share an intimate knowledge of each other, and this is the most precious gift between mortals. That recognition. It cannot be denied.

Because she is not the cause of his pain, and yet she is being punished for it.

Because people have inherent responsibilities to each other to be accountable, regardless of their desires not to be.

Is it his right to pretend she doesn't exist because she knows his truth?

No.

All right, she was reassured. There is right and wrong.

Finally, Bette grew bored of watching Joseph and Hortense stroke each other's inadequacies and assessed that the mutual aid society had gone on long enough. She cued the thug to proceed, as planned, to the final act.

"And Joseph," she asked. "What are *your* limits as an actor?"

"I have no limits," he sputtered. Then raised his eyebrows to signal Bette that he was ready to complete the task. "When it comes to the spiritual truth of my characters, there is nothing I can't achieve. This is not a *hobby* for me."

"Not for me either," Hortense jumped in. "But how far can one go?"

"No limits."

Bette rose strategically from the table to clear the plates. Hortense, now a guest in this house, sat herself down on the sofa, inviting intimacy. Joseph smiled, rose, and went to sit beside her. Cross stage right.

"Some time ago," he said, looking right into her soul, "I was doing a scene in class from *The Immoralist*. By André Gide. I played a homosexual prostitute and blackmailer. An Arab. So, I went out into that homosexual underworld and found some lonely, old fag to pay me for sex."

"You had sex with him?" Hortense was shocked with pleasure. This was the world she had been seeking. Rule breakers who don't get their souls broken. Transgressors who come out ahead.

"Yes."

"For money?"

"I wouldn't do it for free." He looked at her quizzical expression. "I penetrated *him*."

"Oh." She hadn't thought through the specifics, but Joseph seemed to want her to be reassured but still excited. "Of course."

"Then I robbed him. In this very building, in fact. I took his wallet."

"In this building?" Now she was truly shocked by his lack of excuse. "Aren't you afraid?"

"To see the man?"

"Yes!"

"Not at all," Joseph shrugged, with the truth. "What could he say? Besides, they're used to it."

"Who?"

"Fags."

"Oh, yeah." Hortense thought it over. That made sense.

He watched her become persuaded. Now, he had her.

"When I did the scene in class the next day, I had the old guy's money burning a hole in my pocket and my semen in his anus. An actor is under an obligation to live his part inwardly. Only then can he give his experience an external embodiment."

"But, is that . . . is that okay?" Hortense was unusually unsure.

"What do you mean?"

"To treat people that way?"

Bette laughed.

"Stanislavski doesn't say." Joseph's beautiful eyes opened wide enough to take in the sky. "What about you, Hortense? Haven't you ever taken something that wasn't yours? To achieve a higher truth?"

"No," Hortense lamented. "The little I have is so much less than I deserve."

Bette was simultaneously disgusted and interested. Both of these monsters wanted things that weren't theirs. She, Bette, wanted what was already hers. The relationship that she had built and contributed to for most of her life. It was a home that she had worked with Earl to construct. She had cut the boards, painted the walls. She was willing to inhabit it in a different way, share it, even reconfigure it. But she wanted to be

354

part of the decision. To negotiate. She could not come home one day and find the locks changed. That was not right. Earl had promised. He was a man and he had to be accountable. She believed that he could be. She believed in him.

"Perhaps we could do some scene work together."

"You really want to?" Hortense shrilled. "I would love it. Oh, thank you."

Yes, Joseph was doing a good job. Clearly, in two short hours Hortense had come to trust Joseph and believe him. All because he was pretty and had flattered her. Not a word out of his mouth was true. Hortense hated truth and rewarded lies. It was a bit overwhelming to learn how many fellows excelled at being sharks. They seemed to be hidden in every walk of life.

"All right," Joseph said, satisfied.

Bette swirled into their midst now. "This is so exciting, Hortense. Scene work with someone at the Actors Studio. It might be exactly what your boyfriend needs, the kind of artistic outlet that will let him say yes to the television show."

"Boyfriend?"

"Yes," Hortense was caught. She had lied by omission because she wanted something. Now that was out in the open and, so, she was naked.

"Is he an actor?"

"He's an actor," she nodded.

"He lives next door," Bette said, as though discussing the weather. "He has for years."

"Really?"

"Yes," she sang. "Right next door." She filled the dish tub with hot water and LUX.

"Your boyfriend?" Joseph asked Hortense incredulously, as though he had never heard of such a thing. "Next door?"

"Yes," she mumbled. Cheeks aflame.

"And do you also live next door?"

"Yes," she said, flatly.

"Is he a colored guy?"

"Yes." She was surprised now. Somewhere between worried and curious. "Do you know him?"

"Yes, I fucked him," Joseph chortled. He couldn't help showing off. "That's him. That's that aging queer that I rolled."

"I don't . . . What does that mean?"

Hortense was riding the elevator and someone had just cut the cable.

Bette folded her hands in her lap. It was almost over.

"Some failed actor, right? Wants to play Othello?"

"You . . . How . . . ," she stammered. Unlike Valerie, Hortense had no practical graces when it came to defeat.

"Yep!" Joseph laughed out loud. "That's him."

"Bette!" She turned for comfort and protection. "That isn't true?"

Joseph stood and hovered over her, his breath on her face. Bette could see that he was angry and dangerous, prowling for victims. "Of course it's true."

"Bette!"

Then, in his best Orson Welles as Dracula imitation, Joseph spread his wings and boomed *Othello*:

Look to the Moor, if thou hast eyes to see.

He bears the sentence well that nothing bears.

Hortense gasped. She was filled with horror. "Bette, Bette! What do I do?"

Joseph posed by the window, gazing out in silhouette. He was delighted with himself and smoked a cinematic cigarette. A Viceroy he had spotted in a case on the mantel.

"What can you do, my dear?"

"I can't think."

Bette was calm. She smiled the smile of hate, the great smile of joy in someone else's demise.

"Should I leave?"

Here it was. The moment Bette had lived for.

"Your mother misses you desperately, Hortense. She's living on her own now. Outside of New York. On her divorce settlement. And she wants you to join her."

"Mother?" she whimpered.

"Yes." Bette reached for an old opened letter. "She sent you this ticket." She extracted it and placed it firmly in Hortense's limp hand. "It's for a small town . . ." She put on her reading glasses and looked at the return address. "Called Scarsdale."

Hortense stood, empty, with the ticket hanging from her deflated arm. "Should I do it?"

"Do you want to stay *here*?"

"I don't know. What about my career?"

Bette suppressed a laugh. Lied. "It will be waiting for you." Bette recovered quickly enough to again look sincere. "Just go home," she bustled. "And rest.

Be waited on. Fed. Then you can return whenever you wish. The door is eternally open." She knew that this girl would never live in New York again.

"Oh, Bette, what about Earl?"

"Maybe," Bette was very careful now. "Maybe you don't really love Earl."

"Then what do I feel?"

This was Bette's opportunity to give this child an explanation the worm could not create on her own. It was merciful, really. Hortense could use this summary forever as shorthand for her life's greatest adventure.

"You met someone who represents what you want for yourself. To be a good actor. But that is not love, my dear."

"What is love?"

"Love?" This was a question to which Bette knew the answer. "Love is when you truly know them. You have been the recipient of their greatest kindness and their greatest cruelty. You have no illusions. You have seen every lie, every evil, and still you love them. And still, with all the knowledge of their humanity, their complexity, their vanity, contradictions, lies, and weaknesses, you accept them into your heart forever. That is true love."

"It is?" Hortense seemed confused.

"Let me ask you this, Hortense. Knowing what you know now about Earl. Not just the *fact* of it but the deceit, the lack of joy that he has blamed on you. Now, when you think of him, do you have an open heart?"

"No," Hortense said. "I do not."

"Knowing who someone is and still loving them. That is the gift."

Hortense changed before Bette's eyes. She lost the acquisitions of urbanity and became her mother.

"All right," Hortense said. "I'll go. I will go now."

"Goodbye, my dear." Bette swept her to the front door, reached into her bandanna of cash, and handed Hortense five singles. "Take a taxi to the station. Don't look back."

Hortense hovered in the open doorway, she would not return to Earl's apartment. Clutching her ticket and her dollars, she headed toward the stairs.

"Goodbye, Cousin Bette."

"Goodbye, Hortense. May you have everything that you deserve."

Bette watched her walk down the hall, down the stairs. Then she pushed Joseph aside so that she could lean out her second-story window. There she took in the splendor of her block. How she had missed the world! Finally the girl's shadow appeared on the corner, waiting to disappear. Bette watched the light change to green. And, seeing Hortense below, still standing, stunned, on the corner, Bette yelled out, "Cross!"

Hortense looked up as she crossed the street and began walking in the direction of Grand Central Station. The girl was changed. She would go to the station on foot and save the taxi fare in case of emergency. Now she knew something more about consequences.

Bette waited until the girl was out of sight. Then she was happy. Mission accomplished.

Now she just had to get this dirty devil forever out of her life.

As all the anxiety of the past months slowly settled and evaporated into the sky, Bette opened the front door of her apartment and waved a path for Joseph. Without a pause, he pulled out the dolly he'd stored behind her kitchen door, lifted his prize onto its wheels, and rolled his reward out over the threshold and down the hall: his brand new television set that he pushed on the sidewalk, all the way home.

Beat the world at its own game.

Chapter 30

Earl took two days to realize that Hortense wasn't coming back. He put all her belongings into a bag and left them out, first in the hall in front of his door, then in the lobby where they disappeared. A week later he saw one of the queens from the Hotel Albert wearing her light blue frock despite its too-small size. *So be it.* When the apartment was emptied of her influence, he stretched out on the bed, took up all the space, and sighed. There were pluses and minuses to everything. And immediately he longed for a man, and dreamed that night about Anthony, and tried to call Leon's number but it was disconnected. It was all still there, all his feelings, his heart. Only the buffer was removed. Not much had changed. He was still full of holes.

From time to time Earl thought about calling Bette. She had been very quiet ever since that confrontation. She just went to work, came home, went on with her tiny, little life. What a strange creature she was, after all. He did notice that one night sometime back, she had what appeared to be a party. This truly surprised him, as he didn't think she had any friends. And it would be hard to imagine that she had accrued any. At least not enough for a party. Then he decided that she must have loaned her home to someone else for *their* party. And that explained why such a burst of energy was surrounded by the absence of any other traffic in and out of her apartment, as far as he could tell. Just the same old isolation, the same old, lonely Bette. Reading in her chair with her cup of tea. Here, he had been through so much, he had tried so hard to have a better life, but she never changed a thing. Just sat with her book.

Earl went to Alphonso's office and asked for his job back. Alphonso, too embarrassed to discuss it, just said yeah, with his eyes glued to the floor. As Earl suspected, Leon had never been heard from again. And that, sadly, was going to have to be that. He did pass, occasionally, by the Caffe Cino. As predicted, the cops were giving Joe a terrible time, but they had managed to get a show up on its feet, and Earl sat in the back, marveling at all the camping and innuendo happening onstage. It was the kind of thing normally only drag queens would do. But here were men playing the same game. Telling inside jokes about "trade" and "studs" and referring to details of life that only other queers would know. Earl enjoyed himself, he had to admit. It was strange to see it all out in public that way. He wasn't sure there would ever be a real audience for that sort of thing, but it was harmless. Harmless fun.

One night he was going out of his skull and suddenly remembered *No Heaven Like Earth* and got his ass over to 111 East Houston Street, just in time for curtain. Yep, Frank Carter was playing Joe, and *sho 'nuf*, Frankie shuffled that Joe across the floor of Bobby's grocery store. It was exactly the performance those ofays wanted—a Joe who thought nothing, wanted nothing, had never been anywhere, and had no place he had to be. Frank gave them what they wanted and he'd gotten the job.

Coming out of the theater, Earl spotted Lynette, with her new man, a nice-looking Negro guy, nice suit, some kind of professional. They'd been at the play, too, and were waiting for Frankie to get out of his costume. Earl didn't want any trouble, but he caught Lynette's eye, and she waved. She wasn't angry. Her life had gone the way she needed it to go, so why not forgive, right? Why not?

Chapter 31

The following month was a busy one. But finally everything came to an end.

Valerie, Hector, and Bette sat in the empty office, finishing off the last bit of packing. Bette sealed up all the files in boxes, taped them shut. Valerie, meanwhile, put shipping tags on the new office furniture she had only recently ordered.

"I cannot believe that Tibbs Advertising has come to an end," said a dust-covered Hector, glum and somewhat confusedly ashamed. "My father would have been disappointed in me."

"Oh, I don't know about that," Valerie crooned, ever cheerful. "I think your father would have been delighted by all the money we've made."

Hector smiled at her, adoringly. She was still his hero. "Valerie, I will never fully understand how you got J. Walter Thompson to buy us out."

"Friendly fire," she smoked. "Very friendly."

Hector felt sad again, remembering that most of his

share of the profits was going toward alimony. He had retained enough to start his life over here in the city. But that was it. Still, he was amazed by how cheaply he could rent a six-floor walk-up with no closets. He'd already enrolled in a sculpture class. He'd purchased a chess set and some bongos and a hi-fi with some Ella Fitzgerald records. Big gallon jugs of Chianti went for nothing. And he could get a strong coffee anytime of day or night. Food was cheap down here. There was bread at the bread store and cheese at the cheese store and pickles at the pickle store. Everything had its cozy, little, eccentric place. He bought a typewriter and thought about writing a novel called "Connecticut" about a young advertising executive who gives it all up to move to the Village and find meaning in his life. He'd started reading a novel to see how they were made and was halfway through *The Cosmopolitans*, taking careful notes. It was an interesting story about a night clerk at a hotel, a normal young man surrounded by freaks. Clearly there was a market for exactly the kind of story that Hector wanted to tell. So that should make it easier. And it had love, of course. The night clerk still loved the neighborhood girl he'd left behind in a small town in Massachusetts. In Hector's story, the hero would find love with the brilliant, saucy girl from the office. In fact, that morning Hector had begun growing a goatee as a way to make himself a bit more dangerous. Everything was in place for him to finally be a man and let Valerie know the truth of how he felt. How much he cared for her. Hector gulped, scratched his itchy chin, and gathered his courage.

As for Bette. She had raked in quite a significant

sum of money, but there were no plans to be idle. She had promised Earl, to his face, that someday she would find the cash to protect them both. And now she had made her promise come true. She had nothing to do but wait for the opportunity to complete the gift.

Of course, Valerie, too, had plans. She was about to start producing a new television series. A western. It was called *Tumbleweed*. Joseph would be playing the role of the sweet, young priest. She knew he was a thug and could not be trusted, *but we all have our weaknesses*. In a strange moment of decency, she had called up Earl and offered him a part. He could play the lazy, shiftless stable boy. But surprisingly, he said no. Some people just can't spot an opportunity when it slaps them in the face.

"Valerie?" Hector squeaked nervously. "Would you like to go to a poetry reading with me?"

"I'm sorry, Hector," she sweethearted, as if singing *I love you a bushel and a peck*. "I have to wash my hair."

"Oh."

He looked so dejected, she didn't have the heart to end things that way. "Why don't you ask out an exchange student who is just learning English? Or, someone very, very young?"

"Okay," he said, brightening up at the thought of an Anita Ekberg type speaking broken Swedish. He could show her around the Village and be the big man. "Great idea!" Then he left for the men's room to check in on the progress of his goatee.

After all this, Valerie still impressed Bette in the way that no one ever had before. She was a kind of combination role model, teacher, guru, movie star. Her example was filled with warnings, of course, but her impressive set of skills seemed to be without end. And she was adorable. There was no way around that.

"Valerie," Bette said with an open heart. "You know how to refuse people without upsetting them. How do you do that?"

"It's marketing," Valerie smiled, then freshened up her lipstick. "Always make a blow off sound inviting. It gives them something to look forward to. If, for some disappointing reason, you ever need them later, the promise is always there. And you can deliver in person."

"I thought that was it!" Bette's own instincts were much sharper now. "Is there anything that you would *never* compromise?"

Valerie thought for a minute. "No."

"Do you like being that way?"

"I love it."

"I can't imagine it," Bette said.

Valerie put away her lipstick and straightened her collar in preparation for one final act of peppy generosity. She came to Bette and stood before her, offering her this gift.

"Bette, you are so smart. You have many strengths. And yet, you can't make your life work. After some serious study and consideration, I finally have figured out why."

"Why? Tell me!"

Valerie smiled, of course. And selected the kindest, most seductive tone of voice.

"You want truth from people. You want them to be accountable. But they will never, ever take responsibility for what they really feel and do. So . . . so . . . Bette, listen to me! Bette? *Bette?* Are you listening?"

"Yes."

"Bette. Stop caring! IT'S NOT THAT KIND OF WORLD!"

Bette staggered back. This would take a lot of thought.

"Take Hector, for example," Valerie went on. "You think I care about him? He's a dolt, he destroyed his marriage and ruined his family fortune."

Hector walked back into the room.

"Hector!" Valerie gave him the hug of the angels. "It's been wonderful working with you. You did everything right, and everything worked out for the best."

"Thank you," he gleamed. " I feel the same way." He turned to Bette.

She felt awkward and looked to Valerie who silently prompted her to try this new approach.

"Goodbye, Bette," Hector said, waiting to be petted.

"You were a great boss, Hector," she sleazed off her tongue. "And . . ."

"Yes?"

"Youdideverythingright." It wasn't impossible if she said it all in one breath.

"Thank you," he grinned. " I feel the same way." And he left the office a happy, stupid man.

"You see." Valerie pulled on her coat and gloves. "Most people don't want to know the truth. And I'm one of them. So, I know what I am talking about."

"Goodbye, Valerie," Bette said, feeling the tears. "You did everything right."

"You know," Valerie said, kissing Bette surprisingly on the lips. "I feel the same way." And she was gone.

Chapter 32

It took a great deal of strength to let the days and nights pass those next few months, waiting for the reversal of fortune to complete. It was one torturously hot night. In fact, it was the night of July 28, 1958. That was the night of the day that I, the author of this novel, was born in that very building on Tenth Street, down the hall from Bette and Earl. It was horribly hot, I was screaming my head off. Bette couldn't sleep, and so she paced back and forth, folding a pillow over her ears, trying to drown out my wails. She was horrified to think of all the noise I would be making for the next twenty years until my mother married me off. Finally, desperate, she turned on the radio hoping for some kind of distraction as a second choice to peace. Scanning the dial, she noticed more rock and roll than ever, and then found a late night station with a talkative emcee.

It's hot, hot, hot, another scorcher. But that won't keep President Eisenhower from the golf links.

She turned it off. The last thing she wanted to think about was President Eisenhower. Couldn't they find someone better than that? Someone younger, who didn't love being a soldier? Then, I stopped screaming. Bette plopped down in the chair, exhausted. It was the kind of relief that only absence can bring. Quiet. She let the pillow drop to the floor. Then, I started again. Life was new, and I had a lot to say to the world.

Bette leapt up, swung open the apartment's front door and stuck her head out into the hallway. At that very moment, Earl's door also opened abruptly. He couldn't take it either and jumped out of his cell.

"SCHULMAN! Can't you shut that kid up?"

Shocked. They stared at each other. I stopped crying.

"It's a girl," Bette said.

"Why would anyone want to bring a child into this world?" Earl said.

"Why?"

"Happy Birthday," Earl said.

"Thank you so much." Her heart.

"Okay."

"Okay."

And he went back into his room.

She too returned to her apartment, but left the door open and sat silently in the dark. The walls were sweating. Everything was still in the whole big town. Yes, she too had been born on this date. July 28. But in 1907.

She heard it, the creak, as Earl slowly opened his door again. She heard him step toward her apartment, linger in the hallway, and then lean, an apparition, in her doorway, as he had so long been in her heart.

"Just listen," he said.

"Okay," she said, thrilled in her chair.

"Don't say a word. Not even okay."

She mouthed the word *okay*, but he was looking away and missed it.

"All right," he said. "All right. I tried to find an easy out from myself. Okay . . . Okay. There isn't one. And I know my mistake. The person who I picked to cross was *you*. And *you* had nowhere else to go. That's why you couldn't play along, even though I asked you to. It would be giving up too much and getting nothing to replace it."

He panted, regained his breath.

"If there is one thing I have learned it's this: When you leave someone, you have to leave them with a place to go. If they have no place to go, they can't leave."

He coughed.

"So, I tried to make you do something that I made it impossible for you to do: not be yourself. You're a smart person, but you like simplicity. You like things to be known and safe. You don't want to be asked to try anything new. It's not you. And I sprung all that on you with no preparation."

He coughed again.

There was a long silence then. Bette was trembling. Even if everything he said no longer applied, it didn't matter. He had at least thought about it. No one had ever tried to know the truth about her before. She had never before been seen, even if it was mistaken. Her skin sizzled. She waited. He could do it.

"The world . . . ," he said.

He started and stopped. Another long silence.

"The world . . . made me desperate. And you were the only one I could affect. So, I made you desperate."

Finally, Bette, at the age of fifty-one, was getting what she deserved. All these years, these long, sad years, she had waited for justice. And here it was. The truth. At last.

"I expected you," he said, "to give up everything. And no person would just say, 'Okay, take everything.' I wasn't experienced at being superior. Like *they* are. I didn't know how to pull it off."

Then Earl whimpered a little. Then he was fine. Words can't kill anyone. They just require decency, and then they create decency.

"Happy Birthday."

She had seen him. He had spoken to her. The shunning was over.

He had told the truth. He acknowledged her birthday. That's all she wanted. That was her goal from the beginning, basic humanity. It was what she deserved.

"Okay," Bette said. He was the man she had always believed him to be. And he saw the woman she always was. "Okay."

 END

A Note on Style

Honoré de Balzac's novel *Cousin Bette* (1846) is taught as a classic work of nineteenth-century French realism. Balzac was so committed to his task that he wrote ninety novels with a quill pen, worked in Paris while his girlfriend lived in the Ukraine, and died of caffeine poisoning after decades of drinking sixteen cups a day. I've always felt that the job of the novelist is to individuate other people, but it takes an irregular passion to see other people as "real." Both the real and the abstract, ultimately, have to coexist because the will to know others for who they actually are is unfortunately an out-of-social act that transcends the norm. This is what makes artists strange: the desire to see, understand, and articulate what lies beyond the facade. But to puncture someone's facade is to puncture their heart. And the facade of a society is more protected even than its individuals', so the quest to know is accompanied by alienation from those who don't want to know.

My novel also responds to a second iconic realist

work, *Another Country* (1962) by James Baldwin. Earl and Bette occupy the same world, time, and physical space as in Baldwin's novel. Both stories unfold in postwar New York bohemia, where rejected and marginalized people of different races and places on the spectrum of sexuality confront and try to come to terms with each other, both succeeding and failing. The failure is a unique urban failure because it represents a special hope, and is only made disappointing because of the optimism at its root. But for Baldwin, the men are more real than the women, and therefore more important. I want to, with hindsight, reassert into that historic moment that women have as much nuance, desire, contradiction, and, therefore, humanity as men, in fiction as well as in life. They are not pawns in a story, but full human beings with histories, contexts, and reactions. When acted upon unjustly, they experience consequences and they express those consequences. When the women have the same dimension as the men, we have an experience that is interactive. It is dynamic. And therefore more "real."

The Cosmopolitans occurs in the late 1950s in New York City, a place where "kitchen-sink realism" was dominating the works of film, theater, and literature that received approval and reward. At the same time, improvisation and abstraction were biting kitchen-sink's heels. Yet, for example, in painting, the abstract expressionists were benign in the face of McCarthyism, which persecuted realists. While abstraction can have a revolutionary impulse, it can also become cultural wallpaper. Jazz in the 1950s propels as equally toward incitement as it does to Muzak.

From this conjunction of the consequences of McCarthyism on cultural production, a new kind of American realism was established that prevails to this day. It firmly reflects the values of the dominant group, but can have riffs of formal innovation for enjoyment and variation that may be clever or fun. However, these engaging impulses do not disrupt the basic foundational requirements for both characters and authors: That only certain Americans deserve to become protagonists, emblematic of an era. That only certain kinds of writers can be both stylists and have gravitas of content and perspective.

This contemporary American variation on realism is so overbearingly dominant that it now controls how we think about and describe our lives, not just what books we read. We have lost objectivity about this style, see it as neutral or "literary" or "midlist," when, in fact, it reflects values about contemporary social order and control as cohesive, sensical experiences. I have always believed that the form of a novel should be an organic expression of the emotions at the core of the piece. I have never created, nor responded to, work that repeats a known "style" and imposes it on top of its own people and events. In an expansive social moment, the understanding that new representations of under-depicted people and unexplored experiences dictate new styles would be welcomed as a broadening of point of view. We would want to see and internalize how different kinds of people experience the world in a desire to open ourselves to the broad variety of humanity. In a restricted or oppressive period, however, repetition of already known paradigms and ways of writing are embraced and privileged, as though the familiarity itself was a sign of quality.

Only two lines remain from the original *Cousin Bette*, and I leave them to the literary detectives to unearth. *The Cosmopolitans*, in homage to both its source material and the era in which it is set, hovers realistically between French realism, kitchen-sink realism, contemporary American realism, and abstraction. I also try to evoke the era through slight allusion to the Britishized American English that dominated commonly read translations at the time. Whether the source was Flaubert or Dostoyevsky, these novels often sounded, in English, like they were being recited by Katherine Hepburn. And so, that tone, in a way, represents the period for American readers.

The book is distinctly stylized to reflect its characters' specific emotional experience of the world. For it is the specificity of their experiences that guides their perceptions, which in turn produces their actions and thereby creates the story.

Acknowledgments

Thank you to Francoise Meltzer, whose class on nineteenth-century French realism in 1977 at the University of Chicago has stayed with me all my life. Thank you to Jack Doulin, Des McAnuff, Shirley Fishman, Carrie Ryan, Kirsten Brandt, Roberta Maxwell, and my dear Diane Venora for your contributions to the development of this piece. I am grateful to the MacDowell Colony for their life-long support and to the Dora Maar House and the Brown Foundation/Houston Museum of Art for the time to finish the manuscript.

Extra special thanks to Mitchell Waters, Amy Scholder, Tayari Jones, Jennifer Baumgardner, and the amazing team at the Feminist Press.

The Feminist Press is a nonprofit educational organization founded to amplify feminist voices. FP publishes classic and new writing from around the world, creates cutting-edge programs, and elevates silenced and marginalized voices in order to support personal transformation and social justice for all people.

See our complete list of books at
feministpress.org

THE FEMINIST PRESS
AT THE CITY UNIVERSITY OF NEW YORK
FEMINISTPRESS.ORG